Whistler

Roger Taylor

First published in 1994
by HEADLINE BOOK PUBLISHING

First published in paperback in 1995
by HEADLINE BOOK PUBLISHING

A HEADLINE FEATURE paperback

10 9 8 7 6 5 4 3 2 1

ISBN 0 7472 4595 9

Typeset by
Letterpart Limited, Reigate, Surrey

Printed and bound in Great Britain by
Cox & Wyman Ltd, Reading, Berks

HEADLINE BOOK PUBLISHING
A division of Hodder Headline PLC
338 Euston Road
London NW1 3BH

Whistler

Chapter 1

Clouds, dark and ominous, bloomed menacingly out of the north. Slowly, throughout the day, mass piled upon mass, higher and higher, as if those leading the vanguard were being overrun by panicking hordes behind.

Eyes that had been lifted casually towards them in the morning, became narrowed and concerned as the day progressed, for the clouds were grimly unseasonable. Sournatured weather was to be expected as winter fought to hold its ground against the coming spring: dark skies and blustering, buffeting winds bearing cold rains, and perhaps even yet a little snow would offer no great surprises. But this . . .?

This was surely a monstrous blizzard pending, the kind that was rare even at the heart of winter.

'It'll only be a thunderstorm,' some declared, knowingly, though more to hear the reassurance in the words than from any true knowledge.

For there was no tension in the air, no tingling precursor of the tumult to come, raising the hackles of men and beasts alike.

Yet there was something hovering before this dark and massive tide, something that flickered elusively into the senses like an image caught in the corner of the eye that disappears when looked at directly. Something that was unpleasant – menacing, even.

Something primitive. And awful.

None spoke of it.

★ ★ ★

The land that lay in the advancing shade of this strange tide was a great spur that protruded south from a vast continent. It bore the name it had always borne – Gyronlandt. Once, according to legend, it had been a single mighty state glorying in its strength and prosperity, and the name still resonated with that past. Through the ages, however, that same legend declared, Gyronlandt had been riven by terrible civil strife and then by invasions of desperate peoples from across the seas, fleeing terrors and wars of their own. And despite many attempts to hold to this ancient unity – some wise, some foolish – Gyronlandt had drifted relentlessly towards what it was today – a land of a score or so different states living more or less peacefully together. A land that had been thus ever since ringing legend had dwindled into mere history and the thundering rhetoric of mythical heroes had become the ranting and mewling of an interminable list of political leaders in whose wake lay, inevitably, a long tangled skein of unfulfilled promises and broken pacts and treaties.

Nevertheless, the notion that 'one day' Gyronlandt would be united again still held some charm for almost all the peoples of the land, and often formed a rosy backdrop to any revels of a remotely patriotic nature. That the several states were ruled (and misruled) by as many different institutions of government, and that these institutions were frequently changed – sometimes peacefully, sometimes not – did nothing to further any cause towards such unity. Nor did the equally persistent idea that the present disunity was 'of course' due to 'them'. The identity of 'them' varied from time to time, depending on which neighbouring state was in or out of favour, but certainly it was never 'us'.

Gyronlandt was separated from the lands of the northern continent by an intimidating mountain range, across which only occasional traders and other desperate men

2

would venture. The forces that had formed these mountains had also thrown up a craggy rib down the middle of Gyronlandt which culminated at its most southerly point in a region jagged with a jumble of lesser mountains. This was Canol Madreth, the smallest and most central of Gyronlandt's states. It was also the only one whose boundaries had remained unchanged, though this was due mainly to the fact that no one saw any benefit in fighting to annex a land that consisted mainly of mountains and steep-sided valleys of uncertain fertility. Still less could anyone see any benefit in holding sway over the inhabitants of Canol Madreth – the Madren.

To the more kindly disposed of the other peoples of Gyronlandt, the Madren were said to be reserved. Others, less charitably, referred to them as rude and churlish, and frequently linked these attributes with stupidity as well. It could not be denied that the Madren's attitude to outsiders was often an unnerving mixture of chilling politeness and open mistrust, and it did little to endear them to anyone. Not that this seemed to concern them. They considered themselves to be markedly superior to all their neighbours.

And, almost unique amongst the peoples of Gyronlandt, the Madren were religious. Indeed, they had a state religion: Ishrythan. It was a sombre-faced creed involving a stern deity, Ishryth, who together with a triumvirate of Watchers, was responsible for the creation and continuation of all things. Ishryth was forever battling against the depredations of his brother, Ahmral, who, with a trio of his own, the Uleryn, sought constantly to lead mankind astray so that in the ensuing chaos he might remake Ishryth's creation in his own image. Ishrythan was a religion of duty and dedication, not joy or pleasure, promising bliss in the future only for appropriate behaviour now, and heavily larded with threats of eternal damnation for back-sliders. Of the other religions that existed throughout Gyronlandt, almost all derived from the same holy book as the Madren's Ishrythan, the Santyth, though most of them held celebration at their hearts, and in so far as they considered it at all, their followers tended to look upon Ishrythan as at best a misinterpretation of the Santyth and at worst, a wilful distortion, a heresy.

Not that such thoughts were of any great significance for, even among the Madren, few in Gyronlandt held to their religion with any great proselytizing zeal. Such quarrels as existed between the various states were mercifully free from such fervour and were usually associated with trade and commerce, although occasionally tempers would flare over some long-disputed border lands. Whatever the ostensible cause of many of these disputes, there was not infrequently a large element of sheer habit in them.

At the centre of Canol Madreth stood the Ervrin Mallos, Gyronlandt's highest peak. It rose high above its neighbours and dominated much of Canol Madreth. Indeed, its jagged, broken summit could be seen from many of the surrounding states.

The Ervrin Mallos had a curiously isolated appearance, as if it did not truly belong there but had been mysteriously transported from its true home in the great northern range. The Santyth told a tale of a fearsome lord of the earth, then in human form, who had sought to destroy a great army of Ishryth's followers who were preparing to invade the island of Gyronlandt, then an evil place . . .

'. . . and, turning from this, Ishryth saw that Ahmral had given great power unto the chosen of his Uleryn who by his will now moved the isle through the waters of the ocean as though it were the merest coracle. And as the isle was driven upon the shores of the land, so the gathering army of the righteous was destroyed and buried beneath a mighty mountain range. And, so great was his pain, Ishryth cried out, his voice

4

rending the very heavens: "As you have given so shall ye receive," and, reaching forth, he tore from the still trembling mountains a great peak and hurled it down upon the Uleryn, destroying his earthly form forever.'

Children's tales, grimmer by far, told a darker, more claustrophobic story of a terrible king who was entombed for his cruelty and foul magics, and whose last cry of terror at this fate was so awful that the land above could not withstand it and rose up into a great mountain until the sound could be heard no more.

It was also said that the Ervrin Mallos was the resting place of a great prince who, at Ishryth's will – or was it Ahmral's? – lay sleeping until a dark, winged messenger should bring him forth at some time of need. This however, had neither the credence offered by the Santyth, nor the dark certainty of truth that lies in children's whispered secrets, and was generally deemed to be a mere fabrication, although some said that it was in fact a true tale, but one brought by some ancient traveller from another place.

Whatever the truth, the Ervrin Mallos had an aura of deep stillness and mystery about it which had led to its being chosen as the site for the spiritual and administrative centre of Ishrythan: the Witness House. Situated halfway up the mountain, the Witness House was where the Preaching Brothers were taught, and where they returned from time to time for periods of fasting and re-affirmation. Here, too, all matters of theology were debated and decided, as were any matters of a more secular nature associated with the management of a state religion.

And as the dark storm clouds rose relentlessly in the northern sky, a particularly acrimonious debate was nearing its conclusion within the Witness House. For though the Preaching Brothers all wore the same dark garb, and though the Meeting Houses that were to be found in every Madren community were of the same simple and sombre

5

grey-stoned architecture, Ishrythan was not totally free from internal dissension. The Santyth, like all religious books, had many passages capable of more than one interpretation.

Cassraw swept out of the Debating Hall, slamming the heavy wooden door behind him. The boom of its closing mingled with the tumult of voices that its opening had released and rolled along the stone-floored passageways. Followed by Cassraw's echoing footsteps, it was as if the clamour was trying to flee the building before its creator.

Two novice brothers pursuing their duties stepped aside hastily as the stocky, scowling figure strode past them. They bowed tentatively but did not appear to be either surprised or offended at receiving no response. They were just starting to whisper to one another when a second figure passed by them, obviously in anxious pursuit.

'Cassraw, wait!' Vredech called out as he reached a balcony that overlooked the entrance hall to the Witness House. There was both appeal and urgency in his voice, and Cassraw, halfway across the entrance hall, paused.

'Please wait,' Vredech called again.

This time, Cassraw looked up. Vredech leaned forward, resting his hands on the wide stone balustrade. Cassraw was standing at the very centre of an elaborate mosaic pattern that radiated outwards in all directions. As Vredech looked down at his friend, it seemed to him that Cassraw's dark scowling face had replaced the image of Ishryth that was the focus of the mosaic, and that his anger was flowing out to fill the entire hall. Vredech felt a chill of foreboding rise up inside him, and for a moment was held immobile, like prey before a predator. Then Cassraw's voice released him, or rather, tore him free.

'Wait for what?' he said.

Vredech shook his head to dispel the lingering remains of his eerie vision, then, turning, he ran towards the curving stairway. He had no idea what he was going to say when he reached his friend, but was just thankful that he had stopped his flight.

Cassraw watched him as he ran down the stairs.

'Just wait for me,' Vredech said lamely, in the absence of any greater inspiration as he walked across to him.

'For what, Vredech?' Cassraw repeated impatiently, holding out a hand as if to fend him off.

Vredech's distress showed on his face and he turned away from the outburst. Guilt seeped into Cassraw's expression, changing his scowl to a look of irritation. 'Don't do this, Vred,' he said, turning away himself and looking up at the high-domed roof. 'Deliberately throwing yourself in my way and getting hurt.'

'How can you hurt—' Vredech began.

Cassraw rounded on him. 'I said don't!' he shouted. He pointed in the direction of the Debating Hall. 'Ishryth knows, you're my oldest friend and I love you, but they're wrong – and you're wrong if you side with them. The Word is the Word.' He plunged into a pocket of his black cassock and produced a small copy of the Santyth. He slapped the book in emphasis. 'We reject this at our peril.'

Vredech's heart sank, and he could not keep the exasperation from his voice. 'No one's talking about rejecting it,' he said. 'Why won't you just listen to other people's points of view? Why are you suddenly obsessed with this need to take the Santyth so literally? You know as well as I do that it's not without obscurity in places, even downright contradictions.'

Cassraw stiffened and his hand came up again, this time to point an accusing finger. 'That's blasphemy,' he said, his voice soft and hoarse. 'Take care that—'

'That what?' Vredech interrupted, lifting his arms and then dropping them violently. 'I'm not the one who's in trouble. I'm not the one who called the head of the church a heretic. I'm not the one who's being complained about incessantly by his flock. I'm not . . .' he spluttered to a

7

stop for a moment, then seemed to gather new strength. 'And don't you call me a blasphemer,' he said, indignantly. 'Since when is it blasphemy to speak the truth? Where there's doubt, there's doubt, and the blasphemy lies in not facing it, you know that well enough.' He laid his hand on the book that Cassraw was holding. 'These are the reports of men, Cassraw,' he said, his voice softening. 'Wise and revered men, but like all of us, flawed. Subject to—'

He faltered as he sensed Cassraw retreating into the grim silence that was becoming increasingly his answer to reasoned debate – when he was not actually shouting it down. 'All right, all right,' he said quickly. 'Let's not travel over that ground again. But do let's be practical. You'll be lucky if Mueran doesn't have you dismissed from your post if you carry on like this.'

'There are others who agree with me,' Cassraw interjected.

Vredech looked at him, worldly-wise. 'Maybe, but they'll disagree fast enough if their posts are threatened. For pity's sake, put a curb on your tongue. The Church is tolerant enough to accommodate a wide range of different ideas on theological matters. Why risk everything you've got with this nonsense?'

He clapped a hand to his head as if wishing would draw back the ill-considered word. But before he could speak, Cassraw was already heading towards the main door.

'I'm sorry,' Vredech called out, moving after him. 'I didn't mean to say that. It—'

Cassraw had hold of the iron ring that secured the door. 'This church is corrupted with compromise,' he said, his head bowed and his eyes fixed on the ring. 'It must reform. Return to the truth of the Word or we'll all be doomed. It must be made whole again.' He tightened his grip about the ring. 'Like this – unbroken – self-contained.' He turned towards Vredech, his black eyes

8

gazing piercingly. 'Follow me, or leave me, Vredech,' he said, his voice deep and resonant. 'Follow me, or leave me.'

Vredech was suddenly alarmed. He felt events slipping away from him. Cassraw's outburst in the Debating Hall had been a serious matter, but it was repairable, with care: an apology, a little penitence would right it. But he saw now that something strange was happening to Cassraw. He felt a touch of the quality he had sensed in him at times when they were growing up together. A quality that he had thought as long passed as their youth itself. An obsessive, almost fanatical quality that in someone else he might have called evil, though the word did not come to him now.

He hesitated, part of him saying, 'Leave him alone, you're only making him worse.' But the greater part of him forbade inaction where there was pain. He had to reach out – do something.

He laid his hand on the door to prevent Cassraw from opening it, and, with an effort, met the unnerving gaze. 'What are you going to do?' he demanded. 'You've a wife to think of, an important position to maintain – one you strove for and won deservedly. I know you've got problems with some of your flock, but that happens to everyone at some time or another. You can't jeopardize everything like this. Come back with me now. We can smooth everything over with a little care.'

But even as he spoke he knew that his words were not reaching his friend. 'Corrupt with compromise, Vredech,' Cassraw repeated. 'Follow me or leave me.' Then he pulled open the door and stepped outside.

Vredech did not resist. It would be hopeless, he knew. Cassraw had always tended to act more at the behest of his passions than his mind, and only when they were spent would his reason return to him. He'd probably calm down in an hour or so and see the sense of making his peace with

9

Mueran and the others. Surely he wouldn't seriously risk his post with the church? He had no trade to turn to, nor land to live from. Vredech picked up the ring and let it fall. It made a dull thud as it dropped into a well-worn groove in the door. The sound set Vredech's thoughts cascading, they carried him back to the Debating Hall and the excuses he might use to save his friend from the punishment that was surely inevitable.

He had barely taken a step away from the door when a sharp, anguished cry came from outside and tore through his inner discourse. He yanked the door open. Cassraw was standing at the foot of the broad and well-worn stone steps that led down from the door. He was gazing back at the Witness House or, more correctly, he was staring *over* it, his eyes wide with a mixture of terror and . . . ecstasy?

Vredech ran down the steps two at a time, his concern for his friend returning in full and mounting with each stride. Reaching him, he turned to see what he was staring at.

Stretching to the farthest horizons both east and west, the sky was filled with the clouds that been accumulating through that day. But where they had been dark they were now almost black, and what had been a threat of unseasonable ill weather had become a sight of terrible menace. The clouds were piled so high upon one another that they rendered insignificant the Ervrin Mallos and all the lesser peaks about it. Vredech felt himself swaying as his eye was carried irresistibly to their summit.

'Ye gods,' he whispered, taking Cassraw's arm to steady himself, and forgetting momentarily both his cloth and the place where he was standing.

'No,' he heard Cassraw whispering. 'Not gods. But God. He is here. He is come. For me.'

And he was running towards the gate that led out of the grounds of the Witness House. By the time Vredech registered what Cassraw had said, he had disappeared from view. Vredech hurried to the gate after him. Two novice Brothers were returning from the Witness House's garden. They were looking up at the clouds nervously.

'Did you see Brother Cassraw?' Vredech asked, trying not to seem too concerned.

'See him? He nearly sent me sprawling,' one of them replied with some indignation.

Vredech ignored the injured tone. 'Which way did he go?' he demanded.

The second novice pointed. Not along the winding road that led to the town below, but towards the far corner of the high wall that surrounded the Witness House. Vredech grunted an acknowledgement and set off in pursuit.

This isn't happening, he thought, as he half-walked, half-ran, keeping close to the wall, instinctively placing it between himself and the forbidding clouds. This was supposed to be a routine Chapter meeting to discuss routine administrative matters, but somehow Cassraw had succeeded in turning it into a major theological debate. No, debate was not the word – it had been a diatribe. He had latched on to some trivial point that Mueran had made and managed to build a spiralling, self-sustaining harangue out of it. Vredech had been slightly amused at first, as this seemingly coherent string of arguments blossomed out of nothingness. It had been like a metaphor for the Creation itself: out of the emptiness came the Great Heat, and from that, all things. Nearing the end of the wall, he could not help smiling. It was still such, he thought, for that too had gone sour.

Then he was at the corner of the wall. Puffing slightly, he leaned on it for support as he stepped round.

Judgement Day . . .

The words formed in his mind as he found himself standing alone and totally exposed before the black, billowing masses that filled the sky.

He was not aware how long he stood there and it was

11

only with a considerable effort that he managed to drag his mind back to his friend. From here, Cassraw could have moved on down towards the valley or up towards the mountain's shattered summit. There was a small, isolated chapel a little way down the mountainside that the Brothers sometimes used when they felt the need for quiet contemplation. But Cassraw had not run out of the Witness House grounds like a man seeking silence. Vredech scoured the ground rising steeply ahead of him, its dun colours strangely heightened by the oppressive darkness above.

'He is coming. For me.' Cassraw's dreadful words returned to him. Vredech clenched his fists tightly as if the pressure could squeeze the implications of Cassraw's utterance out of existence. The man was going insane.

A movement caught his eye. Vredech gasped: it was Cassraw. But he was so far ahead. And he was almost running up a steep grassy slope.

Vredech shook his head. He would do many things for his old friend, but charge up that mountainside after him was not one of them. It must be fifteen years or more since he had run in a mountain race, and he had done little violent exercise since, being quite content to move at a pace compatible with the dignity of his calling. He was still a little breathless simply after running from the gate.

With a sigh Vredech turned round and headed back.

High above him, eyes wide and fixed on the boiling darkness overhead, Cassraw staggered relentlessly forward, his shoes muddied and scuffed, his cassock torn. In between rasping breaths he implored, 'I am coming, Lord. I am coming. Have mercy on the weakness of Your faithful servant. Do not desert me.'

The darkness seemed to be reaching down towards him, listening.

A silence enfolded him.

Then a voice answered his prayer.

Chapter 2

Dowinne was pacing fretfully from room to room. An unease had been growing on her all day. It was probably the weather, she tried to convince herself, taking her cue from the grim clouds that were steadily building up over the town. But even as this thought came to her, she dismissed it. Whatever was troubling her was deeper by far than any pending storm.

It was not in Dowinne's nature to tolerate difficulties with equanimity and, from time to time, she gritted her teeth and bared them in anger and frustration as she strode about the house. Until she caught sight of her image grimacing out at her from a mirror. It seemed to be snarling at her for this exposure of her inner feelings and she straightened up hastily and forced her face into a bewitching smile.

Something behind the image seemed to be mocking her.

She moved again to the window. The Haven Parish Meeting House at Troidmallos was a well-appointed one, and the living quarters were excellent. As they should be, Dowinne thought. This was far from the poky, down-at-heel Meeting House they had begun with, way out in the wilds, ten years ago, and Cassraw's appointment to it so young was no small achievement. Yet . . .

Yet it wasn't enough.

She folded her arms and squeezed them hard into her body as if to contain the ambitions that for some reason were clamouring to be heard today. Then, secure in the silent stillness of her home, she gave her old desires their head. They excited her. It did not matter what she had now – she would have more. She would be important – powerful. Not just in Troidmallos, but in the whole of Canol Madreth. People would defer to her – would watch their words, their gestures, in her presence, just as she did with others now. And they would seek her patronage. Dowinne could scarcely contain herself at the prospect of what would eventually be hers, *if* she managed the affairs of her husband correctly.

With remarkable perceptiveness she had seen, even in her youth, that the church in Canol Madreth wielded almost as much authority as its secular counterpart, the Heindral, and that her best hope for future wealth and security lay that way. For despite its austere protestations, the church was rich, and its senior figures, though for the most part not ostentatious in their lifestyles, were most agreeably comfortable. More significantly, in political matters the church's opinions and discreet support were always carefully sought because of the influence it exerted over the people. Dowinne particularly appreciated the fact that the church's utterances were substantially unburdened by popular debate and that, above all else, it did not need the affirmation of the people every four years for its continued reign.

Of course, she could not enter the church herself – that was a privilege confined exclusively to men – but she could perhaps do even better than that. By marrying and mastering the right man she could master in turn those whom he commanded. And Cassraw was the right man beyond a doubt. She had judged him to be her own restless ambition given form, and he had confirmed her judgement time after time.

True, his fierce passion had been an unexpected burden to her at first, but she had gradually redirected it into proclivities that she found more tolerable and which had subsequently proved to be useful both as goad and lure. She smiled secretively, instinctively bringing her hand to her face to hide the response even though she was alone.

She must always be careful. She must never fall into the trap of imagining that Cassraw was an ordinary man like any other; that much she had learned through the years. For all his intellect and reason, he resembled a wild animal, and as such he could perhaps be trained, but he could never be tamed.

Her unease returned as she gazed up at the Ervrin Mallos. Within the building clouds she sensed a power which seemed to echo the power she felt within her husband. Unexpectedly, a flicker of self-doubt passed through her. How could she hope to manipulate such a thing? How could she have the temerity?

She crushed the doubt ruthlessly. All storms could be weathered by those with the will.

Yet Cassraw had been behaving in an increasingly peculiar manner of late. His sharp intellect seemed to be feeding upon itself, shying away from the shrewd and subtle conspiring at which he was so adept. It was almost as though he was searching for simpler and simpler solutions. His preaching had become more impassioned, but more primitive, and it was not fully to the liking of all his flock, although, she mused, some of them seemed to be responding to it. Dowinne frowned. They were not the kind of people she wanted following her husband. Not only would they be of little value in furthering his progress through the church, they would probably be an outright hindrance. Still, support was support, even from malcontents and incompetents, and it must surely be usable one way or another. She made a note to turn her mind to this problem in the near future. It was always worthwhile having alternatives available. You never knew . . .

Her thoughts returned to Cassraw. Life would be easier

if she could keep him safely in the mainstream of affairs. Perhaps she had been holding the reins a little too tightly of late. Perhaps she should help him to . . . expend . . . some of his burning energy. She tapped her hand lightly on her chest. After all, it wasn't too unpleasant a prospect, these days.

But, even after this resolution, her unease lingered. She would not be able to settle until he returned from the Witness House. Cassraw had never been desperately enthusiastic about Chapter meetings and, thanks to the bleating of some of his offended flock, he had been on the receiving end of one of Mueran's soft-spoken rebukes only a few days ago. He had laughed it off on his return, mimicking the pompous old hypocrite, but she had felt the rage beneath the mockery and, on the whole, would have preferred that he did not meet Mueran so soon afterwards.

Then, from deep inside her, came an awful intuition that something was terribly amiss. She began to shake and, for an unbelievable and giddying moment, she felt the long-built edifice of her ambitions begin to totter. She caught a glimpse of herself in the mirror again, posture wilting, eyes haunted.

'*No!*' she cried out and, swinging round, she brought her hands down violently on the windowsill. Her right hand caught the base of a heavy metal dish and sent it clattering to the floor, but she made no outward response to the pain, letting it pass through her unhindered, to burn away this unexpected and fearful spasm of weakness.

The effort left her breathless, however. It was the storm coming, she decided. That was all – just the storm. But this explanation held no more comfort than it had earlier.

She looked out again at the mountain. She could just make out the grey-stone Witness House halfway up. It had always seemed pathetically small against the rugged might of the Ervrin Mallos, but now even the mountain looked small against the ominous banks of clouds.

'Come down, Cassraw,' she whispered. 'Come down. Get off the hill before the storm comes.'

'Come, my servant. Come closer.'

Cassraw did not so much hear the voice as feel it suffuse through him. His body began to tremble, and his mind to whirl with a maelstrom of incoherent thoughts. It was as though all that he was, all that he had ever known, was struggling frantically to escape lest it be scattered and destroyed by the power that had just touched him. A preacher both by profession and inclination, however, he instinctively reached out and found his voice. It was hoarse, broken and shaking, but it served as an anchor to which he could cling, if only for the briefest of moments.

'Lord, I see the dust of Your mighty chariot and I am less than nothing even before that. Guide me, Lord. Guide me.' The words seemed pathetically inadequate.

Despite the screaming demands of his body following his precipitate charge up the mountain, Cassraw held his breath through the long silence that followed. Then the voice came again.

'Come closer.'

Cassraw's tumbling thoughts stopped short. He gazed around desperately, not knowing what to do and fearing to repeat his plea. The clouds were above him now, but from the south some residual daylight still lit the mountain, throwing long shadows like an unnatural, pallid sunset. It made all about him unreal, ill-focused and dreamlike; a strange image seeping through to him from some other place – a place in which he did not belong. Only the darkness overhead and his own awareness were real now – the one opaque, oppressive, unbearably solid, the other guttering and feeble. He felt as though he were not standing high up on a mountainside, but cowering in some dark cavern far below, in the very roots of the mountains, with their crushing weight towering above him.

17

Yet he must go upwards. There the Lord waited. Waited for him.

He set off again, clambering recklessly over the rocks, heedless of the damage to his shoes and his cassock, heedless of the cuts and bruises he was gathering as he stumbled and fell repeatedly in the failing light.

Questions tormented him. What was happening? What madness was driving him? Bringing him into confrontation with the leaders of his church, jeopardizing his position both in the church and the community – jeopardizing old friendships, perhaps even his marriage? But these thoughts held no sway. All were carried along by the stark certainty of what he had felt as he had dashed out of the Witness House and turned to see the sky beyond it turned black and forbidding, like the anger of a beloved parent writ large.

And he had been right. With each step he had felt that confirmation. He was right. He was right.

And now the Lord had spoken to him: touched him. Him! Summoned him to his presence on this ancient and most mysterious of hills.

Cassraw cursed his legs for their heavy reluctance as he struggled on.

The chain of seemingly trivial events that had eventually brought him raging out of the Debating Hall flickered briefly before him, taking on the appearance now of a mighty golden pathway along which he had been propelled. 'Your way is beyond our understanding, Lord,' he gasped. 'In the fall of the least mote is Your design.'

'I have little time, servant.'

The voice raked chillingly through Cassraw, reproaching him for this momentary diversion from the call.

'Forgive me, Lord,' he repeated over and over in a frantic litany, as he scrambled up the piles of broken rocks that would lead him to the summit.

Then the strange daylight was gone. He was vaguely

18

aware of a faint haziness from the south, but did not look at it for fear of losing so much as an eye-blink of time on this desperate journey.

He could not forbear a frisson of alarm and despair, however, as the darkness closed about him, but nothing must stop him. He must go forward. He must obey his Lord's command, no matter what the cost.

Then there was light – a dancing, disturbing light that made his shadow jerk feverishly hither and thither over the rocks – but enough to see by, nonetheless. And it was coming from overhead. He made no attempt to look up at its source for fear of what he might see. Classical images of the Watchers of Ishryth, grim and terrible to doubters, filled his mind.

'Great is Your wisdom, Lord. To You are all things known.'

Onwards, upwards, Cassraw struggled, such rational thoughts as he had being swept aside by the monstrous rapture now compelling him forward regardless of his protesting limbs and pounding heart.

And at last he was there, standing on top of the canted, broken obelisks of rock that formed the summit of the Ervrin Mallos. He dropped to his knees with a jarring impact, then immediately dragged himself to his feet again. He held out his arms and, closing his eyes, threw back his head to offer his face to the might of his god.

Such few doubts as he had known were gone now, driven out by the power he could feel all around him.

'Lord, You will do with me as You will, but I implore You, though I am but the least of Your servants, give me the strength to fulfil Your will in the world of men. Great are the sins done there in Your name. Great is the ignorance of Your Word and great the deceit and contention with which it is read.'

He waited.

A coldness touched his mind. He started violently then willed himself to stillness.

'Lord,' he whispered painfully. 'I am Yours. I will serve You with all my being.'

The coldness began to spread through him, and with it a sense of foreboding. Whatever this was, it was but the beginning.

Yet there was a strange quality about it – a *human* quality, it occurred to Cassraw – though he quickly disowned this blasphemous thought and concluded by praying for forgiveness. There was no response.

Still the coldness seeped through him purposefully, growing in strength as it did so.

And then it possessed him entirely.

He waited, scarcely conscious that he existed any more, though he could still sense, deep within him and far beyond his reach, doubts slithering and murmuring. Then the coldness shifted and, for a timeless, searing moment, the doubts flared up, screaming and demanding to be heard. For the feelings that were suddenly flooding into him were far from godlike. Dominating them was a terrible, almost uncontrollable anger.

Anger that so much, built so painstakingly over so long a time, should be lost so totally and so easily.

Anger towards the servants who had betrayed Him by their weakness and folly.

Anger, and something else . . .

Hatred! Deep and implacable. Hatred towards those ancient enemies who had risen to plot and scheme against Him.

And in the wake of this came an overwhelming lust for revenge, bloody and foul.

Yet, too, pervading everything was an almost unbearable sense of loss, and Cassraw could feel the clawing, scrabbling desperation of someone who must hold on to something, however slight, if He were to remain . . .

here? And not plunge into . . . the void? The images eluded Cassraw but he sensed well enough the terror of slipping from this place and tumbling eternally through a nightmare of solitude and powerlessness.

Then everything was changed. As suddenly as it had come, the turmoil was ended. A new awareness moved through Cassraw. A slender hold had been found, and the terrible fall halted. All was not yet lost!

'Be silent, my servant. I must judge you, know the true depths of your faith.'

Cassraw remained motionless, his eyes closed, his head still thrown back to face the black sky. 'As You will, Lord,' he whispered.

Then, where before there had been a coldness, there was now a searching warmth. Though he was waiting for a questioning, a harrowing, nothing happened. Yet something was moving within him. Like the faint rustling of distant trees, elusive and unclear. Then, fleetingly, a grim, malicious satisfaction passed through him.

'These dark and terrible thoughts, these doubts and hatreds are yours, Cassraw,' the voice said, deep and compassionate, though now it was more like a spoken voice than the eerie possession it had been before. *'They are the burden I have put upon you that you might know yourself the better. But you have borne them well and you have not been found wanting.'*

Cassraw was trembling again, though this time with a powerful sense of expectation.

'It is my will that you go forth and bring the truth of my Word to your peoples and all the peoples of this land. A great evil has arisen in the north which must be opposed lest all the world fall under its shadow. This land shall become a Citadel from which my armies will march forth again.'

Cassraw almost opened his eyes. 'Lord, I am no warrior,' he said prosaically. A dark amusement filled him from somewhere.

'*There are many swords, my servant. Yours is your tongue. Wield it well and armies greater than your imagining will be provided. This is my will, and it will be so. Be thou steadfast and true, and let none oppose thee.*'

'But who will listen to me, Lord? And what is this evil that has come about?' Cassraw asked weakly.

'*All will listen to you, my servant, for I have blessed you with my power. And where doubt of my Word exists I shall give you the true meaning.*' A hint of anger seeped into the voice. '*All else will be revealed in due time. Seek not to question your Lord, servant. Seek only to obey and serve.*'

Cassraw's legs finally gave way, and he slumped to the ground. The small, sharp stones driving into his knees began to restore sensation to his body.

'*I must leave you now, my servant.*'

The voice was fainter. The damage that Cassraw had done to himself in his reckless ascent of the mountain began to assert itself.

'Do not leave me, Lord,' he said, holding out his arms.

Again the amusement.

'*Know that I will be with you always, Cassraw. Always. You have but to listen.*'

And Cassraw was alone.

He remained kneeling for a long time, head bowed and arms resting on a flat boulder. Then, slowly, fearfully, he opened his eyes and looked around. The sky was still dark, though now the clouds had the snow-laden greyness of winter rather than the looming menace of before. The call which had drawn Cassraw up the Ervrin Mallos was no longer there, but he could still feel the presence of his Lord echoing and resonating inside him.

He hugged himself and bent forward. 'I was right,' he hissed. 'I was right, I was right.' Over and over, in a mixture of terror and malevolent glee. 'I am the Chosen One. His Chosen. I was right!' Then, with a painful effort he stood up. 'I am Yours, Lord, utterly,' he cried out rapturously. 'Yours! I shall gather up the righteous and bring them to Your Word, and together we shall seek out the sinners in this land and beyond, and bring them to Your Way. Or destroy them.'

Chapter 3

Vredech closed the main door of the Witness House quietly and climbed the stairs that would lead him back to the Debating Hall. He was still breathing heavily and his hands were shaking slightly. The look in Cassraw's eyes, his final, portentous words and then his manic dash up the mountain into what must surely be a monstrous storm, lingered vividly in his mind, adding to his confusion and distress.

Though he knew that Cassraw was fitter than himself, his friend was no youngster and must surely injure himself careening up the mountain like that. And who could say what kind of a storm those clouds presaged, or how long it would last when it broke?

He paused at the entrance to the Debating Hall to quieten his buzzing thoughts. A murmur of voices reached him and he sighed. On the whole he would have preferred to enter into an uproar. At least then he would have been able to intervene in a continuing argument. Now it seemed that the matter had been settled.

What have you done while I've been away, Mueran? he thought bitterly. Used your authority as Covenant Member to have him suspended? Well, not while I've got a tongue in my head!

With an effort he fought down his anger. He must not allow his anxiety for Cassraw to lead him into any rashness. It would be a serious mistake to charge at Mueran

24

like a stupid mountain goat. Tact and diplomacy were required if he was to protect Cassraw from the enemies that his harsh tongue had made.

Vredech took a deep breath and pushed open the door.

The Debating Hall was, like most rooms in the Witness House, plain and simple. It was free from any decoration save for the arched windows which were filled with stone traceries, into which all manner of leaves and vines and, peculiarly, slightly sinister faces had been carved. When a full Convocation was held, the assembled Preaching Brothers would sit on chairs arranged around three walls of the room, while the Chapter Members, the senior Brothers who formed the governing council of the Church of Ishryth in Canol Madreth, sat at one end. Now, however, the Chapter Members were sitting around a long, highly-polished wooden table which occupied the centre of the hall.

All eyes turned towards Vredech as he entered. He bowed slightly to acknowledge this impromptu greeting, then immediately approached Mueran. Whatever had happened in his absence, a more favourable outcome of the whole sorry business would probably be achieved if he did the right thing here, namely attended to the immediate needs of his tormented friend. He did not wait for Mueran to speak.

'Cassraw needs our help,' he said, simply. 'He's unwell. Very unwell. He seems to have had some kind of a . . . seizure.' This provoked knowing looks from a few of the assembled Brothers, but Vredech ignored them. 'He's gone dashing off up the mountain, and there's an appalling storm brewing. If he isn't badly injured, there's every chance that he'll be benighted or snowed in.'

The mood in the hall changed perceptibly. Some of the Brothers showed quite open irritation at this new problem that Cassraw had brought them, but most seemed to be genuinely concerned. Vredech had the impression that Mueran was assessing which group was in the majority

25

before replying, but he swiftly reproached himself for his lack of charity.

'Ah,' Mueran said neutrally, but nodding sagely.

'The sky *was* looking grim this morning. We must send someone to look for him immediately.' The speaker was Morem, a gentle, kindly man, remarkably free from the narrow-eyed shrewdness that typified most of the Chapter Members.

Vredech shook his head and moved closer to the table. He lowered his voice confidentially. 'Whatever problems Cassraw has caused us recently, he's still a senior member of the church, and despite the occasional complaint from some of its noisier members, he is much loved and depended upon by his flock. I don't have to tell you how greatly he's contributed in the past and I'm sure that with help through this . . . difficulty . . . he'll contribute as much again in the future. But he needs *our* help and protection, now. We can't send out the Witness House servants to find him. It'd be all over Troidmallos within the day. We'll have to go ourselves.'

This suggestion caused a stir. Most of the Chapter Members were manifestly too old to be wandering about the upper reaches of the mountain in any weather, let alone in a storm.

'We could send some of the novices,' someone offered tentatively.

Vredech shook his head again. 'The state that Cassraw's in, it's not going to be easy to make him listen,' he said. 'I think he's suffering some deep spiritual crisis. Apart from the common compassion of helping him through this in private, I think only we here stand any chance of being able to get through to him.' He waved down some retorts and, looking at Mueran, became more forceful. 'Those of us who can manage it should go up the hill and look for him, and go now before he gets too far, or that storm breaks.'

26

Mueran affected a look of great concern as if he were pondering the suggestion carefully. Vredech waited. He had launched his final appeal directly at Mueran simply to force the issue. It was a device he had used more than once in the past, knowing that the man disliked taking decisions but disliked being seen as indecisive even more. When faced in such a forthright and public manner, however, he could give his approval in the knowledge that, should it prove to be a mistake, he would be able to lay the greater part of any odium at the main instigator's – the frail servant's – feet. Should it prove to be correct, he would allow himself to bask quietly in the appreciation that would follow. Once again Vredech reproached himself for his lack of charity.

'You're quite right, Brother Vredech,' Mueran said smoothly. 'Dear Brother Cassraw's pain must be our concern. Little is to be served by allowing this matter to become the commonplace of the gossips and still less the Sheeters.' The word Sheeters brought angry frowns to the faces of many of his audience and there was a great deal of knowing nodding.

Mueran turned from Vredech to the others and with a regretful smile said, 'Alas, I myself am long past trekking about the mountain, but those of you with the legs and the youth for it go with Brother Vredech now. The rest of us will wait here and pray for your safe return with our Brother.'

'Perhaps you might also prepare a room and a warm bed for him,' Vredech said, a little more acidly than he had intended.

Mueran's smile barely faltered but his eyes narrowed slightly as he inclined his head regally. Mistake, Vredech thought.

'Practical as ever, Brother Vredech,' Mueran declared unctuously. 'Brother Cassraw had a fine friend in you.'

It was a double-edged remark.

A little later, some eight of the Chapter Brothers were gathered outside the Witness House, clad in such heavy cloaks, scarves and gloves as they could find. There had been more than eight volunteers, but Vredech had had to dissuade several of them. There was no point in taking out such a large group, since they might have to spend more time tending their own than searching for Cassraw.

Those Brothers who were staying behind were either watching anxiously from the top of the steps, or were busily shooing novices and servants about their affairs.

Vredech looked up at the sky and then at his companions. The clouds were lower and more oppressive than ever. He could feel primitive fears stirring deep within him and for a moment, he wanted to flee into the sanctuary of the Witness House like a frightened child. He had to make an unexpected effort to steady himself, and silently, but liberally, he blamed his friend for this disturbance.

Then he noticed that like the rest of the group, he was hunching his shoulders and bending his head forward as if the sky itself were pressing down on him. Consciously he straightened up and stared at the mountain in an attempt to focus his mind on the task at hand. The summit could not be seen from where they were, but he judged that in any case it was lost in the clouds by now. He quailed inwardly at the prospect of the bad weather ahead.

Still, it didn't matter. Cassraw had to be found.

'Come along, Brothers,' he said, almost heartily. 'We've nothing to gain by—'

'A moment, Brother Vredech.' Mueran's voice interrupted him. The company at the top of the steps parted to let him through as he emerged from the Witness House. 'I think a moment's prayer for our lost Brother would not go amiss, don't you?'

Anxious to be off, Vredech managed a commendably impassive expression as he bowed his head in response. He knew well enough that Mueran would take three times as long gently remonstrating with him if he debated the worth of this small exercise.

However, as Mueran, hands clasped and features studiously humble, tilted his head back into his usual preaching position, the lowering sky out-faced him, and for a moment he faltered.

'Ishryth . . . we beseech You . . . guide the feet of our Brothers in their . . . and . . . keep our beloved Brother Cassraw from all harm . . . in his torment . . .' He was both stuttering and gabbling.

Vredech took advantage of a momentary pause. 'Thus let it be,' he said firmly, in case Mueran should recover and begin his usual flow. The traditional response echoed uncertainly through the group, several of the Brothers casting sidelong glances at their revered leader to confirm that he had indeed finished.

Vredech bowed respectfully, then briskly motioned his party forward.

As they walked, there was some discussion about what exactly they should do. Should they divide into two or three parties, or stay together?

'We'd better stay together for now,' Vredech concluded. 'Perhaps when we're nearer the top we might split up – it depends what the weather's like. We must be careful. We're none of us as young as we were and it will certainly reach the Sheeters if we aggravate matters by getting lost ourselves and Mueran has to call in a rescue party from the town.'

They plodded on, stopping occasionally to allow the slower ones to catch up and recover their breath. The sky pressed down on them and the darkness deepened. It seeped inevitably into their conversation.

'I've never seen clouds like this before. They're neither snow, rain nor thunder clouds.' The speaker was Horld, a tall lanky individual who alone among the group seemed to be suffering no physical distress as they climbed. Once a blacksmith, he had turned to the church quite late in life after miraculously escaping from a disastrous fire at his forge. He was famous for the vividness of his preaching, which was permeated by the smoke, heat and clamour of his past trade, and though his pewside manner was the terror of his flock, his compassion and his practical pastoral care made him as much loved as he was feared. Vredech was glad that he had been at the Chapter meeting.

'Judgement Day.'

Vredech started at these words which echoed the thoughts that had come when he had stepped out of the lee of the Witness House wall to stand alone and exposed before the gathering clouds.

'An ominous phrase, Laffran,' he said, struggling with a suddenly dry throat to affect a lightness that he did not feel.

'Just came into my mind, Brother,' Laffran said.

Horld grunted. 'Judgement Day will be darker, hotter and noisier than this,' he said dismissively, but there was an uneasy tension in his manner as he urged the group forward with an impatient gesture.

'Yes, I'm sure it will. And I do believe that Ishryth would have given us some kind of a hint beforehand.' Morem's mild irreverence brought a stern frown from Horld, but seeing his older colleague suffering noticeably with the effort of the climb, he merely put an arm out to help him.

Vredech brought the conversation back to safer ground. 'They are strange, though, these clouds,' he said. 'They must be piled unbelievably high to be so dark.' He looked at Horld. 'And you're right, they don't feel like rain or snow, and certainly not like thunder. Let's just hope that whatever they are, they pass away as quietly as they've come.'

No one seemed inclined to pursue the matter, and the

party moved slowly on up the increasingly steep ground. The light was beginning to fade. Vredech cursed himself for not bringing any lanterns, but he had not envisaged such darkness. He had been caught in the clouds many times before now, sometimes in extremely bad visibility, but this was almost like night-time.

'We'll have to stop,' he said eventually. 'This light's appalling. It's becoming too dangerous to carry on. One of us is going to be hurt if we do.'

'We can't just abandon Cassraw,' Laffran objected.

'No, Vredech's right,' Horld said gloomily. 'We need lights. It's going to be difficult enough just getting back to the Witness House, let alone trying to go on, and still less to actually look for Cassraw.'

There was a reluctance to accept this simple practical logic, however, and for a few minutes the party remained where they were, some resting on the rocks, others peering intently into the gloom.

Abruptly, Horld took Vredech's arm and pointed. His hand was little more than a white blur now.

'There,' he whispered, as though afraid that the others might hear. Vredech screwed his eyes tight and leaned forward but could make nothing out. He shrugged.

'Light,' Horld said, still whispering. 'Up there – see?'

Vredech was about to contradict him when he realized that there was indeed light coming from somewhere. In fact, it was coming from everywhere. Dim, but with a yellowish and, it seemed to Vredech, unhealthy tint, it was marking out the skyline ahead of them. The sight temporarily disorientated him, and for a moment he felt as though he were not truly there. He shook his head to clear his wits.

'What is it?' Laffran asked, his voice unsteady.

'It's the clouds near the summit,' Vredech said slowly. 'They seem to be shining. As if there's something . . .' He hesitated. 'As if there's something . . .' *Inside them*, he

found himself wanting to say. *Something . . . evil.*
Thoughts flooded into his mind, imbued with a tingling,
unreasoning alarm.

Judgement Day.

God is here.

He is come.

For me.

You're like a child in the dark, he shouted silently to
himself in an attempt to deafen this mounting inner
clamour. He was only partially successful, and when he
concluded his remark with a lame, 'I've never seen
anything like it,' he had difficulty in keeping his voice
steady.

Horld grunted and with brusque practicality anchored
Vredech back into solid reality. 'Probably some kind of
lightning,' he announced. 'Shall we go on?'

Vredech thought for a moment. Dark, half-formed fears
were wrestling with his concern for Cassraw and, all too
aware that he was mimicking Mueran, he looked around
the group in an attempt to assess the consensus. Though
he could see faces in the dim light, however, he could read
no expressions. And, disturbingly, all eyes were turned
into deep black sockets.

'A little way,' he decided. 'But move carefully, and keep
together.'

And the group was off again, moving hesitantly through
the eerie light.

'I wonder what it could be,' Morem mused out loud.

'It's Ishryth's will.'

Vredech turned to the speaker. It was Laffran. To his
horror, a violent urge bubbled up within him to curse at
Laffran for his stupidity. They were on this wretched and
now dangerous trail because of Cassraw's ridiculous superstition, and they wanted none of their own to confuse their
judgement. The thought was almost heretical, but it was
the force of his anger that shocked him and he turned away

32

from Laffran sharply. 'All things are Ishryth's will,' he muttered.

'Thus let it be,' he heard Laffran responding.

Vredech lifted a hand to his forehead. He felt as though he were suffocating. *Judgement Day*. The words returned to him again and this time refused to leave him.

'Are you all right?' Morem's voice was anxious.

'Yes,' he replied as casually as he could manage. 'Just a little shaky. Not as fit as I thought I was.' But deep inside him something was turning and heaving, like vomit.

Then he saw them. Shadows.

He froze.

They were moving towards him, black against the unnatural darkness.

Weaving . . .

Swaying . . .

Chapter 4

Vredech stood motionless, paralysed by the conflict between the primitive terror welling up within him and the promptings of his rational mind telling him that what he was seeing was some strange optical illusion. He must be suffering a trick of the senses brought about by the unfamiliar exertion of clambering up the mountain in this bizarre, disturbing light.

He rubbed his arm across his eyes. The gesture should have been comforting but it felt alien and unnatural, as if the arm was not his any more, but some empty shell. And there was worse. He drew in a sharp breath. In the momentary, private gloom behind his closed eyes, where he had sought shelter, the shadows were there also; dancing, at once seductive and repellent, through the dull lights and patterns that hovered there. He opened his eyes in terror. He could feel the cold mountain air filling his chest but it did nothing to restore him. The shadows were still there. They were both beyond and within him, and all sense of normality was gone.

Yet still his reason clung on. Were these something real, or was he indeed suffering from some form of mountain sickness? He should turn to his companions and speak to them, ask them what they thought was happening; ask them what they could see. But he could not. He was unable to move, unable to cry out . . .

The shadows suddenly closed about him.

In the darkness that was not darkness and the now that was not now, a clamour of voices cascaded through Vredech. Voices full of hope rekindled, of an appalling fate avoided. Voices raised in raucous thanksgiving.

But there was no glory in the sound . . . if sound it was. It was more the gloating triumph of barbarian warriors revelling in the slaughter of a weaker foe. No! It was worse even than that. It was something primeval. Something out of the darkest reaches of the human mind. Something from a time before humanity was humanity.

Something to shrivel the mind of even the most depraved.

Under the impact of this revelation, Vredech lashed out, searching for some anchor that might hold him sane and whole amid this horror. Prayer came to him.

Ishryth protect me.

The words formed silently in the darkness.

The tumult did not so much falter as change character at the sounding of this slight clarion. It took on a jagged, unreal quality. Vredech became vaguely aware of his own breathing, shallow and fearful. It focused his awareness still further.

'What is this?'

Vredech felt the question rather than heard it, though its utterance was cold and awful, the very essence of the terrible celebration that hung now in the background.

Then the darkness was passing through him, searching. There were hints of sudden doubt and fear in it. And a burgeoning, terrifying rage. Yet, all too human though these emotions were, there was a quality in them such as could not be sounded by any ordinary measure. Through his growing terror, Vredech sensed his hands trying to move, trying to rise up and protect him from some sudden and unexpected attack. But nothing could prevail against what held him now. Into the silence another prayer came to him, a prayer of denunciation. He roared it into the darkness. 'Leave me, Ahmral's spawn! Leave me!'

His inner prayer echoed futilely about him, inconsequential beyond reckoning. And yet, around its tiny impact something formed.

A dark amusement?

Then . . . relief?

And, abruptly, he was dismissed. He was less than nothing. The merest mote . . .

Briefly the doubt returned, chilling Vredech utterly.

And he was dismissed again.

He was falling. Plummeting into the darkness.

'Vredech! Vredech!'

Voices all about him broke into the darkness and buoyed him up. As did arms wrapped about him.

Vredech's eyes opened on to the lesser darkness that was pervading the mountain. It seemed almost dazzling, so stark was the contrast with . . . wherever he had been.

'Vredech, what's the matter? Are you all right?'

The voice restored him further. It was Horld's, as were the powerful arms holding him. He realized that his fellow Brother was sustaining his entire weight. He willed his legs to support him.

'I'm sorry,' he mumbled, his voice strange in his own ears.

'Are you all right?' the question came again.

He nodded and gently unwound Horld's arms from about himself. 'Did you see that, hear that?' he asked, looking round at his companions.

'See what? Hear what?'

'The shadows. That terrible sound. That presence . . .' His voice faded as normality settled further about him. There was an awkward silence.

'I only saw you suddenly wave your arms then start to collapse,' Horld said, looking at him anxiously. 'You've probably been walking too fast. You're not as fit as—'

'No,' Vredech interrupted, stepping away from him and

gazing intently into the gloom. 'There *was* something here – shadows, moving. You must have seen them!' He put his hand to his head. 'And something worse. Something . . . alive. And awful. And it was in my mind as well.'

Morem took his arm gently. 'I think we'd better head back, Vred,' he said, though the remark was addressed to the others. 'There were no shadows, or anything else. All we saw was Horld grabbing you.'

Vredech wanted to argue. He might not be the man he was but he was fitter than all of them here, save perhaps Horld, and he *hadn't* suffered some hallucination brought on by exhaustion. Ishryth knows, he'd walked the mountains often enough! And he *had* seen what he had seen, heard what he had heard. Worse, he could still feel inside him a lingering after-shadow of the fearful presence that had touched him. It was all he could do to avoid shuddering. Yet he had been too long a member of the Chapter not to be able to stand apart from himself and view his conduct as it would be seen by his companions, with all that that implied. Obviously what had happened had happened to him alone, and if he persisted in questioning the others about it then they would assume, not unreasonably, that he was raving. Infected perhaps in some way by his contact with Cassraw. This little expedition would have to be abandoned and another arranged, which must inevitably involve the Witness House servants or the novices, and which would thus find its way down into the town gossip where Cassraw's spectacular flight would be lavishly embellished with tales of his own apparent derangement. It was unlikely to cost him his place in the Chapter, but it would undermine his authority there and, by the same token, increase that of Mueran and the other timeservers. This was not in the best interests of the church. And as for what the Sheeters would make of it . . .

That settled it. Whatever strangeness had just touched him must be left for later consideration. Now he must attend to the matter in hand.

'I'm sorry,' he said, affecting a heartiness that he certainly did not feel. 'It was just a little dizziness.' He nodded towards Horld. 'You're probably right. I was walking too fast and fretting about Cassraw, and all in this awful light. I'm fine now. Let's press on a little further.'

Horld grunted non-committally. Vredech was certain that had the light been better he would have seen doubt written all over the tall man's face, so he avoided the risk of any further debate by striding out purposefully. The hasty scuffling from behind told him that his immediate problem was over; his decisive action had ended any further interrogation and ensured the continuation of the search. Though the questions set in train by what had just happened were clamouring frantically for attention, he somehow forced them to one side. He was on the Ervrin Mallos, in the dark, looking for his demented friend, in the company of none too robust a team of walkers. He must remain alert, watch and listen for any signs of Cassraw or distress amongst his companions and, not least, he reminded himself, watch his every footstep. Carelessness here could see him pitched over some crag, thereby enabling him to learn the answer to some of life's great mysteries the hard way. The notion made him smile to himself despite his concerns.

'Not so fast, Vred,' came a reproachful cry from behind.

He turned to see his companions some way back, dim figures struggling through the gloom. Reaching out, he rested his hand on a nearby rock. Its cold damp touch felt reassuring. It was here, now, and so was he. He felt lighter.

'Sorry,' he shouted back. 'Must have got my second wind.'

There were complaints when everyone finally caught up.

38

'We should have gone back for some lanterns . . .'

'And more help . . .'

Vredech looked up at the clouds before replying. The dull, wavering yellow light still pervaded them. It had a sickly hue and it illuminated little, but at least it kept total darkness at bay. For a brief, dizzying moment he felt that he was looking not up, but down, down into some terrible pit, into the very eye of whatever it was that had touched him. He jerked his attention back to his companions.

'I don't know,' he admitted. 'We've come a long way and there's just about enough light to carry on with if we're careful. I'm loath to turn back without making a little more of an effort to find Cassraw. He could be in desperate straits by now.'

There was a brief silence.

'Someone's got to find him, sooner or later,' Morem said eventually.

Horld was looking up at the faintly glimmering clouds. 'That's not a happy sight,' he said. 'I'd dearly like to know what's causing it. I've never seen the like, ever.'

'None of us have,' Vredech ventured. 'But light is light. We should use it while we can.'

'And if it goes out?'

Laffran's cold query silenced the group again for a moment. Vredech waited, deliberately saying nothing.

Horld shook his head. 'It won't go out,' he declared. 'Whatever's causing it, it's too vast to be turned on and off like a Meeting House lamp. No, it won't go out.'

There was a hint of the practical man's contempt in his voice and Laffran bridled. 'And if these clouds choose to empty their load on us? Rain, snow, wind – what then?' he demanded. 'It's getting colder, you might have noticed.'

'Then we'll get wetter and colder,' Horld countered, speaking with wilful slowness.

The two held one another in brotherly esteem, as was fitting for men in their position, but there was little affection wasted between them and Chapter meetings were not infrequently enlivened by their petty arguments. Vredech intervened hastily before one developed here. 'To Ishryth's lawn then,' he said, half-suggestion, half-instruction. 'It's not far now. We can review our position there.'

Ishryth's lawn was a gently sloping grassy area where many walkers chose to pause and rest before venturing on the final rocky scramble to the summit. It was sheltered and very pleasant and, given the right weather, offered splendid panoramas of Canol Madreth's mountains.

Laffran and Horld seemed to have no great heart for continuing their argument and, no one objecting to this compromise, the party set off again. Vredech, still strangely buoyed up, paced himself more carefully this time.

As Horld had observed, the light from above showed no signs of diminishing, though it continued to vary in intensity, pulsing slowly and erratically to some indefinable rhythm. Few of the walkers chose to look up at it however, ostensibly being more concerned with watching where they were putting their feet. As they walked on, it grew colder. Not the sharp coldness of a winter frost, but a clinging, damp unpleasantness.

Vredech looked about him at the familiar landscape now made alien. Night in day, a graveyard chill and the whole lit by a light that came from neither sun nor moon, but was . . .? The word *diseased* came to mind but he abandoned it immediately and, reproaching himself for allowing his mind to wander, turned his attention back to where he was walking.

Then, after a slithering and alarming clamber up a narrow gulley down which a small stream was still running, they were walking on to Ishryth's lawn.

'It's brighter,' Morem said in some surprise.

'It's probably because we've just come out of the

gulley,' Horld said, though more gently than he would have addressed such a remark to Laffran.

'Either way, it's no pleasanter,' Vredech said. There was a unanimous nodding of heads from the eight dark-shadowed forms as they each looked around at the soft green grass now rendered dull and lifeless by the touch of the eerie cloudlight.

Motioning his companions to remain where they were, Vredech moved across the clearing towards a rocky edge which he knew would give him a view out over the valley. Only when he reached it did he realize that he was hoping to see Troidmallos far below, its lights shining up to him like tiny welcoming beacons. The town must surely be alive with lights by now, if this vast bank of clouds had moved so far as to cover the peak of the mountain. But there was nothing. Just an impenetrable darkness. There was not even the faint greyness of daylight seeping through to show the edge of the clouds where they had arched over the mountain.

Nothing.

Just blackness.

And silence. No faint murmur of sounds from the valley below, no occasional bird cry, no breeze.

Nothing.

It was as if the world had ended and he and his companions were alone in an endless, empty void.

Vredech did shudder this time. Partly because of the increasing cold, partly from some deeper need. He wanted to pray again, but he steeled himself against the urge. It's just freak weather conditions, he forced himself to think. That's all. I'm not some superstitious savage who retreats into mindless ritual when faced with the unknown. I use the mind that Ishryth gave me. I think. I learn. I strive to fathom his mysteries.

It was true. But it didn't stop him from shuddering again.

The others began to join him. They stood arrayed around him, gazing out into the darkness. There was a little foot-stamping and arm-beating, but it gradually faded away.

'It's frightening.'

Morem's simple admission made Vredech feel slightly ashamed.

'Yes,' he said. 'It is. I suppose we'll just have to be grateful that we're not in the thick of a blizzard or a thunderstorm.'

'Yet,' Laffran added. His slightly sour tone made Vredech smile.

'Now,' he said, turning his back on the emptiness and facing his companions, 'in case the weather has any more surprises for us we'd better decide what to do next. I don't want to leave without a determined search for Cassraw, but the ground's much steeper and rougher from here on and there's precious little in the way of a clearly marked path. We could miss him easily enough and we could end up in difficulties ourselves. And I'm concerned about the temperature.'

'What was Cassraw wearing?' someone asked.

Vredech grimaced. There were no real choices ahead after all. 'Just what he stormed out of the Debating Hall in. No top coat, cloak, nothing.'

'Then some of us will *have* to go on,' Horld announced. 'The darkness is a bad enough problem, but if it keeps on getting colder then Cassraw's soon going to be in very serious trouble, tough though he is.'

'You're right,' Vredech said. He looked at the group, wishing that he could see their faces, read their thoughts. 'While there's still some visibility we'll have to go on.'

'I don't think I can go much further,' Morem confessed. 'That gulley was quite a struggle.'

'We'll split up,' Vredech said, laying a reassuring hand on his shoulder. 'Horld and I still have some wind left.

42

We'll go on to the summit. The rest of you stay here and try to keep warm. Listen for any sound of Cassraw coming back in case we miss him.'

There was no dissent.

'Are you all right?' Horld said softly as they moved away from the group and began cautiously working their way over the shattered rocks that would lead them to the summit.

'I'm fine,' Vredech said. 'Not happy, not warm and not comfortable, but fine for all that.'

Horld grunted. 'That was a very strange turn you had before,' he said.

'It's a strange day,' Vredech replied evasively.

'There's no denying that,' Horld agreed. 'What do you think happened to Cassraw to send him off like that?'

Vredech shrugged his shoulders unhappily. He did not want to discuss Cassraw's behaviour. Indeed, he did not want to discuss anything. Once his thoughts started to run he was far from certain that he would be able to contain them. It was only the physical discipline involved in struggling over the rocks in the darkness that was keeping a torment of his own at bay. But still, he must reply.

'I've no idea,' he said. 'He's always been rather . . . intense. Perhaps it's the problems he's been having with his flock. Some of them are a bit of a pain, and he takes things to heart much more than people realize.'

'I said at the time that I thought he was too young for the Haven parish,' Horld fretted. 'It's a big responsibility. He should've served a year or two more as a Chapter Member before coming to anything like that.'

There was nothing new in Horld's comments. He was quite conservative in his thinking and although he himself had only been a little longer in the church than Cassraw, he was cautious, even suspicious, of younger men coming along too quickly. But he had always spoken his views openly and without acrimony and they were well known.

Vredech had the feeling that, atypically, he was talking around some topic instead of tackling it head on. Taking a risk, he changed the subject abruptly.

'This cold's getting worse. It's starting to cut right through me,' he said.

Horld walked on a little way without replying. Again Vredech sensed an unease within him. Then he stopped suddenly. 'Look,' he whispered. Vredech could dimly make out Horld's arm pointing up into the darkness. He peered after it, but could see nothing.

'What?' he asked.

'There,' Horld said impatiently. 'Look – that light.'

Slowly, Vredech's eyes adjusted. Ahead he saw that a part of the sky was noticeably brighter than the rest. It offered no greater illumination, however. Rather it seemed to be a concentration of all that was unpleasant in the strange cloudlight. He felt a chill of fear as if something might be lurking behind the rocks now silhouetted along the skyline.

'What is it, do you think?' he said, whispering, as Horld had.

'I don't know,' Horld replied. 'But you're right, this cold seems to be getting worse with each step. Come on.' And he was off, moving swiftly.

'Wait,' Vredech called out, though still softly.

But Horld did not seem to be listening. It was almost as though he was being drawn forward by something.

'Wait!' Vredech called again, more insistently. His voice sounded harsh in the cold darkness and Horld stopped and turned.

'Sorry,' he mumbled as Vredech reached him.

Vredech felt a spasm of irritation. 'For pity's sake, Horld, we must keep together! One lost on the mountain is bad enough.' Immediately, regret flooded through him, but he could not find the words to express it. The two men stood staring at one another silently, aware of each other only as darkness within darkness.

Then that very darkness was changing. Sombre shadows were being carved out to give form and depth, though still more was hidden than illuminated. Both men looked upwards instinctively. Vredech drew in a sharp breath, while Horld circled his forefinger over his heart. It was an old gesture invoking Ishryth's protection, long out of favour with the church but much used by many of its followers.

The sky was alive with flickering lights. The dank coldness that pervaded Vredech moved to and fro within him in compulsive harmony with the sight: rising, falling, sucking his breath away with its awful chill. It seemed to him once again that he was in the presence of a great multitude, whirling and dancing in an unholy celebration. Yet was it a multitude? He had the fleeting impression of a single entity, broken and shattered: a myriad gibbering shards trying to become whole again. His body filled with shivering echoes of the pernicious touch he had felt earlier and he raised a hand not only to fend it off but as if, in some way, he could deny the awful synthesis he could feel happening.

'Ishryth,' he heard Horld murmuring, awe-stricken.

The word rang through Vredech and from somewhere deep within him came a great denial. But he could find no voice for it. He was impotent.

The lights danced on, weaving movements growing ever faster and more complex while Vredech sank into despair, consumed by the knowledge that there was something he could do – should do – if he had but the knowledge.

Then, briefly, the lights converged to become like a single star, unbearably bright to the two men after their long journey through the darkness.

And it was over.

The star was gone.

All the light was gone.

Darkness returned, total and absolute.

Both men cried out at their sudden blindness, and reached out wildly to one another. Their hands met fortuitously and tightened upon one another in desperation. Vredech could not have said for how long they stood thus, primitive fears clamouring at them, but eventually he heard his own voice, trembling and breathless, saying, 'We must go down. Very slowly, carefully, step by step. Feeling the way. And we must keep hold of one another.' The sound helped him to regain some control over the screeching tumult filling his mind. Horld made no reply, but his grip tightened further about Vredech's hand. Yet, despite the simple practicality of his suggestion, neither man moved.

'I think I can see again.'

Horld's voice was the merest whisper.

Vredech strained forward to hear him, then he, too, began to see that the greyness which he had taken to be a response by his eyes to the sudden darkness was, in fact, real. He blinked several times and rubbed his eyes with his free hand.

Then Horld's punishing grip was gone and his companion was once again a figure standing next to him, gazing upwards into the dull mottled grey of an ordinary winter sky. The rocks about them emerged from their entombment. The chill about them became the chill of a late winter's day on the mountains, and a slight breeze began to blow.

Relief swept through Vredech, purging away the last few minutes of terror almost as if they had never been.

'It's over,' he said, not knowing what he meant. 'It's over.'

A hand closed powerfully about his shoulder and a familiar, yet unfamiliar voice spoke.

'No, my friends. It begins. It begins.'

46

Chapter 5

Both men started violently and spun round. Horld lost his balance as he did so, but Cassraw's hand on his shoulder stayed his fall and steadied him effortlessly. So heightened were his senses by this sudden shock that Vredech took in Cassraw's entire appearance instantly. He saw the formal black cassock, elegant and well-made, torn and stained beyond repair, with bloody weals showing through several of the larger rents. He noted the grimy face and tousled hair, the scratched and bleeding hands. But, distressing though all this was, to Vredech it appeared to be only the surface manifestation of a far more profound change. For, despite his dark and soiled attire, Cassraw's presence seemed to cut through the gloom as though a light from some distant place were shining on him, like unexpected sunlight striking through storm clouds.

And his eyes . . . Vredech started.

Were they black . . .?

Not just the irises, but the entire orbs . . .?

Like pits of night.

Vredech had scarcely registered this chilling impression when it was gone and Cassraw was again nothing more than his familiar friend, battered and bruised but seemingly whole, and carefully supporting Horld.

Horld, however, was less than grateful, for all that Cassraw had probably saved him from an unpleasant fall. He yanked his arm free and the blacksmith in him opened

47

his mouth and began to abuse Cassraw roundly for the folly of his sudden and silent approach. Cassraw did not respond, but merely stared at him and smiled absently. Meeting no opposition, Horld's tirade foundered awkwardly and the obligations of his latterday calling returned to reproach him for his intemperance. Thus, after a few terse but vivid sentences, his rebukes began to be leavened with more charitable and concerned observations about his returned colleague. Still Cassraw made no reply, though his smile became knowing, like an understanding parent waiting patiently for his clamouring children to fall silent.

'Where have you been? What's happened to you?' Vredech asked a few times while Horld's tirade was plunging on, but even as it faltered into silence so his own questions died. He would receive no answers: he knew this as plainly as if Cassraw had placed his dirt-stained hand across his mouth to silence him.

Then Cassraw was holding their arms and motioning them down the mountain. His grip, though not painful, was quite irresistible and, for a little way, Horld and Vredech found themselves carried along by it. The ground was too uneven for walking thus for long, and after a little while Cassraw released his charges and set off on his own. His pace was not that of a man who had just careened recklessly up a mountain or suffered some great ordeal, and Vredech and Horld fell steadily further behind him.

When he reached the rest of the group waiting on Ishryth's lawn, Cassraw was not only quite a way ahead of his would-be rescuers, but he looked much fresher than they did.

The Chapter Brothers milled around him, bombarding him with questions, but he did not acknowledge any of them other than by nodding occasionally and smiling mysteriously. The questions were redirected towards Horld and Vredech as soon as they arrived but all they could do was shrug.

'We didn't find him, he found us. He was there behind us when the darkness vanished. And no, he hasn't said anything since then,' they replied several times, by some common consent not referring to the enigmatic remark with which he had greeted them.

Morem had trained as a physician when younger and though he had subsequently chosen the church as his vocation, he still had some considerable skill as a healer. 'He's probably in shock,' he offered quietly. 'It takes people in odd ways. He looks an awful mess but at least he doesn't appear to be seriously injured. We shouldn't pester him. He may be more fragile than he looks. I think perhaps we should just go back and let things take their course. He'll tell us what happened when he's ready.'

Even as he was speaking however, Cassraw was moving off again. He went to the rocky edge where, a little earlier, Vredech had stood and stared out into a terrifying black emptiness. Now, though the light was grey and wintry, the scene was more familiar. The lights of Troidmallos could be seen twinkling far below, and the shapes of most of the adjacent mountains could be made out. Cassraw's head moved from side to side as he reviewed the dull panorama, then he nodded to himself very slowly and unfolded his arms until they were held out wide as though he wished to embrace the entire country.

His companions watched in silence, not so much following Morem's advice as simply not knowing what to do. They had little time to ponder, however, for, his brief contemplation over, Cassraw was once again determining the course of events. Striding across Ishryth's lawn he headed towards the gully that would start the descent back to the Witness House.

The return journey gave the Brothers no great insight into Cassraw's condition. In fact, it served only to compound their confusion as Cassraw, though remaining relentlessly silent, continued to take effective command of the group, moving to and fro amongst them, patiently supporting and helping the frailer Brothers who were now beginning to feel the strain of their strange journey.

Finally the Witness House was in sight.

Cassraw stopped on a rocky spur and looked down at it in an almost proprietorial manner, then he turned and stared towards the summit of the Ervrin Mallos. After a moment he nodded to himself as he had at the edge of Ishryth's lawn. It seemed to Vredech that Cassraw was making a decision.

As the group, moving slowly and wearily now, wended its way down the final slopes towards the Witness House, they were greeted by Mueran and several of the other Chapter Members. Mueran had led them forth when the darkness had disappeared, after carefully ensuring that all the novices and servants were kept occupied elsewhere in the building. Vredech thought he noticed a momentary flash of anger in Cassraw's eyes as he caught sight of the Covenant Member approaching, but it was gone before he could register it fully.

He could read the debate in Mueran's eyes, however, even if it lasted only a little longer than Cassraw's seeming anger. Was his greeting to be a rebuke, or a welcome?

Mueran's face became pained and he opened his arms wide. It was to be a welcome.

'Brother Cassraw,' he said. 'We've been greatly alarmed for you.' He looked around at the others. 'For all of you. The darkness seemed to deepen so after you'd left.' He glanced up at the sky. 'I never thought I'd be so glad to see such a dismal wintry sky, but . . .' He chuckled genially in an attempt to lessen the tension but the sound jarred and he concluded awkwardly, 'Ishryth be praised for carrying the darkness from us anyway.'

Cassraw fixed him with a stern gaze. 'Ishryth's will is written on this day truly,' he said, unexpectedly breaking his silence.

Unnerved by Cassraw's stare and uncertain how to respond, Mueran nodded non-committally and said weakly, 'We've warm food and a good fire for you all inside.'

Cassraw's response was an authoritative gesture, which motioned everyone towards the Witness House. A frown flickered across Mueran's face at this cavalier action, but he turned with the rest and, after a short, none too dignified sprint, caught up with Cassraw who was now striding out boldly, his flock abandoned.

Once inside the Witness House, Cassraw maintained the same vigorous pace in the direction of the Debating Hall, drawing the group after him, noisy but too flustered to question him. He seemed to be gathering energy with every step. Mueran was no longer even trying to keep up with him, and kept looking around anxiously for fear that any novices or servants might have strayed from their carefully allotted tasks and be witnessing this scuttling procession. From time to time he lifted his hand as if he were about to call out to Cassraw, but no sound came.

Suddenly, Vredech had had enough. Tired and drained after the ordeal of struggling up the mountain through the darkness, and the strain of the bizarre descent, his patience suddenly evaporated. He ran forward as Cassraw reached the Debating Hall and, stepping in front of him, placed his hand firmly on the door.

'Enough, Cassraw. Enough.' He was out of breath but his voice was nevertheless powerful and angry. The others fell silent. 'I don't know what you're doing, or even if *you* know what you're doing, but some of us who came out to find you are in a sorry state as a result. They need rest and attention *now*.' He looked Cassraw up and down and his tone softened. 'As do you, for pity's sake. Whatever's keeping you on your feet, there'll be a price to pay if you don't get some rest.' Without waiting for a reply he turned to Mueran. 'Warm food and a fire, you said. Where?'

Mueran nodded hesitantly. 'In the Guest Room, next to the Refectory. I—'

'Then let's get up there,' Vredech interrupted. 'Let's wait until we're cleaned up and fed and we've got some normality around us again before we do any talking about what's happened here.'

Several voices spoke out in agreement.

'Of course,' Mueran said. 'You're quite right, Brother Vredech. We must—'

'No!' Cassraw had not moved since Vredech had stepped in front of him. Now, as his voice rang out, his frame became alive with agitation. Vredech winced away from the sound which had been uttered directly into his face, but immediately returned his gaze to meet Cassraw's.

'There are things which you must know,' Cassraw went on, apparently addressing everyone present but still speaking directly and forcefully into Vredech's face. 'Matters of great import. Matters concerning—'

'Enough, I said, Cassraw!' Vredech shouted. 'And I mean it. You've caused enough problems today. You're not well – you need rest. We all need rest.'

Cassraw's eyes suddenly blazed and he reached past Vredech to take hold of the handle of the door to the Debating Hall. For an instant, as he stared into his old friend's black eyes, Vredech felt that he was looking into the very heart of the darkness that had loomed so terribly over them that day. The memory of the dancing shadows and the menacing presence that had reached into him flitted around the edges of his consciousness, threatening to bring with it the babbling host of questions that so far he had been able to hold at bay. But, as during the final part of his journey up the mountain, something else stirred within him, something deep and resolute. And then there was no Mueran, no Brothers, no Witness Hall. Nothing except himself and Cassraw.

And while Cassraw was his friend, he must nonetheless be opposed.

Will against will.

No reason sustained this knowledge. It was simply a truth.

He must not yield.

But it was not a raging power that came to him. He simply said, 'No,' very softly. 'As I love you, my old friend. No.'

And he was once again standing outside the Debating Hall, suddenly noisy now with his fellow Brothers rushing forward to catch the falling Cassraw.

'The people's faith is our charge,' Mueran said at the hastily-convened meeting that followed Cassraw's collapse into unconsciousness. 'We must do what we can to protect the church. News that one of our Brothers has become . . . deranged, because he may have been burdened with too much too soon will give rise to great doubts and distress amongst our flocks.' Then he struck nearer to his true thinking. 'And who can say what the Sheeters will make of it? The truth's going to present us with enough problems, let alone what *they'll* say. The last thing we need is any more controversy about the Haven Parish.'

His assessment of Cassraw's condition was not accepted unopposed however. 'Cassraw's not deranged, he's possessed,' Laffran declared harshly. 'Some servant of Ahmral has entered into him.'

There was uproar around the table, but Vredech, normally a vigorous opponent of such opinions, remained strangely silent even though many heads were turned towards him expectantly.

By default, Mueran spoke on his behalf. 'Those are precisely the kind of remarks we must avoid, Brother Laffran,' he said. 'Possession is an area fraught with difficulty, not least because even today it still carries with it lingering memories of . . . less happy times.' This was Mueran's euphemism for the time of the Court of the Provers, when methods of appalling brutality had been used in the search for Ahmral's servants. A dark time, when the church had been at once more powerful and less civilized, a time before reason had fought its way through to curb the excesses of superstition. An institution set up by the church to protect the faith and maintain its purity, the Court of the Provers had eventually led to the persecution of thousands for the least of deviations from the True Way. It had finally been swept aside by the forces of an increasingly nervous secular state empowered by a sickened populace, but its name lingered as a byword for terror, sadism and savagery, and all that is foul in human nature. It was an era that the modern church of Ishryth earnestly disowned though it was still apt to become overly defensive when reluctantly drawn into debates about it.

Laffran made to interrupt but Mueran ploughed on. 'I'm not going to allow a discussion on that matter now,' he said, with uncharacteristic firmness. 'The church's position is quite clear. The Santyth is, at best, ambiguous on the matter and we favour the search for rational causes for sickness before we invoke Ahmral's personal intervention.'

Though Mueran was merely stating the church's official view on such matters, he was far from happy. Laffran's remark could pitch the gathering into the deepest theological waters and he desperately wanted to keep their discussion on the simple pragmatic level of a sick colleague presenting an awkward administrative problem.

He was spared any further debate by the entry of Morem, who had been attending to Cassraw. He went straight to his seat, dropped down in it heavily and put his face in his hands. When he looked up he started a little, as if surprised to find himself where he was.

'I'm sorry,' he said. 'I was preoccupied.'

Mueran's concerns were not eased by Morem's manner. 'How is Brother Cassraw?' he asked, managing to keep his voice quite calm.

Morem frowned. 'I don't know,' he said. 'He's covered in cuts and bruises. Presumably he must have fallen over a good number of times when he was going up the mountain, but he's suffered no blows to the head or anything else that I can see that should affect him this way.'

Laffran cleared his throat noisily, his jawline taut. Mueran glowered at him. 'Could he just be exhausted?' he tried hopefully.

'We're all exhausted, Mueran,' Morem replied, unusually sour. 'It's been far from the day any of us thought it was going to be. But no one's anywhere near the point of collapse. And Cassraw's probably the fittest amongst us.'

There was an awkward silence. Mueran was at a loss to know what to ask and Morem seemed disinclined to offer any suggestions as to the nature of Cassraw's condition. Vredech looked up. He was having difficulty in concentrating. He wanted to be away from here. He needed to think about everything that had happened today; needed to let loose the questions that were clamouring for release and preventing him from thinking clearly. He turned towards Morem. 'No reflection on you, Morem, but do you think we should call in his physician?' he asked.

Mueran's finger tapped the table nervously.

'I don't think so,' Morem said, after a moment's thought. 'Cassraw will be in some pain for a while, thanks to the knocking about he's given himself, but I've examined him very thoroughly and nothing's broken. Nor is he losing blood. Everything that really matters seems to be all right. Pulses, breathing – calmer and steadier than mine, for what it's worth. Reflexes – fine.' He rubbed his thighs gingerly. 'He should be wide awake and grumbling like the rest of us, not lying there motionless.'

'Well, we've got to do something,' Mueran said pointlessly.

'Perhaps his wife might be able to help,' Morem said, his face lightening a little.

The atmosphere around the table changed. 'We can't bring a woman into the Witness House, just like that,' Laffran exclaimed, eyebrows raised. 'It's . . .' he floundered.

'It's a good idea,' Vredech heard himself saying, cutting through Laffran's confusion. 'If Morem says he's not badly injured that's good enough for me. And if there's nothing physically wrong with him then it's head or heart,' he tapped his head, then his chest. 'Either way, his wife's better equipped to reach him, wherever he is, than any of us.' He became practical. 'Besides, Cassraw would have gone home tonight. She'll be expecting him.'

Thus it was that, despite his reservations about the matter, Laffran found himself escorting Dowinne to the Witness House. Reluctantly, after his announcement that Cassraw had 'had a bit of an accident' he had found it necessary to give Dowinne some assurance that nothing serious had happened to him but that Mueran thought it would be helpful if she were with him. It was near enough to a lie to make him decidedly uncomfortable, and he could do little except smile at her rather weakly in the dim lamplight whenever he caught her eye as they swayed from side to side in the carriage.

It did not occur to Dowinne that it was odd that she should be travelling in one of the church carriages with the blinds pulled down. Had she thought about it at all, she would perhaps have reasoned that although those appalling black clouds had dispersed, it was still very gloomy and quite late in the day. The reality was that Mueran wanted no indication of anything untoward reaching anyone other than those who already knew, and the sight of Cassraw's wife being driven through the streets towards the Witness House would be around the town within the hour.

Her thoughts were elsewhere, however. After the initial shock of Laffran's news, she tried to work out what might have happened, in order to decide how she must behave when she arrived at the Witness House. But to no avail. Apart from one or two servants, women were rarely allowed into the Witness House, and then usually on special ceremonial occasions. Thus, despite Laffran's assurances, she knew that something serious must have happened even though it might not involve any physical injury to her husband. Once or twice she questioned Laffran, but he was evasive and obviously under instructions not to say anything. After a while she leaned back into the corner of her seat and, lifting her hand, rested her head on it. The action relieved Laffran greatly as he had been looking all around the carriage in an attempt to avoid her gaze. Dowinne had always made him feel uncomfortable, and being confined with her under these circumstances was proving to be a considerable ordeal.

In the darkness behind her hand, Dowinne did not find the calm reflection she was seeking. Unthinkingly, she lifted her other hand and tested the bruise where she had inadvertently struck the metal dish earlier. The slight pain brought back the thoughts that had been troubling her all day; the feeling that something bad was about to happen, that forces beyond her and her husband's control were in motion. It was not something that was susceptible to logic, but it was real nonetheless and it was some measure of Dowinne that not the slightest sign appeared on her face, as she faced this unknown, unreasoned intrusion and determined that she would deal with whatever had happened, however grim or strange.

Alert, but calm and clear in her mind now, she lowered her hand and examined her companion. He smiled feebly yet again, and she acknowledged him with an uncertain

57

but calculated smile of her own. 'Not much further now,' he said needlessly, assuming his professional sick visiting manner.

Part of Dowinne's old self had already noted the discreet luxury of the carriage, but now she became aware of the even more discreet quality embedded in its design, as shown by the fact that she had not noticed when they had begun the final uphill climb. It reaffirmed her new intent. She would deal with this pending problem without losing sight of her long-term ambition for a single moment.

When they finally drew to a halt in front of the Witness House, Laffran helped Dowinne down the carriage steps. She had never felt more assured. It wasn't something bad that was going to happen – or had happened, it was only something disturbing – something that brought change in its wake. And that could only be to her advantage.

Chapter 6

Privv was a Sheeter. He liked being a Sheeter – but then, he would. He had always been a worm. Admittedly, a worm with some skill in the handling of words, but a worm nonetheless; most at home when wriggling through the mouldering outer reaches of society or exposing to the light the darker labyrinths of human nature. Not that he considered himself to be so meanly inclined: he could justify his chosen profession, as he called it when he was feeling dignified, with the best of them.

'It's only the likes of us that guarantee our ancient freedom. People are entitled to know what the Heinders are doing in their name. And the Chapter Members of the church, with their secret meetings. And the great merchants. And the Guild Masters.'

And anyone else who exhibited any remotely human frailty that might serve as food for the indiscriminate and ever-greedy god of gossip that Privv so assiduously served.

It did not help that there was a great deal of truth in what he said, of course. More than a few states in Gyronlandt suffered under the heels of autocracies of one form or another, and the first two acts of such governments on coming to power were invariably to disarm their loyal subjects and then ban all the Sheets to ensure that as little as possible about what was really happening would become public knowledge.

Sheeters were a resolute bastion against such eventualities.

59

Sometimes.

They were also a deep pain.

Often.

Privv scowled and scratched himself unceremoniously. He swung his feet down from his desk and walked over to the window again. Not by any definition a sensitive man, he nonetheless enjoyed the view he had from this particular room. To the north stood the dominating bulk of the Ervrin Mallos, halfway up which could be seen, on a clear day, the Witness House. To the east, visible in almost any weather save the grimmest, stood the elegant spires of the PlasHein, home of the Heindral.

Most fitting, he would think in his more sanctimonious moments, that he should have the two great institutions of the state constantly within his view. It was not without symbolic significance. It was where they both belonged. It was the way things should be. Who better to guard the guardians than himself?

But he was in no such philosophical mood now and his eyes were narrowed and fretful as he gazed out at the distant shape of the Witness House. His thumb came to his mouth and he began chewing the nail vigorously.

'You'll be growling when that's all inflamed again.'

The voice was unusual. It was female, high-pitched, hectoring and generally unpleasant. It also existed only in Privv's mind. Not that he imagined it – it was real enough. It belonged to Leck. Privv referred to Leck as his companion, even his partner. Everyone else referred to her as his cat.

'Shut up,' Privv replied irritably. 'I'm trying to think.'

A disdainful hiss, quite clear in its meaning, filled his head, but as there was no specific reply to which he could respond, Privv contented himself with a silent, lip-curling sneer. Most people grow out of their sneers as they reach adulthood but, as was usually the way with Sheeters, Privv had not managed this, and thus one of youth's more

60

regrettable traits had become an adult characteristic. It pervaded most of his thinking. True, it was usually only in the privacy of his own home, as now, that he actually allowed it to show on his face. Though, that said, had he thought about it at all, he would probably have considered it to be a thoroughly wholesome and worthwhile inner quality. He had never been able to differentiate between scepticism and cynicism.

How Privv and Leck came to communicate with one another as they did is not known. Neither could communicate with anyone else in this manner and, as far as they knew, neither came from parents who had the same ability. It was just one of those things. Not that it was unique in Canol Madreth, or for that matter in Gyronlandt as a whole, but it was rare. And it still carried with it faint overtones from the Court of the Provers. To the Judges of the Proving, the ability to communicate with an animal in such a way was, beyond any dispute, the mark of an individual who had had dealings with the Great Destroyer, Ahmral. Indeed, more than that, such an individual might well be possessed by one of His demons, and could therefore look to be lingeringly destroyed for the greater good of the church and, of course, his own soul. Now, in these more enlightened times, the residue of the fear that had brought about such horror showed itself merely in an unspoken but general acceptance that this particular ability was not really attractive in polite society.

Not that Privv cared overly about what was socially desirable or not. It was sufficient for him that he kept silent about his gift and knew how to make the necessary noises to move freely in whatever level of Madren society he found himself. His only real concern was for the accumulation of wealth, followed, a little inconsistently in the light of his chosen profession and his inner disdain for society, by a desire to be both famous *and* respected. He also enjoyed manipulating people and events – though this

61

was as much a hobby, or tool of his trade, as an ambition. Certainly he had no desire whatsoever to volunteer for the constraints offered to the traditional ways of achieving power, namely through the Heindral or the church. As a Sheeter, he was, of course, unfettered, the Sheeting profession being comparatively new to Canol Madreth.

Leck seemed to be very similar in character to Privv – though who could say what ambitions a cat might harbour? She was a true predator however – she *really* enjoyed power, enjoyed it enormously, and as an end in itself. An ordinary, innocuous-looking cat, predominantly white but with various brindled markings scattered indiscriminately about her, she affected a loving disposition, invariably fawning around the legs of anyone who might prove useful, and, of course, purely for pleasure, about the legs of those visitors to Privv's house who particularly did not like cats. She also demonstrated the same general lack of civilized traits – ethics, morality, etc – that characterized Privv. Unlike the Sheeter, though, she did have at least some vestige of an intellectual justification for her disposition, in that she was not human. Indeed, she was inordinately proud of that fact and she had a line in scorn about humanity that could set even Privv's teeth on edge when she chose to use it.

An unlovely couple in almost every way, they tended each other's needs, or rather, served each other's ends with a generally ill grace and little or no affection. Yet they were bound together by ties far deeper than either of them could reach. Ties of which they were scarcely aware, save that they were there and were perhaps unbreakable. Ties that came with their strange shared gift.

'And pray, when you've finished eating your hand, do tell me what object is being given the benefit of your great intellect now,' Leck went on, jumping up onto the windowsill and following his gaze. 'Shouldn't you be finishing that piece on the market officials?'

'No rush for that,' Privv yawned. 'Besides, it'll do them no harm to sweat a little. With a bit of luck they might even try to bribe me, then we'll have an even better story.'

'True,' Leck conceded. 'Unless, of course, it's a really worthwhile bribe.'

Privv chuckled. 'Well, one has to use one's professional judgement in such matters, hasn't one? There are always long-term implications in such matters.'

'You don't normally bother about them where money's concerned,' Leck retorted, stretching herself luxuriously.

Privv shook his head in denial. 'As a puppeteer, I'm always looking out for strings, particularly when they might be fastened to me.'

Leck feigned indifference for a moment, then leaned against him and began to wheedle. 'What's going on, Privv? I smell . . . interesting events. Really interesting. You've been quiet all day, and you keep looking out at the hill. I see the Witness House is quite clear today. Not thinking of joining the church, are you? Not suffering from religious doubts brought on by the passage of the great cloud?'

Privv ignored the sarcasm. It was time to get Leck involved anyway. She could start ferreting for some more information about this business. He made no preamble.

'Something's up,' he said, nodding towards the Ervrin Mallos, 'at the Witness House. Something's happened – something spectacular. And they're trying to keep it quiet.'

'Ah,' Leck purred, her interest engaged immediately. 'Scandal amongst the clerics, eh? Excellent! We haven't had one of those for quite a time. What is it? Adultery, pederasty, or coin?'

Privv shook his head. 'I don't know. But my every nerve tells me they're up to something.'

'Tell, tell.'

Privv returned to his chair. Pushing it on to its back

legs, he swung a foot up on to his desk, rattling a plate on which was spread the congealed remains of a half-eaten meal. He began rocking himself backwards and forwards and chewing his thumb again.

'I met my religious adviser last night,' he began.

'The church's privy cleaner?' Leck inquired.

'The Witness House Maintenance Superintendent,' Privv corrected.

'The privy cleaner,' Leck confirmed. 'I know him – by sight and by smell. One of your occasional creatures.'

'An old friend and one of my respected personal couriers with a continuing interest in the propagation of the truth,' Privv retorted.

Leck sneered. 'A paid gossip, you mean. And whoever heard of a Sheeter with friends?'

'Do you want to hear about this or not?' Privv said irritably.

'You'll tell me anyway,' Leck retorted, 'as soon as you want something done. Suit yourself when – now or later. I'm not *that* interested.' She turned to peer out of the window again.

Privv mouthed an oath at the back of her head. 'I met my man last night.'

'You've just told me that.'

Privv opted for iciness and, with an effort, managed to avoid repeating his opening statement. 'He says there was some big row at the Chapter meeting yesterday.'

Exaggerated shock filled his mind. 'Not another change in cassock design? Not ructions over the prayer-sheet printing contracts?'

'Will you listen?' Privv snapped irritably.

There was a long pause.

'Well, go on,' Leck prompted.

Privv swung his other foot on to the desk and spat out part of his thumbnail. 'My man says that one of the Chapter Members crashed out of the meeting and went dashing off up the mountain. Right up into the thick of that cloud.'

'More cloud madness, eh?' Leck's tone was only slightly caustic. A great many strange occurrences had come in the wake of the passing of the black cloud, and the Sheeters were suffering a surfeit of wild tales which, with their usual talent for imagination, they had categorized under the collective name of 'cloud madness'.

Privv shook his head. 'A little more serious, I think,' he said, 'because about half a dozen of the other Chapter Members – Chapter Members, no less – went lumbering up after him, while Mueran and the others made fairly strenuous efforts to fob off any inquiries by the servants and novices.'

Leck turned and looked at Privv. He smiled at the curiosity he could feel seeping through to him, and remained silent until she eventually demanded, 'And?'

'And they came back down again.'

Leck jumped down from the sill. With a single bound she was on his lap. Her claws dug into his legs and she miaowed close to his face, her mouth gaping wide showing all her teeth – vicious, white and sharp.

'All right, don't lose your temper,' Privv said nervily. 'Just tell me what happened.'

Privv became openly excited. 'My man's fairly certain that it was Cassraw. He was given the name by two novices before Mueran got to them. Apparently, Cassraw came out of the Witness House so fast he nearly sent them both flying. And he was staring up at the clouds and raving about something, although they couldn't hear what.'

'Cassraw, eh?' Leck mused, intrigued. 'The ambitious one. The one who got the Haven Parish amid a great deal of clamour. The youngest ever, and who's had most of his flock up in arms this last couple of months with his stiff-necked preaching about obedience to the words of the Santyth. Do you think he's cracked under the strain?' She

65

purred with relish. 'This'll put the fox amongst the hens. Come on – tell me the rest.'

'The rest is vague, unfortunately,' Privv said, looking pained. 'But it's just as interesting. Apparently, they all came back safely, Cassraw and the others, and shortly afterwards, Mueran told all the servants that they couldn't go into town last night – in case the storm returned and they were needed, he said.'

'And your man?' Leck asked.

Privv shrugged. 'He's an institution. He nods and acts daft, then he goes his own way. Besides, they're not going to dismiss their poor simple privy cleaner for doing what he's done every night of his life, are they?'

Leck cooled a little at this reminder. 'How drunk was he when you spoke to him?' she asked.

'Not at all,' Privv replied unconvincingly, just catching the faint, 'And how drunk were you?' on the fringes of the cat's mind. 'And there's more,' he said, ignoring the inference.

Leck waited.

'He swears that as he was passing the Haven Meeting House he saw Cassraw's wife getting into a church carriage.'

'Really?' Leck purred, interest well alight now. 'Maybe it is adultery, after all. Maybe she's spreading her . . . favours . . . around to further Cassraw's ambition.'

Privv frowned. 'Don't be ridiculous,' he said irritably. 'This has got all the signs of something really worthwhile. A church carriage taking a woman up to the Witness House. Servants not allowed out.'

'Yes, yes. Something to hide. Something to hide,' Leck chanted. 'Where shall we begin?'

Privv thought for a moment. 'We can see if Dowinne Cassrawen is at the Haven Meeting House where she's supposed to be, and if she isn't, then I think straightforward naivety will be our best approach. We can take the trap up to the Witness House. Knock on the door. Bit of talk about some of the things that happened while that cloud was overhead, then ask whether they noticed anything unusual themselves, being so much closer to it than the rest of us.'

'And I'll sneak in round the back. Find out what's *really* happening.'

Morem opened the door cautiously. He had been walking pensively across the entrance hall when a vigorous tattoo had startled him and drawn him to the door regardless of the servants' protocol that it was not the task of Chapter Members to be doing such things. Privv's bulky form filled the tentative space that Morem allowed. He was standing very close to the door and Morem started back a little, momentarily alarmed. However, a pleasant and open disposition protected him from almost everything and, recovering, he bounced Privv's unctuous smile back to him with a welcoming one of his own. Gentle and pleasant though he was, Morem was not a foolish man, and at Privv's announcement that he was a Sheeter, his face clouded a little and he instinctively began to close the door. Privv remembered where he was just in time and managed to refrain from jamming his foot in the shrinking gap.

Instead he made his smile even broader and launched into his opening remarks before Morem could decide what to do.

Morem just about caught the gist of it. 'The black cloud . . . a lot of strange things last night . . . people having vivid dreams . . . hearing voices, singing, calling out . . . strange noises . . . things moving about. The Sheets have been full of it this morning, so I thought . . .'

'Could you wait a moment?' Morem managed to interject. 'I think perhaps you need to talk to someone else.' And, with uncharacteristic alacrity, he closed the door in

Privv's face and scurried off across the entrance hall.

'I'm in.'

Privv nodded as Leck's voice floated into his mind, then he turned around to gaze idly out over the valley, though he saw none of it. He began whistling tunelessly to himself and shifting his weight from one foot to the other. Who would they send to deal with him? he wondered. They wouldn't send old Morem back, surely – that would be *too* easy. Perhaps it would be Mueran – now *that* would be revealing. Or perhaps they would send a servant to tell him they had nothing to say. That would be the most likely. He practised his disappointed look briefly, with a view to engaging the servant's sympathy and starting a conversation. One mustn't let any opportunity pass by. He had his one contact, but the Witness House servants generally were a stern, self-righteous lot, with a quite inflated sense of the worth of their position and difficult to approach in the ordinary way of things. Still, servants were servants after all – paid retainers. A price could always be found eventually. It just needed a careful ear and a little imagination.

The door opened quite suddenly, startling him out of his reverie. He turned and found himself looking up at a familiar face. Any hopes of easy progress faded.

'Well, well. Privv, my favourite Sheeter. How nice to see you again,' Horld said, his voice and demeanour brutally contradicting his words.

Despite himself, Privv's smile faltered and he swallowed.

'Oh,' he said, memories coming back to him of the pieces he had written about Horld many years ago, making wholly unfounded allegations about the blacksmith having destroyed his own forge as an act of spite against his landlord. He had not had the judgement then that he had now, though the pieces had brought him a good deal of fame within Sheeting circles and had

68

proved very worthwhile both financially and profession-
ally. He had continued making cynical innuendoes
about Horld's subsequent conversion to the church for
some time afterwards and had only let the matter go
when other, better scandals had arisen.

This was only the second occasion he had met him
however, and, admittedly not for the first time in his life,
he felt more than a little vulnerable.

Horld stepped forward, closing the door quietly behind
him. He had a powerful presence when he chose and,
standing very close to Privv he gave him the full lowering
benefit of it. Privv was nothing if not resilient, however.
He held out his hand. 'Such a long time, Brother Horld,'
he said. 'Why, we haven't met since before you were
ordained. You're doing very well for yourself these days,
aren't you? Chapter Member and all.'

Habit rather than anything else brought Horld's hand
out to take Privv's. The Sheeter felt a tremor of alarm as
the ex-blacksmith's great muscular fist closed about his
by-now quite clammy hand, and he withdrew it as quickly
as he could without actually snatching it back.

Horld recovered from his momentary politeness. 'What
do you want, Privv?' he asked brusquely.

In the absence of any greater inspiration, Privv rambled
on about the great cloud, as he had with Morem. Horld
looked as if he had a great deal to say, but when Privv had
finished he simply shook his head slowly and said, 'No.
We've had no unusual experiences up here. It was just a
freak weather condition of some kind. People get over-
anxious. Let's be grateful it *didn't* turn into a storm, eh?
There'd have been something to get distressed about then.
Of course, people read such nonsense these days, don't
they? Goodbye.' And he was retreating into the Witness
House almost before Privv could respond.

'What about Cassraw?' he blurted out.

Horld stopped, then half-turned round to him.

69

'Something to hide, something to hide.' Leck's chant resonated through Privv as he read the cleric's posture.

'Do you mean *Brother* Cassraw?' Horld asked censoriously, in his best preaching manner. But Privv had been too long immune to what was left of his childhood encounters with the church to be seriously intimidated.

'Of course,' he said. 'Forgive me.' Then, before Horld could turn back to the door again: 'I hear that *Brother* Cassraw had an accident yesterday.'

Horld looked straight at him, his face unreadable. 'Where did you hear such a tale?' he asked.

Privv shrugged. 'One picks these things up,' he said blandly.

Horld nodded understandingly. 'I'm sure you do,' he said. 'What an interesting profession you've chosen for yourself.' And, though he did not seem to hurry, he was suddenly through the door and quietly closing it.

This time, reflexes took Privv forward before he had time to think and the heavy door closed painfully on his foot. It did little to ease his distress that Horld gave the door a good push as though perhaps the hinges might have jammed, before apparently realizing that it was Privv's foot that was causing the problem.

'Dear me,' he said in a voice noticeably lacking in regret. 'You must be more careful. You're going to injure yourself doing things like that.' He looked at Privv. 'Did you want to ask me something else?'

Then he opened the door to release Privv's foot.

'Brother Cassraw,' Privv said, through slightly clenched teeth. 'I believe he had an accident last night.'

'Ah. The titbit you . . . picked up,' Horld said. 'I can't imagine where you heard about that, but it's quite true. Brother Cassraw went for a breath of fresh air yesterday after a long meeting of the Chapter, and unfortunately, the light being rather bad, took a bit of a tumble. He'll be sore for a day or two, but if it's likely to be of any interest to your readers you can certainly reassure them that nothing serious has happened to him.'

He laid a hand on Privv's shoulder, as if to turn him gently back on his way down the mountain, but Privv held his ground.

'He went out when the thickest storm clouds anyone's ever known here were overhead,' he exclaimed, his eyes too wide and eyebrows too arched.

Horld nodded. He was reluctant to bend the truth any further and was well aware of the fact that in resisting a powerful urge to throttle this individual, he was being too easy with him. Leaving his hand on Privv's shoulder he risked another step towards perdition, however.

'Brother Cassraw's a vigorous and inquiring individual,' he said. 'Ever curious. While we were content to watch from shelter, he wanted to be amid it all. And the clouds were a remarkable sight from up here. He presumed that the worst he might suffer would be a wetting, so off he went.' He shrugged as if that were the end of the tale, but Privv's silence and his enthralled and expectant face lured him into continuing. 'When he'd been out rather longer than we thought he would, we became a little concerned and a few of us went to look for him. We met him limping down.'

Before Privv could provoke him into further admissions, Leck's voice floated into his mind. 'I'm getting nothing here. They're all too busy preparing a meal to be gossiping. I'll tell you what though, these people eat well. Some way this side of pious frugality for sure.'

Privv did not reply. 'Could I perhaps have a word with Brother Cassraw?' he asked Horld. 'I'm sure my readers would be interested to hear his impressions of the clouds as seen from up here.'

'No,' Horld said categorically and a little too hastily. 'I'm afraid we're in the middle of a meeting right now. Perhaps you could go down to the Haven Meeting House

71

and make an appointment to see him. I'm sure he'd be happy to speak to you when he has the time.'

'I've just been there,' Privv retorted. 'But there's no one there except a housekeeper. Apparently his wife was called out urgently last night.'

He felt Horld's hand closing about his shoulder.

Something to hide, something to hide.

Suddenly, like a rasping saw-blade, a hissing, in-drawn breath cut across his growing elation. He felt the hairs on his neck and his arms tingle and rise. Then his nostrils were full of intense and heady scents, his ears full of strange, exaggerated sounds and his mind full of utterly alien images. Instinctively his hands came up to squeeze his nose and rub his neck violently to shake off the sensation. But Leck's powerful and fearful response would not leave him.

He began to sway unsteadily.

Chapter 7

'For pity's sake, cat, what are you doing?' Privv cried out silently as Leck's screaming emotions swept through him.

'What's the matter?' Horld's voice reached him through the uproar, faint and distorted, as though the speaker were far away. And the tall figure of the cleric framed in the door to the Witness House seemed to be at once near and yet distant, standing at both ends of a long, howling tunnel. Somehow Privv managed to nod by way of reply but he could not speak. Whatever Leck was reacting to, her response was threatening to overwhelm him utterly. Privv took a deep breath. He must exert every ounce of his will to reach into the cat's mind and calm it, or he would be swept along totally by its now ravening animal nature. Bad enough when this happened in private, but here . . .

The consequences didn't bear thinking about. He must resist while he still had some semblance of his humanity about him.

Yet he had no inkling of what was happening. On the rare occasions when this had happened in the past it had been as a result of Leck's reaction to being unable to escape the unwelcome attentions of a dog. But this was not the case now, Privv knew. The emotions engendered by such incidents, though powerful, were not as bad as this. And too, they were quite distinct; loaded with massive, visceral violence which the deeper reaches of his humanity could at least appreciate. He was usually content to let them ride for fear that any interference on his part might mar his partner's ability to defend herself. But this was different. And he was being drawn further and further in.

He felt Horld's arms about him, supporting him.

No, he cried out to himself. *Not here. This mustn't happen!* Yet even as these thoughts came to him, others, scheming and ambitious, arrived with them. He was going to get inside the Witness House. He was going to be the centre of some confusion as the Brothers fussed about him. Opportunities were opening.

But these compensations were like corks in a buffeting ocean. And Privv was drowning. Images whirled and twisted through him as his mind fought against Leck's fearful insistence. 'Cat!' he screamed desperately through the inner mayhem, hoping that the simple call might distract her, but the sensations did not even waver and, abruptly, a deeper part of him was awake. When he reached out again, his will was brutal and cruel. This was now a conflict with the unalloyed animal ferocity of his partner for control of the common ground of their psyches, and in such circumstances there could only be one leader. Thus menaced, his own primitive nature rose to the fore, worse by far than any animal's.

'Enough!'

The command, laden with savage meanings far beyond anything in the word itself, hurtled through the mysterious by-ways of their joining. Leck's spirit bridled against the impact with her own screaming rage, filling Privv's mind with a spitting fury of glittering teeth and claws. But it yielded before this greater menace nevertheless.

The whole incident had lasted perhaps only a few seconds but, as the uproar began to recede, Privv found that he was being almost carried by Horld towards a long bench-seat at the opposite side of the entrance hall. He had a fleeting impression of Morem somewhere also. I'm inside, he thought jubilantly, momentarily forgetting what had happened to bring him there. Then Leck's rage returned.

'Don't you ever do anything like that again,' came a blistering outburst.

Though sorely tempted, Privv managed not to respond to the anger. Leck had been downed completely and that which was human in her would not only need to abuse him, but could be allowed to with impunity. He let Horld sit him down on the bench.

'Are you all right?'

His own question to Leck coincided with Horld's and the words resonated unpleasantly in his head. He raised his hand gently to fend off Horld's inquiry, saying softly, 'A moment, please.'

'Leck, what in the devil's name was all that about?' he demanded.

Unexpectedly he received no further abuse. Leck was icily calm.

'A good word, devil,' came the enigmatic reply. 'I need to think.'

'But . . .'

The word echoed back to him through a special silence. Leck had withdrawn. Privv, head lowered so that Horld could not see his face, grimaced. Leck had been deeply disturbed and her language had been hung about with images that he could not begin to interpret. He reached out, more gently this time.

'I don't understand,' he replied. 'What's happened? Has something threatened you?'

Still there was no reply.

Privv swore inwardly, but had neither the strength nor the desire to launch another assault on his partner. Something very strange had occurred – something the like of which he, and, he suspected, she also, had never known before. But he could not go chasing about the Witness

House to find out what, and he knew well enough that he would gain nothing by badgering her. Besides, rare opportunities were opening up for him here. Horld was still leaning over him, his face genuinely concerned 'Are you all right?' he asked again.

Privv looked up sharply, making Horld start. 'Yes, yes,' he nodded. He searched for a convenient lie. 'I think I've been working too hard lately,' he said, then realized as soon as he had spoken that it was not a reply likely to induce sympathy in Horld. 'But I'm fine now, thank you,' he added hastily. With an effort, he set his concerns about Leck aside. Whatever had happened had happened. She was obviously in no danger now and, doubtless, he would learn about everything in due course. Thus, at least partly unburdened, the opportunist in him began to reassert itself fully.

'If I could perhaps sit a moment,' he said, looking around the entrance hall with its ornate mosaic floor, sweeping staircases and fluted columns rising to the high domed roof. 'It's very calming here. And would it be an imposition to ask for a glass of water?'

Horld pondered the request, his mistrust of the Sheeter returning in direct proportion to Privv's recovery. 'No, not at all,' he said slowly, but he looked around for a servant to undertake the errand rather than risk leaving Privv alone. At that moment, however, Morem appeared bearing a glass of water and a large blanket and looking very businesslike. Privv rejected the blanket with a gesture, but gulped down the water greedily. He was parched – indeed, his throat was painfully dry. Fear, he realized. Leck's fear. He reached out again tentatively but, though he could feel the cat's presence, there was no acknowledgement.

Morem was looking at him, at once concerned and shrewd-eyed. He was hefting the blanket purposefully, apparently loath to relinquish it before he had put it to good medical use. Privv stood up to demonstrate his returned well-being.

'Thank you – Brother Morem, isn't it?' he said, returning the empty glass to him in order to still the fidgeting blanket. Morem smiled broadly, lured on by this unexpected recognition. As he was about to speak, though, Horld, his face darkening, stepped protectively between them. He laid a comradely, but strong arm around Privv's shoulders and began ushering him towards the door.

'Well, if you're sure you're all right now I'm afraid I'll have to see you out. We still have our meeting to finish, and it's already been a long one.'

'I understand, of course,' Privv managed, risking a brief stop. 'And I'm sorry to have been such a trouble. But as I'm here, I wonder if it would be possible to have a word with Brother Cassraw? If I picked up a rumour about his being hurt, then it'll be all over Haven Parish tomorrow. A word in my Sheet would help to stop a lot of foolish gossip.'

Horld moved him on again. 'I'm sorry. As I just told you, Brother Cassraw's resting. He's less than happy about his little tumble and he certainly doesn't want to be disturbed.' He looked significantly at Morem. 'As Brother Morem will confirm. Besides, I doubt anyone will be seriously interested in such a trivial incident, do you?' he concluded as they reached the door.

Untypically, Privv had almost been reduced to stammering as Horld opened the door and pushed him gently, but determinedly through it. 'Well, thank you . . . er . . .'

His eyes looked past Horld and back into the entrance hall. Coming down the stairs was Cassraw.

'Ah!' he exclaimed, his face lighting up.

Both Horld and Morem caught the look and turned round. Morem reacted with unfeigned surprise, but Horld merely kept his arm across the doorway to keep Privv out.

77

'There you are,' he said to Privv, without looking at him. 'As I said, Brother Cassraw's fine. No reason for anyone to be concerned. I'm afraid you've had a wasted journey. Still, I'm sure that you'll find plenty of other things to . . . reassure . . . your readers about.'

But Privv was not one to be hindered by politeness when need arose.

'Brother Cassraw,' he shouted, waving his hand past Horld. 'Brother Cassraw. Can you spare me a minute?'

He sensed Horld's great hand curling up into a most unclerical fist, but he broadened his smile and redoubled his waving. Cassraw had by now reached the foot of the stairs and was being accosted by an anxious Morem. He nodded to something that Morem was saying, then looked towards the door. Horld, considerably unsettled by the sudden appearance of the man he thought was still lying comatose in his room, was about to push Privv bodily away from the door and slam it after him. He had visions of Privv bombarding Cassraw with questions and being treated to the eerie nodding and smiling that had hall-marked Cassraw's conduct prior to his collapse. He was already reading the consequences amplified beyond recog-nition in Privv's Sheet.

Even as he was bracing himself to give this wretched man a good push, Cassraw called out, 'Who is it, Brother?' moving Morem to one side. He sounded quite his old self again.

This time it was Horld who stammered. 'It's only a Sheeter, Brother Cassraw. He's just leaving.'

'Brother Cassraw – a minute, if you please.' Privv continued his barrage regardless of this exchange.

Cassraw stared at him for a moment, then raised his hand and beckoned him forward. 'Let him in,' he said to Horld. 'I'm sure we can spare him a minute or two. We mustn't turn our backs on these new ways, must we?'

Horld could have disputed that at great length but, with

blatant reluctance, he lowered his arm. Released, Privv bustled past him and made straight for Cassraw like a dog sighting food, Horld staring after him in open distaste. Cassraw redirected the Sheeter towards the bench-seat and then sat down beside him. Horld, shepherd-like, hovered over them both while Morem stood back and watched uneasily.

'We have to get on with our meeting, Brother Cassraw,' Horld said significantly. 'There is a great deal to discuss yet.'

Cassraw nodded. 'I know,' he said. Then he turned to Privv, confidential. 'I'm afraid my little walk yesterday not only cost me a bruise or two, it's caused no small number of administrative problems so I can't talk for long. What is it you wanted to see me about?'

Before Privv could answer, Cassraw gave a slight start. Then he smiled and shook his head. 'Come on,' he said to someone other than Privv and, reaching down, he picked something up. 'I don't know how you got in here, but you've been haunting me ever since I left my room, haven't you?'

He placed the burden on his knee.

Privv found himself looking down at Leck, nestling comfortably in Cassraw's lap.

Cassraw held open his arms and addressed the assembled Chapter Brothers. His hands and face showed the damage he had suffered the previous day, but he was groomed and immaculate and, seemingly, in complete control of himself.

'My friends, what can I say?' he began. 'My apologies, certainly. And my thanks – for your patience, and for your prayers. And my special thanks to Brothers Vredech and Horld and the others for their courage and compassion in venturing out into the darkness to find me. Not to mention their good practical help in bringing me back

79

here.' He turned to the head of the table. 'Brother Mueran, in particular I ask your forgiveness for more than the trouble I caused yesterday. My behaviour of late has left much to be desired. I'm all too well aware of that now.' He clasped his hands and looked upwards. 'The ways of Ishryth are indeed often beyond our knowing, and whatever led me into my . . . escapade . . . yesterday, and held me in that mysterious sleep through the night and most of this day has brought me to my senses.'

He held out the torn and stained cassock that he had been wearing. 'I shall hang this in a special place in my living quarters at the Meeting House, to serve as a constant reminder of the folly into which men can be led by their arrogance.' His manner eased and he smiled in self-reproach. 'And, to ensure a reminder of a different kind, should you at any time find me setting my face against the ways of the church, or being obdurate beyond reason in debate, then I give you my permission here and now to turn to me and say: "Brother Cassraw, remember the lessons you learned in the darkness."' Then, with a slight, deprecating wave of his hands, he sat down.

There was a spontaneous burst of applause from several of the Brothers, and most of the remainder were nodding in approval and relief at this speech. For though it had been short, its simplicity and the openness of its delivery had held all its hearers spellbound: Cassraw was a considerable orator when he chose. Only Vredech seemed to be uncertain about this sudden change of heart by his friend. It showed on his face and, unfortunately, Mueran noticed it. With yesterday's awful problems apparently evaporating before his eyes, and the prospect of normality returning once more, he felt a great burden being lifted from him and he was desperately anxious to ensure the complete unanimity of the Chapter in accepting Cassraw's recantation. It had been fortuitous that Cassraw had suddenly emerged from his strange coma in time to appease that wretched Sheeter, but one couldn't be too careful. Sheeters could present the slightest disagreement as Schism, and the slightest misdemeanour as scandal. A unified front was essential, if only for the next few days, until Cassraw had made his peace with those of his flock whom he had offended.

'Brother Vredech, you seem unhappy,' he risked.

Vredech felt himself the focus of the surprised but good-natured attention of his colleagues. Under its pressure he forced his face into a smile that he did not feel. He looked at Cassraw who was still standing, his head bowed, as if awaiting judgement. He felt the will of the meeting and the great momentum of the minutiae of everyday life seeking to reassert itself. Let everything be as it was. He was not immune to such pressure. Change is a fearful thing.

'I'm sorry,' he said with a disarming shrug as he gathered his thoughts. 'I'm a little out of sorts. I slept badly last night, despite the day's exertions.'

'I doubt any of us slept well,' Mueran said, allowing himself a tone of gentle rebuke. 'With Brother Cassraw lying unconscious amongst us.'

Vredech was anxious now to be away from this scrutiny. Words seemed reluctant to come to him, however, and it was only with the greatest difficulty that he managed to say, 'I'm truly glad that Brother Cassraw is back with us in every way.'

It was enough for Mueran. He turned to Cassraw and motioned him to sit down. Before he did so, Cassraw turned and looked at Vredech, his face full of gratitude and thanks. He was the Cassraw whom everyone knew and loved, the man whose diligence and ability had been such that he had shown himself suitable to receive the Haven Parish.

No! Voices deep inside Vredech called out in denial.

This was *not* that Cassraw. He was different. Something was askew, not right.

Not right.

He pushed the voices down, crushing them with his own need to be at ease with everything again. At his acknowledging nod, Cassraw finally sat down. He leaned forward, resting his arms on the carefully folded cassock.

Mueran speedily guided the meeting through such of the business as had been abandoned at Cassraw's explosive exit the previous day, and the Chapter Members dispersed quickly and without ceremony.

As they were all milling about the entrance hall, Cassraw formed a natural focal point for the activity. Watching him from some way away, Vredech found himself noting that while everyone took Cassraw's hand and wished him well, one or two spoke to him at length, heads inclined forward, as though they were lowering their voices, despite the din all about them. Like plotters, the thought occurred to him. A twinge of guilt came in its wake. Where could such a ridiculous idea have come from?

He shrugged it off. He was tired after a bad night, that was all. Cassraw was well and with them again, that was all that mattered, surely?

Another unwelcome thought came to him. Could it be that he was jealous of his old friend, his star now apparently ascendant again? Although they had entered the church together, Cassraw had risen further and faster than Vredech had. But then, he had not wanted what Cassraw had wanted. He had wanted only what he had subsequently managed to achieve. There had been no competition between them. Still, one never knew. He smiled to himself. All the time we find new measures of ourselves, he thought. And, like the rest, he gravitated towards Cassraw, shook his hand and wished him well.

Yet even as he did so, the voices returned.

Not right.
Not right.

Privv's trap clattered down the winding road that led from the Witness House.

'All right. Truce,' he said, after a long silence. 'I'm sorry I did what I did, but you were completely out of control. I'd have been spitting and clawing on the floor if I hadn't stopped you somehow.' He could not avoid some self-pity. 'And it took it out of me, I can tell you. I'm still feeling shaky.'

He could not match Leck's sense of injury, however. 'Oh, you don't have to tell me. I know how it is with you humans only too well,' she said, her tone massively injured. 'Anything goes wrong – kick the cat. Besides, what's wrong with spitting and clawing? They're infinitely preferable to some of the things *you* get up to. Especially with—'

Images began to form in Privv's mind. 'Yes, very well,' he said hastily. 'I've said I'm sorry. Let's leave it. Tell me what it was all about, anyway, and what were you doing, crawling all over Cassraw?'

'My job,' Leck replied tartly.

The answer caught Privv off-balance. His elation at succeeding in entering the Witness House, together with speaking to Cassraw under such circumstances, not to mention Leck's bizarre outburst which these successes had momentarily eclipsed, had so preoccupied him that he had almost forgotten why he had gone up there in the first place. Leck's terse reminder deflated him somewhat.

'Ah yes,' he said weakly, adding, 'and well you did too, finding Cassraw and all. Pity there's no worthwhile story though.'

'I wouldn't say that,' Leck retorted.

'What? "Chapter Member goes for a walk and falls over",' Privv sneered. 'It'd have to be a quiet day indeed for that to rouse anyone's interest. I think I'll liven up that business with the market officials. It's beginning to look really promising. I wouldn't be surprised if there isn't a Heinder lurking in the background there somewhere.' He began to speculate. 'We haven't had a decent PlasHein scandal in—'

'Days,' Leck said scornfully. 'And you made that one up as well. Let someone else do the next one or you'll find yourself on the Keepers' special list.'

Privv shrugged dismissively. 'Sheeters' privilege,' he parroted. 'Can't touch me for reasonable speculation. Besides, no one denied it.'

Leck did not argue. 'Suit yourself,' she replied, with considerable indifference. 'But don't blame me if you get the dawn knock.' She yawned and scratched.

Privv gave her a sulky look, and they rode on in silence for a little while. As they drove through the ornate gates that marked the end of the church's official territory, they nearly collided with a carriage travelling along the public road. It was, as usual, Privv's fault, though the details of his error were by no means fully clarified in the exchange of abuse that followed. Nevertheless, it brushed away the uneasy atmosphere between the two.

'What *was* all that business about up there?' Privv asked as he finally regained control of the pony. 'It wasn't some dog, I could tell that.'

Immediately, a wave of confused emotions swept through him. He glanced down at the cat to see if there was any outward manifestation of this, but she was lying motionless, apparently asleep. Her voice, though, was wide awake and sharp. 'I don't know,' she said. 'It was something to do with Cassraw. There's something odd about him. Very odd. Something I've never felt in any human before.'

'What do you mean?' Privv asked.

'I just said I didn't know, didn't I?' came the irritable

response. 'Why don't you listen?'

'How would you like to walk home, cat?'

'It'd probably be safer than riding with you. Do you want to hear about Cassraw or not?'

'Sorry, go on,' Privv replied gracelessly.

Suddenly, Leck was earnest. 'This is important, Privv,' she said. 'There's something *really* strange about Cassraw.' Then, rather embarrassed: 'I even tried to reach him.'

Privv looked down in surprise. 'And?' he asked after a moment.

'Nothing, of course,' Leck replied, after a short pause. 'But . . .' She hesitated. 'It was almost as if he were keeping me out. It was very peculiar.'

Privv felt let down. 'The man's a cleric, for pity's sake,' he said. 'They're all a bit peculiar. We should know. They've given us some rare stories at times – better than any we could make up.' He laughed.

Leck's response was caustic. 'Those were just ordinary humans,' she said, 'doing what you all do. Nothing strange about them at all, just more guilt and hypocrisy. Cassraw's different.' She hesitated again, then sat up suddenly. 'He's not human,' she blurted out, almost as if against her will. Her unexpected movement coupled with the force behind her words made Privv jump, but before he could say anything his mind was filled with wild, animal images.

'Stop it. You'll have us over,' he said, nudging the cat with his foot.

Leck hissed at him viciously. 'And you stop that,' she snarled, raising a paw, its claws extended. 'I'm trying to think. That . . . man . . . frightened me witless when I first saw him.'

'Why?' Privv asked.

'I've told you, I don't know,' Leck snapped back. Again, strange images surged into Privv's mind. This time he did not react.

85

'Why were you all over him then?' he asked quietly when Leck seemed to be more settled.

'Because he's . . . powerful,' Leck replied after a long silence. Her voice was thoughtful. 'We must watch Cassraw, Privv. Be his allies. Things are going to happen all about him. Spectacular things. Dangerous things.'

Chapter 8

Vredech threw his cloak on to a chair and slumped into another one. He put his hands to his head. He had hoped that the leisurely ride down from the Witness House and through the town would have settled and relaxed him, but it had not. If anything, he felt more tense and disturbed now than before Cassraw's seemingly miraculous recovery. He took a deep breath and laid his hand on a copy of the Santyth that was resting on a small table by the chair. It was an old, battered copy and its position on the table was both permanent and one of honour, as it had originally belonged to his father. By an irony which Vredech always appreciated, his father had been that rarity in Madren society, an unbeliever. 'Some good tales in there, lad. And a deal of wisdom – no denying. And some fine writing. But the Great Creator of all things? Ishryth?' He would shake his head. 'No. Men's work, this. Only men would create a creator in their own image. I doubt they meant any harm by it, but it's men's work all the same. Men railing against the dark. As ignorant as the rest of us.'

He had set great store by reason and would bring it to bear formidably on any problem foolish enough to cross his path, but he had been neither a bigot nor a proselytizer for his beliefs.

'You need to use your head all the time, lad. Knowledge is always your greatest protection.' He would strike his chest. 'But your faith's what you find in your heart. It's beyond reason and thus debate and it's to be held in silence, not prated from a pulpit. Most of these people use what they call faith as an excuse for straightforward lack of clear thinking. Laziness, that's all their faith is. Laziness. I've no time for it. It's blasphemous.' It was a conclusion that used to make him laugh heartily.

His words still resounded about the room for Vredech. It had been a source of disappointment to him that his only son had turned to the church, and, unusually, there had been some unpleasantness about it at first. However, sure in the knowledge of what it was that he really valued, he had, in the end, stuck by his own creed, wished his son well, and supported him when he could, even through the doubts that must assail anyone following such a vocation. They had been friends up to the end and thus his support had continued after his death.

Resting now in the shade of his father, Vredech began talking to himself. It was a conscious aping of the old man: 'Gets those tricky thoughts to the forefront of your mind, those little swine lurking about below the surface, getting ready to ambush you at some dire moment.'

'Cassraw's my friend. I don't think I'm jealous of him.' Vredech said, dragging out his most reprehensible concern. He tapped the Santyth. 'I certainly wouldn't have wanted the Haven Parish. Dowinne, maybe.' He cast a look about him at this, even though he knew the house was empty. 'I know he can be a pain, but more often than not it's he himself who really suffers. And I *was* glad to see him back safely off the mountain, for all he was . . . odd.'

The black clouds loomed into his mind again.

Judgement Day.

Not right.

Not right.

Vredech swore and stood up. The sudden action made him giddy, and he sat down again, his head back in his hands. 'Get hold of yourself, man,' he muttered. 'Relax.

Take it easy for an hour or so. You've had a queer couple of days and a bad night.'

This reminder of the previous night only brought him upright and tense again, for where he should have slept deeply, following an afternoon's activity the like of which he had not known in many years, he found himself wide-awake, his body agitated and his mind tormented. He had twitched in and out of sleep repeatedly, for the most part unable to tell which was which, as memories of the day buffeted him relentlessly. Cassraw suddenly there beside him, strange, commanding – mesmeric almost – and now lying still and silent, yet somehow, Vredech sensed, alert and listening. And, terrifying, dancing black shadows that had brought with them that truly awful presence, searching into him, discarding him. Had it been real, or was it just some trick of the light and the circumstances that his body and senses had misunderstood? It had felt real enough, but where did that leave him? If it *was* real then what awful thing was it? And what had happened to Cassraw, who had presumably been nearer to the heart of it? And if it was not real, then what was the matter with him, that he should suffer such a vivid hallucination?

He leaned back in the chair, stretched out and closed his eyes, with the intention of ordering his thoughts once and for all. Almost immediately, he was back in the Debating Hall, with Cassraw staring at him across the long table – the old, familiar Cassraw. Waiting for his approval . . . his support? And still there was a wrongness about the scene, though he could not identify it. A wrongness that slithered away from him tantalizingly, its very movement illuminating Cassraw's face with the jaundiced light that had emanated from the sinister black cloud under which all this strangeness had occurred. Indeed, Vredech saw, Cassraw's face *was* the light. And too, he was the cloud, vast and overwhelming, looming over the entire land and

89

beyond, eyes penetrating, face marked with the arrogant indifference of supreme power. Vredech wanted to fall to his knees in mortal fear before this manifestation, for he knew that though he was insignificant beyond imagining, yet his every thought was known and understood, and he was deeply unworthy. Nothing could stand against such might, nothing be hidden from it. His obedience, his obeisance, was demanded. But he would not yield. It was an abomination: it had to be opposed. He wanted to cry out against it, raise his fist in defiance, however futile.

'You are but a man, Cassraw,' he bellowed into the echoing vault. 'Frail and flawed as are we all.'

Laughter came back to him, scornful and crazed. 'Frail, old friend? Frail? God is come for me. Follow me or . . .'

'Leave me,' Vredech said.

'Follow me or die. Die and be doomed forever. I am the Judgement Day. All things are to be weighed. Mine is the new Word.'

Cassraw's face filled Vredech's vision.

He felt his chest tightening, his shoulders throbbing, as if the sky itself were pressing down on him.

'You're only a man,' he gasped.

'*You* are the man.'

The face grew larger still, until it was but a single eye, its black iris like a huge, dead moon.

Vredech stared into it, scarcely able to breathe. Then, black against the blackness, an army of shadows was about him, wheeling and dancing, full of mocking, horrible sounds. He flailed his arms as if to fend them off but to no avail. They were there and not there. Inside and outside him. Growing. Growing. Louder and louder.

Then all was silence, terrible and total, as it had been on the mountain in that fearful moment before Cassraw had reappeared.

Vredech waited, his breath frozen within him.

A hand closed about his shoulder.

Dowinne and Cassraw travelled back from the Witness House in one of the church carriages, Cassraw's own small trap being returned by one of the servants. Dowinne's pale blue eyes were fixed relentlessly on her husband, and her hands were twitching restlessly. Her shoulders were raised and tense. Cassraw, by contrast, was staring calmly out of the window, watching the valley scenery move slowly up and around them as the carriage descended the mountain road.

The sound of the wheels changed as they moved through the gates at the end of the road and turned on to the public highway. The change prompted Dowinne to speak.

'Well?' she asked.

Without turning from his vigil, Cassraw raised a hand as if to fend off the question. Dowinne leaned forward and slapped it aside none too gently. Cassraw turned to her sharply, making her start, but she held his gaze.

'Well?' she repeated, more insistently. His look became quizzical. 'That's the second time you've done that,' Dowinne said, as though answering an unspoken question. 'And I didn't like it very much the first time. Now tell me what's been happening. Everything. Right away.'

As she drew a breath to continue, Cassraw smiled and raised his hand again. 'When we get home,' he said simply. The smile was captivating but his voice was an odd mixture of command and concession and Dowinne's resolve faltered. 'When we get home,' he repeated.

'Very well,' she said emptily, her brow furrowing as Cassraw turned again to stare out of the window. The carriage was travelling quite slowly now, not because they were moving up yet another of Troidmallos's many hills, but because they were passing through a part of the town that was dominated by the workshops, offices and ware- houses of Canol Madreth's larger merchanting companies, and the streets were very crowded. Apart from pedestrians and riders there were all manner of carriages and carts jostling for position in the wide streets: light traps used by the PlasHein messengers, ornate and dignified company carriages, jangling public carriages with their noisy drivers, and even some of the great six-horse wagons that hauled timber and cotton and kegs of oil and wine and all the other commodities that served Canol Madreth's trading needs. Cassraw's eyes moved leisurely over the scene. Occasionally, from amid the bustling crowds a hand would be raised in greeting which he acknowledged with an inclination of his head and a small but definite movement of his hand.

Briefly, Dowinne toyed with the idea of questioning him again, but she did not pursue it. Perhaps he just needed to clarify his own thoughts before he could tell her anything. Besides, she'd have plenty of time when they got home and she wouldn't have to be looking over her shoulder to assess the reactions of others if she had to deal with any obduracy on Cassraw's part.

As Cassraw quietly acknowledged another passer-by, Dowinne set aside both her concerns and her dudgeon and let the luxury of the carriage enfold her. For this journey at least she could enjoy being a distinguished foreign visitor, or some other civic worthy, powerful and respected. As her gaze followed her husband's, she noticed with pleasure many eyes turning towards the carriage. And, too, rippling through the crowds, there was a slight, but conspicuous and steady rhythm of circling hands as people made the old sign of the ring over their hearts. Not all of them elderly by any means, she noted.

'Deep in our people, religion,' Cassraw said, without turning. 'Obedience to the old ways. Good.'

Uncertain to whom the remark was being addressed, Dowinne remained silent, content to bask in the imagined respect of the crowd and the very real comfort of the church carriage.

Then they were entering the part of the town which was the preferred residential district for people unburdened by concerns about money – the merchants, the Heinders, high-ranking civic and governmental officers and the plain rich – the Haven district. Great stone houses, built many storeys high and topped with steep pitched slate roofs in the Madren tradition, stood in imitation of the mountains around them. Some were ranked in impressive, curving rows, others stood isolated amid their own grounds. They would have dominated the streets and made them oppressive, had they not been widely spaced, with ample gardens or open areas around them, and had the streets themselves not been wide and airy. Dowinne looked at these monuments to conspicuous prosperity and felt a glow of pride. The Meeting House, lavish though it was in comparison to most Meeting Houses, did not begin to compare with houses such as these, and Cassraw and she did not possess the kind of wealth that they represented, but for all that, they *were* there, living in the Haven, tending the spiritual needs of the rich and powerful. Her thoughts echoed Cassraw's words. It was good.

Yet, just as the black clouds had appeared from nowhere to darken the land the previous day, so Dowinne's concerns returned to mar her pleasure and darken her thoughts. What had happened to Cassraw during his 'little walk up the hill', as Mueran had called it? And what had possessed him to do such a thing? In the turmoil of her arrival at the Witness House she had not thought to question the Covenant Member about such things but, as she had sat helpless by Cassraw's motionless form through the night, fretting and at one stage almost praying, those and many other questions had come to her. And something *had* happened, beyond a doubt. For all his affability after he had suddenly woken, for all the peace he

93

seemed to have made behind the closed doors of the Debating Hall, her husband was different. The good-natured, apologetic exterior that looked like the old Cass-raw was only a mask, a shield. Behind it lay something very different.

'Come on.'

Cassraw's voice startled her. He was standing in the doorway of the carriage, his hand extended towards her.

'Come on. We're home,' he said.

Catching sight of the carriage driver standing behind her husband, Dowinne quickly gathered her wits and smiled winningly. 'Sorry, my dear,' she said, taking the offered hand. 'Just daydreaming.'

As the door of their living quarters closed behind them, however, the smile vanished instantly, to be replaced by a look of angry sternness. 'Now,' she demanded of her husband's retreating back, 'Tell me everything that's been going on before you take a single step further.'

Cassraw stopped and turned. He stared at her intently. His face wore a strange expression and, for a moment, Dowinne was afraid. She had always known that violence bubbled just beneath the surface of her husband, but she had known too that it was well-harnessed, and that his various passions were, at least in part, a release for it. But she was no prey animal. She knew that to flinch was to bring down on her the very thing of which she was afraid. And if the worst came to the worst, she knew also that her own nature was not without its savage streak.

'When you've quite finished gazing at me, Enryc,' she said coldly, 'perhaps you'll answer my question. Tell me, for mercy's sake, what's been going on. I get dragged up to the Witness House at a moment's notice to find you . . .' she waved her arms about vaguely . . . 'asleep, uncon-scious, I don't know what. Your clothes ruined, you cut and bruised. Mueran's babbling on about how you'd gone for a walk and "had a fall", Morem trying to be reassuring and failing dismally. And both of them lying about whatever had happened.' She paused, but as Cassraw made no effort to reply she continued almost immediately. Laying a hand on his arm, she softened her manner. 'I've never had such a night. You frightened me half to death. I didn't know what to do, except sit there and hold your hand and hope.'

'And pray,' Cassraw prompted, unexpectedly reproving. 'Pray for His mercy to guide you through your trial.'

'Oh yes,' Dowinne heard herself replying. 'Of course. And pray. That goes without saying.'

Her mind was suddenly racing. Never in all their time together had Cassraw made such a remark to her and it caught her badly off-balance. She knew what was expected of her as the wife of a Preaching Brother, and she observed the forms of Ishrythan not only meticulously, but sometimes more knowledgeably than her husband. Having been brought up in a strictly orthodox family she had behaved thus all her life and it was little trouble. But actually *believing*! That was surely for children and the weak-minded? Noting quite early in life that hypocrisy was far from uncommon and that no one ever really seemed to be punished for their misdeeds unless they were caught by some human agency, Dowinne had long assumed that the image of the stern and forbidding Ishryth that dominated the religion was just another means of political control. She had taken it for granted that Cassraw thought as she did and that his choice of the church had been purely a means towards gaining wealth and power. It had necessarily been a tacit assumption, however. As her childish awareness had grown she had learned too, that such topics were not for open discussion. Total immersion in her chosen role was essential, and the least crack in her shield could be the presager of catastrophe.

Had she been wrong all this time? Had Cassraw's protestations of faith, his passionate sermons, all been *sincere*? The past few months came into a new focus. She had presumed, or, more correctly, hoped, that Cassraw's increasingly primitive preaching was part of some scheme he was hatching to win further popular support for himself within the church. She had not attempted to discuss it with him as she knew he preferred to develop his ideas fully before he brought them to her. In her worst fears she had imagined that he was overworking, but Cassraw was a strong, tireless individual, not given to many forms of physical weakness. Now it seemed as though she might well have been wrong. The prospect chilled her and, for the second time in two days, she felt the entire edifice of her life tremble. Sensing the blood draining from her face, she turned away quickly and began unfastening her cloak. She desperately needed a moment to compose herself.

It didn't matter, she decided frantically. It wasn't that important. If she'd been wrong, she'd been wrong, that was all. It didn't really alter anything. She would just have to be even more careful to keep her shield about her.

Yet, she couldn't have been so wrong, surely? It wasn't possible that she'd misread the man for so long.

Something *had* happened up that damned hill. And she needed to know what, more than ever now.

She had come full circle. On firmer ground again, her composure returned. Folding her cloak carefully and laying it delicately over the back of a chair, she confronted her husband.

'Well?' she asked.

'Well what?'

'What happened?' Dowinne allowed herself a note of exasperation.

'Your prayers were answered,' Cassraw replied, without an inkling of humour. 'I returned.'

Dowinne put her hands to her head. 'But what happened?' she demanded again. 'Why did you suddenly decide to go wandering about the mountainside in the middle of a Chapter meeting? And into that storm, of all things. And where did you fall, and why, and who found you, and what were they doing looking for—'

'Enough, Dowinne,' Cassraw interrupted, raising both hands as if to fend her off. 'So many questions.' He put an arm around her shoulders and moved her across to a seat by the window.

'*Speak to her*,' the voice within him said. '*As you know how. She is too strong to oppose and too valuable to dispense with. She will be your right hand, as you are Mine.*'

The words chimed with Cassraw's own thoughts.

He smiled. Dowinne had not seen him smile like that for a long time. 'Curb your impatience, my dear,' he said. 'I'll tell you everything as soon as I've got it completely clear in my own mind.' Dowinne made to speak but he raised a hand to silence her. Then he turned away from her slightly and looked out of the window as if he were afraid to meet her gaze.

'As you may have guessed, these last few months have been . . . difficult,' he began. 'Much about the church has been troubling me.' His hand fell to the pocket in which he kept his familiar copy of the Santyth, and he patted it reassuringly. 'But I went about seeking answers the wrong way. Offended people with whom I should be friends, turned people against me who should be my allies, showed disrespect to the Covenant Member . . .' He shook his head. 'All bad things. Serious misjudgements. I won't excuse them.' He looked earnestly into Dowinne's eyes. 'But it's all behind me now. Something . . . wonderful . . . happened to me yesterday.' He raised his hand again in anticipation of further questioning. 'I can't tell you what, not yet – the time's not right. I'll have to ask you to trust me.' His face became alive with excitement. 'But great changes are coming, Dowinne. And I . . . *we* . . . will be riding them. Riding them on into a new era, one in which His Word will reign supreme, in which Canol Madreth will be again the centre of a Gyronlandt united within the church.'

Dowinne kept her eyes fixed on her husband's face throughout this declamation, searching desperately with her every sense for the signs about him that would confirm what his words were telling her, namely that he had become unhinged. But there was nothing. Though his voice and manner were excited, they were not hysterical. Nor was there anything in his gestures, his expression, or in those most revealing traitors, his eyes, that indicated that he was other than quite sane.

It *was* a scheme, she decided. He had seen the folly of his conduct of the last few months and had decided to change direction. But a united Gyronlandt . . .

Despite his appeal, she would have to probe.

'I can see you rising to the position of Covenant Member, Enryc,' she said, 'but a united Gyronlandt? And within the church? Twenty or more different states with every conceivable form of government and religion, or lack of it, all of them larger and more powerful than Canol Madreth: even the most ambitious of politicians would hesitate before promising something like that.'

There was no reproach, however. Instead, Cassraw simply nodded and smiled again. He gave a dismissive wave of his hand. 'Politicians,' he sneered. 'Mountebanks and charlatans. Men with dreams far outstripping their meagre abilities, yet without vision beyond the next Acclamation, or even the next crop of Sheets.' He stood up and looked out at the Ervrin Mallos, dark and solid against the grey sky. 'They clatter around without any semblance of true guidance.' He shook his head. 'They have no conception of the nature of the institutions that they ostensibly command, none at all. They're blind, Dowinne, blind to a man, but I will bring them the light to see by. The One True Light.' He fell silent. 'As for their religions,' there was a darker note in his voice now that drew

Dowinne's attention sharply, 'they are heresies, all of them. They will fall before what is coming like wheat before a scythe. There will be a grim harvest.'

Dowinne experienced a frisson of excitement as Cassraw spoke. There seemed to be a power about him that she had never known before. She reprimanded herself. Stay calm. Stay quiet. Above all, listen!

She probed again. 'I've never doubted your vision, Enryc,' she said. 'Not ever – you know that. But what you're saying now seems as wild as any politician's Acclamation speech.' Then, dangerously, 'Or as foolish as the rantings of one of those spurious religious leaders who spring up from time to time to prey on the gullible and foolish.'

Cassraw's eyes blazed.

Dowinne braced herself, though she could not hazard for what.

She is of Us. Do not doubt. She will not be lightly won. Lead and she will follow.

With an effort, Cassraw set his anger aside. 'I am neither, Dowinne. If you don't know that, then watch me, and learn. You will be by my side in this as you have been in all other things before.'

Again she felt a power within him that was new to her. He was not insane, nor was he naive or foolish. He was strong and whole, and filled with a purpose whose end she could not see but which would be one after her own desires.

Abruptly, he reached out towards her with both hands. 'Will you trust and follow me?' he said, very softly.

This time the power in him almost overwhelmed her. Doubts whirled about her mind, but beneath them another knowledge rose to urge her on.

She stood up and took the offered hands. 'Yes, my love,' she said. 'I will.'

Chapter 9

Vredech leapt up out of his chair in terror and spun round, his mind scrabbling for sanity. He became aware of a cry mingling with his own, and as his eyes began to focus, reality slipped away once more as he found himself gazing into Cassraw's face, its eyes wide and fearful, its mouth agape.

His mind teetered at the edge of an abyss.

The mouth began to move. Slow, lumbering words reached him.

'I'm so sorry, Brother Vredech,' they said breathlessly. 'I didn't mean to startle you. I . . .' There was a trembling but relieved breath. 'You gave me a rare fright, jumping up like that and crying out.'

Vredech's vision cleared and, somehow, he found his own voice. 'Skynner. Keeper Skynner,' he gasped, slapping his hand on his chest as if to still the frantic pounding of his heart. The two men stared at one another for a moment, then simultaneously began a babbled round of mutual apologizing. Eventually they both became coherent and Vredech motioned his visitor to a seat.

Haron Skynner, a bulky man of middle years, was a Keeper – a Serjeant Keeper, to give him his rank – one of that august civilian body which maintained order on the streets of Troidmallos at the behest of the Heindral. It was not a clearly defined duty and the Keepers were judged primarily on their success at controlling the town's more troublesome individuals, rather than on the legal niceties of how they achieved this. But, for the most part, they were respected, if not always loved. And generally, they were competent and honest. Not that Keeper Skynner and his colleagues were above occasionally welcoming largesse from the local traders as tokens of gratitude for their good offices. Hardly ever money – that was really beyond the pale – but a meal here, a piece of beef there, a loaf, a fowl, a favourable discount on this or that. It was not approved of officially and, in fact, ran directly counter to the formal procedures laid down by the Heindral governing the conduct of Keepers, but one has to be realistic, flexible, in these matters, hasn't one?

'What do you want, Haron?' Vredech asked, as the waves of his panic finally subsided.

Skynner gave a long, regretful breath. 'It's Mad Jarry, I'm afraid,' he said.

Anticipation of what was to follow set aside Vredech's immediate concerns and, lifting his hand to his mouth, he tilted an imaginary glass. Skynner nodded.

'Who gave it to him?' Vredech asked, frowning.

Skynner shrugged. 'None of our local innkeepers, for sure,' he replied. 'They value their Consents too highly – not to mention their property. It might have been young lads, for a lark, or maybe someone was just careless when he was around. You know what he's like when he gets the urge for a drink.'

'Indeed I do,' Vredech acknowledged, standing up wearily. 'Where is he?'

Skynner stood up as well, clutching his cap apologetically. 'I'm really sorry for giving you such a fright,' he said. 'I can see you're tired. You needn't come if it's too much trouble. We can deal with him. I just thought that . . . after the last time . . .' he raised his eyebrows and left the sentence unfinished.

For a moment, Vredech was tempted. Jarry could be a

considerable handful when he was drunk but then, as Skynner's expression was reminding him, if the Keepers had to deal with him they would probably have little choice but to resort to force – and who could say what consequences might flow from that?

As he debated with himself Skynner was continuing, 'I heard you had a little problem up at the Witness House.' His wilfully casual manner made Vredech chuckle and his hesitation vanished. Poor Mueran, he thought, imagining he could keep anything secret in Troidmallos. From past experience he knew that it was not only pointless, but foolish to equivocate with Skynner; he liked and respected the man. Besides, the Keepers having the proper tale would help to dampen down the more foolish gossip that was likely to be abroad soon. He kept matters simple and told the truth. Most of it, anyway.

'We had a difficult meeting,' he said. 'Cassraw went out to stretch his legs and clear his head and unfortunately had a nasty fall. The light went very suddenly under that cloud. He was lucky to get away with just a few bruises.' Then he added his own political contribution, with a knowing smile. 'If you heard anything substantially different from that it'll give you some measure of the worth of your informants.'

Skynner grinned. 'I'll take due note of your advice,' he said.

'Come on,' Vredech said, reaching for his cloak. 'Take me to Jarry. I'll do what I can. Chapter meetings are not my favourite activity at the best of times and this one was particularly trying, even without Cassraw's misfortune. A bit of active pastoral care will blow the cobwebs off me.'

'Don't make it too active, Brother,' Skynner remarked. 'I came to you to avoid that.'

Jarold Harverson – Mad Jarry to everyone who knew him – was a very large and powerful man. He was also strange.

102

Some called him stupid, others simple. Children generally loved him, except for those who had been infected by their parents' fears; they ran from him in terror, or around him pelting him with scorn and anything else they felt brave enough to handle. Such physicians as had looked at him from time to time had shaken their heads and, in the absence of any greater wisdom, had declared that his 'condition' was attributable to a dangerous fever he had suffered when young and that nothing could be done for him.

Despite their natural sternness, the Madren were kinder than many in their treatment of such as Jarry. Other states in Gyronlandt hounded and persecuted them, not infrequently locking them up in the foulest conditions or subjecting them to the outlandish treatments of physicians who were even less inclined to admit their ignorance than their colleagues in Canol Madreth. The Madren, for the most part, though wary, watched and tended and made allowances for such people, taking what care they could to ensure that they hurt neither themselves nor others.

A few said of Jarry that, 'he sees with other eyes'. Though he had no clear idea what it meant, Vredech had a sneaking sympathy for this notion, for Jarry's manner was often at once absent and attentive as if indeed he were in some other place. And he could be so heartbreakingly gentle and sensitive at times that more than once Vredech had felt truly humbled before him. Yet at other times he was undeniably odd, running about frantically as if trying to escape from some awful pursuer, ranting and raving in what seemed to be a coherent foreign language, though no one could identify it. Sadly, too, he also possessed the darker nature that is humanity's inexorable lot. He could be violent – very violent. Though it was only under one circumstance – when he had been drinking.

Drink was viewed with great suspicion by the church in Canol Madreth, largely, in the view of outsiders, because people enjoyed it. Be that as it may, the disapproval existed and while accepting that it could not eradicate drink as a social vice while large sections of the community regarded it as a social grace, the church expected its Preaching Brothers to inveigh against it heavily from time to time. They were also required to be conspicuously abstinent, thus providing a fairly steady source of scandals for Privv and the other Sheeters. It was, however, the efforts of the church through the years that had bound Canol Madreth's innkeepers to their Consents – a bizarre tangle of petty statutes and by-laws with which they were required to comply in order to ply their trade. The complexities of the Consent Laws were a source of endless complaint for the Keepers, the innkeepers, most of the public and nearly all outsiders. The latter in particular could often be found staring open-mouthed at the list of restrictions which were posted on each inn door and which told them why they would have to remain thirsty for the next few hours.

On the whole however, innkeepers complained only so far – there was no saying what mess the Heindral would make of the Consent Laws if they revised them yet again. It was unheard of for the Heindral to reassess the need for, and value of, any statute totally. Their universally consistent method of adjusting to social change was to tack bits and pieces on to existing statutes. Their laws were thus often festooned with obscure and difficult amendments, not a few of which were often irrelevant in that the conditions which they were intended to deal with had long passed away. And, to a man, innkeepers were careful. Substantial financial penalties awaited anyone who was foolish enough to flout the conditions of his Consent.

Hence Skynner's certainty that Jarry had not received his drink from any authorized source – not that the source was of any great relevance at the moment. Regrettably, there were times when Jarry actively sought whatever solace it was he found in drink and, for any person so inclined, the drink was always there to be found. Why Jarry should be so driven no one could say. Had it been asked, the church would have probably fallen back on its dogma that Man was naturally evil and would necessarily do such things unless restrained by the threat of retribution – divine or secular. Vredech was personally inclined to the view that whatever worlds Jarry saw into sometimes became so awful that he simply sought oblivion. It was not a view he discussed with anyone, though it came to him again as he walked alongside Skynner towards the place where Jarry had last been seen.

Perhaps if I could see what he sees, I might be able to help him more, he found himself thinking. The thought had an unusually strange force and he set it aside with an inward shudder; he had looked into enough strange worlds of his own these past two days. Now was a time for simple, down-to-earth practicalities. His expertise as a negotiator was needed, if Jarry was to be spared what must inevitably be a severe beating, and doubtless several Keepers spared injury. And there was always the fear at such times that greater harm than bruises and sprains might occur, leading to Jarry being jailed, perhaps permanently, for the public good. It was a peculiarly horrible thought. Although he had a home, maintained by various relatives and friends of the family, Jarry did not like being indoors. Apart from hunger and tiredness, only the fiercest of weathers would keep him inside. Jailing him would be hurling him headlong into the very worst of the worlds to which he was witness.

A figure came running toward them. It was another Keeper. He acknowledged Vredech with a brief but respectful nod then spoke to Skynner. 'He's off again. It looks as if he's heading for Mirrylan Square.' He looked anxious. 'He keeps pestering people – shouting at them.'

Skynner frowned. 'What have you done?' he asked.

'Just kept an eye on him, like you said,' came the reply. 'I know well enough how he responds to our uniforms when he's like this.'

Skynner made no comment but turned sharply into a narrow alleyway. Vredech and the Keeper swung in behind him and the trio moved in single uneven file, stepping around and over the debris and litter that cluttered the alley floor. Every now and then, Skynner's long stride would give way to a trot as his anxiety drew him on. Thus, when they emerged from the alley Vredech was slightly breathless and quite flushed. He put his hand on Skynner's arm to slow him down. The big man did so, albeit reluctantly.

A noise reached them. It was someone shouting.

'He's in the Square,' the Keeper said, pointing. Vredech saw a small group of Keepers gathered at the far end of the street. It was apparent from their movement that they were endeavouring to watch what was happening around the corner without being seen. Some of them were swinging their batons.

'Put those away right now,' Vredech said grimly as he reached the group. One or two looked at Skynner who merely furrowed his brow angrily at them for their hesitancy in doing as the Preacher bade them.

Vredech looked round the corner into Mirrylan Square. It was one of Troidmallos's older squares and, though its age showed in the buildings around it and the well-worn and rutted cobbles, it always had an open, airy feel to it which made it more popular than many of the town's newer squares with their carefully maintained lawns and trees.

Now, however, the people standing around the edges of the square were not interested in the subtle mysteries of its charm. Their attention was on the centre of the Square, where stood a small stone tower which marked the site of a long-sealed well, and their mood was one of uncertain

106

excitement, plus no small amount of expectation. Motioning Skynner and the others to stay where they were, Vredech stepped forward and began walking towards the tower. Donning his Preacher's manner he looked round at the watchers sternly as he passed. Most of them shifted a little uncomfortably under his gaze, but he did not pause to give them any further reproach. Instead, he concentrated on the hulking figure of Jarry pacing to and fro at the foot of the broad steps which served as a dais for the tower. He had a half-empty bottle in one hand and was gesticulating violently with the other, at the same time calling out something that Vredech could not make out.

Aware that all eyes would now be on him, Vredech straightened up and tried to keep his anxiety from his face. It was no easy task as a large part of his mind was occupied with asking: 'What am I doing here?' Jarry was larger even than Skynner and fully as strong as his powerful muscular frame indicated. And, right now, there was a frightening momentum in the long strides he was taking. Vredech took in the old tower with its stained and spalling rendering and its steeply pitched slate roof, dotted with spheres of moss. It was scarcely the height of two men to its eaves, but Jarry's size so distorted its perspective that Vredech had the impression he was looking at a picture taken from some child's book showing a great giant guarding a mighty tower fortress.

Oddly, the impression did not fade immediately, and for a terrifying moment he felt as though he were shrinking as he neared the formidable figure. He stopped and deliberately composed himself. His father's words came to him. 'See things as they are.' Simple, but profound advice which, though far from easy to follow, had more than once been of great value to him. Then the scene in front of him was Jarry and the old Well Tower. And Jarry was Jarry, for all practical purposes a child trapped in a man's body. Vredech began advancing again, this time at an easy pace and in a direction that would ensure that Jarry would see him before he was too close. He smiled.

'Jarold,' he called out. 'What's the matter?'

Jarry lowered the bottle from his lips and began looking from side to side frantically. Vredech took a deep breath and walked up to him.

'What's the matter?' he asked again, looking into the distant, fearful eyes, red-rimmed and bloodshot with the spirits that Jarry had been drinking. Anger flashed, brilliant, in Vredech's mind. Whoever had done this needed horse-whipping! He set the rage aside quickly lest Jarry, his senses never dull, and perhaps heightened now by whatever had made him start drinking, might feel it and respond badly. It was he however, who detected Jarry's mood, as a great wave of terror flooded over him. Vredech felt tears coming into his eyes.

'Jarry, don't be afraid. It's me,' he said, a little hoarsely. 'Brother Vredech. Don't you recognize me?'

There was a long pause, then a crash that made him start violently. Jarry had dropped the bottle which had shattered on the cobbles in a glittering spray of liquor and broken glass. Almost before Vredech could register what had happened, Jarry was standing in front of him, his huge hands resting heavily on his shoulders. Ironically, Jarry's movement was so fast that Vredech did not have time to be frightened. The big man bent forward and peered blearily into Vredech's face, searching. Vredech tried not to flinch away from the stink of spirits on Jarry's breath. Then, abruptly, Jarry was looking past him and his expression was changing – becoming vicious and angry. Vredech glanced quickly over the great hand holding his shoulder to see a group of Keepers closing rapidly, obviously fearing that he was being attacked.

'Go back. There's no problem. I'm all right,' he shouted, though more in hope than certainty.

The group hesitated. Vredech felt Jarry's hands shifting

on his shoulders; he was about to release him, presumably with the intention of moving to attack the Keepers. He seized one of the great hands as strongly as he could and shouted, 'No!' loudly and commandingly into Jarry's face, following it with another earnest appeal to his would-be rescuers. 'Go back, quickly. Get out of sight. Now! You're only going to make him angry.'

With some reluctance the Keepers did as he asked, and as soon as they started to move back Vredech returned his attention to Jarry. He tried shaking the hand he was holding, to draw Jarry's menacing gaze away from the retreating Keepers, but it had no effect that he could notice. Rather it seemed that he was merely succeeding in shaking himself, so solid was Jarry's posture. Despite his growing concern for his own safety, he felt a twinge of sympathy for the Keepers who might have to subdue this skull-crushing power if he failed. No wonder they had drawn their batons!

Then Jarry was talking. Gabbling nonsense at him, his hands opening and closing painfully about his shoulders. 'Stop it, Jarry, you're hurting me,' Vredech said, still managing to sound authoritative in spite of the fear that was coming to him in earnest now. In desperation, he placed a hand under each of Jarry's wrists and pushed upwards in an attempt to ease the pressure. It succeeded partially, though he felt his knees start to buckle under the strain. Unused to physical contact, still less violence, he wanted to shout and bellow to make this ludicrous conflict stop, but from somewhere a wiser inspiration came. 'Enough, Jarry,' he said, very softly and gently. 'Enough, you're hurting me. You don't want to do that, do you? I'm your friend, remember? See, the Keepers have gone. Let go of me so that we can talk properly. Then you can tell me what's the matter.'

As he had hoped, it was the tone rather than his words that reached through to his antagonist. The hands slid off him. His legs, suddenly unburdened, felt unsteady and he took hold of Jarry's arm momentarily for support. Jarry stared at him again, flickers of recognition coming into his blinking eyes. Then there was only fear again. His mouth opened to emit a cry that voiced it clearly. Vredech winced at the man's pain. He reached up and took the great head in his two hands. 'You're safe, Jarry,' he said into the din. 'No one's going to hurt you. Listen to me. *No one's going to hurt you.*'

Jarry's arms rose up and waved about in denial. 'He's here,' he said, his voice shaking, but quite clear. The unexpected lucidity made Vredech start.

'Who is?' he asked simply.

Jarry shot a fearful glance upwards, then bent forward, bringing his face so close to Vredech's as to be almost touching it. 'He is,' he whispered hoarsely. 'Him.'

Vredech shook his head. 'I don't understand,' he said. 'Who's here? Has someone been frightening you?'

Jarry let out a pitiful whimper, then looked at the hand in which he had been holding the bottle. His eyes became lost and vacant.

'It's gone, Jarry,' Vredech said. 'You dropped the bottle and it broke. Anyway, you know it's not good for you. It only gets you into trouble.' He wanted to ask who had given it to him, but even if Jarry could remember, it was unlikely that he would divulge the name of his benefactor, and what Jarry needed now was to talk, not to retreat into some haunted silence. 'Why did you start drinking, Jarry?' he asked instead. 'You haven't done it for a long time.'

'Drink. Drink,' Jarry said, looking at his empty hand, then at Vredech. 'Must have a drink.' He was becoming very agitated. Fighting an increasingly powerful urge to flee, Vredech held his ground.

'No,' he said unequivocally. 'No drink. It's bad for you. You'll get hurt and you'll hurt other people.'

'No. No. Jarry not hurt. Drink.'

'Why?'

Jarry lowered his head and started squeezing his hands together fretfully.

Vredech laid his own hands on top of them and bent forward to look into Jarry's face. 'Why?' he asked again, gently.

'Hide. Jarry hide.' Then, explosively, he let out a great cry and threw his arms into the air, sending Vredech reeling. As he staggered to regain his balance, Vredech caught sight of the Keepers racing across the Square towards him, batons waving. At the same time he saw that Jarry was standing motionless, his hand wrapped over the top of his head. Scarcely thinking what he was doing, but knowing that no command of his would stop the Keepers attempting to restrain Jarry, with all that that meant, he lunged forward and placed himself between them and the swaying Jarry.

He held out his hands protectively. 'I'm all right,' he shouted. 'Leave him. It was just a misunderstanding.' He caught Skynner's eye. 'Please, Haron. Please.'

'He's dangerous when he's like this Brother,' Skynner replied heatedly. 'You nearly measured your length on the cobbles just then. I can't—'

'He's here. Jarry hide. Jarry hide.'

Jarry's cry interrupted him. It was followed by a moaning cry that was so pitiful that even some of the hardened Keepers looked distressed by it. Vredech, still holding out a hand to fend off his would-be defenders, turned back to him. Jarry's face was now buried in his arms. Skynner motioned his men back a little.

'He's going down,' one of them whispered, infected by Vredech's concern.

And even as he spoke, Jarry sank slowly to his knees, then, his hands still wrapped about his head, he bent forward, as if to make himself as small as possible. His

111

keening continued steadily. Vredech knelt beside him. As he did so he noticed that the watching crowd was growing bolder in its curiosity and starting to move forward. He gave Skynner a significant nod in their direction and he immediately dispatched his men to send the sightseers on their way.

Vredech could do no other than put his arms around Jarry and make soothing noises. 'You're safe now. No one's going to hurt you. No need to hide.' All he received by way of reply, though, was the undiminished moaning.

'What's the matter with him?'

Vredech looked up to see Privv standing nearby, being prevented from coming any closer by a Keeper's baton. Vredech turned away to hide the distaste on his face. He knew Privv of old as a result of some indiscretions by members of his flock and, despite his religious principles, he found it hard not to despise him and other Sheeters of his ilk, who wilfully peddled anything that was hurtful and claimed it as a precious civic trust. He had heard about Privv's antics at the Witness House and, like Horld, viewed them with the utmost suspicion. And, though he could not have said why, he had been unsettled by the news that Cassraw had talked to the wretched man so freely.

'Someone gave him some drink,' he said. A malicious sprite rose inside him and he turned back towards Privv. 'It wasn't you, was it?' he asked, his face stern. He took some pleasure in Privv's slight start. Don't like your own tricks, do you? he thought. But the Sheeter recovered on the instant and affected a hurt look.

'Why would *I* do such a thing?' he asked, eyes wide. Vredech did not reply but turned back to tending the downed Jarry.

'Move on, sir,' the Keeper said. 'There's nothing for you here.'

Privv took no notice. 'What was he babbling on about before?' he asked Vredech around the ushering arm of the Keeper.

'Go away, Privv,' Vredech sighed. 'There is nothing for you here – just a poor unfortunate soul who's been frightened by something he's imagined. He'll be all right shortly, if he's left alone.'

Privv wrinkled his nose thoughtfully, then shrugged and walked away, his thoughts turning to how he could describe the incident and still cast a discreetly bad light on this surly preacher. Vredech had always been a nuisance. He was a Chapter Member, for pity's sake; he shouldn't talk to people like that just for doing their jobs! Privv searched the dispersing crowd for familiar faces from whom he could get the full story of what had happened here. He often found that the truth was quite useful as a starting point for a good story.

Privv was already far from Vredech's mind as he turned his attention back to the still motionless, whimpering Jarry. As he looked at him, a large drop of rain splattered a dark star noisily on the cobbles at his feet. Jarry started as if there had been a thunderclap. His eyes widened as he saw the wet stain, now being joined by others. Tentatively he reached out and touched it with the end of his forefinger. His hand jerked away convulsively.

'Come on, Jarry,' Vredech was saying. 'Let's get you home. It's starting to rain.'

But Jarry was rubbing his finger, as if he were trying to wipe something particularly unpleasant or painful off it. He kept glancing up at the sky and Vredech noticed that he was trembling.

'He's here,' he said in a childish whisper. He brought his finger close to his face to examine it. 'He was up there. Now He's down here.' Vredech could do no other than look upwards, but there was nothing to be seen except the grey clouds and the dancing black dots of rain falling towards his upturned face.

'Who is?' he asked awkwardly. 'Who's here? Who's frightening you like this?'

Skynner returned and crouched down beside him. 'The rain'll shift the rest of the audience. Have you found out what's the matter with him yet?'

Vredech shook his head. 'I'll get him home, if I can. He might tell me about it, if he remembers when he's recovered.' He lowered his voice. 'But he's scared to death of something . . . or someone.'

Skynner shrugged. 'It's a great pity he's not more scared of me,' he said with rueful practicality. 'Still, he seems quiet enough now. If you're happy about him I can leave you a couple of lads to help, but I'll have to get the rest of them back to their duties. A little disruption like this is all some of them need to quietly disappear for an hour or so.'

A hand plucked at Vredech's sleeve before he could reply. It was Jarry's. As he caught the big man's gaze he noticed for the first time that his eyes, like his own and Cassraw's, were black. 'I saw Him rising to fill the sky, His great night cloak swallowing up the holy mountain and covering the whole land. I heard His cries turn from despair to rejoicing, a terrible rejoicing, as I travelled the dream ways.' He clawed at Vredech's arm. 'Horrible. Horrible. And now He walks amongst us again.'

Taken aback by this unexpected burst of eloquence, Vredech could merely ask, 'Who, Jarry?'

Jarry swallowed, as if the words were likely to choke him.

'Ahmral, Brother. Ahmral,' he said, very softly.

Skynner chuckled and reached down to hoist him to his feet. He winked at Vredech. 'Don't fret yourself about that, Jarry,' he said. 'You're not the first person to see the devil when he's had a drink too many.'

Vredech said nothing. Jarry's words had transported him back to the previous day when he, too, alone in the darkness, had heard a terrible rejoicing. And when he, too, in his fear had cried out, 'Leave me, Ahmral's spawn. *Leave me.*'

Chapter 10

Troidmallos quickly settled back into its normal routine. Or apparently so. The mysterious cloud with its threat of a terrible storm that never came soon lost its worth as a topic of conversation and speculation, not least because the weather generally began to improve. Winter had its occasional dying fling but, on the whole, grey skies became bluer, and cold, damp winds became warmer and drier. Then a faint green sheen began to appear on trees and bushes, announcing that spring was definitely on its way. The church held to the line that Cassraw had gone out for a walk to refresh himself after a long meeting and had fallen when the light suddenly deteriorated. The Chapter was remarkably unified in its silence about the real reason for his angry departure from the Witness House, his odd behaviour when he reappeared, and his even stranger collapse and recovery. Privv had the deepest reservations about what had happened, scenting closed ranks and secrecy with the sensitivity of a dog scenting a bitch on heat, but Cassraw's open admission of the events left him virtually nothing to work on. And he was loath to fabricate anything too fanciful for fear of losing that intangible thread of goodwill that had prompted Cassraw to talk to him and which, he was sure, could be woven into a rope of rare value with care and time.

As for Jarry's escapade, in the absence of a spectacular and violent conclusion, that merely provided a sour little item in one or two of the less widely read Sheets.

But changes had occurred. A subtle tide was starting to run, for many bizarre things had happened during the night following Cassraw's mysterious transformation. People had suffered vivid dreams: some, appalling and fearful, others, full of the promise of unsettling desires. Others claimed to have heard noises – unworldly singing, eerie chanting, even screaming. And some said they saw . . . things . . . flitting about the streets – dark things, like shadows, but with no one there to cast them. A handful of these tales were picked up by the Sheeters, mistold and forgotten except by those involved, but far more people were touched that night than chose to talk about it, and in all of those the memory of the experience lingered . . . and lingered.

Only the Preaching Brothers had any measure of what had happened as, one after another, members of their flocks – some guiltily, some bewildered, many frightened – trooped in for hesitant discussions about this and that until they plucked up courage to talk about what they had really come for – a dream, a vision, a sighting. But the Preaching Brothers did not meet one another very often and, in any event, had no reason to discuss such pastoral matters even though some of them had been distinctly peculiar. Thus the measure they had went unnoticed.

The tide swelled, unheeded.

Besides, more serious things were afoot. A respected Madren merchant, travelling abroad, had been murdered.

Canol Madreth's immediate westerly neighbour was Tirfelden. Larger and more populous than Canol Madreth, Tirfelden was also a livelier place by far. Not that this was always to the advantage of its citizens. A few decades previously it had emerged from a long period of tyranny and oppression and since then had enjoyed a system of government not dissimilar to that of Canol Madreth, except that where the Madren had some three major political parties, the Felden had no less than fifteen – or seventeen, or thirteen, etc – depending on the pacts, coalitions, alliances and realignments that were current at any one time. Further, the Felden, who lived beyond the constant sobering presence of the central mountains and away from the aegis of a stern religion, were generally a more flamboyant people than the Madren, and very apt to act first and think afterwards. Whether this was the cause of their long tradition of violent changes of government or the effect of it cannot really be determined, but they did not hesitate to take to the streets whenever the government of the day was doing something unpopular.

In the absence of any brutal oppression from above to unite the people, this form of political enthusiasm usually manifested itself in street fighting between the many factions that were constantly clamouring for 'fair and even treatment'.

The Madren viewed the Felden with some disdain while the Felden viewed them in their turn as sour faced, humourless and obsessively religious. Nevertheless, business was business, and there was some trade between the two countries, mainly in timber. This enabled the Madren to exchange some of their dark forests for iron and associated products which the Felden mined and worked.

It was in connection with this trade that two Madren merchants were in Tirfelden at a time when feelings were running high over some proposed legislation. Heady with the openness of Tirfelden society, which made the strictures of their homeland seem particularly suffocating, the two men had sought entertainment in a local inn and, being unused to the potency and uncontrolled availability of the Tirfelden ale, had ill-advisedly ventured into a particularly heated argument. When this resulted in their being abused and generally held to scorn along with their country and their religion, they had retorted in kind and,

117

in the ensuing mêlée, one man had been killed and the other badly hurt.

The response of the Tirfelden authorities to this incident was less than satisfactory as far as the Madren were concerned. Strong in hypocrisy themselves, they were particularly sensitive to it in others and the expressions of regret and horror that they received were deemed to be markedly lacking in sincerity, particularly as little or no attempt appeared to have been made to find the offenders – allegedly some of the more volatile supporters of the then dominant government party. They considered their suspicions confirmed when the incident became a matter of debate in the Tirfelden Congress.

The Congress was not an ideal forum for temperate debate at the best of times and the fate of the two Madren soon became a shuttlecock to be buffeted about the chamber as the various factions sought to score points against one another. An official Madren observer stormed out of the chamber in a fury before the debate had ended, and demanded a formal apology and compensation for the families of the two men from the Tirfelden government. In the face of the man's considerable anger this was promised, but when he had left, it became, in its turn, the subject of another Congress debate. Although this new debate was a little more sober than the first, it was not without national indignation at what was regarded as the high-handed manner of the Madren civil servant, and the offer of compensation was reduced. By this time the matter had reached the ears of the Sheeters and a wide variety of gory tellings of the incident were being distributed about Canol Madreth. News of the Tirfelden Congress's unsavoury haggling amplified these tellings and as a result of being repeatedly told of the public's outrage at this affair, the Heinders began to feel themselves under pressure to 'do something'.

In reality there was little or no such pressure. Those

who read of the affair responded in many ways, ranging from indifference to genuine concern and sympathy, but few pestered their Heinders to take any kind of action. And, it could not be denied, such sympathy as was felt was tempered by the fact that the two men, 'had been drinking, after all . . .' with all that that implied. Retribution for one's sins was a strong element in Ishrythan. However, folly begets folly, and in responding to something that was not in reality there, the Heindral succeeded in creating a genuine crisis for itself.

The term of the government was well into its second half and thoughts were already beginning to turn toward the next Acclamation when the Tirfelden incident occurred. Thus, as in the Tirfelden Congress, the matter became an opportunity to jockey for position in the eyes of the voting public. The party in power, the Castellans, unexpectedly mooted the idea of expelling any Felden currently resident in Canol Madreth and seizing Felden assets. This was a bold gesture, delivered with great panache, and would undoubtedly resound well when the voters were being wooed in due course. It was put forward however, only in the fairly certain knowledge that the other two parties would, for once, unite and vote against it. And indeed the main opposition party, the Ploughers, played their part admirably, speaking in powerful but calmly measured tones, and dwelling on the outrage that 'they too', felt about the fate of 'this highly respected merchant'. However, scared senseless at what they thought the Castellans wanted to do, they suggested that a 'more effective and even-handed measure', would be to refrain from trading with Tirfelden, on the grounds that the Felden needed timber more than the Madren needed iron. For a while there was some robust debating, the Castellans being pilloried as dictatorial and even war-mongering, while the Ploughers were labelled as naive appeasers and cowards and quite indifferent to the fate of

119

the people who worked in the forestry trade. Then the leader of the third and smallest party began to speak.

The Witness Party had been the smallest for many decades now, and such power as it had wielded from time to time had been dependent on how nearly equal the other two parties were. Unlikely ever to hold real power in the near future, it had the privilege of advocating outrageous ideas, but it knew its place and would not resort to anything foolish when matters of importance were being discussed. What was special about the Witness Party was its religious element. Unique amongst the parties it actually had Preaching Brothers in its ranks, and it would unrepentantly point out the moral and religious aspects of any subject being debated. Its speakers were often greeted with an unconscious but heartfelt sigh as they rose.

Now there was an almost respectful silence as Toom Drommel stood up to outline his party's view. Expectation filled the chamber – expectation that Drommel would castigate the Castellans for their belligerent proposal, with its appalling disregard for basic justice in seeking to punish Felden citizens who, quite patently, had had nothing to do with the murder of the merchant and were entitled to look to the Madren authorities for protection not persecution. He would then turn on the Ploughers to reproach them for their economic naivety in imagining that loss of trade with Canol Madreth would make any material impression on Tirfelden. Finally, he would conclude that his party would vote against both suggestions, thereby releasing both parties from the need to do anything without seriously undermining his own party's standing. The matter would then drift out of the public limelight and be sorted out by officials from the respective governments.

Quite unexpectedly however, Toom simply said: 'We shall support the Castellans in their proposal,' and then sat down.

For a moment it seemed that the Castellans were about to lose their leader as he turned first red then purple, but somehow he survived the blow and was on his feet in seconds.

So was everyone else.

Privv, high in the spectators' gallery, rubbed his hands gleefully. He knew quite a few Felden and he could see stories developing that would last him for weeks – and make him quite a lot of money in the process. He saw what the Ploughers and the Castellans had failed to see, namely that while Toom Drommel and his party had no great desire to be associated with either the economic ineptitude of the Ploughers, or the strutting posturing of the Castellans, they also had no desire to be seen as a party that could not make up its mind, or take a stern stand where the safety of Madren citizens was at stake. They had therefore decided to call the Castellans' bluff. For in supporting them, the Witness Party would appear to be strong and resolute in the defence of their country's citizens abroad – a very useful attribute to be displaying during the approach to an Acclamation, while at the same time showing the Castellans to be weak and uncertain. For there was no way in which the Castellans could implement their proposals without causing a major rift with Tirfelden – a much larger and wealthier nation.

Privv waited for the inevitable outcome. When the uproar subsided, the leader of the Castellans would end the debate without a vote and scurry off to a panic-stricken meeting with his party officers to try to find some way of extricating himself from this problem without the retreat being too public or too humiliating.

Toom Drommel sat with his arms folded, quietly smiling to himself, and Privv observed him intently. He had misjudged this man. He had always regarded him as another bigoted pain in the neck, but there was obviously much more to him than met the eye. He had judged the

Castellans' complacency and political carelessness to a nicety and had done them no small amount of harm with his brief statement. He had also done his own party a great deal of good. As he watched the man, sitting motionless amid the hubbub, it dawned on Privv that Toom Drommel was a force to be reckoned with. And he really was going to push his party forward at the next Acclamation. Interesting times were coming, Privv thought to himself. Interesting times.

The church's only declared interest in the affair of the slaughtered merchant was one of simple compassion for the man's family. It had, of course, a permanent and considerable interest in all political developments, but it was discreet, not to say meticulous, in ensuring that it was seen to be above any petty power chasing, and in this case it confined itself to watching and weighing events.

Apart from taking due note of happenings in the Heindral and dealing with routine church business, two other topics were occupying the attention of Mueran and his staff at the Witness House. One was the change that had come over Cassraw, and the other was the change that had come over Vredech. Where before, the mention of Cassraw's name had brought a weary frown to Mueran's brow as he braced himself for yet more complaints from the Haven flock, or another diatribe on the Santyth from the man himself, it now brought a pleasant smile. Complaints had changed to compliments. Since his strange 'attack', Cassraw seemed to have become a different and much more amenable person, and he was proving himself to be a worthy incumbent for the Haven Parish. He had seemingly set aside his growing obsession with the minutiae of the Santyth and was throwing himself wholeheartedly into his pastoral work, moving around tirelessly, helping and advising members of his flock, talking to them, listening to them, whatever the circumstances required. And his preaching was becoming almost legendary. Attendances at his Meeting House were higher than they had ever been, as backsliding church members returned to the fold and people travelled from other parishes to listen to him. He had even established a special organization to look after the needs of a group of troublesome youths who had been the bane of the area for some time. Mueran had some reservations about the name that had been chosen for this organization – the Knights of Ishryth – but Cassraw had laughingly reassured him. 'You know what young men are like. They have to look manly – if only in their own eyes. I doubt I'd have been able to catch their attention with a name like the Haven Parish Group for Santyth Appreciation.' Then, a hand on Mueran's shoulder – firm and full of good-natured resolution – 'You needn't fret. They're a little wild, but they're all good lads at heart, and better we keep them occupied than leave them to their own devices.'

Yes, Mueran mused, Cassraw was shaping up nicely. He was back once again on the track which had seemed to be his from the outset – the track that could eventually make him Covenant Member. Mueran laid a great deal of emphasis on the word 'eventually', however.

Vredech though, was a different matter. Since that same incident, the first complaints ever about him began to reach Mueran. Vredech was becoming morose, bad-tempered, lax in the performance of his parish duties. Some even hinted that his faith was less than sound. Concerned, Mueran called him to the Witness House and after a lengthy talk with him apparently diagnosed nothing more than tiredness. 'Feeling for the pain of others is one of the more burdensome attributes we must bring to our ministry, Brother, but it carries a heavy price if we don't learn how to detach ourselves from it.' He copied Cassraw's hand on the shoulder. 'I think that what happened to Brother Cassraw the other week disturbed you more than you know, but he's fit and well now while you still seem to be labouring through the darkness. If you wish, I can arrange for a relief to take over for a couple of weeks to give you a rest, let you build up your reserves again.'

But Vredech smiled and declined the offer with thanks, at the same time promising to take note of Mueran's good advice and be a little less personally involved in the troubles of his parishioners. In reality, Mueran's offer of a relief shook him badly. The last thing he needed now was to be left alone to his own devices. Work was perhaps the only thing that was keeping him sane. Nevertheless, he had heard the serious undertones in Mueran's words and he knew that he ignored them at the peril not only of his future in the church, but even his Parish. This realization helped him to turn and face what was happening to him.

But what *was* happening?

That same evening, after his return from the Witness House, he sat alone before the cold ashes of a dead fire and determined to search into the cause of the darkness that seemed to have settled on him like a damp, clinging cloak. Certain things were obvious. The dominant one being that he was not sleeping well. He could not recall ever dreaming in his entire life, but sometimes now, when he closed his eyes, he would find himself looking at the dancing shadows that had surrounded him on the mountain. Black on black, they were like bottomless pits . . . He would open his eyes, fearful of what he might see or what might happen if they . . .

If they what?

There was no answer. Just the fear of some unknown consequence.

And he would hear again the din of that awful celebration; primitive, barbarous, stirring reaches deep inside him that should not be disturbed. Even now, his hands rose to his ears with a nervous twitch. What in Ishryth's name had happened on that mountain? What did it all mean? And why were these . . . memories . . . if memories they were, haunting him so?

Was he going insane?

'No, no,' he muttered to himself. He was confused and angry – frightened even, he conceded. But insane, surely not. What he had seen he had seen, and what he had heard he had heard; he was sure of it, even though for some reason the others had not. He clung to reason. Insanity cast a shadow before it. He had had no fever, nor any other signs of physical illness, nor had he now, except for the dragging uneasiness in his stomach – though this, he knew from past experience, was because he was worrying. It would go when he had accomplished two things – found out what he was worrying about and done something about it.

He stiffened his resolve. He would remain in his chair that night until he had examined every aspect of that strange day and come to some conclusion. It would be a vigil. He prayed a little, but it was more from habit than true need and the words hung hollow and empty in his mind. That did not concern him too much. Ishryth was not an easy god, given to smoothing the way at the behest of any slight appeal. Ishryth helped those who helped themselves, and those alone. Vredech knew that only in his striving would he see the hand of Ishryth.

His resolution renewed, he closed the window shutters to lock out the night and then turned off all the lamps in the room save one, which he turned down until it gave out little more light than a solitary candle. It was a comforting light, however, turning his room into a cave of restful, clear-cut shadows. He leaned back in his chair and tried for a while to order his tumbling thoughts. After a few minutes however, he smiled slightly. Some lessons always had to be relearned. He had been through enough emotional and spiritual crises in his life to know what he needed to do, and struggling to control this tumult was not

125

it! Not without some effort he abandoned the attempt and gave his thoughts free rein.

To an outside observer, Vredech was merely a man sitting alone and motionless in his chair. A man resting quietly after the toils of the day. Inside, however, a great flood was in spate as a roaring torrent of thoughts cascaded through his mind. He made no effort to stem it.

Let it run.

Let it run.

There would be no conclusion, he knew. This was not the ordered sorting of facts and events, this was a painful, frightening changing of the landscape. When it had passed, all would be the same and yet different. He would see more, and clearly. And even if he did not like what he saw he would look at it squarely. *See things as they are.*

It was a wretched, wrenching time, but finally the flood was gone.

Vredech woke with a slight start. He had no recollection of when he had drifted into sleep, or what he had been thinking about last. All he had was a lingering impression of a sound, a note, fading into the distance.

He felt drained. His hands were trembling slightly, and as he raised one to his brow he realized that he was perspiring. He let his eyes drift about the room, just content to rest for a moment after his peculiar, effortless ordeal. The shadows reshaping his room swayed as the lamp, its light a little too low, guttered slightly. This is a good place to be, he thought, and a true prayer of thanksgiving formed inside him.

Then he resumed his quest, turning his mind back to the darkness that had covered the Ervrin Mallos. The shadows, the noise, the cold presence that had probed and then discarded him . . . whatever else they had been, they had been real. He was still resolute in that. They were no figment of his imagination brought on by concern for Cassraw or exhaustion. His hand tightened about the arm

126

of his chair. They had been as real as this chair. Either that or he was totally insane and, by definition, he could do nothing about that. And he could not avoid the feeling that Horld had seen or felt something too, though he had no idea how he might raise the matter with him.

But if they were real, what were they? And what did the whole thing mean? It had not been, as Cassraw had ranted, a visitation from Ishryth. Judgement Day! The words and his own response to the clouds at the time mocked him now. He and the other Brothers had all behaved like primitives, cowering in their caves when lightning tore the sky apart and thunder declaimed a measure of their insignificance. Amongst other things, that particular response had been theologically unsound. The passages in the Santyth that referred to that dread day spoke not of darkness but of a searing light and, in any event, they were written in so strange a manner that some scholars had even suggested that they could be interpreted as meaning that the day was so far in the future that it might be the distant past. A bizarre, oddly disturbing idea. And, on less academic grounds, of course, everything was still here, life continued. Further, he had no reason to doubt the long-established principle of Divine Intervention – Ishryth did not perform tricks for the edification of the childish and the gullible. These apart, it was the all-too-human attributes which had pervaded everything that convinced Vredech that something other than Ishryth's will had been at work that day. But as to what, he was no nearer to an answer. And whatever else it had been, it had been a visitation of unbelievable power.

Vredech stared fixedly at the ashes of the now dead fire. Nothing came to him. All that had happened had been quite beyond anything in his experience.

For a while, bleakness descended on him and everything about him seemed to take on the grey barrenness of the ashes in front of him.

Then something stirred again. Unable to pursue his reasoning further, he would have to look elsewhere. He would have to look at what the consequences of the day had been. He would have to turn his mind towards the centre of the disturbance – to his friend, to Cassraw.

Chapter 11

The prospect made Vredech churn with guilt. The Santyth protested that men were Ishryth's greatest, most
valued and mysterious creation. A man should not examine another as though he were some interesting insect or
plant. Still less when that other was an old friend. But
what else was to be done? Something had happened within
the shade of that cloud which had affected him and
affected him badly. How much more so then might
Cassraw have been affected, who had already been disturbed when he had plunged into the heart of the thing
with such demented enthusiasm? Others such as Mueran
might be happy to regard the man who came down from
the mountain as a considerable improvement on the one
who went up it, but that was wrong. That was the easy
way, the way of acceptance without inquiry, without
testing. It was the luring shortcut that could lead only to
the wilderness, to blindness and paralysis. Vredech recognized his father's influence leading his thoughts forward.

Too many questions hung about Cassraw. What had
there been in that strange distant look on his face when he
had first emerged from the darkness – aloofness, arrogance? Fanaticism – madness, even? Perhaps all of those
and more. What had caused his mysterious collapse when
Vredech had finally opposed him at the doorway of the
Debating Hall? What had caused his equally mysterious
awakening the following day, when the Chapter was on the

verge of outright panic about what to do with him? It was surely no act of disrespect or dishonour to seek answers to such questions, and Vredech steeled himself to the task.

Slowly, he began to relive the moments from Cassraw's sudden reappearance out of the darkness, to his departure from the Witness House. He remembered the anger that had flickered briefly into his old friend's eyes when they encountered Mueran and the others coming to meet them. He recalled with a shudder the cruel look he had seen when he denied Cassraw access to the Debating Hall, and the fearful clash of wills that had come in its wake. What had prompted him to stand so firmly against Cassraw's determination? And where could such a determination have come from? What had Cassraw intended to do?

And who *was* this Cassraw who had been restored to them? Despite appearances, Vredech found it difficult to accept that he was the man he seemed to be, the man he had once been – tireless, thoughtful, helpful, a true Preaching Brother. Vredech's guilt returned twofold. What in the world was wrong with such attributes?

They're false, came a reply, cold and clear like freezing water dashed in his face. *They're a mask, a shield, a disguise that he's wearing. And knowing that, how can you* not *seek to know what lies behind it?*

This condemnation of Cassraw would not go away. Vredech thought of Cassraw's behaviour over the last few months. More and more insistent on the literal truth of the Santyth, he had been directing – or misdirecting – his considerable energy into offending virtually everyone whom it was possible to offend. With his heightened awareness, Vredech could see now that it was Cassraw who had been working his way relentlessly towards a collapse. And now he was supposed to be well and whole. His old self again . . .

Never!

Not right.

130

Not right.

But if he was not what he seemed, then what was he? What *demon* lurked behind the mask? Vredech was jolted by the appearance of this word in his mind, but in its wake came the memory of Jarry and his tormented insistence: 'He was up there. Now He's here . . . He walks amongst us again . . . Ahmral.'

Vredech stood up. The shadows etched about the room shifted restlessly as his sudden movement caused the lamp-flame to waver. Both intuition and reason told him that he must take note of such strange, unheralded thoughts, but even to come near to imagining such a notion as Ahmral in human form, was ridiculous. He tried to laugh at his foolishness but found that he could not. Not since the time of the Provers had Ahmral been seriously conceived of as a personal entity, a demon, who could possess people or work individual acts of malice against them. Granted He was still conceived of as such by some of the less sophisticated members of the church, but theological opinion, and of course, reason, identified Him simply as a metaphor for the evil that was inherent in humankind: a real enemy and one to be fought constantly – but a person? A creature? That was ridiculous, even dangerous.

The idea would not be crushed, however. Still lingering inside him was the dreadful resonance he had felt when he had looked into Jarry's black eyes and heard him announce the coming of Ahmral: the resonance that had brought to his mind, like a drowned body rising to the surface of a lake, his own frantic denunciation of Ahmral on the mountainside.

He sat down again and began tapping his fingers nervously on the arms of the chair.

'More primitive than I thought,' he said out loud, as if the admission would in some way protect him.

But where was he now? Where had his precious reasoning led him? Back through the centuries into the time of

131

the Provers. Back into unreason and superstition, where Ahmral could be found as a scapegoat in all things.

Angrily he stopped his fingers twitching by clutching the chair arms tightly. He could feel his heart beating and his breathing was shallow and rapid. He wanted desperately to abandon this foolishness, to get back behind his own everyday mask, pretend that everything was as it had always been. Perhaps he should stop worrying about Cassraw. After all, what was he doing that was harmful? He should also have a word with Morem to see if he had anything to help him with his sleeplessness . . .

He let the thoughts trail off into emptiness. Nothing was changed. The greater part of him insisted: finish your vigil, Preacher. The dawn is still far away.

He could not turn back, the thoughts that were consuming him not only could not, but should not be hidden behind *any* mask. Masks were for dealing with the trivial awkwardnesses of life, not for living behind. That way madness truly lay.

The thought brought him back to Cassraw, and from nowhere came the name of Dowinne. Puzzled, Vredech allowed his mind to linger on her. He was still attracted to her, but that was an unspoken and long-buried desire. She was someone who lived behind a mask, of that he was sure. Charming and clever, hard-working and capable in her constant support of her husband, Dowinne seemed to be an ideal Preacher's wife. But Vredech had always sensed a disturbing quality about her, as if the eyes that looked out of her did not belong to the gestures that the hands were making, or the words that the mouth was speaking. He shook his head. Enough was enough. He couldn't be analysing everyone! Perhaps she was just shy and put on a show to hide it. And thinking about her only unsettled him. Besides, she certainly had nothing to do with what had happened to Cassraw on the mountain.

He let Dowinne go, and closed his eyes.

The shadows were about him again!

For an instant his mind teetered giddily on the edge of panic. He heard his breath being drawn in with a chesty, animal squeal but somehow he took control of it. For the first time since he had seen the shadows on the mountain, Vredech remained calm in their presence. Whether they were something real that would be occupying his room when he opened his eyes, or whether they were some product of his own disturbed thinking, he would study them this time, come what may.

He waited, motionless, ignoring the voices that arose to call his sanity in doubt once again.

And then he saw . . . felt? . . . that the shadows were no longer weaving and dancing. They, too, were waiting.

What are you? he thought.

What are you? the question echoed back at him. The shadows shivered at the touch of his voice, and as they shivered, they changed. Yet the act of changing was not perceptible. Vredech simply found his perspective suddenly different. Were these things here, close by and bounded by the limits of his blind vision or his familiar, solid room, or were they towering creations scattered far and wide across a vast plain? Nothing guided him.

Was this a dream? No, it couldn't be. He did not dream. Never had. Yet what else could this bizarre and haunting scene be? No answer came.

All was still. Nothing was happening. Just shadows, near or far, waiting.

For what?

And yet . . .?

And yet, even as he looked at the motionless forms about him he knew that he was in his room. Under his hand lay the arm of the chair. His back and his head rested against the familiar contours. And there were the faint scents of his chilly room in his nose. He knew that if he opened his eyes he would see the grey ashes in the fireplace

133

and the soft formed shadows thrown by the single lamp.

Or would he?

Were these sensations only memories? No more real than the landscape he now found himself in? For he *was* in a landscape, he knew, as surely as he knew that he was also in his room. And if he stepped forward, then he would be both sitting in his room and walking through this strange, silent place.

These are not the ideas of a sane man, he thought.

This is a dream.

But, cold now. No. You cannot dream. This is not a dream.

Should he open his eyes? Could he expunge this eerie world with its watching shadows? Doubt. No, this must take its course, he determined. He must await events.

Thus he waited. Relaxed in his chair, relaxed in the world of the shadows that had come to him. Time was nothing. There was no past, no future. Dawn was no longer far away: it simply *was* no longer.

Yet though no movement was to be seen, all about him was change. Wherever he looked, there were shadows near – or far – but always the scene was different when he returned to it. Sometimes subtly, sometimes massively. And, indeed, were these things even shadows? How can there be a shadow without a light and a form to create it? And there was neither light nor form here, only darkness within the darkness.

But if not shadows, then what?

He peered at one intently. It seemed to him that it sensed his scrutiny. And again, though he saw no change, his perspective was different. This was not a shadow, nor yet solid. It was an opening, he thought, though the idea came to him rather as an old memory recalled than a reasoned conclusion. Yet it did not have the feeling of an opening as to a cave or a tunnel, but more of a door, a portal to . . . somewhere else.

Abruptly and alarmingly, he felt a dizzying sense of vertigo, as though if he were to move now he would find himself hurtling into some unknown depths. Oddly, the sensation was not without pleasure.

His thoughts disturbed the landscape. Imperceptibly, a restlessness was beginning to pervade it. It was as though other doors were opening and winds were soughing through them, bringing with them the sounds and scents of those other places, and . . .

. . . listening ears and watching eyes?

Am I but one of a multitude? he thought, as the echoing silence tingled through him.

Then part of the changing darkness was a sound. He leaned forward to catch it and as he did so, so it became clearer: three notes, high and plaintive. Now here, now there. Sometimes long, sometimes short, and to an uncertain rhythm, but quite definite. And with a power that commanded attention.

Vredech's eyes twitched convulsively behind his closed lids. And the shadows were shadows again, dancing, flitting. Regret swept over him as if he was responsible for this sudden change. Don't go, he cried out silently. Stay. Explain. What are you? What's happening? Why . . .?

But time had returned. Now was the endless making and unmaking that is the way of things of the world. The shadows were slipping away from him, like smoke in the breeze. Yet the sound remained. Over and over, the same three notes. Always the same and never the same. Notes from a flute. Wilful and deliberate. And from time to time there was a rasping quality about them that turned their plaintiveness into a stark and chilling bleakness.

Vredech searched the whirling gloom.

Someone else was sharing this mysterious world with him . . .

'Travelling the dreamways.' Jarry's words came back to him.

135

And the player was there.

There had been no sign of his coming but Vredech could see him, standing only a few paces away, a dim, unclear shape in the darkness. Then he moved forward and his features and form became gradually more visible.

Almost as if I were the light, Vredech thought, though he was both too occupied examining the newcomer and too afraid to ponder the strangeness of the idea.

Similar in height to himself, but thinner and more angular, with a shape that gave the impression of crookedness though no apparent deformity was visible, the man had wide, wild eyes set in a lean face that was topped by a mane of equally wild hair, and fringed by a thin straggling beard. Long, bony fingers were moving slowly along a glistening black flute, and red lips were pursed purposefully over a mouth-hole. The sound cut heartbreakingly through Vredech.

Then the eyes narrowed slightly and focused on Vredech. As they did so, the playing stopped, the final note fading gradually. The flute moved away from the mouth, paused, and then twisted in a slow elaborate arc from hand to hand as if it had a will of its own until it was finally trapped between the thin man's arm and his body, with his bony hand wrapped around the protruding end.

Vredech gaped. The man leaned forward a little, his eyes narrowing further, and his head tilting slightly as if a different view might clarify what he was seeing. Then his brow furrowed and the hand holding the end of the flute brought it to his mouth. Not in a position to play, but rather as though he were whispering to it confidentially.

'Who are you?' Vredech heard himself asking.

He was not prepared for the gamut of emotions that ran across the man's face. There was uncertainty and fear, mingling with relief and happiness, sorrow and acceptance. And no small amount of anger.

The preacher in Vredech reached out to him. 'Don't be

136

afraid,' he said, though even as he spoke it occurred to him that the phrase was meaningless. What did he know of the hurts that lay in this place? Still, he could not have remained silent.

The man appeared to be whispering to his flute again. Then, suddenly, the flute was levelled at Vredech, a cross between a stabbing sword and a teacher's pointer. And one of the wild eyes was squinting along it.

'Who are *you*?' asked the mouth. The voice had a strange accent, and the words were uttered with a staccato clarity.

'I am Allyn Vredech, a Preaching Brother in the church of Ishrythan,' Vredech replied without thinking, the answer being almost jolted out of him by the impact of the speaker's words. The shadows danced.

The eye squinting along the flute glazed momentarily as this information was accepted.

'I suppose it was foolish to ask,' the newcomer said, though apparently to himself. Then he straightened up and the flute twirled slowly from hand to hand. Vredech found himself being examined as though he were some unusual plant or sculpture. 'Perhaps I should have asked, what are you? Or even better, where are you? Where are we?'

Vredech opened his mouth to make some form of reply, but the figure continued. Again Vredech had the feeling that the questions were being spoken in his presence rather than being addressed to him.

'Am I to be released? Am I to awaken, at last?'

He raised the flute to his lips and the three notes came again, very softly, idly, while the eyes widened and focused once more on Vredech. They were both expectant and scornful.

'I don't understand what you mean,' Vredech said hesitantly. 'I don't know where this place is, except that I might be dreaming. But why my dream should bring such a creation as you to me, I cannot think.'

The figure crouched low and slowly blew the three notes again. Then he leaned forward and peered at Vredech with sudden concentration.

'Well, well,' he muttered, screwing up his face as if trying to remember something. 'Straight out of my childhood, aren't you? Eyes of night. Eyes of night.'

He swayed from side to side, his mouth pursing and whistling soundlessly, then:

> 'Eyes of night,
> Dreams aflight,
> Darkling gaze,
> Travel the ways,
> Find the heart,
> That's your part.'

He seemed pleased. 'Fancy that,' he said. 'It's a long while since I've heard that, I think. Question – did you bring the verse, or did the verse bring you? Strange, haunting image. How can I know? Finish the verse for me . . . what have I called you? Ah, Preacher, wasn't it? Finish the verse, Preacher.' He flicked his hands upwards and froze in position like a child at play, his head cocked on one side, expectant, challenging.

Vredech was spellbound by these antics, curiosity overriding his alarm and the returning doubts about his own sanity. Furthermore, though he had never heard the verse before, he found it peculiarly disturbing. He did not dwell on the sensation.

'You called me nothing,' he said slowly. 'You asked me who I was. I told you – I *am* a preacher. And I don't know your verse at all.' He tried to be prosaic. 'It sounds like a child's rhyme of some kind.'

The man tapped a long bony forefinger on his lips as he listened. 'Strange, strange. Why should I want a

138

preacher?' he said absently. 'Why a preacher?' The flute was at his mouth again and two or three disjointed and pensive notes drifted from it as he continued to stare at Vredech. Then he addressed him directly. 'Why a preacher, Preacher? I made you come here. In fact, I *made* you. Tell me why.'

> 'There's the weave,
> Time to grieve,
> Fabric's torn,
> 'fore all was born.'

Vredech spoke as the words came into his head. He took in a sharp breath. He had never heard them before but they brought a terror with them that was totally disproportionate to their meaning.

'Aha!' the man exclaimed triumphantly. 'Never heard the verse, eh?' Then the triumph faded, to be replaced by a look of resignation. His angular figure drooped. He looked around. 'This is such a strange place. I thought . . .' He shrugged. 'Still, I never was good at self-deception. You can go now. I'll move on to whatever's next.' He was talking to himself again. 'Whatever's next.'

He did not move, however. Instead he brought the flute up and began playing a lively jig, boisterous and foot-tapping. Vredech felt his spirits lift and he became aware of the shadows dancing again. But the man's face showed none of the joy that was in the music and he kept his gaze fixed on Vredech.

Quite unexpectedly, he lowered the flute. The shadows arched high and paused, caught in the middle of the dance. 'Am I going to wake now?' the man asked. 'Is that it? Are you standing over me, Priest – watching, waiting?' He gazed around again and then returned to his intense scrutiny of Vredech. 'I've never been here before. Nor ever created anything as dreamlike as you, with your fairy-rhyme face. Am I going to wake?'

Vredech winced away from the pain in his voice. 'I don't know what you mean,' he said. 'And I don't really know why I'm talking to you. You're only a figment of my imagination, after all. Something that will disappear when I open my eyes.' Then, a little indignantly: 'And what's wrong with my face?' His hand relinquished its grip of the chair arm and rose to touch his cheeks. He needed a shave, he decided, but that was hardly call for the newcomer's odd remarks.

What am I doing? he thought in sudden exasperation. Behaving as though this person is really here. He's my creation – he can only be my creation. But why would I invent such a bizarre character? And where did that strange verse come from? He shivered. The words of the rhyme seemed to touch something deep and terrifying within him.

Perhaps that was the way with dreams. He had heard it to be so. No logic, no sense, all manner of disjointed events jumbled together, sometimes feelings of terror for no apparent reason. But he did not dream.

The man was speaking. 'There's nothing much wrong with your face, night eyes,' he said. 'You're as I would imagine you to be. But let's be clear about who's the figment of whose imagination.' He played a rapid, piercing trill that seemed to tear into Vredech. 'I'm the real one, the one lying somewhere in a sleep from which I can't waken. You're the—' He stopped, paused, and then threw up his hands. 'What am I doing?' he cried out. Vredech found himself grimacing at this echo of his own thoughts. The flute was flicked towards him again, agitatedly. 'What am I doing, talking to you as if you existed.'

Vredech followed an impulse. 'Who are you, sleeper?' he asked, returning to his first question. 'I told you *my* name. I'm Allyn Vredech, a Preaching Brother in the church of Ishrythan in Canol Madreth.' Then, rather self-consciously, he added: 'I suspect I'm having my first dream ever.'

The flute, on its way to the mouth again, stopped sharply. 'Night eyes can't dream,' its owner said disparagingly. 'You should . . .' he hesitated. 'I . . . I . . . should know that.' The thin face became concerned and, incongruously, the bony hands twirled the flute so that it wound up the straggling beard until it was tight under the man's chin. They repeated the process in reverse, and the flute was swung up to tap the red mouth thoughtfully.

'Why would I have you say that?' the man said. 'Why should—'

'You didn't have me say anything,' Vredech interrupted sharply. 'I am my own self, within Ishryth's writ. I say what *I* want . . .'

'Like verses you've never heard before?'

The mocking rejoinder stung Vredech. 'If I can conjure this place out of nothing, and a creation like you, then I can presumably conjure up some childish poem.' He was almost shouting. Then, somewhat to his own embarrassment, he became wheedling. 'Now tell me who you are. It's only fair, isn't it?'

The flute brayed out a distorted, breathy note that made Vredech start.

'You know I can't answer that,' said the man, the still-playing note distorting his voice eerily. 'I can give you all names, so it tells me nothing that you have them and proudly announce them. But you know that mine is gone. That's why you taunt me, isn't it? Perhaps if I had it I'd awaken, and be rid of you all.'

'What do *you* call yourself then?' Vredech asked, increasingly intrigued by this strange dialogue.

The man hunched up his shoulders warily. 'I'm not sure I want to carry on with this,' he said. 'You know what you call me.'

Vredech shook his head. 'No, Whistler, I don't, I—'

'Aha! Two times, Preacher. Two times.' The eyes were wide and wild in triumph again, and the flute circling from hand to hand. Then it was at the mouth once more and the three plaintive notes were sounding, over and over, the player moving his head from side to side and swaying hypnotically. They were echoing all around Vredech as the man spoke. 'Get out of my dream, night eyes,' he said, his voice full of anger. 'False guide. Wake me or leave.'

'I . . .'

'*Wake me or leave.*' Strident.

Vredech reached out, appealing. 'No. I . . .'

The man's face became livid with rage and it seemed to Vredech that it filled his entire world. As did the screaming voice.

'GO TO HELL, PRIEST!'

Vredech's eyes jerked open and he was on his feet before he realized that the strange shadow-strewn world was gone and he was in his room again. It did not help that all around him were echoing the strange man's despairing notes mingled with his savage execration. Vredech clapped his hands to his ears but the action seemed only to trap the sounds in his head. Staggering slightly he reached out to steady himself on the mantel shelf. As he did so he caught sight of his reflection in a small mirror that stood there. It had been in his family for years, a simple black frame, oddly smooth, housing a silvered glass that showed not the least tarnishing to mark its great age. As a child he had sometimes stared into it so intensely that after a while he would feel that he was the image and the room in the mirror was the reality: vivid, perfect, and quite unreachable.

It had chilled him then, but he was chilled now for a different reason. For the face that looked out at him from the darkened room with its unsteady flickering lamp shadows, had eyes whose sockets were black as coals.

142

Chapter 12

Eyes of night,
Dreams aflight,
Darkling gaze,
Travel the ways . . .

The words rang in Vredech's head like a knell and, with a cry, he jerked away from the fearful image in the mirror. His mind clamouring for escape, he pressed his fingers hard into his closed eyelids. You're still half-asleep, he thought frantically. You've just woken up. It's only the lamplight. It's . . .

He gave up. There was no alternative but to look again to see if that first glance had shown him the truth.

His hands were shaking as he forced himself to take hold of the mirror. At first he could not focus, bringing on a spasm of earnest blinking until eventually his vision cleared. Standing where he was however, his eyes were heavily shaded. Hands still unsteady, he moved the mirror and twisted himself around until the faint lamplight was shining on his face. Almost childishly, he pulled a long face, widening his eyes manically in unconscious imitation of the dream figure who had just so violently ejected him into wakefulness.

For a terrifying instant he thought he was staring again into the black orbs that the mirror had shown him before. But as he blinked again, the image was gone. His own face, twisted awry, gaped wildly out at him, but his eyes were quite normal. Relief swept over him.

'Of course. Of course,' he whispered as, composing his features, he slowly returned the mirror to the mantel shelf. 'What else did you expect, foolish man?' He moved back to his chair, massaging his brow with his fingertips and repeatedly muttering, 'Foolish man.' He turned up the solitary lamp and then lit another. The light blossomed to fill the room, and though some of the shadows deepened at its touch, the room became more its familiar self again.

Night eyes, night eyes. He shivered at the memory of the words. So many images, he thought. So that was a dream, was it? It needed little imagination to see why people would sometimes come to him for advice after such an experience. It had been so vivid: at once real and unreal. Easy to doubt one's sanity in that strange place – wherever it was.

It must have been as his father had once suggested – perhaps in reality he dreamed regularly but normally did not remember. Now, for some reason he had. That was not an idea he should have any difficulty in accepting, surely? And, despite widows' tales to the contrary, he knew that dreams came only from within. What he had seen, heard, felt, could only have been of his own making, no matter how strange.

'Night eyes can't dream.' The words came to deny this conclusion. He remembered the Whistler's voice, dismissive, scornful almost, that such an obvious thing should have to be mentioned. But apart from the strange reference to his eyes, the idea that he could not dream had been his own for as long as he could remember.

Then he suddenly recalled the sight of his fellow Chapter Brothers as they had struggled up the mountain through the darkness in search of Cassraw. At one point the light had been so strange that they, too, had had eyes whose sockets seemed to be full of night. The memory relaxed him. So that was where *that* idea had come from.

As for why he should choose to create strange figures and dialogue just to torment himself, that puzzle must be left for some other time. The fear for his sanity was almost gone now, driven into nothingness by the solidity of the ordinary world that had once more closed about him.

He leaned back in his chair and stared at the ceiling. Slowly his breathing grew quieter, his heart began to beat more steadily, and his hands stopped trembling. His thoughts returned gradually to the problems that he had been considering when he first sat down, although he felt oddly reluctant to move away from the vivid intensity he had just left.

Still, he could ponder his new experience any time. At the moment he had more important considerations to deal with than his first dream – his first *remembered* dream, he corrected himself. He dropped his hands on to his knees noisily and sat up straight, signalling to himself that he must now move on. Tonight was to be a vigil still. He had to find a solution to his unsettled disposition of late, and sleeping – dreaming – the night away was hardly likely to help.

Yet something had changed. He was different. As in the shadow-strewn landscape he had just left, his perspectives had changed, though he could not have said in what manner. Perhaps the thoughts and ideas that had come to him in the dream had been his father's, 'little swine lurking about below the surface, getting ready to ambush you'. Perhaps the whole thing had been some kind of catharsis . . . a purging, a purification. Certainly it had taxed him in ways he had never known before. The place, if 'place' was the correct word, though eerie and disturbing, had seemed as real as this room. And the strange figure of the Whistler with his haunting tune – from what depths had he arisen to test Vredech with taunts about his very existence? 'I *made*

145

you,' he had said. '*I* made *you*.' And he had trapped him twice, first with the verse, and then with his name. That had been truly disturbing. What self-flagellation did he represent?

As for that verse – that damned silly verse! That was not remotely familiar, yet Vredech knew it now as though he had known it all his life, and it kept running through his mind, demanding attention. Why should he find it so alarming – no – why did he find it downright frightening? He mouthed it silently to himself, searching for signs within it that might help him to track down its source. But there was nothing there, and it still held a terror of some kind which was not to be found in the simple meaning of its words. Furthermore, he noted, it brought back to him the intense reality of his dream-world. For a heart-stopping moment he thought the firm contours of his room were fading again.

Angrily he dashed the impression aside. No doubt at some time in the next few days he would recall the verse as having been learned at school, or from his mother or grandmother, and all would then be clear to him. If he kept on worrying at it, he was merely postponing that revelation.

He went to the window and opened the shutters. It was dark out and all he could see at first was the reflection of himself silhouetted against the lighted room. He looked at it pensively for a moment and then, bringing his face close to the glass, he peered through it at the dimly-lit streets of the town. Rain on the window blurred such street lamps as were lit. As he gently closed the shutters again, he made a decision. Picking up his cloak, he walked quietly out of the room.

The shadows wavered slightly as he left, leaving the door open, then, moments later, they flickered and danced a little more urgently as cold air from the street wafted into the house and sought out the lamps. They became still again as the sound of the Meeting House door closing faded into the silence.

That night there was a murder in Troidmallos. A peculiarly nasty one.

Skynner was bleary-eyed and irritable when he arrived at the scene and nothing happened there to improve his demeanour. Murder was not a common crime in the town but he had had the misfortune to encounter a few in his time as a Keeper. Ironically, for all the horror associated with such a crime, the cause and the culprit usually took little finding. First he would question the spouse and any other 'loved ones', then the immediate relatives, followed by close friends, and perhaps business partners and the like. Very quickly from that would emerge a picture that would almost inevitably direct him towards his goal – usually some pathetic, inadequate individual with precious little control over his own destiny, and, by the time of his discovery, often utterly destroyed by the forces that had led him or her to such violence.

Sometimes a murder would ensue from youthful brawling, and these, too, were usually easy to solve. Occasionally there would be an abrupt and vicious end to a dispute, or a realignment of authority within the criminal elements that Troidmallos shared in common with every other community in Gyronlandt. In such cases, Skynner would investigate with sufficient diligence to satisfy his professional conscience but would meticulously avoid any excess of zeal. Generally he viewed them with a pragmatic air as: 'One less for me to worry about. Pity more of them don't do it. Save us all a lot of problems.' It was a commonly held view.

As a rule, however, he took little relish in bringing murderers to justice, as such affairs were invariably hallmarked by a squalid pettiness that left him feeling soiled.

As he followed Albor, the duty Keeper who had discovered the body, into a narrow alleyway between two warehouses, his mood was therefore mixed. His expectations of a rapid conclusion were quite high, but already he could feel the taint of what the next few days would bring as he saw himself once again having to wade through the dismal lives of the victim and who knew how many other wretched creatures. He set the prospect aside. It was unavoidable so there was no point in suffering it twice. Now he must steel himself for whatever grim spectacle lay in wait for him, knowing that he would have to bear it with seeming indifference as befitted an experienced Serjeant Keeper. Albor's unusual reluctance to go into details however, unsettled him a little.

Halfway along the alley they reached a small circle of rain-soaked Keepers, all with their night lanterns turned high as if some form of extra protection were needed to keep the night at bay. The circle parted silently as he arrived and, maintaining the silence, he and Albor stepped through the gap. Quickly he noted the faces of his men. Except for Albor they were all fairly junior. One was obviously distressed, and a couple were grinning uneasily, while the rest were trying unsuccessfully to keep their faces unreadable. Curious, nervous, and ashamed of both, Skynner thought. Another problem for him. But he could not prevent his own lip from curling back as he crushed down the remains of his own reluctance to do what he had to do next. Crouching down, he turned back the sheet that someone had placed over the body. Albor brought a lamp close to the upturned face. The fine rain danced silver and black through its light. Skynner's brow wrinkled unhappily as he found himself looking into the fear-filled eyes of a young man. For the first time, though for no reason that he could have explained, his routine expectations of a rapid solution to this affair started to falter.

'Anyone know him?' he asked without turning round, at

the same time throwing back the sheet entirely. There was an intake of breath behind him as the lamplight exposed a lacerated throat and a tunic covered with a random pattern of gore-stained slashes.

'If anyone's going to be sick, get down the alley now, and then get back here at the double. You're Keepers and you're on duty,' Skynner growled unsympathetically as he turned round and glared at his men. No one moved, though all faces were now drawn and tense. 'Does anyone know him?' he repeated angrily. 'I don't want to spend all night out here getting soaked while you lot gather your wits.'

There was some hesitation.

'Well, look at him, for pity's sake!' he shouted as he stood up. 'He won't bite you, poor sod. Whereas *I* will.'

This was sufficient to galvanize his men. It appeared that no one knew him.

'Marvellous,' he muttered caustically, looking round at the warehouse walls bounding the alley. Glistening darkly with rainwater, they stretched up into the night beyond the bobbing lantern-light, like sinister observers. Neither witnesses nor inhabitants would be found around here. 'Well, he might have died here, but he certainly doesn't live here, that's for sure,' Skynner announced. 'We'll have to wait for someone to come looking for him. Failing that, I suppose we'll have to get his picture posted up.' He shook his head and swore softly to himself, then he began going through the man's pockets. 'Empty,' he said, his voice a little surprised. 'Look around. See if there's a pack or a bag lying about somewhere.'

There was a brief flurry of activity in the alley, but nothing was found.

'Robbery,' Skynner concluded, though he was frowning. Street robbers usually worked in groups of three or more and used intimidation, or at worst clubs rather than knives, precisely to avoid risking killing people and thereby bringing the Keepers relentlessly down on them. Perhaps something had gone wrong here. The lad had argued, resisted. Someone had panicked or . . .

Or what?

He looked at the gashed throat and the mass of wounds in the young man's chest, then dropped the sheet back over him with an extravagant gesture to disguise his response to the thoughts that were beginning to come to him. This killing had not been the result of an accident during a scuffle. It had been frenzied – and that betokened a jealous lover, a betrayed husband. Yet all the man's possessions had apparently been taken away.

A savage, unrestrained killing *and* robbery. It didn't make sense. Or rather, it made a kind of sense that he did not really want to think about. And something else was troubling him, too, though he could not bring it into focus.

He looked at Albor and grimaced, keeping his face away from the others. 'Get a cart and take him to the buriers. I'll need to have a good look at him in daylight, see what's really been done to him. Leave a couple of men here to stop people walking through until we've given the place a proper search in the morning.' He turned to the others. 'The rest of you get back on duty. There's nothing else to be done here tonight.'

He stood silent and thoughtful as his instructions were implemented. Albor remained by him, standing close and confidential, instinctively demonstrating his superiority to the more junior Keepers now milling about the alley.

'You think we'll find anything?' he asked as the group dwindled to the two who had been posted on guard.

Skynner eased him out of earshot of the two men. 'I hope to Ishryth we do,' he said. 'But I doubt it.'

Albor raised an eyebrow, detecting the unusual note in his superior's voice. Skynner answered the unspoken question. 'It's got all the earmarks of a lover's tiff.' Albor allowed himself a slight knowing smile at this heavy professional irony as Skynner continued: 'But wives and sweethearts don't normally rob their heart's desire after they've killed him, do they?' The slight smile became a slight nod. 'So . . .' He seemed reluctant to spell out his conclusion and his voice dropped even though he could not be overheard by the two junior Keepers. 'So it might be a random killing. We might have a lunatic on our hands – someone who kills people for no reason, except some weird desire of their own.'

Albor remained silent. Skynner's simple statement made as powerful an impression on him as any amount of ranting and shouting, and though he had no experience of such a killing, he was experienced enough to see the implications. If it had happened once, then . . . And neither laws nor Keepers could protect anyone from a murderer who would strike thus. He shivered slightly. He did not want to think about it. Indeed, he found it almost impossible even to imagine such a thing, notwithstanding, or perhaps because of, the presence of a mutilated corpse.

'I've heard about things like that, but a long time ago,' he said reassuringly. 'I'll grant this is a bad one, but you're probably worrying unnecessarily. There'll be a jealous lover somewhere, I'll wager.'

Skynner did not reply. His conviction was growing, and the thing that had been silently nagging at him came into focus. 'It *is* a lunatic,' he said eventually. 'You saw the man's eyes. That wasn't someone fighting to keep his money, or trying to beat off a jealous lover. He was looking at something truly frightful.'

'He *was* being stabbed,' Albor remarked, in an attempt to move away from this conclusion. 'He's hardly likely to have been smiling, is he?'

Skynner gave a slight nod but his demeanour did not change. 'We've got an ordinary person doing some

151

ordinary thing here, suddenly faced with an unprovoked, unexpected and unstoppable attack. Suddenly faced with his worst nightmare. It's all in his eyes.' He started walking slowly towards the mouth of the alley, motioning Albor to follow him.

There was such certainty in his voice that Albor did not even consider debating the point. Besides, the man's eyes *had* given him the creeps.

'If you're right what can we do then?' he asked.

'Personal awareness and luck,' Skynner said flatly.

Albor looked at him quizzically.

'That's what my old Serjeant told me when I was a pup,' Skynner expanded. 'Personal awareness and luck. Said he'd realized that, the last time this kind of thing happened here.'

Albor was openly surprised. 'I've never heard of any . . . lunatic . . . murderer in Troidmallos,' he said.

Despite the rain, his interrupted sleep, and his dark thoughts, Skynner felt his spirits lift a little at the memory. The two men emerged into the street where their horses were tethered.

'Nor will you,' Skynner said, mounting. 'It was all discreetly forgotten in the end.' Albor leaned forward a little, detecting the change in tone. He did not have to prompt Skynner into continuing. There was nothing quite like Keepers' gossip. 'Ten people this fellow killed,' Skynner went on, holding his hands out in demonstration. 'Ten. Smashed their heads in.' One hand folded into a fist and struck the palm of the other. 'One every two weeks or so. 'Course, there were no Sheets in those days, just the daily postings, but apparently there were crowds around the posting points, and the whole town was in a state verging on panic. Heinders were yelling at the Chief to "do something", the Chief was yelling at the High Captains, High Captains yelling at Captains and so on, right down the line. One of the Witness Party Heinders even tried to get an emergency law passed to forbid people from carrying cudgels.'

Albor's mouth dropped open. 'You're not serious,' he said with amused incredulity.

'Oh yes,' Skynner confirmed. 'Just like it is today, there's no end to the ridiculous things that a Heinder will suggest rather than admit he can't do anything.'

'I presume nothing came of it?'

'With most of the Heinders around him armed to the teeth, some of them even hiring private guards, and ordinary folks organizing armed patrols? It certainly didn't.' He paused. 'Awareness and luck,' he said softly to himself. His mood darkened as he realized he was describing what might come to pass again if he was right. 'It was a bad time by all accounts, Albor. Difficult to imagine. The whole town full of frightened people. One person holding tens of thousands in sway.'

But Albor was not interested in social subtleties. 'What happened in the end?' he asked.

Skynner pursed his lips appreciatively. 'Some woman got him – a little old lady. Strange really, he'd always attacked men before. But who knows what these people think? Anyway, according to my old Serjeant, this old dear was walking home past Haven Park when a man appeared in front of her shouting something wild and waving an iron bar at her. At this, she's supposed to have folded her arms across her bag and said something like, "Stand aside, young man, I wish to pass," even as he was walking towards her!'

Albor was enthralled, and Skynner was beginning to enjoy himself. 'But as the man's arm goes up to add number eleven to his list, out of the old lady's bag comes her best carving knife.' Skynner thrust his hand forward in imitation. His horse lifted its head and shook it. 'Not a flicker of a pause. Up under the ribcage, into the heart, end of murderer. Thus let it be.' He chuckled loudly. 'It

153

seems that the old lady was once a butcher's wife.' His chuckle became a full-bellied laugh.

Albor was suspicious. 'You're making it up,' he risked. 'I've never heard of any of that.'

Skynner shook his head. 'No, it's true to the best of my knowledge. There were other officers who remembered it. It was a tale they came out with almost every time there was a murder. The reason it's not commonplace is that the murderer was the son of one of the wealthy merchants – a big supporter of the Castellan Party – you know the kind of thing. And, as I said, there were no Sheets in those days. The daily postings simply announced that an unknown man had been killed while resisting arrest and the whole business quietly faded away.'

The two men shared a brief spell of professional good fellowship in the glow of this tale as they rode quietly along, but the bloodstained body under the sheet soon returned to dispel it. Skynner began making plans for the immediate future. He would catch as much sleep as he could salvage from the rest of tonight, then tomorrow he would inform his Captain and set about the happy business of examining the body. He puffed out his cheeks in rueful anticipation. At least he could leave the Sheeters to the Captain. On the whole he'd rather deal with a dead body than the likes of Privv and his ilk. Somehow it felt more wholesome.

Chapter 13

Cassraw sat pensively in the room that served him as an office for dealing with the considerable workload that tending the Haven parish presented him with. It was a typical Meeting House room, plain and spartan. It had a high arched ceiling, but despite this, its long, narrow shape and the poor lighting gave it a somewhat claustrophobic atmosphere. Had Cassraw chosen to look from the window that was providing this inadequate light, he would have seen a fine spring day bustling about its rich and varied business, with a strong wind tousling the trees and shrubs of the large Meeting House garden and hurrying bright white clouds across the blue sky and over the mountains.

But Cassraw had little eye for such things. His gaze was on a far future: on a vision that had been given to him on the mountain and which grew daily. A vision of a Gyronlandt united again under the rule of the church, its various decadent and irreligious governments overthrown by a fervent people yearning to fulfil His will, yearning to come together into an army that would sweep His enemies not only from Gyronlandt but from *all* the lands where they were to be found. It was a heady prospect.

He reached out and laid a hand on his favourite copy of the Santyth. At first he had been concerned about some of the messages that had come to him in the wake of his fateful encounter on the Ervrin Mallos. Sometimes, albeit rarely, the voice within him spoke as clearly to him as if He were immediately before him. Cassraw's legs shook even at the thought of the power that he felt when this happened. At other times the voice was distant and vague, its meaning obscure if not completely unintelligible. This must be a failing on his part, he was sure – a weakness of faith, something he must seek out within himself ruthlessly and destroy. And, strangely, he was having dreams now. Dreams full of strange shifting landscapes and black shadows that were not shadows, and where other things prowled, searching, watching, listening. He had never dreamed before.

Vredech.

The name came unbidden and, as was always the case these days when he thought of his old friend, he was filled with uncertainty.

At some time, in some place, he had disputed with Vredech, he was sure. He had declaimed his power and his transfiguration into the Chosen One. He had filled the world with his being. But Vredech, small and insignificant, had defied him – defied him, even though in the end he had reduced him to less than the merest mote.

The memory was vivid but the time, the place, were gone. It must have been in a dream, he presumed.

Cassraw set the memory of his friend aside. It had the quality of a tiny buzzing insect, offering no threat, but ever there, reminding him of something, though he could not say what. He turned his mind to the thoughts that had recently been tormenting him. Thoughts the like of which he had never before experienced, not even in his wild and angry youth. Thoughts full of lust and violence. Thoughts markedly at odds with the words of the Santyth. He had prayed desperately for guidance when these had begun to manifest themselves.

And his prayer had been answered.

'*You are the Chosen One. My vessel. You are not as others,*

156

nor as you were. All comes from Me. Obey. That which has been written shall be written anew.'

Cassraw patted a copy of the Santyth that lay on the desk before him. It was a frequent, reassuring gesture. Already he saw in many of its verses meanings that had previously been hidden from him. And he had been told that where there was obscurity, inconsistency, new verses would be given to him. A thrill passed through him even at the idea.

But now was not the time. Neither the church nor the people were ready yet for His new interpretations, still less new revelations. Now was the time for silently driving roots deep into the fertile ground of the Madren people. Roots that would grip firm and strong in the hidden darkness so that when the plant finally bloomed, no power of man would be able to draw it forth.

Little by little, His will would be done. With the patient inexorability that wore down mountains, each deed done in His name, however seemingly slight, would set in train irreversible consequences, like ripples from an idly-thrown pebble spreading across the silent surface of a mountain lake.

He looked up from the book and his eye fell on the glass-panelled door of a cabinet. In it, distorted and fragmented, was a reflection of part of the garden, and there, too, twisted and hunched by the irregular panes was Dowinne. He turned to look at the true image of his wife through the window. She was standing motionless, apparently deep in thought, her hand resting lightly on the trunk of a tree, staring at a small ornamental pond.

She too had changed since that first night following his return from the Witness Hall. Throughout their married life it had always disturbed him a little that, though affectionate enough, there had always been a quality of uncertainty – dutifulness, even – about her lovemaking. Now however, there were times when she would seize him with a breathless, exhausting passion as if some wild and long-hidden creature within her had suddenly been released.

It is fitting, he thought. She senses His presence within me. She yearns to be one with Him, as I am.

And she pleases Him.

A discreet tapping on the door drew his mind back to matters of the moment. A servant entered. 'Heinder Drommel is here, Brother Cassraw,' she announced.

He nodded and made a hand gesture by way of reply. The woman bowed and backed out of the doorway without comment. Cassraw flicked open the Santyth and began studying it earnestly.

'Brother Cassraw?'

Cassraw smiled broadly as he stood up and extended his hand towards the speaker, a tall, thin man whose naturally straight posture was exaggerated by a nervous stiffness. 'Heinder Drommel,' he said warmly. 'Thank you for coming to see me.' He motioned him to a chair.

'Who could refuse an invitation from the church's most famous preacher?' Drommel said, sitting down a little awkwardly as if reluctant to bend any part of himself.

'You'll have me guilty of pride,' Cassraw replied, raising one hand in denial while the other came to rest on the open Santyth. 'I but spread the Word that He has left for us, and tend to the spiritual and moral needs of my flock.' Drommel looked as if he was about to say something, but Cassraw forestalled him. 'You, on the other hand, tend to their . . .' he paused . . .'their secular needs. You strive to keep justice in our laws, to ensure that our streets and highways are kept free from danger and open to the passage of the worldly goods that we require. You look to the safety of our borders, situated as we are, small and weak amid decadent and godless lands.'

Slightly unsettled by this last reference and by the

158

apparent trend of the conversation, Drommel intervened: 'What we might look to do and what we can actually do are, sadly, two different things for a small party such as ours. Whenever possible, we try to bring a little morality into the proceedings of the Heindral but alas, we are not often successful. Matters are often arranged for the best interests of the few rather than the many.'

'We live in an imperfect world, Heinder.'

A thin humourless slit cut Drommel's face. It was a smile. 'Rendered thus by ourselves, if I remember my Santyth,' he said.

Cassraw waved a conceding hand. 'Indeed,' he said. 'But remediable by us also.'

He leaned back in his chair, his face suddenly serious and controlling the silence that hung between the two men. After a moment, he spoke. 'You'll have to forgive me, Heinder, if I'm a touch hesitant about what I'm going to say next, but just as you risked venturing into the Santyth just now, so I'm going to risk venturing a little way into your territory.'

Drommel's eyes widened slightly. He was intensely intrigued. The church was not above discreetly meddling in politics, but it concerned itself strictly with the realities of Canol Madreth's political life and only made its wishes known to either the Castellans or the Ploughers, whichever happened to be in power, and then only through its Covenant Member. Despite the fact that the Witness Party was often praised for its moral stand on various issues and even had Preaching Brothers amongst its ranks, it was never seriously expected to actually do anything, so it was never even approached. What, therefore, could Cassraw be up to?

'This business with Tirfelden,' Cassraw said, his voice intense and powerful. 'I'm no expert in these matters, but I have the feeling that your party was expected to disagree with both sides and thereby ensure that no real action

159

would be taken.' He looked straight at his guest. 'Why did you support the Castellans?'

Drommel managed to disguise a nervous start as a look of attentiveness. Whatever he had been expecting from this interview it had not been an interrogation. He was half-inclined to be indignant, but even though he began weighing the consequences of risking a quarrel with a man who could possibly rise to become Covenant Member in due course, it was Cassraw's actual presence that deterred him.

He settled for a haughty line. 'A man was killed, Brother – a respected man who had travelled abroad in the quite legitimate pursuit of his business affairs. One of many such whose activities benefit us all in one way or another by helping to preserve our prosperity. This is not a matter for foolish political games. A strong response is necessary if our people are to feel safe as they go about Gyronlandt on our service.'

'He was in his cups,' Cassraw said sternly.

Drommel responded in like manner, pointing towards the Santyth that lay under Cassraw's hand. 'An activity of his own choosing, which though perhaps foolish, is legal both here and in Tirfelden, and in any event not one that deserves the death penalty.'

Cassraw's expression did not change, slightly unnerving Drommel. Untypically, he blundered on rather than risk trading silences with this unexpectedly powerful individual. 'The Ploughers with their foolishness would merely have injured us all. Such things as we trade with Tirfelden can be obtained from other countries, albeit more expensively. They would simply turn away from us and trade elsewhere.'

Still Cassraw's expression did not change. 'But your way might lead to violence,' he said.

Drommel shook his head. 'Violence is begotten only by violence, and we shall be using none. We're a civilized

160

people, after all. There's no reason why expulsion of their people should not be conducted in an orderly and peaceful manner. And such assets as are seized will be released in due course, after an appropriate deduction to compensate the victims' families.' He gave a slight shrug, which seemed to use the whole of his upper body rather than just his shoulders. 'Besides, I doubt it will come to that. If we remain resolute then the Felden will behave in a sensible manner before the matter goes too far.'

'And if we don't?'

Drommel's nose twitched. 'You mean if the Castellan Party retreats from its position? Then everything will be as it is now. Neither we nor they will vote for the Ploughers' ridiculous scheme. Put simply, nothing will be done.'

'You will not retreat from yours if they hold?' Cassraw said quietly.

Drommel was pondering the question even as he was shaking his head. He could not read this Preaching Brother, and the whole atmosphere of the room and the interview was disturbing him profoundly. His every political instinct was crying out to him to be alert.

To his relief, the old servant interrupted the proceedings at this point, entering without knocking and bearing a tray on which stood two glasses.

'A fruit juice,' Cassraw said as he took the tray and silently dismissed the servant. 'My wife has a rare way with the trees in our garden and an even rarer one with their fruit. This will refresh you – keep you in good voice for the PlasHein.' He smiled disarmingly. To Drommel it was like the sun emerging from behind a dark cloud and his mood relaxed, although little of it showed in his rigid posture.

He murmured his thanks as he took the glass and followed it with a compliment after he had drunk a little.

'You will not retreat from your position?' Cassraw said again as he settled back in his chair.

'No,' Drommel said, seeing little alternative. 'Our people must be able to travel abroad in safety. They must know that their government will act firmly should anything happen to them.'

Cassraw laid down his glass and tapped the Santyth thoughtfully. Drommel waited, still wondering why he had been asked here and what Cassraw's true interest was in this affair. He was, after all, neither merchant nor trader.

Cassraw's voice was reflective when he eventually spoke. 'You recall, some weeks ago, dark clouds coming over the land, plunging us into night in the middle of the day?' he said. Drommel nodded, disconcerted by this abrupt change of direction. 'And I've no doubt that you heard about my own little escapade?' Drommel nodded again and made to reply, but Cassraw raised a hand to stop him. 'For a while, after my tumble, I lay in the darkness, stunned, in some pain and, I'll be honest, frightened. I did not know how badly I'd been hurt, but it *felt* bad, and I realized that my colleagues,' he smiled again, 'not the youngest or the nimblest as you'll appreciate . . . I realized that even if they managed to get up the mountain to look for me, they might well not find me in the thickening gloom. And if the threatened storm broke, then I could well die where I lay. As it transpired, of course, I was only a little cut and bruised, and, to shame me for my lack of faith, my colleagues did in fact venture into the darkness to seek me out.' He leaned forward a little, and his presence filled the room. 'But in that brief time, thoughts and memories cascaded through my mind like a river in spate. Many happy ones, some sad. Some regrets for things I'd done that I shouldn't have but, worst of all by far, regrets for things that I had *not* done when I should have. They tore at me, Heinder. Ripped away much that I had taken for granted about myself.' He paused and Drommel found himself struggling not to turn away from

162

his piercing gaze. 'Evil prevails when good lies abed,' he concluded, simply and starkly.

It was an old Madren saying, but from Cassraw's mouth all triteness left it. It was as alive and true and vigorous as the first time it had been uttered. More, it was a call to arms. A small part of Drommel ruefully noted that it was fortunate that Cassraw had never entered politics, for he would have been a formidable opponent. The greater part of him however, was simply swept along.

'It was almost as if He Himself had led my feet astray and plunged me low so that I could learn that lesson.'

Then Drommel felt the pressure leave him. Cassraw was leaning back in his chair again, relaxed and smiling. 'You are right to do what you are doing in this matter of Tirfelden,' he said, reverting to their previous topic as suddenly as he had left it. 'And I shall say so. I am no politician, nor do I want to play any politicians' games. But right is right and I can no longer lie abed when wrong is liable to be done.'

'I'm at a loss to know what to say,' Drommel stammered. 'We always think of ourselves as a party that in many ways represents the ways of the church in politics, and your support for our cause will be welcome. But in all fairness I should warn you that you will risk being severely rebuked, censured even, if you attempt to bring the church into the arena of politics.'

'I understand what you say, Heinder,' Cassraw said. 'But unless something is done, my heart tells me that the Castellan Party will find a way of retreating from their declared intention, and that will be a step into the darkness for all our people.'

'A little strong, I think, Brother,' Drommel ventured.

The presence returned. 'No,' Cassraw declared. 'There is little to be gained from euphemism. As you said yourself, a man has been killed. A family has been deprived of its heart, its support. Our society has been lessened by the loss. Those that the people have acclaimed must not betray the people by inaction. And they *will* retreat, won't they?'

There was such force in this last question, that Drommel almost stammered his reply. 'They were taken aback by our support, without a doubt,' he said. 'And I know there's been a great many hasty meetings of their senior officers and ministers of late.'

'You mean yes,' Cassraw said, still forceful.

Drommel hesitated. He was becoming increasingly concerned by the tenor and direction of this conversation. It was all very well for some preacher to theorize about what a government should or should not do under ideal circumstances, but *he* was a politician, and pragmatism was everything. He had to deal with the realities of balancing the innumerable and, not infrequently, incompatible claims of individuals and groups whose support was necessary if he was to retain office. And retaining office was essential if he was to be able to do anything at all of value. The last thing that was needed now was this Tirfelden business being inadvertently stirred up by someone like Cassraw careening about recklessly. The only reason that the Witness Party had supported the Castellans' blustering nonsense was to put them in a position where they would have to back down, thereby enabling the Witness Party to point out their weakness and indecisiveness during the approaches to the next Acclamation. The whole notion of expelling foreign residents was, of course, fraught with hazard, and could not be allowed. If circumstances arose that obliged the Castellan Party to maintain its stance, then the Witness Party would in the end have to withdraw its support, thereby leaving them open to the same reproaches. It was not a happy prospect.

Yet, for some reason, he could not take this man head on. He had such force about him. Then, he reflected, a man who had risen so quickly through the church would necessarily have exceptional powers of eloquence. Drommel found himself thrashing about in search of a way to avoid a confrontation and to escape this man's alarming presence.

Then his years of experience in the PlasHein came to his aid. He was concerning himself unnecessarily. What could this man do? Preach a passionate sermon, perhaps? But that would serve little purpose. It would be a rare sermon indeed that prompted people to take real action about anything. And even if he did so animate his congregation that they began to pester their Heinders, what would that mean?

Nothing, of course. Heinders were being pestered all the time and all were masters of the noncommittal response that enabled them to avoid any issue. He began to feel easier. Let this man rant. He might perhaps have some sway over the minds of a few people, but he had no control over their actions and that was what mattered.

'I do mean yes,' he replied. 'You must forgive me if I have a politician's gift of using four words where one would suffice. But, in that one word, yes, they will step back from their original proposal now that our support has made it possible.'

Cassraw nodded. 'We will not allow it,' he said softly.

To his considerable surprise, Drommel found himself almost rallying to this unexpectedly gentle declaration. He crushed the response swiftly.

'I doubt we can stop it, Brother Cassraw,' he said without risking any amplification of the conclusion.

Before Cassraw could reply, the delicate chimes of a distant bell percolated into the room. Cassraw looked surprised. 'I'd no idea it was so late,' he said, standing up. 'I get so engrossed when I start talking. You'll have to excuse me but I've another visitor due any moment, I'm afraid.' He shrugged apologetically and held out his hand. Drommel needed no urging. He was more than relieved at being given the opportunity to leave this place. As he held out his hand, Cassraw took it in both of his in a powerful encompassing grip which was both intimate and determined. It was almost as though he were accepting a pledge of fealty. And though Drommel was a full head taller than him, he nevertheless felt measurably smaller.

'Thank you for giving up your time to come and see me,' Cassraw said, ushering him gently towards the door. 'It's been both helpful and instructive. I see we're of like mind. You may count on my support, and I, presumably, on yours.' Far from certain what this last remark meant, Drommel made a vague gesture as he opened the door. A cat was standing in the doorway, its head inclined to one side.

'Ah, I think that belongs to my next visitor,' Cassraw said. 'It's apt to follow him about.'

Drommel did not like cats at all. And, as he had feared, it stepped forward and rubbed itself affectionately against his leg.

His skin started to crawl. Then the sensation was suddenly gone, for Cassraw's hand was on his shoulder, like a healing touch. 'You must be with me, Heinder Drommel,' he said softly, 'lest you find yourself alone in the darkness one day with the dogs of your conscience baying for you. You must be with me. We are at the beginning of great changes.'

Drommel moved quickly away from the Haven Parish Meeting House, telling himself that he'd best avoid encounters such as that in future. Amateur politicians could be lethally dangerous. But, despite himself, his heart was singing out. Here was a man of fibre. Here was a man of true power; a man who knew Ishryth's will and would speak it against all the urgings of compromisers and backsliders.

Cassraw bent down and picked up Leck who looked at him through half-closed eyes. He chuckled. 'Weak, weak,

weak,' he said as he stroked the cat. 'He's ours, cat. As will they all be in time.'

Two men rode out of the bleak mountains that formed the northern border of Gyronlandt. At first glance they appeared to be ordinary travellers, if such an expression could be applied to the few people who traversed the mountains, but a close examination would have shown that their horses were particularly fine and their clothes, though simple in style, were both well-made and practical. And it was some measure of these two that they had passed through the mountains in the winter and emerged not only alive, but looking substantially untroubled by the journey.

One was similar in both age and build to Vredech while his companion was a little shorter and more heavily built, and nearer to Horld's age.

The younger of the two spurred his horse alongside his companion. 'You've been very quiet these last few days, Darke,' he said. 'Is something bothering you?'

The older man reined his horse to a halt, gazed out over the rolling foothills that marked the north of Gyronlandt, then turned in his saddle and looked back at the mountains. He did not speak for some time but his questioner did not press him.

'I was wondering why we ventured through those mountains at such a time,' he said eventually.

'What?' came the disbelieving reply.

'I said—'

'I heard you,' the younger man interrupted, though not unpleasantly. 'It's an odd time to be asking *that* question. We came here to find out about this place and its people, as we've done everywhere else.'

'We could have gone east or west at that mountain range. Why did we head south?'

'Because we've been in the saddle so long our brains are addled. We could also have gone back home.'

167

Darke laughed a little at his companion's manner. 'True, Tirec,' he said. 'And we will, one day. But . . .' The laughter faded.

'Something *is* troubling you, isn't it?' Tirec said, more soberly.

Darke frowned, then rolled his shoulder as if it were stiff. Tirec noted the gesture and his eyes narrowed in concern.

'You're getting sharper in your old age,' Darke said.

'It's the company I've been keeping,' Tirec retorted. 'And you're the one who taught me to listen to the voices that whisper in the silence.'

Darke looked pained. 'It's . . . nothing,' he said after a while, though with some effort.

'It's *everything*, if it brought us through those mountains in winter,' Tirec insisted. 'And you don't need me to tell you that, do you? Speak it before we ride another pace.'

For a moment, Darke seemed set to dispute the younger man's command, then he said, 'I haven't the words yet. Just . . .' He patted his stomach. 'Bad. Very bad. I . . .' He abandoned the sentence and clicked his horse forward. 'We'll carry on, south,' he said purposefully. 'Mark the way.'

Tirec, now openly concerned, watched him for a moment before moving after him. 'As soon as you get some words, speak them,' he said, frowning.

Darke nodded. 'Of course.'

Then he looked at Tirec penetratingly. 'And you, stay quiet.' He patted his stomach again, then his head. 'Be aware.'

Chapter 14

'Do you still think he's not human?' Privv said, taunting.

Leck did not reply.

'Very wise, no answer,' Privv went on. 'It strikes me he's all too human.'

'You're a fool, Privv,' Leck said witheringly.

'And you're still sour because he gave you the creeps the first time you met him,' Privv replied with airy contempt as he swung his feet up on to his desk and began chewing his thumbnail with relish.

'Your funeral,' Leck commented coldly. 'It's no fur off my tail what happens to humanity. In fact, it could be quite entertaining.'

Privv felt generous. 'Come on, don't be such a misery. He's just odd, that's all. We never meet church people normally. You're not used to them. They must all be a bit strange, to go on believing in Ishryth and the Santyth once they've grown up. All we need concern ourselves with is the fact that he's going to let me – *me!*—'

'Us,' Leck interjected.

'Us then,' Privv conceded with a wave. 'He's going to let us "represent his views in the Sheets".' He mimicked Cassraw's voice, badly. 'Discreetly, of course.'

'He's using you.'

'Us,' Privv mocked.

'He's using *you*,' Leck repeated. 'You're his kind.'

'Of course he is,' Privv said, gritting his teeth purpose-

fully around the edge of his thumbnail. 'Everyone uses us.
And we use them in turn, only better. That's the Sheet
business, isn't it? Using people. What's to the point is that
for all his Preacher's dignity and talk, he's just as venal
and self-seeking as any market-trader on the lookout for
something to his advantage. I tell you—' He swore as, in
his enthusiasm, he tore a piece of skin from his thumb.

His head filled with Leck's disgust. 'When are you
going to learn?' she spat. 'You're always doing that. It'll be
sore for days now and I'll have to put up with your
incessant grumbling. I don't know what it is about you
creatures.'

Privv snarled at the cat then sucked vigorously on the
damaged thumb, filling his mouth with the acrid taste of
blood. Leck's claws extended and her mouth gaped wide
to reveal her teeth. 'Stop that!' she hissed furiously.

'Well, shut up then,' Privv snapped, spitting on the
floor. Then he swore again and unearthing a dirty
kerchief from somewhere, wrapped it tightly around his
thumb. 'As I was saying, he's just another man looking
for a way to gain an advantage. He's always been
marked as someone who'd rise to the top, but he doesn't
want to wait. He wants it *now*. And he sees us as a way
to help him.'

'I love it when you gloat,' Leck said coldly.

But Privv was impervious. 'So do I,' he smirked.
'Whatever happens, we'll be the ones who benefit from
this. Either he'll get there, in which case we'll still have his
ear – an ear right at the heart of the church, Leck – just
imagine. Or he'll fail, and if he fails then it'll be spectacular for sure, *and* we'll have all the details of his antics.
There's a fortune to be made here.'

'It's a tempting prospect, without a doubt,' Leck conceded reluctantly.

'Do I detect a hint of enthusiasm after all?' Privv
probed.

'It's what we do best.' There was an odd note in her voice.

Privv frowned slightly and looked at her. 'But?' he said.

Leck's tone was oddly concerned. 'But he's strange, Privv,' she said. '*Really* strange. It's as if there's something hidden in him. Something primitive, violent.'

'Wasn't it you who said we should watch him? Things were going to happen around him – spectacular things?'

'Oh yes,' Leck replied. 'I'm even more convinced of that now. Especially finding Toom Drommel there as well. But *we* – you and me – must be careful. Take a predator's word for it, he's dangerous. We must make sure there's more than one way out of whatever we get involved in with him.'

'You worry too much.'

'I don't worry at all,' Leck said quietly. 'I can scale a wall twice your height and run through a gap you couldn't get your foot in, if I have to. It's you who'll get the worst of it if things start to go wrong. You know what your kind are like.'

'What things, for pity's sake?' Privv began, then dismissed the question immediately. 'Oh, never mind. I'll be careful. I'm sure nothing's going to happen right now, is it, this very evening? It'll be all right if I spend a little time quietly relishing today's business and the views from my windows – church and state – with me in the middle and with ears and eyes in both of them.'

'Between hammer and anvil,' Leck muttered, turning over and closing her eyes.

Privv did not hear her.

Cassraw, too, was sitting relishing the view that lay in front of him. As ever, it was a view of his future. The paving of its way, having already been started, was proceeding apace. And what materials he had to work with! Drommel, crafty and astute, but an egotistical, power-craving weakling who could be manipulated like sculptor's clay. And that slithering wretch of a Sheeter, Privv, who could scarcely keep the lust from his eyes when he offered to make him his 'discreet' confidant. They were the first volunteers for the army that he was beginning to forge – and fine ones, at that. They would serve admirably.

But others were needed, too. Others better suited to the things that armies traditionally did. He picked up his cloak and toyed with it for a moment. Then he laid it down again. It was not a cold evening, and he would achieve greater anonymity if he walked out openly than if he went about cloaked and hooded.

As it transpired, there were few abroad to see him anyway. The evening might not have been cold, but it was still too windy to draw people out in leisurely appreciation, and such few as he did encounter were too occupied with their own errands to pay much heed to a passing Preacher.

As he strode out, the sound of his footsteps beat an unclerical tattoo into the long-shadowed twilight.

He soon passed through the broad familiar streets that surrounded the Meeting House, directing himself towards the narrow, more unkempt streets that lay to the east of the Haven Parish. They were fringed by older, once-prosperous but now derelict properties. Originally built for the gentry of the day, their owners had gradually moved on to better things, and over the years the houses had been bought by companies and individual merchants, either for use as business premises or for the housing of their workers. Now, the notion of the company house had fallen into disfavour, and though still owned for the most part by companies and merchants, most of the properties were rented. Initially this had been to anyone who was prepared to pay what was asked. Subsequently, however, many owners had to choose between taking tenants at whatever rent they could afford or allowing their houses to stand empty. In both cases the nett effect was that properties were neglected. The aura of deteriorated gentility that the buildings exuded heightened the feeling of general degradation that pervaded the area.

To Cassraw, who had spent some time here when he was a novice but who later would only have come here in reply to the most earnest of appeals, the decay of the place was like the rich smell of fertile ground. It was here that he had already begun to cultivate the shoots that he could see ultimately growing in rank after rank to cover the land. For here dwelt those with the least material possessions and the greatest anger and bitterness. Individuals who, either through temperament or upbringing, looked always to others as the source of their ills and who, by virtue of that same trait, stood always ready to break those restraints that are necessary for the preservation of any ordered society. Individuals who were all too easily manipulated.

'Not the safest of areas for you to be walking alone in, Brother Cassraw.'

The voice broke through Cassraw's soaring reverie and made him start. He turned to see a figure silhouetted against the low red sun which was shining around the jagged edge of a partially demolished house. He screwed up his eyes and lifted his hand to shade them.

'I'm sorry if I startled you, Brother,' the figure said. 'I'm afraid we get into the habit of staying out of sight in places like this if we want to see what's going on. Cute as Ahmral's imps, some of the ones you get round here, if you'll pardon the expression.' He smiled broadly. 'I'm Keeper Albor. Can I escort you anywhere?'

Cassraw had recovered his composure. 'No thank you, Keeper,' he replied. 'I'm just on my way to see one of my flock.'

'Might I ask who that would be, Brother?' Albor inquired, inadvertently professional in his manner.

173

Cassraw ignored the question. 'Albor . . .' he muttered thoughtfully. 'Ah, I remember. Weren't you the officer who found the body of that murdered lad the other week?' Flattered at this recognition by the famous, Albor forgot his own question. 'Very nasty business that,' Cassraw continued. 'Are you any nearer finding out what happened?'

Albor shook his head soberly. 'I'm afraid not, Brother. We found out who the lad was.' He looked around. 'Lived not far from here actually,' he went on, pointing vaguely. 'Bit of a rascal, between you and me. Shouldn't really say it, but he was no great loss. It was his friends who came asking about him, oddly enough.' He faltered and looked a little embarrassed. 'They said he was out looking for a woman, I'm afraid, Brother.'

Cassraw grimaced and gave a sigh that was almost a growl.

'It's the way of young men,' Albor shrugged, hastily deciding not to report the fact that, judging from the state of the man's clothing, he had found one immediately prior to his murder.

'*Some* young men,' Cassraw corrected sternly. 'Most are capable of controlling their baser instincts until such activities can be sanctified by marriage.'

Albor held his peace.

Then, in unconscious imitation of Drommel's plea earlier, Cassraw added, 'But still, grave though it is, fornication's hardly a sin that demands a life for expiation. And you have no idea who might have done such a deed or why?'

'None, Brother,' Albor replied. He lowered his voice. 'We've spoken to the women who trade in that area, but they know nothing. In fact, they're all scared half to death. They think as Serjeant Skynner does, that it was a madman who did it, and that he'll do it again sooner or later.' His face became pained. 'He was terribly cut, that young man. Never seen anything like it when we stripped him off. Physician says he was stabbed a lot after he was dead. Frenzied, he said.' He shuddered and ran his hands down his tunic as if trying to wipe something from them, and it took him a moment to recover. 'We've put extra men on patrol round there, of course, but we can't do that for much longer. Nothing much else we can do now except hope, I'm afraid, unless someone takes it into their mind to confess or a witness turns up.'

Cassraw nodded sympathetically and laid a sustaining hand on Albor's arm. 'You have a difficult task, Keeper Albor. We are all in your debt.' His manner became determined. 'I will help you. I will speak on this matter at my next service. Who knows, a person who would do such a thing may well indeed be very precariously balanced.' He tapped his head. 'A word from the pulpit might topple him into the realization of what he's done and bring him forth.'

Albor gaped openly and a gamut of emotions ran across his face. It was a peculiar enough experience discussing such an event with a Preaching Brother, but the prospect of it being mentioned in a sermon had, frankly, shaken him, and he was a man who took a strong Keeper's pride in the fact that he was not easily moved. But, Ahmral's teeth! A Meeting House was no place to be talking about a murder, still less the murder of some scapegrace on the roam for a prostitute. The church didn't get involved in such matters!

Then, with sudden and appalling vividness, the terrified look on the victim's face filled his mind. It was as if he were standing in the alley again, with the fine damping rain falling all around, streaking the lamplight. This had happened several times since that day and at night he was sometimes almost afraid to close his eyes when he lay down to sleep. He flinched inwardly. No one deserved a death like that and, he supposed, anything that might stop it happening again was worth a try. For happen again it might well – Skynner was invariably a shrewd judge of such matters. But, the *church*? He'd never heard the like. The opportunity for Keepers' gossip arose to dismiss the young man's phantom. Wait 'till he got back to the Keeperage and told the others about this! He looked at Cassraw shrewdly. This was quite a man, coming out with ideas like that. A man to get things done. Not something he normally associated with Preachers.

He made a resolution to attend the next Haven Meeting House service.

'Is something wrong?' Cassraw asked.

'I'm sorry,' Albor stammered. 'You took me by surprise. It's not usual for the church to get involved in such matters.'

Cassraw's face darkened momentarily and Albor regretted his assumption of informality. But no outburst came. 'He is involved in all things,' Cassraw declaimed. 'It is not for us, His servants, to decide what we wish to do. We must follow the words of the Santyth, must we not?'

Albor found himself nodding in reply to this unexpected and forceful catechizing.

'It may not have been so in the past,' Cassraw went on. 'But many changes are coming, Keeper. Many changes. Be ready. Be with us.'

Before Albor could make anything of this last remark, Cassraw was suddenly brisk and hearty. 'But I must let you get about your duties, my friend,' he announced, slapping Albor's arm manfully. 'I don't want to get you reprimanded for being late on patrol, eh?' Then, after another resounding slap and a brief wave of his hand, he was striding off.

Albor stared after him, as bewildered by this abrupt end as he was by the whole encounter. He lifted his hand, about to call after him, but let it fall almost immediately. He shouldn't really let the man go wandering about alone

176

here. But he *was* behind on his patrol, and Cassraw was not walking like a man uncertain of where he was or where he was going. Still less did he look as though he needed or would appreciate an escort.

His hesitancy decided his actions for him and as Cassraw's determined footsteps carried him swiftly into the reddening gloom, Albor gave a slight shrug then turned and set off in the opposite direction.

Cassraw maintained his resolute pace until he was satisfied that a bend in the road had taken him completely from the view of the watching Keeper. Like Albor, he was unsettled by what had occurred. The murder had struck him with unusual force when he had first heard about it, but there had been the inevitable distance between the event and the reporting of it to protect him from too deep a response, and it had soon faded. In truth, his mind had been fully occupied with matters far more significant than the miserable slaying of some fornicating malefactor in a Troidmallos alley. He had shown an interest in front of Albor purely for the sake of appearance and to prevent the Keeper from questioning him, but the brief conversation had disturbed him – brought the corpse before him in all its gory horror – a horror enhanced by the very ordinariness of Albor's description. And what had prompted him to say that he would speak of it in his next service? It was an action liable to cause quite a flutter amongst his fellow Chapter Brothers, for the church rarely involved itself in the ordinary affairs of the people, and *never* in matters such as this.

A lamplighter's cart clattered into the street.

And yet the idea intrigued him. There were opportunities here. He could do it. Already phrases were forming that he could feel had the makings of a fine oration. He must do it in such a way as to avoid controversy. He must link his every word to the verses of the Santyth and he must arrange his arguments so that they could be used to sway Mueran himself. As indeed they might well have to.

He watched a sour-faced lamplighter pursuing his trade, muttering to himself each time he came to a damaged lamp. Precious few lights left around here for him, Cassraw thought. Light wasn't in the interests of many of the folk who lived in these peevish streets.

Then, a surge of confidence. Yes, he would do it. All was change now. Just as this grumbling artisan was using his screeching flints to bring some unwanted light into this place, so he, Cassraw, would bring His One True Light into this benighted land from such small chances. It had been no idle whim that had prompted him to speak to Albor as he had. It had been His will. Such was the subtlety of His ways.

'Thus let it be. Thus let it be,' he murmured softly.

He looked around to see exactly where he was. The light in the street was strange. The purpling sky, flecked with moving clouds, some pink, others darkening and leaden, was bright enough to heighten the darkness of the street, and the street lamps were so few and weak they could only illuminate their immediate surroundings until night was fully here.

A gust of wind blew dust in his face, making his eyes water. As he rubbed them irritably, the street lamps welled up into hovering discs of light and the shapes of the houses became blurred and indistinct, their darkened windows and doorways resembling the vague dancing shadows that were haunting his night-time hours.

Then his vision was clear again and the image was forgotten. He saw his destination, but some caution made him wait until the lamplighter had gone further down the street, before he crossed over and slipped down the steps that would lead him there.

He wrinkled his nose at the stench that greeted him as he reached the foot of the stairs. Cats he recognized. And worse. All hanging in a miasma of decay and dampness.

He took out his small lantern and coaxed it into life. As with the street lights above, it seemed to heighten the darkness rather than penetrate it, almost as if the light was reluctant to leave the lantern for fear of being absorbed by the very air itself. As his eyes adjusted, Cassraw began to make out the walls of the subterranean passage somewhere along which lay the home of the person he intended to meet.

Fighting down a momentary wave of nausea, he set off, advancing warily, anxious to avoid whatever might be lying on the uneven paved floor of the passage. Not that it was easy, for, albeit weakly, his lantern was illuminating the misshapen heaps of debris and rubbish that had been stacked along both walls of the passage; in many places they had spilled across its entire width, making impromptu barricades for him to negotiate.

Just as his eyes adjusted, so did his nose, though mercifully, where his eyes had opened, his nose seemed to close, dimming the stomach-churning effect of the rotting detritus accumulated by the inhabitants of these subterranean dwellings. This place was as far from the Haven Parish as he could begin to imagine.

He stopped. How could people live like this? he thought. He remembered the place as it was when he had been an earnest novice, struggling for the first time with the realities of pastoral care in the latter years of his training at the Witness House. Then, he had been almost overwhelmed by compassion for the people obliged to live here. They at least made some kind of effort to maintain a degree of respectability, of cleanliness. The passages, natural traps for rubbish, were swept and scrubbed and occasionally given a thorough clean out. And the dingy damp rooms that stood off the passages were similarly tended. Now, taking the state of the passages as a measure of the homes here and the attitudes of the current tenants, he could feel little more than contempt. These people were not worthy of his compassion. Wilfully allowing such deterioration when all that was needed was a little endeavour, was verging on the blasphemous.

Knots of anger began to swirl within him. He realized that he was standing with his head bent forward and his shoulders rounded, offended by what might be lying underfoot and oppressed by the low arched brick ceiling above, despite the fact that it was a head higher than he was. The knots suddenly came together and a rush of defiant rage flowed through him, straightening his posture and lifting his spirits above the clinging taint of the place. As he set off again, his footsteps echoed through the passageways as they had echoed through the streets above. Occasionally the rhythm of his progress was interrupted by a clatter as a mighty kick dislodged some obstacle from his path.

He glanced along each side passage as he came to it and, as if in response to his resolution he noted that here and there were doorways which were illuminated by lanterns and in front of which the passageway was well cleared. ' "And the flame shall never truly die",' he said softly to himself, quoting the Santyth. ' "But shall burn unseen in the dark places of the world until the righteous shall come again".'

His thoughts cried out in response: 'And they are come now. Come to bring the light to all men. Come to sweep away the heretics and sinners. Come to judge.'

A gust of air struck him and a soft, moaning sigh enveloped him. It was as if the building was breathing, responding to his silent proclamation. And from then the passageway was alive with noises that he had not noticed when he first entered. The low echoing rumble that was the synthesis of all the lesser sounds that permeated the maze of passageways carried in it, occasional and indistinct, but identifiable: the closing of a door, footsteps, voices – the general clatter of people living too close to one another.

He looked carefully at the next side passage, holding the lantern high. There, decorating the padstones of its arched entrance were two peculiarly ugly carvings – leering sprites, crouching with their knees drawn up high as if preparing to spring on unwary passers-by. Placed there doubtless by some builder with a sense of humour, they were patently not Madren in origin. And, for all their grotesqueness they were fine pieces of work. So fine that Cassraw jumped slightly as they seemed to move at the touch of the light from his lantern. And even as he recovered himself and held the lamp steady so that he could examine them, he thought he saw one of them flickering an eye at him malevolently.

Guards, he thought, for no reason that he could immediately fathom. He shook off the notion as an idle fancy. He was where he needed to be.

A few paces further along the passage brought him to a doorway on the left-hand side. A rusted and long-defunct lantern hung outside it, and stout timbers and several rows of iron bolt heads bore witness to the fact that the door was heavily reinforced. Cassraw looked at it for a moment, then, as it bore no striker, he struck it with his clenched fist. The door was as solid as it looked and the blows stung his hands. The sound of them echoed back to him from the passage walls and, as if in defiance, he struck again, harder, ignoring the pain.

He was raising his fist to strike again when the clatter of a bolt being drawn stopped him. Others were drawn, and the sound of muffled cursing reached Cassraw as the door began to open. It opened very silently. Cassraw noted it. Whatever else was neglected in this place, hinges were not. Comings and goings were secret matters. It was good.

Then he was looking at a figure silhouetted, as Albor had been only a little earlier, except now the light was not

181

coming from the setting sun but from the three or four lanterns in the room behind.

He identified the figure, nonetheless. Taller than he was and well-built, it was a young man, and while his face was hidden, his posture was undoubtedly belligerent. Cassraw's eyes widened with the passion of a fiery conviction and his hand came out to rest on the man's shoulder before he could speak.

'Yanos. I am Brother Cassraw. I have come for you. The Knights of Ishryth need you.'

Chapter 15

Yanos started back from this sudden and strange confrontation.

'Who the hell are you?' he demanded angrily.

Cassraw took advantage of the movement to step purposefully through the doorway, causing his involuntary host to step back even further.

'Brother Cassraw, as I just told you,' he replied simply but with the same power. He could see the young man properly now, and he was not a prepossessing sight. Tall, but with a slouch that sacrificed height for menace, Yanos was blessed with an oval face that might have been good-looking were it not for the surly eyes and a mouth that apparently spent most of its time sneering. The whole was topped by long black hair which hung, dank and neglected, about his face and shoulders.

Cassraw awaited no ceremony. If he was to use this man, he must tame him in his own lair, and to that end he must be totally committed. Keeping his gaze fixed intently on Yanos's face, he reached behind himself, took hold of the door and swung it shut. It closed with a dull thud. Strangely, Cassraw felt a tremor of excitement at the sound of his escape being sealed.

There were two other young men in the room. They stood up. Like Yanos, they were both taller than Cassraw and, he presumed, more than a match for him physically.

'Ah. Your lieutenants, I presume,' he said, turning his

intimidating gaze towards them. 'I was told you'd probably be here. That's good. You may sit.'

The two men looked at one another in disbelief then started to move towards him. Cassraw held his ground, however, and with his already staring eyes widening further, he barked: 'SIT!'

Neither man did so, but they both stopped and looked hesitantly at Yanos who, baring his teeth, lunged forwards to seize this unwelcome visitor.

'You *dare* to lay hands on a Preaching Brother?' Cassraw's hand shot out and levelled an accusing finger at him. Years of preaching had given him considerable vocal skill and in the confined space of the room his powerfully projected voice seemed to come from every direction. Yanos froze.

'Sit down!' Cassraw repeated fiercely to the two others. 'It remains to be seen whether you two are worthy.'

Still the two men did not do as they were bidden, but the ebb of such determination as they had could be read on their faces as clearly as if they had dropped on to their knees. Whatever their ultimate destination in life, most Madren were strongly touched by the church in childhood, and this pair were too young to have developed the layers of indifference and worldly hurt that were necessary to oppose anyone with the skill and the will to work this rich, deep vein. They looked again to their leader.

But Cassraw was not going to allow anyone an advantage.

'You are loyal Madren, are you not?' he demanded of Yanos.

Yanos scowled uncertainly. Cassraw repeated the question, slowly but with a subtly menacing undertone, as if he was beginning to suspect that he might be in the presence of treason.

It squeezed a reply out of Yanos. 'Yes, but—'

'And you believe in His holy word, as enshrined in the

184

Santyth?' He held out his copy.

Yanos, the hero of many a sneering denunciation of the church amongst his peers, floundered openly in the face of Cassraw's massive insistence. He made an effort to avoid the issue. 'Get the hell out of my place, you—'

'*Your* place, Yanos Yanoskin? *Your* place?' Cassraw's gaze moved airily around the sparsely furnished room as he spoke, then snapped back to his faltering antagonist. With great disdain, he reached up and delicately tapped one of the iron bars that tied together the shallow brick arches forming the ceiling. It vibrated with a low hum. 'You have attested documents of right of domain?' he said, eyes wide again. 'Or a Keeper's indulgence? Or perhaps you've got deeds of possession somewhere?'

'I . . .'

'You *are* a loyal Madren, aren't you?'

'I . . .'

'A true believer in His word?'

Cassraw bent forward, keeping his burning gaze fixed on Yanos. Like a hunting dog, he could sense his prey about to stumble and fail. But this was no fleeing doe, this was a dangerous man, still capable of reaching for that last resource and turning to fight: and fight for his very life. He had to be unbalanced.

Cassraw's manner softened abruptly. He took hold of Yanos's arms in a grip at once firm and supporting. 'Yes, you are,' he said, the accusation in his voice becoming a fatherly reassurance. 'Of course you are. There is no doubt about that. Many things I've heard about Yanos Yanoskin of late, and not all good, I'll admit. But that he was a traitor to his country, a godless heretic, never. And Canol Madreth needs you.' He turned to the others. 'And men like you, to face the trials ahead.'

'Who told you . . .? What . . .?'

This time Cassraw did not interrupt, but stood patiently waiting, the benign elder, ensuring thereby that Yanos, unable to support himself by offering opposition, finally fell. The young man's unformed questions stumbled to a halt, leaving a gaping silence hanging in the room.

'May I sit down?' Cassraw said regally as he felt one of the others about to speak. 'We've a lot to talk about.'

Unexpectedly released from his interrogation, Yanos found himself peculiarly anxious to appease his tormentor. He responded to the opportunity for action like a fish swallowing bait, and with exaggerated enthusiasm he kicked some rubbish out of the way, snatched up a chair and planted it firmly in front of the crude table that the group had been sitting around before Cassraw's explosive entrance.

Cassraw sat down as though the battered chair were a throne and, with an authoritative gesture, motioned the others to sit also. Surreptitiously he swung one leg under himself. Sitting thus, he would be the tallest there. As the others sat down, he slammed his copy of the Santyth in the middle of the table, making them start. He noted with some relish the uneasy glances that this caused.

Now would be the testing time.

For an instant his confidence wavered. He had heard of Yanos from members of his Knights of Ishryth. The man was undoubtedly a hero to some of them, and held in sneaking regard by many others. Tales abounded of his fighting ability and courage, his defiance of authority and his general refusal to accept the hide-bound norms of Madren society. Cassraw's immediate reaction had been to denounce such tales, to dismiss them scornfully as idle fancies for the amusement of children, or to dash them into nothingness with arguments full of cold reason. But he had felt a spark being struck within his Knights that he could well use to ignite them so, instead, he chose not to condemn, but to listen. The very absence of censure ensured that he was drawn into the confidential heart of the tales and, by discreet questioning, he had formed his

186

own assessment of this would-be mythic figure. A leader of some kind, without a doubt, and cunning also, though neither educated nor given to reasoning.

But he saw too, a man already turning sour under the unwritten restrictions that hedged Madren life. A man who, left to his own devices, would eventually overstep the mark and draw down the weight of the Keepers on himself in earnest. It came to Cassraw that Yanos had the qualities that could be used to transform his Knights of Ishryth into the kind of group that he was going to need, and for some time he had been toying with the idea of recruiting him. He had been at somewhat of a loss as to how to achieve this however, until, flush with his success with Toom Drommel and Privv, he had felt suddenly that this was the moment, and that he must seek out a confrontation unhindered by any form of pre-arranged plan or argument. He must have faith. Faith in himself, faith in the future, and faith in the inner voice that even when unheard was surely guiding him.

As he looked at the three faces, now focusing on him with expressions that displayed bewilderment, curiosity and irritation in more or less equal parts, all of his doubts passed. Had he not just drawn into his web the leader of the Witness Party and one of Troidmallos's most influential Sheeters? These three before him were children by comparison, almost literally so. All that need trouble him now was exactly what he was going to do with them.

'Before I begin, we'll say a short prayer,' he said powerfully, taking up the Santyth and looking down on his congregation. 'Then I'll tell you about the Knights of Ishryth, and the part you will play when you are one of them.'

Later, as he walked back towards the Haven Meeting House at a pace markedly more relaxed than the one that had carried him away from it, he mused on the day's happenings. So much so fast. Of course, it could only be thus when he followed His guidance, but nevertheless he marvelled at the changes that had occurred in the passing of so short a time. He took in a deep breath. The wind had dropped and the night air was tainted somewhat with the smell of the burning street lamps, but it was still cool and luxurious after the dank staleness that had pervaded the cellarage and which still clung to his clothes. Still, a little water, a little toil, would remove that, while nothing would remove the seeds he had sown in the minds of Yanos and his two henchmen. For a moment his thoughts soared again into a distant and glorious future, but he reined them back almost guiltily, suddenly afraid that the very consideration of such rewards might in some way jeopardize them. The path forward could only be long and hard, because that was His way, and nothing lay ahead for those who lingered on it, indulging in idle speculation. He must occupy his mind now with guiding the events that today's endeavours would set in train. Only in a ploughed field could new crops be grown.

Then, on an impulse, he changed direction.

He walked for some time without noticing where he was going, his head working out plans, conjecturing on possibilities, considering contingency arrangements, on and on, round and round. There would have been little point in his going home and attempting to sleep, so preoccupied was he.

Abruptly, almost as though he had been struck a violent blow, his thoughts evaporated and he halted. For a moment he stood motionless and bewildered. Where had he wandered to? He looked about him slowly, trying to find some identifying landmark. It was not easy. The street was deserted and the lighting poor. High walls hemmed him in; they were simple and functional in appearance and, at first glance, windowless, although after a moment he noticed some windows well above the street level. They were sealed with bars and heavy iron shutters.

Warehouses. He knew where he was now.

He cursed himself softly for his lack of attention. It'd be a long walk back home now and he'd better set off right away. Yet for some reason, he was reluctant to move. Something was holding him there – something troublesome.

Then he remembered that it was near here that the murder had occurred. He felt a sudden surge of terror. Brought forth by the darkness around him it rose up from his own inner night, primitive and ancient, effortlessly setting aside all reason, religion, and the other trappings of civilization. Transfixed, he could do no other than stare wide-eyed into the dark shadows that waited between the pools of light thrown by the flickering street lamps.

Gradually, his reason regained a tentative foothold. It told him that he knew where he was, and that all he had to do was walk. Broader, well-lit streets were nearby, and people going about their evening's affairs. In any case, whatever had happened here a few weeks ago was unlikely to recur in the same place, was it? Yet his reasoning lacked power, and still his feet refused to move.

Go to the place.

He started. Was this the Voice within him speaking, garbled and indistinct – or was it some bizarre whim of his own?

Go to the place.

He began to sweat. He could not risk interrogating something that might be the command of his god; he must simply obey it. Awkwardly he began to move forward.

'We've put extra men on patrol round there, of course.'

Albor's words came back to him. They should have been a relief, but for some reason they added to his alarm, for even as he moved, he felt impelled to avoid discovery. His hands were shaking now. Surreptitiously he slipped into one of the shadowed parts of the street. At least there

189

he could see without being seen – could collect himself a little.

As he felt the shade close about him, however, he realized that he did not know exactly where the body had been found. But even as the thought came to him his eye was drawn to the dark maw of an alleyway directly opposite. It was like a gateway into another world – so dark that even the puny lights around him seemed dazzling.

Go to the place.

Shaking, and scarcely master of himself, he moved forward. As he reached the alley, its darkness seemed almost palpable. Unsteadily he groped for his small lantern: whether he would be seen or not, nothing would possess him to enter that gloom without light. It took him some time to strike it into life, then he found himself oddly reluctant to open the shutter. A blaze of light would not only expose him like a beacon but would deepen the darkness about him tenfold. He had a fleeting vision of himself surrounded by a dome of blackness punctuated by pairs of glistening eyes. He clenched his teeth and forced the image from his mind.

Yet he *must* see.

Tentatively he eased the shutter back to release a narrow beam of light, carefully avoiding looking at it as he did so. The darkness receded a little and the walls and cluttered floor of the alley began to appear. He stepped forward hesitantly, moving slightly sideways and keeping close to the wall on one side. Every few steps he turned and looked back at the dim outline of the entrance to the alley.

What was he doing here? he eventually began to ask himself.

Go to the place.

It was as though some unseen hand was guiding him further and further away from the street, deeper and deeper into the darkness gathering about him as though to crush out the flimsy light of his lantern and leave him alone and howling.

'Lord protect me.' Neither threat nor reward could have restrained his whispered prayer.

There was a pause that might have been the darkness holding its breath, then it was all around him. A silent shrieking filled his mind, tearing at his nerve ends like nails drawn down glass.

It was here!

Cassraw's legs gave way under him. He fell to his knees, then slumped forward on all fours. The lantern slipped from his hand and rolled over, sending a brief dance of shadows across the walls of the alley before going out. Cassraw scarcely noticed however, for as the cold touch of the flagged ground impinged on his hands, the sensations clamouring at him increased manifold. There was lust, primitive and all too human: grasping, possessing, devouring. And mingling with it was a breathless terror – terror such as even a nightmare could not contain – a terror full of dreadful flickering images, glinting steel and glaring eyes, and teeth, clenched in a terrible smile. Then there was another sensation. His mind tried to shy away from it, but deeper desires drew him inexorably into it until he could no longer deny the echoes that were ringing out within him in recognition.

It was bloodlust – a singing and ecstatic joy at the destruction of another life!

Cassraw cried out in horror and shame, and with an almost unbearable effort, tore his hands from the ground. He tumbled over heavily. Vaguely aware of the stone flags cold against his cheek, he clung to the solidity of the contact, sensing that it was all that kept him here: should he lose it, he would be plummeted into some other place and lost forever.

He could see shadows dancing all about him, luring him on. He closed his eyes, but it was to no avail. They were all about him, as they had always been. The alley and the shell of the man that lay huddled there became a vague and distant memory from some other time. Here were the entrances to the worlds he should roam. Here was truth. Here was . . .

But he was not alone . . .

Someone was watching him!

'Another priest,' a voice said. The accent was strange and the tones clipped and sharp. Cassraw blinked as if that might clear the shadows from him, but nothing happened. Yet now he could see the figure, although he could not tell whether it was near or far.

Lean and crooked, it bent forward to examine him, lifting a long bony hand to its eyes as it did so.

'Why would I want another?' it asked itself. Then a shining black stick swung from behind its back and into its other hand before pointing at Cassraw. 'Have I given *you* a name, night eyes?'

But before Cassraw could reply, the figure seemed to be immediately in front of him, peering into his eyes – into the very depths of him.

'Ah,' it breathed out, a sound full of anger and contempt. 'You again, you abomination. Well, I don't need you. I know my own soul well enough by now. There's nothing else to be learned, no depths I have not plumbed while I've been here. I need no more demon guides such as you.' The stick was suddenly at its mouth and biting music was ringing in Cassraw's ears. Then the figure was far away, dancing manically. 'I won't have you here again, with your horrors and your blood-letting. I won't have you. I renounce you, priest.'

Then close, a high shrieking note, rasping and awful, and the wild-eyed face filling Cassraw's vision.

'GO!'

And Cassraw was in the alley again. Breathing heavily and fearfully, but alone in the Troidmallos darkness.

Echoes of the frightening images of the last few minutes, if minutes they had been, hung about him and filled his mind with questions, but relief swept through him as he took in the stale odour of the alley and the cold touch of the flags under his hands. Whatever had just happened to him, it was over. He must get up and get himself home, away from this dreadful place and the awful memories that seemed to be lingering in the stones here. He could ponder all this at his leisure.

He looked around in an attempt to orientate himself. The dim street lighting marked out the narrow entrance to the alley.

And close by, black against this feebly-lit background, stood a figure.

Chapter 16

Vredech's pen wilted from his hand. Scarcely aware of what he was doing, he folded his arms on the desk and slowly sagged forward to rest his head on them. Beside his papers stood a plate bearing the congealed remains of a barely touched meal. His housekeeper had left it for him, venturing again the plea, at once anxious and stern: 'You must eat something, Brother. I'm sure you're losing weight, and you're looking far from well.'

She had known him for a long time and freely took motherly licence with him, though her natural relish for ailments, both her own and others', and ability to discourse on them at length to any available audience, had caused Vredech to stop listening long ago. Christened 'House' by Vredech as a result of some long-forgotten joke, she was an excellent and caring housekeeper, and for the sake of domestic harmony he had gradually developed a knowing nod and a reassuring smile with which to deflect these unwanted concerns. They were by now a reflex response which could be invoked by the sound of a certain in-drawn breath, or the placing of the hands on the hips in a particular manner. She, in turn, had an upward glance to indicate that she had clearly seen through his game and would be undeterred from doing what she took to be her duty.

Of late, however, this gentle ritual had foundered. Her observations had become more earnest and more strident as it seemed that Vredech had set his foot upon a path of self-neglect that could only end in personal disaster for him.

'You should see a physician,' she had said eventually, rather more vehemently than she had intended. Vredech was shocked at the rage that welled up inside him and he barely managed to stop himself from cursing her for her interference. It was only an anxious movement of her hands that had prevented the outburst. Something about the gesture reminded him that she cared for him a great deal.

'Just church affairs, House,' he lied. 'They're preoccupying me more than usual, that's all.'

There was no upward glance in reply, just a bowed head, a troubled brow, and a penetrating look which he had been unable to meet.

For Vredech knew that no physician could help him. No potions or pills could cure madness, and madness it was that was creeping up on him, surely? You're not going mad if you think you are, it was said, but what else could explain the things that had happened since the fateful night of his vigil and his disturbing encounter with that figment of his imagination he had called the Whistler? After a lifetime without dreams it seemed now that he could not sleep without finding himself enmeshed in bizarre fantasies. Some were frightening, some gentle and evocative, some quite embarrassingly not to say disturbingly, for a voluntarily celibate Preaching Brother – of the flesh. The majority were just rambling streams of incoherent nonsense full of distorted fragments of what seemed to be everyday occurrences.

But they were not his!

None of them.

They were other people's.

They couldn't be otherwise. He might not have dreamed before, but he did know that dreams were intensely personal, a deep reflection of the inner character of the dreamer. Almost everything that had ever been related to him had been confirmed by the teller as being such, and where the events of a dream were seemingly obscure or irrelevant, he had learned that a few careful questions would often reveal the presence of some private fear, some desire, that could not otherwise be spoken of.

And there was none of this in the dreams that he had been having. There were familiar sights and places, sometimes familiar people – even himself on a couple of occasions – but the associations and memories that went with those sights and places were not his, the people were not as he knew them, and even the images of himself had been so different from the way he imagined himself that on each occasion it was only the thoughts of the dreamer that had told him who it was.

The dreamer . . .

All the time, it was the dreamer who was creating these visions, not him.

But such a thing couldn't be. He could not enter someone else's dream, could he? And the only people he had ever known who imagined they were someone other than who they actually were, had been insane – sometimes dangerously so.

The thought terrified him. What was happening to him? What was *going* to happen to him?

He had scanned the Santyth for guidance, but there was nothing in the Dominant Texts and only a passing mention in the Lesser Books – those texts generally regarded as being uncertain in origin, myths almost, and of symbolic value only. Here were a few colourful and unannotated tales about heroes who moved in worlds beyond this one – Dream Warriors, Masters and Adepts of the White Way and other such fanciful names. Once, such tales might well have entertained him, or perhaps given him an idea on which to base a sermon, but now they simply left him frustrated and angry and then, inevitably, full of self-reproach for thus condemning his holy book.

And prayer, too, had given him neither solace nor guidance. Not that that was any great surprise. That kind of solace was given only to those who for various reasons were beyond helping themselves. Obviously he must not be. Somewhere a solution lay within him, and he must struggle to find it if he was to be helped by his god.

Now, however, he was afraid to go to sleep for fear of what would happen. Not because of the incidents in which he might find himself involved – he was curiously unaffected by these – but that very detachment, that sense of being an intruder, frightened him desperately, confirming as it seemed to do, his failing reason. Not eating, not tending to his duties, or indeed at times even himself, came as a consequence of his nightly resistance to sleep. He would walk the streets endlessly, often having no recollection of where he had been when he found himself returning home, mentally and physically drained.

That had started on the night of his attempted vigil. He had set out full of determination, hoping to use the night air, the silence, and the steady rhythm of his steps to order his thoughts and to put himself at least on the way to some kind of an explanation. But it had not happened. The encounter with the Whistler seemed to have unleashed something within him that was restless and quite beyond his control. For all its strangeness, the incident had been so vivid, so intense, that at the time he could not bring himself to doubt its reality. Nor did he even now, when he thought back to it. But what did that mean?

And the haunting sound of the flute echoed constantly through his head.

Repeatedly he would set his thoughts on one track, only to find shortly afterwards that he had deviated from it and returned to the Whistler and his poem and his insistence that it was *he* who was real and Vredech a mere image that

197

he had created. It was a chillingly awful recollection. At times he felt that if he closed his eyes, the buildings about him might silently fade into nothingness, and the people, too, and the hills, and the mountains – everything – even his own memories.

Round and round the ideas had gone, always bringing him back to the Whistler.

Since he had returned that night, exhausted yet too agitated to sleep, and having no idea where he had been, his moods had swung wildly from elation into depression, with no prior warning of either. For the most part, however, he fancied that, apart from his housekeeper, he was managing to keep his agitation from the members of his flock, though he kept having to find excuses for avoiding people, and his pastoral work was definitely suffering.

By chance he had discovered that if he slept during the day, he was less troubled, though in reasoning that this was because fewer people were dreaming at that time, he knew he was confirming his own diagnosis. Nevertheless it was all he could do to cope with the demands of his body for rest.

He jerked upright violently, catching the plate with his arm and sending it skidding towards the edge of the desk. The plate was stopped by a book, but the knife and fork on top of it continued on their journey and clattered to the floor. Vredech, already tense, stiffened further at the noise. Everything about him was aching – his neck, shoulders and back – and he seemed to be permanently groggy. There was no mystery to this. If he continued sleeping fitfully and in chairs, this must be the inevitable consequence. Rubbing his temples he looked around at the chaos on his desk. Papers, pens and books were strewn everywhere, and the plate with its now greasy burden reproached him. That had been his favourite meal. House didn't make it for him very often, being a regular churchgoer and having the natural Madren uncertainty about anything that gave enjoyment. It had been there a long time, by the look of it. He couldn't even remember her bringing it in, and yet she must have made some fuss about it, doubtless trying to persuade him to eat.

He stood up. The room swayed alarmingly and he took hold of the desk for support. Whatever was happening to him was getting worse. He was still sufficiently lucid to see that he was physically destroying himself and on the verge of wrecking his career, but his ability to remedy this situation seemed to be slipping away from him.

Yet something had to be done: he could not continue like this. No matter how ill he felt, how fearful, how tormented, still he must strive. He must seek out and face the cause of his pain.

Vredech clenched his fists and ground his teeth together then forced himself to set about the task of tidying his desk. He was an orderly person. He did not work like this. He must re-establish the steady rhythm of his life, beat back this demon that was pursuing him, by . . . by what means? By application to his work. By logic. By reason.

The confusion on his desk seemed to grow as he stared at it however, and his hands dithered vaguely, moving hither and thither but accomplishing nothing. His spirit wavered. There was so much to do. Where could he start? He wanted to lie down and rest. Find oblivion in the darkness . . .

'Move it one piece at a time,' he muttered grimly to himself. 'One piece at a time. I have a place for everything. Move, damn you.'

His hands obeyed, though they were shaking.

He released a breath that he seemed to have been holding all his life.

Then he saw that his hand was screwing up a piece of paper. Screwing it tighter and tighter, as if to crush it out of existence. The hand looked like someone else's. Why was it doing that? What was on the paper? He'd made no decision that it wasn't wanted. It took a deliberate effort to stop the hand and retrieve the paper, and a further one to flatten it out and read it.

It was nothing – just the opening sentences to a sermon, written in a spidery scrawl that was like a caricature of his own. He allowed the hand to finish the work it had started, while the other began to riffle aimlessly through the rest of the papers on the desk. There were so many.

'Can't go on,' he heard himself say. 'Too much. Too much.'

He was so tired. And so afraid. His insides felt both empty and full. A leaden core of a stomach to an empty shell of a man.

Then the room lurched violently, and something hit him very hard.

'Welcome back, night eyes,' the Whistler said. He played a short, mocking phrase on his flute.

'Where is this place?' Vredech asked. All about was a dull greyness, like a mountain mist, though without the dampness and the piercing cold. Mysteriously, all his turmoil had gone. He was relaxed and completely at ease, almost as if he had come home in some way.

'Better ask where *you* are, than that,' the Whistler replied.

'Where am I then?' Vredech obliged.

'Where you were before. If it was before, and not after – I don't know. It's difficult.'

'Where am I?' Vredech persisted.

'In my dream – what did I have you call yourself? – Vredech, wasn't it? Allyn Vredech. Funny foreign-sounding sort of a name – where could I have got it from? You're in my dream, Allyn Vredech. All things where I am are in my dream. I create them.' He gave a massive

200

shrug. 'I don't know how. Still less, why. But I create them, then . . .' His voice tailed off and the flute was at his mouth. Low sombre notes came from it.

'You're troubled,' Vredech said.

'Indeed, indeed, indeed.' The Whistler executed a jigging dance step to each word, angular elbows flying. 'Why else should I bring me a priest but to debate dark matters of the soul?'

Vredech wondered why he felt so easy in himself. Had he slipped finally into madness? The question did not trouble him. He was content to feel whole again – no matter where, or under what circumstances. What he was now was what he wanted to be. The shaking wraith of a man haunting his Meeting House was of no value and little interest. When – *if* – he returned there – or was expelled from here again, he mused with some humour – he would take this feeling back with him and be whole again there as well.

And for all its strangeness, this place had a solidity that had been lacking in all the dreams he had had . . . or had 'visited'. If what was happening was not a fantasy conjured out of the depths of his own fevered imaginings, but indeed the true reality, while Gyronlandt and all that went with it were mere dreams, then so it would have to be. It was probably as well he'd awakened eventually.

He was only mildly puzzled by the fact that he was accepting these disturbing conclusions so readily.

I will not oppose. I will not resist. I will be. And I will be content. All things are Ishryth's gift. I ask forgiveness for my doubts, Lord.

The Whistler leaned forward wide-eyed and flicked his fingers teasingly in Vredech's face. 'But if I'm troubled, you seem easier, Priest. You were quite agitated when we met last.'

Vredech smiled. 'I am easier,' he said. 'Perhaps I've come to like the way you've made me.'

The Whistler's head cocked on one side. 'Ah-ah,' he said, waving a long forefinger warningly. 'No tricks now. You lost the argument last time, remember? Knew the poem. Knew my name. And I was obliged to dismiss you.' The bony fingers emitted four great cracks as he snapped them at Vredech. 'Now behave yourself and do what you have to do. Talk – debate – teach me something about myself.'

Vredech gave a conceding nod. The Whistler trapped the flute under his arm like a soldier's baton and looked at Vredech suspiciously.

'What do you want to debate?' Vredech asked.

The Whistler turned away and slumped a little. The low, mournful notes came again. 'You know, don't you?' he said. 'Just as I must know. Why don't *you* tell *me*?'

'I don't think that's the way you do it,' Vredech replied.

The Whistler turned back to him, his head bent massively to one side, and his face puckered up with puzzlement. 'You *are* different, aren't you?' he said. 'I must be getting quite perceptive or . . .' He twitched his head upright, and left the comment unfinished. 'Very well. I've seen Him, you know?' he said.

Vredech shook his head. 'You have to tell me, remember?'

The Whistler scuttled over to him and crouched down on his haunches, his flute wedged between his legs and his body and his arms wrapped tightly around his knees. 'Came to me like you, He did. Night-eyed and black-bearded and in your priestly robe.' He looked Vredech up and down disparagingly, then flounced up the lace that was decorating his own broad collar. Vredech realized that it was the first time he had noticed how the man was dressed. 'Though it's a poor garb for a priest that I've given you, I must admit,' the Whistler continued. 'I've done better in the past . . .' He frowned.

'Or the future?' Vredech risked a taunt.

202

The Whistler waved the remark aside. 'Anyway, I've done far more lavish creations, some of them quite wildly ostentatious.' He curled his nose in distaste. 'Then, I suppose ostentation is rather silly in the servant of the Great Creator, isn't it?' There was venom in the words 'Great Creator'. 'It's not as if we could do anything that would impress him, is it? While, on the other hand, we could well irritate him beyond measure, couldn't we? With our strutting arrogance.'

Vredech, in his turn, waved the subject aside. 'Who is it you've seen?' he asked simply.

A finger was raised for emphasis. 'You hold me to the point. That's good. I'm apt to ramble,' the Whistler said. Then his face contorted. 'Him,' he said. 'I've seen Him. The one who always comes when there's going to be blood-letting and horror. The one who brings the worlds together.' A high keening whine suddenly came from his throat. 'I won't have it,' he said, bringing his face so close to Vredech's that it was almost touching. 'I won't have it. Enough's enough. I have a measure of the darkness within me. I need no more lessons.' His expression became at once vicious and triumphant. 'I threw Him out.' His arms flailed wildly and his fingers snapped, like breaking twigs in an autumn evening. 'Threw Him out. Never managed that before.'

Abruptly, he was standing, and the end of the black flute was being poked against Vredech's breast like a sword. 'But I think He might come back. Can you stop Him? Can you keep Him away? I don't want to do it again. All that pain. All that suffering. It's so real.'

'I don't know,' Vredech replied.

'Then what use are you to me?' the Whistler bellowed, suddenly in a rage.

'I don't know,' Vredech said again, wilfully calm. 'That's for you to judge. But where will you be if you dismiss me again? Any nearer to an answer?'

The Whistler looked at him for a moment and then walked away. Vredech watched him dwindle against the grey background. No sky, no ground, nothing. What is he standing on? he thought. Or, for that matter, what am I sitting on?

Looking down, he could see nothing. Tentatively and rather self-consciously, he pushed his hand under his behind. There appeared to be nothing there. Yet he must be sitting on something! He dismissed the problem. It was hardly one of any significance. But still . . .

The Whistler was returning, swelling against the perspective-less background. 'What am I to do with you then?' he asked.

Vredech chose to ignore the question. 'Where is this place?' he asked.

The Whistler grimaced. 'All places are my dream, I've told you once. Why don't you pay—'

'No,' Vredech interrupted. 'I mean, where is *this* place? Here. It's not where we were before. That was all darkness, and full of strange shadows. This is . . .' He gesticulated vaguely. 'This is . . . nowhere.'

The Whistler looked around, idly tapping the flute against his pursed lips. 'It certainly looks like nowhere ought to look, I'll grant you,' he said after a moment. 'Rather unimaginative. Perhaps I'm going through a dull phase. What with this and your rather humdrum robes, maybe . . .'

Vredech suddenly reached up and seized his wrist. It was thin and stiff, but it was undeniably human flesh and bone. And *very* strong. The Whistler's eyes opened in a mixture of surprise and anger, though he made no effort to free himself. 'Don't . . .' he began.

'You're lying,' Vredech said, shaking the wrist. 'Tell me about this place, and you, and the one you saw who was like me, and the pain he brings. Tell me everything.' He released his grip. For all that he had offered no resistance, the Whistler snatched his arm back like a child retrieving a withheld toy. Very gently, he ran his other hand down the wrist and, bringing it close to his face, examined it in great detail, from time to time looking over it at Vredech.

'You must tell me,' Vredech insisted.

'Perhaps not as dull as I thought,' the Whistler said.

Vredech made a broad gesture to indicate the greyness about them and raised an expectant eyebrow. The Whistler chuckled, took a few paces back and then played a series of repeated notes followed by an upward scale which he seemed to be playing long after Vredech had stopped hearing it.

'I think this place is . . . Between. Yes. Between.'

'Between what?' Vredech demanded.

The Whistler shrugged. 'Between my dreams, of course. Or perhaps at the edge. Or perhaps both. Maybe we're at the edge of between.'

'I've no idea what you're talking about,' Vredech said. 'Why won't you answer me properly? If this place is yours, where is it?'

'I don't know!' the Whistler shouted, suddenly angry. 'I've never been here before. I told you what I thought. We're between. Stuck between the dreams. Look!' He brought face and flute close to Vredech's again and blew a rippling cascade of notes. 'See?' he said, more quietly, placing his arm around Vredech's shoulder and making a broad sweeping gesture with his flute across the surrounding greyness. 'Nothing. Nothing at all. I play my flute and the ways open or the ways close. But here, nothing.' His grip about Vredech's shoulders tightened. 'You've locked me in limbo, Priest. You or Him. I threw Him out. Hurled Him from me. Black-eyed abomination. Then I was here.' He stood up suddenly. 'Or perhaps I'm dead.' He cocked his head first to one side then the other, like a great bird. 'Is that it, Priest? I'm dead? No one ever woke me – I just died?'

'I don't think either of us is dead,' Vredech said, as if he were a disinterested spectator. 'I wasn't well before I came here, but I certainly wasn't dying.'

The Whistler burst out laughing. 'Before you came here,' he echoed, shaking his head. 'A nice touch.' He held the flute against his ear. 'And there's a deal of life in the old bone here, for sure. I suppose if we feel alive, we'll have to assume we *are* alive. Failing that, then if I'm dead, you must be my guide to the world beyond. And I don't think you're that, are you?'

Vredech shook his head. 'Sorry,' he said.

'But I don't like this place, Priest,' the Whistler continued, sober again. 'Not while He's around. I want to be away. I won't have Him come again. I must be able to move . . . to escape to my other dreams.'

'Tell me about Him,' Vredech said.

'What's to tell?' the Whistler replied. 'You're mine – you must know.'

Vredech found himself peculiarly patient. 'If, as you say, I'm yours, then presumably you must have brought me here to ask you that question,' he replied. 'If I'm *not* yours, but in fact *you* are *mine*, then I too, need to know the answer that's wrapped in you.'

The two men looked at one another.

'Tell me about Him,' Vredech said again, forcefully.

Slowly the Whistler lifted the flute to his mouth and blew out the three haunting notes that Vredech had heard before their first encounter. Several times he repeated them, each time a little differently. When he spoke, he uttered some of the words across the mouth-hole, adding an eerie echoing quality to his voice.

'Many times I've met Him,' he said, though more to himself than to Vredech, 'in many different guises. But He's always the same. He used to fool me, but I recognize the scent of him now – the *stink*. Corruption, pestilence and death.' He raised his head and tested the air like a hunting animal. 'Then I look into the eyes – and through them. And there He is, looking back. Ancient, malevolent. Always the same. Always waiting. Never tiring. Waiting for the events to unfold that will give Him what He wants.'

Despite his continuing feeling of ease and well-being, Vredech winced inwardly at the deep pain that came from this mysterious individual. Deliberately he reminded himself not to question the reality of what was happening. Whatever was to be revealed now would be important no matter what the apparent source.

'What does He want?' he asked.

The Whistler crouched down on to his haunches again and, one eye closed, squinted at Vredech along the length of his flute. 'Everything,' he replied. 'He wants everything. And He wants to destroy it. He would see the whole world a charred cinder wandering lost through the stars. He would see all the worlds thus.'

Vredech found that he was unable to speak for a moment, so awful was the desolation in the Whistler's voice.

Then he said, 'Why?'

The Whistler's head jerked up sharply. It seemed as though he was going to make an angry rejoinder, but apparently changed his mind. 'I don't know,' he replied with genuine puzzlement in his voice. 'I've never asked.'

'Do so next time you meet Him,' Vredech said.

Fury lit the Whistler's face. 'There isn't going to *be* a next time!' he shouted. 'I won't allow it. Not again.'

Vredech's voice was calm. 'I doubt you'd shout so loud if you thought that was true.'

The Whistler stood up and his hand shot forward, clawed and menacing. 'Enough, Priest. Remember what you are,' he snarled.

'I know what I am,' Vredech replied, waving the gesture away. 'And where I come from. I'm Allyn Vredech,

Chapter Member of the Church of Ishryth. Even now, I'm lying in the Meeting House, in Troidmallos, chief town of Canol Madreth. The question is, what are you, hovering alone in this grey twilight, proud possessor of a great insight that enables you to see into the heart of some world-destroyer? What world, Whistler? What worlds? And who is this great warmonger?'

The Whistler twitched violently and backed away from this onslaught, dwindling in the greyness. He began to play the flute loudly in a manic jig. Vredech stood up to follow him. The playing stopped.

'Who do you think it could be, Priest?' the Whistler shouted. 'All things here are mine. All things here are me. You are me. This greyness is me. The great warmonger is me. ME! I create these things to torment myself.'

'Why?'

'Stop asking that question.'

'According to you, it's you who's asking it.'

The Whistler's face became angry again. 'Don't get clever with me, Priest. Or . . .'

'Or what?' Vredech almost sneered. 'You'll dismiss me? I doubt it. Blow your flute, make your faces, rant and shout. But I won't go.'

The Whistler's eyes widened insanely and the flute came to his mouth. But he made no sound. Instead he just stared at Vredech. Then, very softly, he said:

> *Darkling gaze,*
> *Travel the ways,*
> *Find the heart,*
> *That's your part.'*

His eyes narrowed. 'I've made so many people,' he said. 'So vivid. So real. And they all pretend they *are* real, especially when I make a world for them as well. But you're strange. Why would I make anything like you, with your frightening eyes? Why would I lock us here, in this endless grey nothing? Of all the things I've made, I've never . . .' He put his hands to his head. 'I sometimes think I've forgotten the memories of a million lifetimes, Priest. It's not easy, never waking. Not even knowing which way time runs.' He began to fiddle with his straggling beard. 'Darkling gaze, travel the ways. I wonder if you *are* real.' Then he grinned and waved a finger at Vredech. 'No, no. That way lies madness – and I don't want to be raving when I wake, do I? But you're interesting, there's no denying that. I wonder what you're here to make me learn.'

'About Him?' Vredech suggested. 'You've still told me nothing, like who He is, why He is, or what He looks like. You ramble. You avoid. You get angry. Why don't you just tell me about Him?'

The Whistler abandoned his beard with a flourish. 'Why not?' he said with sudden decisiveness. 'Just give me a moment.'

And he was gone.

209

Chapter 17

Cassraw stared up at the looming figure, his mouth suddenly dry and his insides hideously mobile. It did not matter that for the moment he had lost the wits to decide whether to remain silent, or to speak, or to call out for help, as his tongue was stuck to the roof of his mouth.

One old habit did not desert him, however, and instinctively, his hand groped towards his pocket to pat the copy of the Santyth there. The figure's head inclined slightly, then there was a violent oath, a flurry of movement, and Cassraw found himself blinking into an unbearably bright light.

He raised a hand to shield his eyes, but something knocked it aside painfully.

'Stay still,' a powerful voice commanded. 'And keep your hands where I can see them, unless you want your skull cracked.'

Cassraw could do no other, his fear having been supplemented by the pain in his hand. He screwed up his eyes and made to turn his face from the light.

'Stay still!'

Something then struck his leg violently, numbing it, and something – a stick? – was preventing his head from turning. Then it was gone, but a hand was gripping his chin and forcing his face into the light. It was not a hand to be argued with.

'Ye gods,' came the voice again, now full of surprise and

concern. 'Brother Cassraw. What the dev—. I mean . . . what are you doing here? Have you been attacked? Don't move.'

The light was taken away from his eyes, and the hand that had been clamped on his chin was joined by its partner in urgently testing his limbs for signs of injury.

'It's Serjeant Skynner, Brother. Do you recognize me? Are you all right? Tell me what's happened.'

The changed tone, coupled with the familiar name, restored Cassraw's senses as rapidly as the Keeper's sudden appearance and violent assault had scattered them, though he still felt assailed, albeit not physically. His mind raced. He must have a plausible excuse for being found here in this both ridiculous and suspicious position, or much that he had gained of late could be lost.

'I'm all right, Serjeant,' he said, struggling inwardly to set aside the eerie experiences of the last few minutes so that he could concentrate on a simple, legitimate excuse. 'Perhaps you'd help me up?'

The request was scarcely made when he was hoisted to his feet as easily as if he had been a small child.

'And can you look for my lantern for me, Serjeant?' Cassraw said, looking to take charge of events before Skynner could recommence his questioning. 'I dropped it when I tripped over something.'

Skynner's curiosity was not so easily deflected, however, and he was asking questions even as he opened up his own lantern fully and began searching about the alley. 'What in the world are you doing out here, Brother? It's hardly the most sensible of places to be wandering alone.'

'He is always with me,' Cassraw replied, gradually gaining control over his voice again.

Skynner paused temporarily in his search then continued as if this had been a perfectly reasonable answer. 'Thus let it be,' he said solemnly, without looking up. 'But, with respect, Brother, if you're going to walk around

211

here at this time of night, by all means put your faith in Ishryth . . .'

'. . . but carry a big stick.' Cassraw finished the saying for him.

Skynner found the lantern. He straightened up to his full height and looked down at Cassraw as he returned it to him. 'Indeed, Brother,' he said. 'Ishryth helps those who help themselves, but this is a foolish place to be tempting Providence.'

'I stand theologically rebuked,' Cassraw replied with a smile and a slight bow. He was relaxed now: he had his tale. He must set aside all consideration of what had really happened to him until he had convinced this astute and suspicious officer. 'I'm afraid I allowed my pastoral concerns to sweep aside my commonsense.'

Skynner was genuinely curious but he could be nothing other than professional in his manner. 'And what conceivable pastoral concerns would bring you to this alleyway, Brother?' he asked sternly.

Cassraw had struck his lantern and was affecting to check it, carefully testing the shutter and adjusting the intensity of the light. Seemingly satisfied, he put a hand on Skynner's arm and began moving him towards the street.

'I was visiting one of my flock earlier this evening when I met a colleague of yours, Albor. We talked for a few minutes about this and that, and amongst other things, the topic of the murder of that poor young man happened to come up.' Cassraw paused and looked thoughtful. 'It was really very strange. Some impulse told me that I must not stand back from this incident. I think the church stands a little too aloof at times, don't you?' He did not wait for an answer. 'So I told Albor that I would mention it at my next service.' He became genial, aware of Skynner's sudden startled glance. 'I'm not quite sure who was the most surprised, he or I, but if there *is* someone amongst us who may be teetering on the edge of his sanity, then a voice from the church, by its very unexpectedness, may do at least as much as the posted notices and the reports in the Sheets.' He waved his hand airily, indicating that this was, in any event, a trivial matter, not worthy of further discussion. 'Anyway, after I'd visited my parishioner I set off towards home, having, I'm afraid, forgotten about my promise, when it all came back to me with terrible force. I was suddenly overcome by the horror and tragedy of what had happened.'

They had reached the comparative brightness of the street now, and Cassraw felt easier with each step he took away from the intense gloom of the alley, although he had to resist the temptation to keep turning round in response to the feeling that something there was still watching him, calling out to him softly.

He forced himself to continue. 'I felt that in some way *I* had died a little with that youth – indeed, that the whole of Troidmallos had died a little. I knew that I would not be able to rest until I had done something. The Lord moves us in ways we can't begin to understand, Serjeant. Sometimes we must simply follow. So, I followed my instincts and they led me here. I thought, a prayer . . . a blessing on this awful place, maybe . . . to exorcise some of the terrible memories that must be lingering here. I don't know – I was far from clear in my thinking. Unfortunately, I was also far from clear about where I was walking and I tripped over something and went headlong.' He chuckled. 'I seem to be doing that a lot lately. Lost my lantern, my dignity and my pious intentions all in one go.'

Skynner smiled tentatively, then Cassraw staggered slightly and caught his arm. 'I'm afraid my leg's still a little numb, where you kicked me,' he said. 'Are you always so rough with your . . . clients?'

Skynner cleared his throat awkwardly. 'I didn't kick you, Brother,' he lied. 'That's against regulations. I hit you with my stick.' He cleared his throat again. 'And to be honest,

213

with all due respect to your calling, you're lucky I wasn't a great deal rougher, dealing with someone loitering down an alley where there's just been a particularly nasty murder.' He allowed his professional manner to falter a little and his voice became genuinely alarmed. 'You frightened me half to death, Brother. If you'd made any attempt to get to your feet before I recognized you, I wouldn't have been bothering too much about regulations, I can tell you.'

'We must thank Him for His guidance in bidding me stay still, then,' Cassraw said. Skynner grunted, non-committally.

They were nearing a more brightly lit part of the town and both pedestrian and road traffic were increasing. 'I can get one of the Keeper Wagons to take you back to the Haven, if you wish, Brother,' Skynner offered.

Cassraw shook his head. 'No thank you, Serjeant,' he replied. 'I'm still troubled by this unhappy business. I'll think as I walk.' He raised a hand in reassurance. 'I promise I'll go down no more dark ways tonight.'

'Or any other night preferably, Brother,' Skynner said.

'I must go where He leads me, and He is everywhere,' Cassraw said.

Skynner came as near as he dared to rebuking a senior member of the church. 'That's your province, Brother, and I can't debate it with you, but these streets are mine, and there are places where your cloth won't protect you.'

Cassraw looked as if he wished to dispute this point, but he simply said, by way of parting message: 'I'm indebted to you for your vigilance, Serjeant. I could well have been injured back in that alley and your appearance was most timely. And I'll certainly forgive you the blow you struck. There was no true malice in it. Now I'll take up no more of your time.' And he turned and walked away, still limping slightly, before Skynner could pursue the matter.

Skynner took a step forward as though to follow him, then stopped. He watched Cassraw until he disappeared

214

into the evening traffic however, and he was frowning. He was sure he'd heard more than one voice down that alley. But he'd seen no one running away, and there'd been no one else hiding there, he was sure. He'd had quite a thorough look when he was pretending to search for Cassraw's lantern.

Must have been cursing to himself, he thought. Even a cleric's entitled to the odd oath when he barks his shin on something. But he was uneasy. Cassraw's tale was bizarre, to say the least. It wouldn't be a complete lie, he was fairly certain about that, and he fully expected that a word with Albor would confirm some of it – although the idea of a murder being mentioned in a sermon was startling enough in itself. But it was not the truth either, or he wasn't a Serjeant Keeper.

It was not a happy conclusion. Skynner was a moderately devout follower of the church, despite his constant contact with the darker side of human nature, and Cassraw was one of the Preaching Brothers for whom he had a genuine respect, even though he did not particularly like him. But if he had not been telling the whole truth – and he hadn't – then what in Ahmral's name had he been doing down that alley?

It could be morbid curiosity, of course. Murder held a fascination for the oddest people, and this crime was still being gossiped about extensively, not least because no culprit had yet been found, nor even a suspect. But it did not seem conceivable that Cassraw would have succumbed to such prurience. Besides, wandering about round there at night took no small amount of courage for someone who was not familiar with the area and its denizens.

There were a few other possibilities, each of them improbable: a woman; a secret meeting in connection with church politics; even that Cassraw was the murderer. Skynner let them all go. It seemed that his judgement about Cassraw's honesty might have been wrong. Perhaps he *had* told the truth after all.

But Skynner's instinct cried out against this. His judgement was sound enough. A lot of strange things had happened lately – all since that damned black cloud had appeared over the town. Poor old Jarry, thinking that the devil had come again and rambling about it still, by all accounts. People claiming that voices had told them to do things. Others saying they were being followed by strange shadowy figures. It seemed that every eccentric in Troidmallos had become more so. And Cassraw's escapade had to be put with these until he found out otherwise.

A crier sounded the time, startling him a little. On an impulse, he decided to pursue the matter immediately.

As he strode through more familiar streets, Cassraw did as he said he would: he thought about what had happened. Or rather he watched as the events of the last hour tumbled through his head over and over. At first the dominant feature was the most recent, and most physical: his encounter with Skynner. This had shaken him badly. He had felt an aspect of the man's power which he could never have known under normal circumstances. For a moment, he had been a criminal, and as such he had been seized, quite literally, by the law. His leg was still sore where Skynner had kicked him, and his jaw was aching a little where it had been gripped. And he had no doubt at all that he would have been brutally beaten if, in panic, he had tried to flee. Yet, oddly, the experience had been exhilarating. The intensity of the focus of an unyielding intention had stirred him in some way. It had the purity of simplicity. The simplicity of the mailed fist. Thus we learn. A new element entered into deepening resolutions. He would become His mailed fist. Iron, implacable to those who opposed His will. And so, too, would be his men: his iron fist writ large.

His men. He relished the thought. His contact with

216

Skynner was swept aside by visions of the future of his Knights of Ishryth, transformed – no, revealed in their true splendour – to bring order to His followers and terror to His enemies. It was a heady vision, in which the steady rhythm of his feet on the roadway became the marching feet of thousands.

Yet amid this rapture came memories of the other events that had occurred in the alley. The terrifying, primitive emotions that had possessed him as he had stumbled to the ground and into the lanternless darkness; the burning desires of the flesh and the fearful, murderous bloodlust, hideously intermingled; that strange figure which had peered into his eyes as if searching out his very soul. *And then rejected him!* Cassraw clenched his fists and his jaw tautened.

Rejected *him* – the Chosen One – as if he had been some unwanted cur. It was intolerable. Rage filled him.

But other questions still burned through his anger. Who had he been? For a brief moment, Cassraw shook violently as it occurred to him that the figure might have been the murderer, returning to the scene of his atrocity. Yet, that could not have been. There was no one else in the alley – Skynner would have seen him for sure. Besides, their mysterious meeting had not happened in the alley – they had been somewhere else. An inner certainty of this allowed Cassraw no reasoned reservation. But if not the alley, then where? Where could such a land, with its luring shadows, be – other than in one of his strange new dreams? That there could be no answer merely served to heighten the power of the question.

And had the figure been as real as it had seemed, or was it just a figment of his imagination? But why should he create such an illusion? An illusion that had judged him with such withering contempt. His mind twisted with fury again at the memory. Yet if it was not an illusion, what was it?

Then, blindingly. It was a test!

How else could he have been so powerfully drawn to that place? How truly impulsive had his decision been, to visit Yanos? And how accidental his meeting with Albor? And how else could his unthinking footsteps have carried him there? Even the alley itself had lured him like a dark beacon. It had been a test, beyond a doubt.

But had he failed or had he passed? Or was judgement still pending?

He gripped the copy of the Santyth in his pocket, hoping for guidance. He tried to recall the figure that had appeared to him and the words that it had spoken. But no face came to him, and only fleeting hints of a lean angular form, shielding its eyes as it peered into him, and then prancing grotesquely away. Some of the words it had spoken he remembered, though they meant nothing to him – abomination; demon guide; night eyes. But the contempt he recalled in its entirety, and as he recalled it so his fury returned and was fed.

By now he had stopped walking and was standing rigid with tension in the full glare of one of the street lights. It took him a wilful effort to release his clenched fists and the knuckles ached as he did so, as did his jaw and almost every part of him as he forced muscles and sinews into movement again. Then, aware of his visibility, he brought his hands together and bowed his head as if he had suddenly been inspired to pray, looking about him surreptitiously as he did so to see if anyone had been witness to this silent outburst.

Satisfied that his strange behaviour had gone unnoticed, he set off again. Had that perhaps been the purpose of the test – to give him a true measure of his righteous anger when assailed by doubters and scoffers? If so, then it had been successful. He would know how to deal with such in the future.

The conclusion brought him back to his plans for Yanos

and the Knights of Ishryth. A sword must be forged that would sweep all before it. A sword that could glisten untarnished through an endless bloodletting, should His will be defied. Once again, the sound of his footsteps became the feet of thousands, and he was oblivious to all things until he found himself passing through the tall iron gates of the Haven Meeting House. His soaring dreams faded sourly, however, as he approached the darkened doorway to his private quarters. A lamp should have been burning there. He must rebuke the servants tomorrow. The Meeting House should be a constant source of illumination in every sense. It should shine through the night of Troidmallos as it should shine through the spiritual night of Canol Madreth and the whole of Gyronlandt and beyond.

He paused as the thought took wings. His eyes were drawn upwards, towards the invisible bulk of the Ervrin Mallos. *There* was the place for a true beacon, one that indeed would light the whole land and act as focus for the many powers that he could sense hovering about him, awaiting that single tiny grain that would coalesce them into a mighty whole.

There was a stirring within him. A listening? A prompting?

Then, as if clouds were slowly being blown away to expose it, there came to him a vision of a great place of worship rising out of the jagged peak of the mountain: a many-towered temple, glittering arrow-sharp and sunlit against the grim black clouds that presaged the coming of His chariots.

Cassraw stood silent and awe-stricken before the ramping splendour of this sight, then sank to his knees, his hands clasped. 'Thus let it be, Lord. Thus *shall* it be. Through such shall the One True Light be drawn down amongst us again, to spread across the worlds.' His voice was hoarse with emotion.

219

He knew that in some way he did not understand, he had been tested and found whole, and that this vision had been granted him to show him the way forward. With this single binding thread, the tangled weave of careful plans, vague hopes and fanciful speculations that had been shifting and changing within him since his encounter on the mountain, came together to form a tapestry, in whose pattern, at once subtle and open, delicate and iron-shod, the entire future could be read.

He knew, too, that though this present intensity must surely pass, the vision would remain with him for ever and that, as with the Santyth, he had but to look into it to see what he must do. Indeed, he had but to be aware of its existence to know what to do.

He had no conception of how long he remained kneeling on the stone pathway, but slowly he became aware of normality re-forming about him. And, too, there was a presence. He looked about him as he stood up. A figure was standing nearby. Unlike the figures he had met in the alley, this one he recognized, even in the dim light that was reaching him from the street. She was standing as she had been when he had seen her earlier that day, her head slightly bowed.

'Dowinne,' he said quietly.

'Enryc,' his wife replied, almost formally. 'I was reading. I had no idea how late it was.' She hesitated and inclined her head a little as if listening to something. When she spoke again her voice was low and full of messages that of late had become very familiar to him. 'I was beginning to be concerned about you. The servants are long asleep.'

Cassraw felt his chest tighten. He reached out. His wife's hand closed about his purposefully. 'This has been a rare day, wife,' he said. 'Such things have happened as I can scarcely believe. Such visions.'

'I feel the change in you,' Dowinne replied, almost

220

whispering now, leading him forward. 'Words are not necessary.'

'But I must tell you,' Cassraw insisted as they stepped through the doorway into their private quarters.

Dowinne closed the door behind them. 'Yes,' she said. Her arms folded irresistibly about him. 'But not yet. They are words of power and success, I can tell. But behind them is the spirit which is beyond the words. Let that possess me as it now possesses you. Share it with me, here, now.'

Chapter 18

Vredech waited in the grey silence. He asked himself the same questions that the Whistler had asked. Why should he create such a place as this? And why a character such as the Whistler, a figure who sounded no familiar echo along the tunnels of memory? And where could he have conceived the pain that the man exuded, and the images of destruction that he conjured? Apart from the odd youthful folly, he himself had known little violence in his life, and he knew nothing of the reality of war other than from reports of the skirmishes that occurred from time to time between neighbouring states. Even here there had been nothing which could be regarded as a large-scale war. As for the massive horror such as the Whistler spoke of, Vredech had met that only in ancient history, and in myths and legends.

He rubbed his eyes. The monotonous greyness was beginning to hurt them. It had not been noticeable when the Whistler was there with his garish clothes and frantic movements, but now he could not stop his eyes from straining to focus on something where nothing existed. He had been caught in mountain mists in his time, even once during the winter, when a brilliant whiteness had merged sky and ground frighteningly, but even then there had been contrast. Here, the greyness was total, and uniform in every direction.

His head began to ache, and his sense of ease to fade and

he began to feel a little afraid. He closed his eyes. Relieving colours washed before him, flowing patterns growing and diminishing. And amid them, dancing through and around them, shadows.

He opened his eyes abruptly.

The Whistler was standing in front of him, looking at him intently and still rubbing his wrist. All around them was the darkness in which they had first met, full of shadows, black in black, near and far.

Without really knowing why, Vredech felt a surge of relief. Then he latched on to the prosaic to quieten himself further. 'I didn't hurt your arm, did I?' he asked.

The Whistler released his wrist as if he had been stung. 'No, no. Of course not. How could *you* hurt *me*?'

'Where are we now?' Vredech asked.

The Whistler's eyes widened and his thin face cracked into a broad, knowing smile. Teasingly he flicked the flute to his lips and played a rapid flurry of notes. Though he could see nothing specific, Vredech felt the darkness around him changing.

'Where we always were,' the Whistler said off-handedly, standing up. 'In my dream.'

'But the greyness – the limbo?'

The Whistler gave an exaggerated shrug. 'A whim, a fancy. I moved away from it. It was tiresome.'

'You're lying,' Vredech burst out.

The Whistler's lips pursed in mock outrage, then he spun round on his heel. The flute seemed to follow a separate path of its own, glistening black in the darkness, but when both stopped, the Whistler was in an affected fencing stance and holding the end of the flute against Vredech's throat. 'You're very free with your abuse, Priest,' he said. 'That's twice you've called me a liar.' He clicked his tongue reproachfully. 'Three times is a declaration of war, I've heard it said.'

Vredech swung his hand up to strike the flute away, but

the Whistler casually moved it at the last moment and, meeting no resistance, Vredech staggered slightly. The Whistler caught him. 'Fortunately, I'm not religious myself,' he declared pompously. 'And thus not given to violence.' Vredech found he was scowling and clenching his fists. The Whistler clicked his tongue again and turned away. With an effort, Vredech composed himself and moved after him. As they walked together Vredech felt that it was as though the shadowy landscape about them was moving also – sometimes fast, sometimes slow, and that it was this that was determining their progress.

At first, Vredech was inclined to continue his dispute. The man was lying, he was sure – his eyes, his manner, left no doubt. He had no idea where they had both been, or how they had come away from it.

Yet he had flitted mysteriously away from the greyness, seemingly at his own behest . . .

Vredech's certainty evaporated and he was flooded with doubt. His feet became leaden and his head ached again. Suddenly he wanted to stop and sit down. Do nothing. Just sit. The Whistler was some way ahead of him, still visible despite the darkness, as though he carried a light all his own. A jaunty tune drifted back to Vredech. He heard it almost reluctantly, trying to resist it as it moved through him like a breath of cold, wakening air, until finally it jerked his right foot into a rhythmic tapping. Trailing behind this intrusion came the memory of the sense of well-being he had had but moments ago when he found himself in the presence of this strange man – wherever it had been. He remembered, too, his resolve to carry the feeling with him when he awoke again. He smiled a little. Nearly forgot to carry it through my dream, let alone into my waking hours, he thought.

If he had created the Whistler, then he had created the lies he was telling, and in concerning himself about those, he was concerning himself too much about his own inner

224

searchings – those tenuous, aching thoughts that could only make themselves heard in this bizarre fashion. And in so doing he was denying them the only answer they could give him. He must let them take their course freely, let them provide him with their answer subtly, silently, unknowingly.

'Whistler,' he called out. 'You were going to tell me about the man you've seen.'

The Whistler turned round. 'Not a man, Allyn Vredech, Preaching Brother. A demon. A natural force of destruction and terror.' He bent forward, eyes wide. '*My* demon.'

Vredech reached him. 'So you've said. You seem inordinately proud of Him, really. Why would you make such a monster?'

The Whistler opened his mouth to answer but no sound came. Instead, his mouth remained open, and he stopped moving. The effect was disturbing. Vredech had not realized how much the man moved until he was so suddenly still. The restlessness that had pervaded the Whistler seemed now to pervade the landscape and Vredech became aware of shadows trembling all about him.

'Well?' he insisted, more forcefully than he had intended to the motionless figure. Then he heard himself providing his own answer. 'Perhaps when he has reduced these worlds of yours to cinders, you'll awake.'

Stillness and silence formed about them both.

Slowly, the Whistler straightened up, standing tall and relaxed, motionless now in a different way.

'That's a dark answer, Priest,' he said, his brow furrowed. 'Darker than I think I have the stomach for. I'm beginning to see why I made you.'

'Answer then,' Vredech said simply. 'I'm intrigued to know what we think.'

'No games, Priest,' the Whistler said. 'Play your part properly.'

225

'Answer then,' Vredech repeated.

The Whistler looked down at his flute, hanging lifeless and dull in his hand. He brought it to his mouth, then lowered it. His face was suddenly drawn and haggard. Vredech felt his hand wanting to reach out and comfort him.

'If what you say is true, then why should I constantly oppose Him? Why should I battle with Him through world after world, time after time, when I could let Him have His way – perhaps even aid Him?' He bared his teeth in an angry snarl and his hands came up like claws. 'Tear all this down. Obliterate it. Reduce it to the primordial dust from whence it came. With nothing here, I would wake, wouldn't I?' He turned to Vredech, his eyes pleading.

Vredech could not speak.

'Why, Priest?' the Whistler shouted. '*Your* question. Why?'

Vredech's mouth was suddenly dry with fear, but he spoke as the thoughts came. 'Two answers, Whistler, perhaps three. You would be left alone with Him in a wilderness of dead worlds.' He swallowed. 'But that couldn't be, because He's your creation, and when His task was done you would no longer need Him, and having truly nothing here, then indeed, you might wake.'

The Whistler leaned forward, listening intently. 'And the other?'

Vredech, his face tense with the effort of speaking, met his gaze. 'The other is that . . .' He hesitated. 'The other is that . . . He is not your creation.'

'But yours!' the Whistler exploded, all animation again. 'As am I, I suppose.' He spun round and brought the flute down to slap into the palm of his hand, before swinging it up to point accusingly at Vredech. 'Another of your games, Priest? Damn you to whatever passes for hell in your black-clad religion. I'm not some gullible peasant to be cowed and swayed by twisting words and blustering oratory. I see what I see, and I see it for what it is. I've spanned dreamways beyond your imagining, floated sun-carried amid the glittering cities of the clouds, trekked through deserts of eye-scorching sand and eye-blinding snow, led legions into battle, conquered . . .' He stopped and waved his hand wildly as if to stop the flow of memories. 'And you, you black-eyed crow, you rake across my soul with your probings just for a game.' He raised the flute high behind him as if to strike Vredech.

'The other is that He's not your creation or mine but *real*!' Vredech roared at him. His face flinched away from the intended blow while his feet carried him forwards as if welcoming it. 'As am I. As are you. As are all the things you've ever known. *Real*, Whistler.' His voice faded into the faintest of whispers. 'Not your creation, nor mine, but someone else's.'

The Whistler, his hand still poised, stared at him, his eyes searching Vredech's face desperately.

'Real.' He spoke the word very softly, as if testing it for some mysterious power. 'Real.' Slowly he lowered his arm and, equally slowly, he lifted the flute to his mouth. He blew a solitary note, long and steady, but growing softer and softer. To Vredech, it was like a shining silver rope. He had a vision of it twining out into the darkness, on and on, twisting its eternal way through the stars.

Even when the Whistler stopped playing, it seemed to Vredech that the sound was continuing, and would continue for ever.

'The Sound Carvers taught me to play this,' the Whistler said, shaking his head sadly. 'Strange, elusive people. But the noises I make are scarcely a shadow of theirs. I wonder if I'll meet them again? There's so much I want to ask them now.'

Vredech did not speak. The terrible violence that had radiated from the Whistler but moments ago was gone

227

utterly, and his voice held such poignancy that to have interrupted would have been like a gratuitous cruelty.

The Whistler looked at him. 'You're a rare one, Allyn Vredech. The best I've ever made.'

'Or met on your wanderings,' Vredech added, forcing a smile. 'And I'm hard pressed to know where I could have conjured you from. I never had much of an imagination.'

The two men stared at one another for a long, timeless moment.

'There is no answer, is there?' the Whistler said, looking at his hand as if he had never truly seen it before.

'I'm not sure we're asking the right question,' Vredech replied.

'A priest's answer, for sure,' the Whistler replied, his mood lightening.

'A thinker's answer,' Vredech said in mock reproach.

'Another priest's answer,' the Whistler announced definitively.

'Let's discuss our situation, then. Let's reason – like priests.'

The Whistler laughed loudly, making the shadows dance. 'Reason and priests. Oil and water.' He laughed again. 'First you call me a liar, then a priest. You're certainly free with your abuse, night eyes.'

'I think you'll survive any abuse *I* can offer you.'

The Whistler was playing again, the three notes that Vredech had first heard, though a little faster, their character one of curiosity almost. 'True, true, true,' came the Whistler's voice across the mouth-hole.

'Tell me about the man,' Vredech risked. 'Whatever, wherever, whenever, we are – *whoever* we are – it is *he* who brings the pain to you.'

The Whistler stopped playing and gazed upwards as if he were looking for something. 'I'm not sure I know how to talk any more,' he said. 'You've given me such strange doubts.'

228

'A priest's answer,' Vredech said.

The Whistler looked at him sharply, his eyes mocking. 'Priests never doubt,' he declared.

'True priests always doubt,' Vredech retorted instantly.

Then, simultaneously, the two of them said, 'A priest's answer!' and burst out laughing.

'Be silent, night eyes,' the Whistler said, with heavy friendliness as their laughter faded. 'I have a tune to play.'

And the air was suddenly full of bouncing, irresistible music that left Vredech no choice, despite his priestly dignity, but to lift his hands and clap them in response to its pounding rhythm. The Whistler was bobbing and jigging as he played, his body marking out its own dancing counterpoint to the swirling music.

Abruptly he stopped, leaving Vredech with his hands thrown wide, expectant. 'You're no drummer, Priest. But there's hope for anyone with music in him.' His eyes were sparkling and his face flushed. Vredech smiled broadly, as though this were considerable praise. Then he saw that the Whistler was motioning him to turn around. As he did so, a strange sensation under his feet drew his eyes downwards. He was standing on grass! And he was casting a shadow across it!

He looked up.

At first he could not make out what he was looking at, so used had he become to the world of shadows in which he and the Whistler were conversing. Then he saw that he was standing on a hillside and looking across a broad, rolling landscape towards a distant sky, red with the light of a setting sun.

'Where . . .?'

'Shh,' the Whistler replied very softly, coming to his side.

Vredech did as he was bidden, and for a few silent minutes the two men stood and watched the fading sun. Long, deceiving shadows disguised the land over which he was gazing, but Vredech could make out trees and wood-lands and fields and, he thought, dwellings of some kind. A broad river wound golden through it, and the air about them was soft and warm and full of evening birdsong. Vredech could feel a great peacefulness passing over him.

A dull thud drew him out of his reverie. Looking around, he saw that the Whistler had sat down on the grass and was lying back, his hands behind his head. He sat down beside him.

'Where are we?' he asked, unable to contain the question now.

'Here,' came the reply. 'We're only ever here.'

'Stop that, and answer properly,' Vredech demanded sternly.

The Whistler chuckled to himself at this response as he brought the flute to his eye and peered along it, swinging it slowly across the reddening horizon. 'You'd be none the wiser if I told you,' he said. 'It's just a world I made once. I carry it with me for when I need to lie down and think.'

Vredech shook his head. 'Even *I* could imagine some-where as gentle and peaceful as this,' he said.

Unexpectedly, the Whistler gave him an approving look. 'Good,' he said. 'Do so, then. And carry it with you always.'

The remark brought Vredech's earlier thoughts back to him; how he was going to carry this sense of well-being back into his own world when he returned there. It seemed to stir something deep inside him.

'Would you rather I'd carried you to some land deso-lated by plague and famine, devastated by the passage of warring armies?' the Whistler said.

'I'd rather you told me about Him,' Vredech replied. 'Talked about the heart of your concerns.'

The Whistler sat up and wrapped his arms around his knees. 'Why the interest?' he asked. 'He's my bane, not yours.'

230

Vredech spoke the answer before he had even thought about it. 'Because He's in my world now,' he said. 'And whether you're real or figment, you're here to tell me about Him.'

The Whistler cocked his head on one side and studied Vredech carefully. 'I know nothing about Him,' he replied. 'He *is*, that's all I can tell you.' He picked a small white flower and held it out to Vredech. 'He *is*. Like this flower, like this hill, that sunset.'

'You don't scream denial at the flowers and the sunset,' Vredech said, taking the flower. 'You don't run away from them, flee into worlds of your own making.'

'You flee the forest fire, the flood, the tempest . . .'

'Stop it,' Vredech said, his face pained. 'Stop running. Just tell me who He is and why I have to know about Him.'

'He is me . . .'

'Stop it, damn you!' Anger surged through Vredech, as savage as it was unexpected.

An echoing spasm flitted across the Whistler's face, but his voice was calm when he spoke. 'Very well,' he said. 'We agreed we'd not debate that, didn't we? Who is He, then? He is Evil personified. His guise is always different, but *He* is always the same. It's almost as if, at the beginning of time, out of the heat of the Great Creation, He came together as a whole when He should have been scattered through all mankind, like a . . . tempering, sobering influence.'

Vredech watched him cautiously, wondering whether he might not suddenly shy away from the topic into some irrelevancy. But the Whistler seemed totally absorbed. The setting sun shone red on his face. 'It's almost as if,' he hesitated, 'as if the whole process of the Creation had gone wrong. "Fabrics's torn, 'fore all was born".'

Despite himself, Vredech felt his eyes widening in shock. This was sacrilege! The Creation was Ishryth's and

231

it was perfect. It had been marred only by the natural sinfulness of man. It—

He stopped himself. Sacrilege or no, he must listen. Whatever was happening here, this was something that had to be heard.

The Whistler was shaking his head, as if rejecting the idea himself. 'He wanders the worlds like a lost spirit – no, like a predator, a parasite – in search of a host.' He fell silent, rapt in thought, his eyes fixed and staring, the flute swinging slowly from his hand like a pendulum.

Not 'my worlds', Vredech noted. Though it was part of their agreement, it made him feel deeply uneasy. He risked a comment. 'You sound as if you're talking about Ahmral – the devil,' he said. 'A supernatural manifestation of—'

The Whistler's hand came up sharply to silence him. Its long forefinger waved from side to side hypnotically. 'There is nothing supernatural, Priest. There is only the darkness where your ability to measure the natural ends. And it's up to you, above all, to shine the light into it. He is all too natural, all too human, and He carries with Him the essence of all that is dark and foul in the human spirit, all that wallows in ignorance.' The long hand tightened into an agonizing fist. 'He's as real as my fist. And though He normally uses others to fulfil His benighted will, should the whim take Him, He'd throttle you with His bare hands, throw your babes into the fire, ravage and slaughter your women – *and His heart would revel in it.* Supernatural!' He spat.

There was such scorn in his voice that Vredech wanted suddenly to turn away from the very course that he had set the Whistler upon. Wanted to taunt him back into quarrelling about their mutual reality. 'But you said that He was you, your creation, your darker self.' But the words would not form. Nor could he force himself to remember that he was listening to the ramblings of someone who was nothing more than his own creation. His senses forbade all forms of solace. Everything around him cried out that both he and the Whistler, and this silent, summer-evening world, were all real, for all it defied reason.

There is only the darkness where your ability to measure the natural ends.

He was impaled on that. Immovable.

Damn him!

The Whistler was talking again. 'If He's in your world, Allyn Vredech, and something prompted you to say He was, then He's one of you – a priest. That's how I saw Him.' He frowned, as if trying to recall something. 'And He's hung about already with an aura of carnage – drawing it in. Feeding on it. He'll be plotting, thinking, deceiving, seeking power. You'll probably find Him gently sowing disorder and discontent where He affects to bring calm and tranquillity. Find Him, Priest. *Kill Him.*'

This pronouncement seemed to cut through the balmy evening air like an icy mist. The very simplicity of its utterance gave it a chilling quality that no emotional ranting could have done, and Vredech started back in horror.

He began to stammer out, 'I can't . . .' then some furious, but almost childlike reaction welled up inside him. 'Why haven't you killed Him, if you know Him so well, if you've met Him so often?' His voice was shrill.

The Whistler seemed reluctant to answer and there was a long silence. 'I have,' he said, eventually. 'And so have others.'

'Then why . . .?'

'It's not enough,' the Whistler answered before the question was asked. 'Killing His body brings a respite to His victims of the moment – no small thing, I can assure you. But it merely cuts Him free from His own voluntary bondage. Releases Him to wander, to find another place, another time, another host. To begin again. He is endlessly patient.' He turned to Vredech, his face grim. 'And each time He comes, He spreads His ways a little wider, a little deeper. Endlessly, endlessly patient.'

'I don't understand you,' Vredech said. His head was beginning to ache again. 'If He's dead, He's dead.'

The Whistler's mouth curled into a sadly ironic smile. 'Don't you believe in souls in your religion, Priest?' he asked.

The remark flustered Vredech for a moment. 'Yes . . . the soul is that part of man that returns to the body of Ishryth on death. It's not some . . . entity, capable of wilfully taking possession of others.'

The Whistler chuckled softly to himself and shook his head with the sadness of a parent who knows he cannot begin to explain some profundity to his child. 'Never mind,' he said. 'Just accept my word in this. The death of His body is merely a setback.' He chuckled again, a little more loudly. 'One He strives murderously to avoid, I'll grant you, but only a setback for all that.'

He lay back on the grass again, his face suddenly pensive.

Vredech waited.

The Whistler played the three notes again, long, slow, plaintive. He played them several times, then he closed his eyes. 'Weak,' he said softly. 'He was weak. It comes back to me now. He was holding on like a failing climber. Clinging desperately to the tiniest crevice in a rock face. Desperately.' His eyes opened suddenly and the flute gave out a rising and anguished shriek. 'He's met a terrible foe,' he said, sitting up sharply. 'Someone who's succeeded in destroying not only His body but has reached almost into the heart of Him and struck again – scattered Him far and wide. Reduced Him to what He should have been.'

'I don't understand you,' Vredech said. His headache was getting worse and he was finding it increasingly difficult to keep pace with the shifting realities that were implied in what he was hearing.

The Whistler held up his hand for silence. 'I've heard of people – rare people – with the gift of change. Those who for some reason lie nearer to the essence of all things than most, and who can transmute it at will – air, water, earth – life itself.' He stared into the dull red sky. 'They say He searches for them always. He can use them – they ease His way between the worlds. But He fears them, too. All making is unmaking, and with their unmaking, they can destroy Him.'

He stood up suddenly. 'He is weak, He is weak, He is weak,' he said, almost rapturously. 'Perhaps now the slaying of His body alone might release that frantic fingerhold He has here. Dispatch Him for ever.' He began to move about agitatedly, looking this way and that, the flute flickering red in the dying sunlight. 'I must find Him. And I must find the changer who did this to Him.' He came to a halt, between Vredech and the final glow of the setting sun. 'As must you, Priest. Find Him. *Kill Him.*'

Vredech could stand no more. He could see only the vaguest outline of the Whistler etched into the darkness, and his head was throbbing unbearably.

'None of this is real,' he cried out furiously, making to stand up.

A scream and a startled cry greeted this outburst, and light flooded painfully into his face.

Chapter 19

Vredech closed his eyes and jerked his head away violently. The light swayed unsteadily.

'Dim the lantern, quickly,' a man's voice said, and Vredech felt powerful hands at once supporting and restraining him. The light faded. 'Gently, Brother, gently,' the voice went on. 'Don't struggle. You're safe. You must've been having a dream.'

Out of habit, Vredech mumbled, 'Don't dream,' but it was barely intelligible.

'Yes, yes,' the voice said, comfortingly but not listening.

'Whistler?' Vredech said uncertainly.

'What?' came an amused inquiry, then to someone else: 'I think he's still dreaming.'

'Is he all right?' a woman's voice asked anxiously.

There was a noncommittal grunt by way of reply. 'Brighten the lantern a little.' Vredech felt the returning light through his closed eyelids. 'Are you all right now, Brother?' the man asked. 'It's me, Skynner. You've had a fall by the look of it. Is anything hurting?'

Vredech's mind raced. Where was he? Was this another dream? Where was the Whistler? The hillside – the sunset?

'Brother?'

'I knew something like this was going to happen,' came the woman's voice again, sounding agitated. 'He's been neglecting himself so—'

'Be quiet,' Skynner said brusquely. 'Get me some water and a cloth to bathe his head.'

Vredech opened his eyes. As they slowly focused, he saw the indignant form of his housekeeper bustling from the room. Then his view was dominated by Skynner's face. There was some concern in it but the Serjeant was smiling. 'I'm having a deal of trouble with preachers falling over tonight,' he said. 'I'm beginning to think you've all broken your vows of abstinence.'

As Vredech's vision cleared, so did his mind. The perspective was strange, but he could see familiar furniture. This was his study, in his Meeting House, in Troidmallos. Skynner and House were fussing over him for some reason.

And he was on the floor!

Had a fall, Skynner had said. Yes, that was it. He must have had a fall.

The throbbing pain in his head interrupted his reasoning and he began to move his hand to it. Skynner restrained him. 'Let me have a proper look before you start meddling with it,' he said with authority. Vredech offered no resistance. Back home he might be, but the memory of the Whistler was still with him, clear and sharp. A real incident of barely a minute ago. Real and solid. Nothing like the vague memories he had had of . . . other people's dreams. He chased that thought away almost in panic. He had enough to contend with at the moment determining which reality was the true one, without fretting about whether he was suddenly having dreams now . . .

No! He mustn't even think like that. There was only one reality. Here was here, what he had known for most of his adult life. The world, or worlds, of the Whistler were some fabrication of his own imagination, however vivid they might seem. He must cling to what he had here, to what he knew. The word cling unsettled him, though. His hand tightened about Skynner's arm.

The big man winced. 'Steady,' he said, gently prising Vredech's grip open.

'Help me up,' Vredech said.

'Just wait a moment until I've finished looking at you,' Skynner ordered, his hands still prying through Vredech's hair.

Vredech protested irritably. 'Get me up, for mercy's sake. You're no physi . . . ouch!'

'Yes, there it is,' Skynner said knowingly, probing the spot on Vredech's head again, regardless of his protests. The housekeeper returned carrying a bowl of water and a cloth. Skynner motioned her to put it down on a nearby chair which she did with a conspicuous show of injured dignity despite her still obvious concern for Vredech.

'It's just a bruise,' Skynner diagnosed, wetting the cloth and placing it on Vredech's head. 'Skin's not broken. It'll be sore for a while, but—'

'An expert in blows to the head, are you?' Vredech interrupted sarcastically as he took the cloth and repositioned it.

'Oh yes,' Skynner acknowledged with a smile, tapping the baton that hung from his belt. 'A considerable expert.'

Vredech shook his head, to his immediate regret, and Skynner laughed unsympathetically. The housekeeper's indignation bubbled over, and without speaking she pushed the Keeper to one side and bent down to look at her employer. 'Are you all right, Brother?' she asked.

Vredech remembered just in time not to nod as he replied. 'Yes,' he said, patting her arm but looking past her at Skynner. 'Help me up,' he demanded, anxious to avoid House's ministrations. His head hurt like the devil and he wanted to be free of these people so that he could think, but the only way to achieve that would be to feign well-being.

Skynner hoisted him to his feet and placed him in a

238

chair. 'Always a good idea to sit on the culprit,' he said, with an encouraging grin. Vredech gave him a puzzled look. The Keeper patted the arm of the chair. 'Banged your head on the way down by the look of it,' he said.

Vredech nodded very slowly.

'It's lucky Keeper Skynner came along,' House intervened, unhappy at being on the edges of this event. 'I was just going to bed. I wouldn't have found you until the morning. Frightened me to death, you did. And I couldn't have lifted you on my own.' She turned to Skynner, gathering momentum. 'I've been telling him for weeks now to take more care of himself, not to work so hard. He's not been eating, not been sleeping properly. He should go and see—'

'Thank you, House,' Vredech managed, in the hope of stemming the pending torrent of concerns. 'All's well now. Let's be thankful that Ishryth guided Serjeant Skynner to our door when I was in need.'

'Thus let it be,' House intoned with a small but very respectful bow, just restraining herself from circling her hand over her heart.

Vredech levered himself forward in the chair and wet the cloth again. House was hovering by him as he wrung it out and lifted it gingerly back to his bruised head. Her hands were fidgeting nervously. Vredech reached up and took hold of them. 'Don't fret,' he said kindly. 'I'm all right now, truly. I just lost my balance reaching for something and tumbled off my chair, that's all.' She looked down at him unhappily. As she was about to speak again, his eye let on the dinner plate that had fallen when he had. He frowned. 'I'm sorry about the mess.'

Thankful for a simple practicality to attend to, House fluttered. 'I'll clean it up right away, Brother,' she said. She could not leave her complaint unvoiced, however, and as she was leaving the room she said, 'But it'd have been better if you'd eaten it in the first place.' She could be heard muttering to herself as she walked down the hall-way.

Skynner was grinning. 'I didn't realize you were married, Brother,' he said, after a moment.

Vredech held out his hand. 'Enough,' he commanded, with a grimace and such priestly firmness as his aching head would allow. 'Now, what can I do for you?'

House returned before Skynner could reply and for a few minutes the two men were bustled to one side while she fulfilled her duties, zealously and efficiently sweeping up the debris of Vredech's fall. Vredech mustered his best smile of reassurance and thanks when he eventually dismissed her. As soon as she had gone, however, he leaned back in the chair wearily and pressed the cloth to his head.

Skynner's face became concerned. 'You never tumbled off your seat,' he declared. 'You passed out for some reason. And you look like death. You really should—'

'Haron, I'm indebted to you for helping me just now,' Vredech interrupted determinedly. 'The least you've spared me is the consequences of spending a night on the floor, and I'm obliged. You've also probably spared House the heart seizure she'd have had if she'd been alone when she found me lying here in the morning, and I'm even more obliged for that. But I presume you weren't making a social call at this time of night. What can I do for you?'

Skynner looked a little embarrassed. 'It's awkward, Brother,' he said. 'Very awkward, actually.' He slapped his hands together and shrugged expansively. 'In fact, I'll leave it. I can come back tomorrow when you've rested.'

'Sit down, Haron,' Vredech said irritably, indicating a chair. 'All I'm suffering from is a little overwork, a headache and a mild loss of dignity, none of which is of any great consequence. You, on the other hand, wouldn't have come here at this time on any trivial matter, so tell me what it is then you can get about your business and I can hold my head in peace.'

240

Untypically, Skynner dithered for a moment, avoiding Vredech's gaze, then he cleared his throat self-consciously and, as though he were giving evidence before the Town Court, he recounted the tale of his meeting with Cassraw earlier that evening.

Vredech listened with increasing disbelief, his concerns about himself fading for the moment. Skynner finished with an uncomfortable statement to the effect that none of this was official, just for his guidance. Confidential . . .

'I understand,' Vredech said. 'I'll mention nothing to anyone without discussing it with you first. But what do you make of it?'

'I've no idea,' Skynner shrugged. 'That's why I came here.' He lowered his voice and looked from side to side uneasily. 'With all respect, I couldn't avoid the feeling that Brother Cassraw was lying to me – but about what I've no idea. I'm fairly certain that he was quite alone – there was no one else in the alley – and I got the impression that he was very agitated, excited almost.'

There was an awkward pause, both men reluctant to pursue this remark. Skynner changed direction. 'As for talking about the murder from the pulpit, I don't think the Chapter's going to be too happy. If he actually does it, that is.'

Vredech frowned. 'Nor do I,' he said. 'That kind of thing's just not done. The church has a long tradition of not meddling in temporal matters.' His face became grim. 'Since the Court of the Provers, in fact. And for that precise reason – the church is grossly unsuited to running the affairs of the country. I can't imagine what he's thinking about. There's all manner of legal and constitutional pitfalls lying in wait for him, not least his career.'

'The murder's obviously distressed him deeply,' Skynner said. 'Perhaps he finds it hard just to stand by and do nothing.'

Vredech made a vague gesture then asked unexpectedly:

241

'Is it liable to do any good, discussing it in a service?'

Skynner was openly surprised at the question. 'I can't see it doing any harm with regard to finding the murderer,' he said after a moment's thought. 'I still think whoever did it is seriously deranged. We've been through all the man's friends and enemies and found no likely suspects. It's possible that a word from the pulpit – the voice of Ishryth, as it were – might well provoke some response, but . . .' He left the sentence unfinished.

Vredech looked at him narrowly. 'Go on,' he prompted.

Skynner hesitated. 'I've no experience of this kind of killing,' he said. 'To be honest, I lie awake worrying about it, and I haven't done that in many a year.' He leaned forward intimately. 'I try to think about Jarry, and the few others we've got who're – not altogether with us. I try to put myself in their place, think about what could drive them to such a thing.'

'And?'

'I'm little the wiser for it. I know some of them say they hear voices. Some of them simply seem to want attention,' Skynner went on uncertainly. 'As I said, a plea from the pulpit might well provoke a response – but it might not be the response we want.'

It took Vredech a moment to understand. 'You mean there might be another killing?' he said, eyes widening.

Skynner shrugged.

For want of something to do, Vredech damped the cloth again, wringing it out with such force that it hurt his hands. Meticulously he shaped it into a flat pad and, wincing slightly, returned it to his bruised head.

'I shouldn't have burdened you with this,' Skynner said hurriedly, making to stand up. 'It's all conjecture. And it's Brother Cassraw's problem after all, not yours.'

Vredech motioned him back into his seat. 'Brother Cassraw's problem is the church's problem, and that makes it mine also,' he said.

But Skynner was not to be persuaded. 'No, Brother,' he said. 'I mustn't stay any longer, I've still got my rounds to do. Besides, I need to think about this some more – perhaps sleep on it.' He looked down at Vredech. 'If you'll forgive a word of advice from someone who's not only cracked heads himself but who's had his own head cracked more than a few times, you'll do the same. Let your body get on with its healing – it's wiser than any amount of physic.'

Vredech protested, but within minutes of saying fare-well to the Serjeant Keeper, he was preparing to go to bed. Only when he was actually in bed did he realize that it was the momentum of years of habit that had carried him there. He had been so preoccupied with the injury to his head and with Skynner's bizarre tale about Cassraw that he had forgotten the fear of sleeping that had been dogging him for weeks now.

And, indeed, as he lay there, his concern for his sanity returning, he realized that, for some reason, it had lost much of its force. His earlier intuitions had been right. Something *was* grievously amiss, something deeply myste-rious and frightening. It had come on the day that the black clouds had loomed over the land like Judgement Day, and lured Cassraw up towards their heart. He recalled with extraordinary vividness the cold alien pres-ence that had touched him amid the dancing shadows and, too, Cassraw's condition when he had first emerged from the darkness: the gleam in his eye, the authority of his manner – the *arrogance*! And then, seemingly, it had all vanished after his strange collapse and equally strange awakening. But had it disappeared? Since then, Cassraw had been like a strained copy of the man he had been many years before: efficient, diligent, hard-working, filling his Meeting House with the power of his preaching. What was there to be faulted in this? Vredech had no answer, but the Whistler's words rang in his ears.

'He'll be plotting, thinking, deceiving, seeking power.'

Then too, he recalled, 'He's one of you. A priest – hung about already with an aura of carnage – drawing it in, feeding on it.'

What had Cassraw been doing in that awful alley? Excited, Skynner said he had been. Vredech closed his eyes as if the darkness of the room was insufficient to hide the thoughts that were coming to him. Part of him wanted to thrust them away, but another carried with it the open curiosity that had pervaded him when he had been in the presence of the Whistler. Had this awful figure of which the Whistler had spoken, taken possession of Cassraw? Certainly the Cassraw who had strode down the mountain had been charged with some great resolution. And, on being opposed at the door of the Debating Hall, had he not retreated from immediate exposure, to return later, patience renewed, to plot and scheme in silence?

Reproaches filled Vredech's mind, but he ploughed relentlessly on. Cassraw's apology to the Chapter had restored their goodwill towards him in its entirety. The vision of Cassraw surrounded by the Chapter Brothers – himself included – almost like acolytes, as they had been leaving the Witness House, returned to complete the picture for him.

It could be, Vredech decided, that he was being unjust – perhaps even obsessively so. Seeing things which simply were not there. Motivated perhaps by some hidden jealousy of his friend. But it could do no conceivable harm to watch, to listen, to think – could it? And perhaps the Whistler was nothing more than a figment of his imagination, yet there had been an honesty in their last encounter that seemed to have washed away many of his torments, even though he had been given no easy comfort. Here also, what harm could be done by pondering this meeting, this vividly intense meeting?

He smiled to himself. It could not have been real, of

course. *This* was real: blankets, sheets, pillows, familiar sounds and smells, Skynner, House, a whole lifetime of memories. Yet, as he was hovering halfway between sleeping and waking, and his hand came up to lie on the pillow by his face, was there not a faint hint of the scented evening flower that the Whistler had given to him on the hillside?

The question barely formed itself before he slipped into sleep.

That night he found himself dreaming again, or visiting someone else's dream. He was, and was not, the dreamer. At once a spectator and a participant. Strange images came and went; bizarre, illogical events unfolded quite sensibly. But now he was unconcerned. He was quieter. He would watch and listen, and learn. To debate reality too closely was to pick healthy flesh until it became the open wound that was feared in the first place. He would be what he was, where he was. He would not be afraid of the darkness that stood where his ability to measure the natural ended.

When he woke the following morning, Vredech's headache was gone, although the bruise was still tender, and he was relaxed and rested. He got out of bed slowly and performed his rising habits with a gentle delight as though they had been part of one of the sacred ceremonies of Ishrythan. As indeed perhaps they were, he thought.

He offered a silent prayer of thanks to Ishryth for giving him the strength to learn.

Then he ate a substantial and smiling breakfast to appease the stern and searching eye of the goddess of his hearth.

Cassraw stared out across the crowded Meeting House. It was good. Every place on the stern upright benches was full, people were actually sitting in the three aisles, and the open space at the back of the hall was crowded. Through the open doors beyond, he could see the heads of many others craning to see and to hear what he was about to say. Pride surged through him. No one – *no one* – had filled a Meeting House like this since the great days of Ishrythan when attendance had been a matter of law, and failure to do so a matter to be accounted for before the Court of the Provers.

Very slowly he looked across the entire congregation, as if to impose his will on each member of it individually. An unusually high number were robed and hooded, following the old tradition that worshippers should enter the church in humility and free from all outward show of vanity. They added a mysterious dignity to the atmosphere of the place. Of those who were unhooded, he recognized many of his own flock, but for each of these there must have been two strange faces. Laggard attenders from his own parish? People from other parishes? Even some foreigners, judging by their dress. But it did not matter. Nor did it matter whether they were drawn by the rumour of what he was about to say, or by his rapidly spreading fame as a great preacher. It mattered only that they were here, because in being here, they were his. For he was the Chosen One and this was *his* Meeting House, and what was said and done here was determined by him and him alone. All who came to listen would be brought to know that, and would lay themselves open to receive His word. They would learn that they must sacrifice their own petty concerns and desires for the greater good, for the restoring of the church of Ishrythan to its former splendour and power, so that His will might once again sweep out across the world and bring order to all.

Something inside him stirred in expectation.

'Great is Thy power, Lord,' Cassraw said.

'Thus let it be,' the congregation intoned.

Cassraw's prayer had been a spontaneous utterance, not the beginning of the peroration he had been intending. Nor had it been spoken with the power that he knew he

246

could use to overwhelm a large audience. The congregation's response therefore was totally unexpected. Its ragged but massive power rolled over him like a great wave, and for a moment he felt as if he were drowning in it. Panic swept through him; his planned words fled. He was going to be left gaping and foolish before this mob, this motley assortment.

He had been abandoned!

And as if to accentuate his peril, his eye lit on Privv, leaning against the wall at the back of the hall. He was here for one reason only, to find something to write in his Sheet. Cassraw knew only too well that though he might at the moment have secured Privv as an ally, it was an uncertain alliance, and a rambling, incoherent performance now would see him doubly damned – once before this immediate congregation and again through the successive distorting lenses of the Sheets as the tale was told and retold through the following days. Then he saw Albor standing near to Privv. Difficult to recognize out of his Keeper's uniform, he stood expectant and respectful, but to Cassraw he felt like the hard focus of this entire happening: the solitary speck about which it had all coalesced. He could willingly have cursed him into oblivion for his unknowing part in the gathering of this crowd.

Cassraw's hand tightened purposefully about the rail that fringed the pulpit while he fought to regain control of himself. Years of experience held him motionless, save for his eyes as they continued their now sightless examination of the congregation. Not the slightest indication of his inner turmoil radiated from him.

And finally he was looking into the eyes of his wife, sitting immediately below him and dressed in a simple black robe with the hood drawn back. She made no movement nor gave any perceptible sign, but he felt her presence flooding powerfully through him. He was filled with desire for her. And even as the echoes of the unexpected response were dying away, Cassraw's doubts left him.

The presence within him bloomed.

All was well. It had been but another trial. Had he not been told? *'Know that I will be with you always, Cassraw. Always. You have but to listen.'*

He spoke.

'Darkness came upon the land.'

His words filled the hall, silencing the petty shufflings of his audience.

'And I ascended into it and was struck down.'

The silence deepened.

'And as I lay alone in the darkness, full of pain and fear, He revealed a vision to me.'

'Praise Him. Praise Him.'

The cry, not loud, but full of passion, rose from someone in the congregation. There was some head-turning. That kind of enthusiastic participation was a feature of the smaller, rural Meeting Houses, where a simpler, less sophisticated religion might be practised. It was not done in the most urban Meeting Houses and certainly not in the Haven.

The heads turned sharply back to Cassraw however, at his next words.

'Praise Him, indeed, my child. Praise Him, indeed. For in this vision I saw our country, as from a great height. I saw our country, divided and weak, the butt of its neighbours' whims, and on the verge of being led into a terrible decay.'

Silence.

'And as my eyes misted over at this sight, so I was raised still higher, until I could see all the lands of Gyronlandt. The *divided* lands of Gyronlandt. And I could see its many peoples being led inexorably into sin and destruction by base rulers and false gods. Being led, my children, into a

248

future when all must surely be torn asunder.'

He lowered his voice almost to a whisper. 'And the vision spread such things before me as I can scarcely tell you. I was shown far distant lands. Lands unknown to us.' His voice grew gradually louder. 'Unknown except for the taint of Ahmral that could be seen upon them also. Dividing kin against kin. Paving the wide and downward road into the everlasting perdition that awaits those who turn their faces against the Lord.'

As Cassraw's voice rose to fill the hall, Vredech, seated near the back, his face concealed in the darkness of a deep hood, frowned. He had listened carefully to his friend's sonorous voice, rising, falling, pausing, rushing on, burying itself deep into its audience, subtly carrying it along. Now he was frowning, not only because of what Cassraw was saying but because, despite himself, he felt the hairs on his arms tingling at the touch of this powerful oratory, and it was only with an effort of will that he forced himself to listen to the true content of the words, and their practised manipulation.

'Thus let it be, thus let it be.'

The solitary voice, louder now, and full of judgement, rose again from the body of the hall. Several others echoed it. Cassraw straightened up and leaned forward.

'Thus it *will* be, my children. Thus it *will* be. Is it not written so?' And as his voice rose with the question, so his hand slammed down on the ornate copy of the Santyth that rested on the lectern by his side. The sound made the whole congregation start.

Cassraw caught them before the movement could turn into an inattentive restlessness.

'But . . .' He paused and scanned the congregation as he had at the beginning. 'Thus it will be with us also.'

'No,' came the voice again.

'Yes.' Cassraw's contradiction swept the denial aside. 'Unworthy as I am, I have been chosen to bring this vision

249

to you. And if, having been given this vision, we stand aside, then yes, thus it will be with us also. If we do not first mend our own ways and then, strong in our own virtue, reach out to these benighted peoples to bring them to the truth then, yes, thus it will be with us also.'

Silence.

'For in my vision I was shown also what can be brought to pass. I was shown how warring differences can be transformed into peace, into calm and tranquillity. As I turned from this awful sight, I saw in the distance, bright against a golden sky, a solitary silver star. His star. The One True Light.'

'Praise Him, praise Him.' Many voices were raised now, picking up the rhythm of Cassraw's speech.

'And by its light I saw our small land here made whole, and from this mended land I saw multitudes marching forth to win the hearts of all the peoples of Gyronlandt and unite them under His sacred banner.'

Vredech shuddered. He had come secretly out of genuine concern for what he had believed Cassraw was about to do, and so that he might have an accurate account of it. But now he knew that he himself would have to raise what he had heard with the Chapter. Perhaps even ask Mueran to call a special Chapter Meeting with the intention of reprimanding Cassraw.

Yet even as these thoughts formed, part of Vredech was responding to what he was hearing. For a moment it seemed as though he were standing on the Ervrin Mallos again, amid dark, flickering shadows. Voices lured him on. 'Follow. Follow. Let all be united under the church. Let there be peace, let there be order. Follow.' The prospect, heightened by Cassraw's telling, genuinely thrilled. And the effect of the words on those around him was undeniable. The congregation was becoming a single entity, all reason gone. A single will. The will of Enryc Cassraw.

The realization sobered Vredech. As on the mountain, and for no logical reason that he could fathom, he called out silently, 'Leave me, Ahmral's spawn, leave me.'

He thought he heard a distant laughter.

Cassraw was continuing, his voice rolling on. 'My children, Canol Madreth is nearing a time of testing, of proving. We shall need all our strength, all our resolution. I am a poor vessel to bear the burden with which I have been charged. But carry this hesitant and inadequate telling of the wonder of my vision away with you. Ponder it. Let it sustain you, guide you, when the time for decision comes. For that time will be sooner than you realize.' He paused significantly and held up his own small copy of the Santyth. 'Much more was shown to me. Much more. What was dark and confused has been made clear and lucid. I shall speak further of it at another time.'

'Thus let it be. Thus let it be.'

Cassraw made no response, but stood with his head bowed for a long time, as though in private contemplation. When he eventually looked up, his face was grim. As too was his voice, even more powerful and penetrating than before as he continued. 'To those of you who doubt this revelation, know that He sees all, knows all. No secret can be hidden from Him; no crime concealed. If your heart is soiled with evil thoughts, if your hands are stained with goods or coin dishonestly won, with cruel deeds . . .' he paused . . .'or with blood,' the phrase hung in the air, 'know then that you are discovered and that unless you purge yourselves of these sins, the time of your punishment is near. *Very* near. As it is for all those who defy His will.'

The light in the hall seemed to dim in response to this ominous conclusion.

Then Cassraw held out his hand, the fingers stretched wide. 'Go in His peace, all of you, and prepare yourselves for what is to come. I shall remain here to pray for you all

251

for a little while. When I have finished, the doors will be opened again and those of you who wish to begin the purging of your sins and set your feet back on the true path may return. Thus let it be.'

The congregation's response of, 'Thus let it be,' was far from automatic. It was larded with excitement and passion and cries of, 'Praise Him, praise Him.'

Vredech sat motionless, stunned by what he had heard and shaken by what he had felt. He was an experienced enough preacher himself to see that Cassraw's words had been rambling rhetoric, theatrically and, he had to concede, brilliantly presented with the specific intention of provoking an emotional response from his congregation. To a certain extent this was a respected tradition in Ishrythan – 'Put the fear of Ishryth in them. Put them by Ahmral's fireside.' And congregations expected fearsome, rousing sermons from time to time, sermons that would send them home shivering and bring them to the Meeting House more diligently for the next few weeks. Their effect was both cathartic and restraining: they were adult versions of the frightening tales told to and loved by children. Horld's 'fireside' sermons were particularly famous for their colourful rhetoric, and vivid, not to say technically sound, representations of Ahmral's furnaces. In his absence, they were a source of some envious jocularity amongst his peers.

But there were unwritten rules to such sermons. They must be built around a text from the Santyth and, in the end, uplift and sustain; hold out hope of redemption, albeit through sweat and toil, the foregoing of self-indulgence and, not least, regular attendance at the Meeting House. Cassraw had not observed these rules. His words had actually been less overtly frightening than those of many another preacher, but they had not been taken from the Santyth, and they had been full of dark and unresolved portents. And menace, Vredech realized slowly, quite awful menace, though whether it was the words, or the way they had been spoken, he could not say. Probably both, he decided.

And, too, Cassraw had made openly political statements. Vredech had come in fear of hearing some indiscreet reference to a secular matter in the form of the murder. To have heard again the old cry of strength through a united Gyronlandt was almost beyond belief. For a frightening moment he wondered whether he had not slipped into an eerie dream again. He half-expected to see the Whistler appear in front of him. But no. He put his hand on the back of the bench in front of him and looked around the hall. This *was* the Haven Meeting House, and he had heard what he had heard. A united Gyronlandt! For mercy's sake, what atrocities had not been committed in answer to that obscene siren call?

He stood up and looked at the departing congregation. The sight of them further heightened his concern. One thing about Cassraw's harangue was certain: he was a powerful preacher, and no part of it had been fortuitous. The whole thing had been deliberately planned to have a specific effect on his audience. And the congregation was not leaving as it normally would, in a subdued and patient shuffle, taking the leisurely walk along the aisles as an opportunity to return, as it were, from the spiritual world to the 'real' one. Vredech saw anxiety and urgency, and too, some bewilderment and fear. There was even some nervous laughter – an unheard-of sound in a Meeting House. But, most frightening of all, many of the faces he could see were alight with . . . the word that he did not want to hear crawled, hissing, into his mind like a serpent.

Fanaticism.

Ishryth protect us, he thought, and his hand almost circled about his heart. What dreadful tinder had the fire of Cassraw's words struck light to?

And how did it come there to be so easily lit?

'I saw Him rising to fill the sky, His great night cloak swallowing up the holy mountain and covering the whole land. I heard His cries turn from despair to rejoicing; a terrible rejoicing as I travelled the dreamway. Horrible. Horrible. And now He walks amongst us again.'

'He was holding on like a failing climber.'

The words of Jarry and the Whistler flooded suddenly into Vredech's mind, making him start. Whatever the Whistler was – strange reality or figment – Jarry was real and solid, and his reaction to the cloud had not been all that dissimilar to his own. Then more of the Whistler's words returned to him. 'You'll probably find Him gently sowing disorder and discontent where He affects to bring calm and tranquillity.'

Calm and tranquillity – Cassraw's very words. For a moment, Vredech felt sick, and his turmoil about the true nature of the Whistler returned to him. The coincidence between Cassraw's words and those of Jarry and the Whistler could well be just that – coincidence, but he could find no solace in this. Cassraw's sermon had been truly frightening, as, too, had been its effect on the congregation.

Vredech stood up and joined the crowd. As he reached the Meeting House door, he turned and looked back. Cassraw was standing motionless in the gloom of the pulpit, his head bowed, a stark black form against the pale grey of the stonework. Like an entrance to some other place, Vredech thought. Or from it . . .

He dismissed the thought angrily, disturbed by it.

Outside, the brightness of the afternoon made him blink for a moment, and the dark-clad figures dispersing about him blurred into dancing shadows. Then they were people again. He noted a number of young men wearing the sash of Cassraw's Knights of Ishryth, and a frisson of distaste skittered across the surface of his deeper concerns. Try as he might, he found it hard to warm to Cassraw's notion that this group served any useful purpose. He was not disposed to debate it with himself here, however. It was a trivial matter indeed in comparison with what had just happened.

He noted, too, that a large number of people were simply standing, waiting.

Waiting to have their sins purged, I suppose, he thought angrily. Not content with making political pronouncements from the pulpit, Cassraw was approaching outright blasphemy with such an idea. Vredech wanted to throw back his hood and denounce these people for the fools they were, chase them back to their homes to ponder their sins and learn from them, not seek to have them in some way undone. Calmer counsels prevailed, however, and, head bowed, he walked quickly down the steps of the Meeting House and off along the path that led towards the main gates.

As he strode out, he heard footsteps running behind him. He turned and a hand took his arm lightly.

'Allyn,' a woman's voice said.

Chapter 20

The woman was as tall as Vredech, with long black hair framing a slim, well-defined face. Her figure, too, was slim – though even dressed in a dark formal robe and cloak, the impression she gave was one of wiry toughness rather than willowy softness.

The hand on his arm tightened a little in confirmation of this.

'I was looking all around the congregation for you.' Her voice fell to an amused whisper. 'I didn't think you'd be here in secret, but as soon as I saw you getting angry at the people standing around here I recognized you. There was no mistaking that posture.'

Still preoccupied with his response to Cassraw's sermon, Vredech stared at her vacantly for a moment. Then his mouth dropped open.

'Nertha! What are you doing here?'

The woman raised her eyebrows. 'How nice to see you, Nertha. It's been such a long time. How are you? Well, I hope.'

Vredech floundered. 'I'm sorry,' he stuttered. 'You caught me completely by surprise. I didn't recognize . . . I mean, I never expected . . . I—'

'Coherent as ever, Preacher,' Nertha said mockingly, though the gentle taunt did not reach the brown eyes which were searching anxiously into the darkness of Vredech's hood. Her hands rose a little, nervously, as though to throw it back, but changed their mind.

Vredech looked around at the crowd. People were still leaving, but the number of those who were standing about waiting was growing.

'I must get away from here before I do something foolish,' he said. 'Come on.'

A group of Cassraw's Knights of Ishryth were standing by the gates and as Vredech and Nertha approached, one of them stepped forward.

'Do you not wish to have your sins purged, pilgrim?' he asked politely, but with an air of slightly surprised dismay.

Vredech stiffened. ' "At the Day of Judgement shall your sins be weighed and judged",' he said, quoting the Santyth. 'And think on this, young man: "Follow no prophets, for I shall send ye none".' His voice was soft but the anger in it was unmistakable. The youth's smile became vacuous and he glanced uneasily from side to side, as if searching for a response to this rebuke. Vredech gave him no opportunity to find one, but strode past purposefully. Two others who were approaching, obviously bearing the same gift, turned away sharply and headed towards easier prey.

Nertha followed Vredech. 'What in the world's happening, Allyn?' she asked, pacing easily alongside him. 'I've never heard preaching like that before. And who are these people in the sashes?'

'What are you doing here, Nertha?' Vredech interrupted, the anger from his encounter with the youth still colouring his speech. He knew it for a mistake as soon as the words were spoken.

'I'm here because House sent me a message saying she was worried about you,' Nertha retorted, reflecting his anger back at him and adding her own. 'Though I don't know why I bothered. You always were a bad-tempered sod when the mood took you.'

Vredech raised his hand. 'Peace, Nertha,' he pleaded. 'I'm sorry. I'm afraid, answering your question, a lot's been happening lately, not least within the last hour. And most of it bad.' He put a hand to his head. 'You must forgive me. My mind's still reeling from what I've just heard. I can hardly believe it.' Then, he forced himself to veer away from the subject and attempted some social nicety. 'House worries too much, but it's good to see you again. I think about you . . .'

'Every few months or so.'

'A lot, I was about to say.'

He stopped walking and threw back his hood. He was smiling, though the smile became a little strained as he watched Nertha's eyes examining him shrewdly. They were filling with open concern.

'I've been a bit out of sorts lately,' he began defensively.

'You look awful,' Nertha pronounced.

Vredech grimaced at the typical bluntness. 'I've been a bit off-colour lately,' he persisted, taking her hand reassuringly and setting off again. 'But I'm through it. I'm sure House has told you that I'm eating and sleeping properly now. She *is* my regular jailer, you know. And I presume you've seen her, since you apparently knew where to find me.'

Nertha grunted, non-committally.

They turned into a side street. It was very steep, obliging them to walk more slowly. The change of pace seemed to dissipate some of the tension between them. Vredech smiled again. 'House shouldn't have worried you – she knows I'm all right now. By the way, how did she know where you were?' Without waiting for a reply he went on, a little too heartily: 'Never mind. I mightn't be married, but I know enough about the endless cunning of women. Speaking of which, shouldn't you be assisting your learned Felden doctor in his work instead of chasing across the country after me?'

His manner forced a smile out of Nertha. 'No,' she said. 'He's packed me off.' Vredech's false geniality faded and

258

his eyes widened with surprise and pending indignation. 'He said he'd taught me all he could and that I'd have to learn on my own now,' she added. The indignation became open admiration.

'A considerable teacher,' Vredech said. 'I wish I'd had some like that when I was a novice. Some of them still haven't let go. Still, there was no need for you to come all this way.'

'Someone other than Ishryth has to keep an eye on you.'

Vredech let out an exasperated breath. 'Just like Father. As irreverent as ever, I see,' he said.

Nertha grinned. 'You hear, you mean,' she said, gently mocking again. 'But I've most dutifully been to service today, haven't I? And respectfully dressed, too.' She swirled her cloak.

Vredech eyed her suspiciously.

'Mind you, that was only because I was visiting the sick,' she said.

'As *irredeemable* as ever,' he concluded.

'I'm afraid so, Brother brother. I've not seen anything yet that will make me change my mind. In fact, after what I've just heard I'm not only even less enchanted with Ishrythan and your chosen vocation, I'm quite alarmed.'

It was an old debate, long exhausted between them, and substantially free from rancour now. Nertha had been found abandoned as a baby, and had been taken in and reared by Vredech's parents as one of their own. Though they knew of their true relationship, she and Vredech had grown up together as brother and sister and as friends – albeit at times stormy ones – an inevitable consequence of living under the influence of such a father. Only when Vredech had turned to the Church had there been any serious breach between them. Nertha, ironically taking more after her adoptive father than his true son, had taken much longer to come to terms with the decision. Subsequently she had gone to study medicine in Tirfelden under the aegis of a noted Felden physician.

Vredech frowned. 'That's not the church, Nertha, that's Cassraw. I don't know what's happening but . . .' He gesticulated vaguely. 'I have the feeling that I'm on some huge wagon that is beginning to move, and which nothing will be able to stop until it comes to a terrible crashing end.'

'Well, that's quite dramatic, but not very helpful,' Nertha said. 'You wouldn't care to be a little more specific, would you?'

Vredech smiled faintly as he heard his father's voice yet again. 'I'd be delighted to be more specific,' he said acidly. 'But unfortunately I can't.'

The top of the street opened out into a small square. Surrounded by buildings which were smaller than was typical in Troidmallos, the square had a pleasant, airy atmosphere, and offered an excellent view not only of the Ervrin Mallos, but also many of the neighbouring peaks. As was normal on Service Day, there were quite a few people 'taking the air'. Some were sitting on benches, talking, reading, or dozing, while others strolled to and fro in a leisurely manner. Such children as were present were unnaturally stiff in their Service Day clothes and Service Day manners, and were patently unhappy.

'Ah, the Madren at play,' Nertha said.

Vredech refused to rise to the bait. He felt suddenly as though a burden had been lifted from him. 'I'm really glad to see you, Nertha,' he said as the two of them instinctively slowed down to match the gait of the strollers. He looked at her intently. 'You're probably the only person I can speak to about what's been happening, without you thinking I'm going mad.'

Nertha smiled and did what she had been wanting to do since their first encounter. She reached up and touched his face. 'You've lost weight,' she said.

Vredech did not argue. 'I know,' he said. 'But that's

260

over with now. I told you, I'm through that.' Briefly he became a small boy again. 'Ask House, she'll tell you I'm eating and sleeping properly now.'

'Well, apart from your chronic religious mania, which goes on undiminished, you seem alert enough,' Nertha conceded. 'And you're intriguing me with your hints and suggestions.' She linked his arm. 'Tell me everything.'

And, as they walked on through the town, he did.

Even as he talked, Vredech was more than a little surprised that his tale did not emerge into the daylight sounding awkward and embarrassed, a night phantom which shrivelled at the touch of the sun. As he had when young, he told her everything that he could recall. Not logically – for it was hardly a logical tale – but at least chronologically. Once and once only did she look at him narrowly to see whether this was some kind of a joke on his part. She did not look thus again, and on the few occasions afterwards when she seemed inclined to interrupt, she remained silent.

As did they both for some time after he had finished. 'I see what you mean about being thought mad,' Nertha said eventually. 'If it wasn't for the fact that I know you so well, and that you've no imagination worthy of the name, and if I hadn't heard Cassraw's bizarre sermon with my own ears, I'd probably have concluded you were.'

'But?'

'But I don't know,' Nertha said. 'My eyes tell me you've been ill without a doubt. My head tells me you've probably had some kind of a brain fever. But my heart . . .'

She looked around. They were walking along a tree-lined avenue, through one of the most prosperous parts of the Haven Parish. Stout timber balconies on corbelling stonework, ornate windows and decorated doors, steep roofs broken by ranks of delicate chimneys and occasional, seemingly random, turrets and spires, marked the houses of the area, both private and community, that stood with

261

unassailable confidence amid their well-tended gardens. Now and then, an expensive carriage trotted past the two walkers. No fantasy could survive such conspicuous reality. Yet . . .

'My heart tells me something else. Even here, there's something odd . . . in the wind. I don't know what it is.' Nertha suddenly pulled a wry face. 'It's probably because I've been fretting about you for days, while I've been travelling, that's all. I can't, in all conscience, bring myself to *believe* in this Whistler character you've invented. It's just not possible.'

'You know everything there is to know about reality then, do you?' Vredech asked, immediately wishing he could bite back the words. Her familiar assertive tone had provoked him a little, but he didn't want to become involved in a pointless debate.

'I know there's a difference between discussing interesting possibilities into the early hours of the morning with friends, and actually believing in them,' she replied, more gently than he had expected, as if she, too, wanted to avoid one of their old arguments. 'I must start from where I am.' She held out both her hands, unbalancing Vredech slightly. 'I must take these and what they can touch as real, philosophical considerations notwithstanding. I must fix a point to stand on even if I concede that it's arbitrary, you know that. That's why . . .' She waved her hand to end the remarks, and returned to her main concern.

'It's odd that you've started to dream after all these years. Perhaps, as you say, it's some trick of your mind that's making you discuss problems with yourself that you can't otherwise face. I've known similar things in patients before, and we all do it to some extent. Whatever the cause, whatever the . . . reality . . . I can see no harm coming from just . . . listening . . . to such inner debates. Thinking about them.' She looked at him anxiously. 'If you're at ease with that.'

Vredech smiled. 'I am – reasonably,' he said. 'Though it's taken its toll to get that far, as you can see. And don't worry, Cassraw might think that Ishryth spoke to him on the mountain, but I'm not mad enough to go telling anyone except you what's been happening to me.' He laid his hand over hers, still linked through his arm. 'But the Whistler was intensely real. Very different from a dream. Or at least the dreams I've been having . . . entering . . . anyway. I seized his wrist at one point – he felt very solid, and very strong – and I could still smell the evening flowers from that hillside when I . . . came back. I have to follow Father's advice – keep an open mind. Can you do that?'

Nertha raised her eyebrows as though she had just been given the benefit of the wisdom of a precocious four year old. '*Me* keep an open mind? I shan't even grace that with an answer, you shaman,' she retorted with affected indignation.

'You just dismissed it all out of hand a moment ago,' Vredech reminded her.

Nertha floundered. 'Not completely. I said—'

'You dismissed it out of hand. "Just not possible", you said.'

Nertha's mouth briefly became a straight peevish line. 'That was just—'

'A manner of speaking?'

'A first reaction to a very strange story,' she replied sternly. 'Which, you'll concede, it is. If one of your flock had brought it to you, what would *you* have done?'

Vredech accepted the point.

'I'll keep my mind open all right,' Nertha went on, quite intense now, 'because I trust you completely and because I trust that's the way through to the truth of what's going on. Speaking of which – if, as you say, you seem to be over whatever was troubling you, then I think perhaps you need to turn your mind to some serious practical problems.'

'Cassraw, you mean?'

'Cassraw indeed,' Nertha replied. 'The man's raving, and, with his talent for oratory, probably dangerous. Who knows what harm'll come of it, if people start to believe him?'

Vredech grimaced. 'I'll have to go to the Witness House tomorrow. Talk with Mueran. Not that I think he's going to be much use, but it's church business and I can't do anything on my own.' The grimace became a frown. 'That wretched Sheeter Privv was there too. He must have smelt something in the wind. Cassraw's sermon was grotesque enough but I shudder to think of the version that will be all over Troidmallos tomorrow.' He stopped suddenly and looked keenly at Nertha. 'That's what you said, isn't it? Something in the wind.'

Nertha returned his gaze with studious blandness. Vredech recognized the look.

'My turn,' he said knowingly. 'What did you mean?'

Nertha wrinkled her nose and made a vague gesture with her free hand. 'Nothing,' she said, after rather too long a pause. 'It was just . . .' The hand waved again.

'A manner of speaking?' Vredech offered again.

Nertha nodded. 'In this case, yes,' she agreed, now avoiding his gaze.

'You were a little out of sorts with the travelling? Concern for your Brother brother?'

'Yes, I . . .' She stopped and coloured a little.

Vredech went on in the same helpful tone. 'You thought you could fob me off with any old tale?'

'All right, all right,' Nertha said darkly. 'I'm sorry. I should know better than to try to out-wriggle you, you worm.'

Vredech became unexpectedly serious. 'Open minds, Nertha,' he said. 'It's important.'

'Why the concern over a trivial remark, Allyn?' Nertha asked.

'Nothing's trivial, Nertha, we both know that. Only from the least can come the greatest. You made the remark, it's come back to me, you're embarrassed by it. It's enough. Bear with me. Tell me why you said there was something odd in the wind.'

'I don't really know,' Nertha said, after a long pause. 'It's just a feeling I have. It may be, as you said, the travelling, the worrying. I don't know.'

Vredech waited. They had left the Haven Parish and were nearing his own Meeting House. The high clouds overhead were thickening, taking from the streets the faint wash of pleasant sunlight. A breeze had started to blow, bringing with it a slight chill.

Nertha made a peculiar gesture. She ran her thumb across the tips of her fingers as though testing the delicacy of fine silk. 'I have this feeling of . . . difference . . . all around,' she said. 'Almost as if something's actually in the air. I can't explain it. It's not nice, Allyn. It's a bad feeling.'

Once he would have taunted her mercilessly for such a remark, and a fine quarrel would have ensued. Now, he simply pressed her hand.

'A bad feeling,' she went on, almost talking to herself now. 'That's why I didn't want to acknowledge it. I never do.' She turned to Vredech. 'They're not usually a good omen, my bad feelings. They frequently mean I can't help someone any further.'

Vredech met the pain in her eyes. Dealing with suffering was ground common to them both.

'But that's people you're talking about,' he said. 'Your own kind. Not a town.'

Nertha shook her head. 'It's me,' she said. 'Me, being open to whatever's around me. Picking up the signs too subtle for my eyes, my ears, my nose, my hands.'

Vredech smiled slightly. 'So you brought your reason to bear on your intuition in the end, did you?'

265

Nertha shrugged. 'They don't exclude one another. Besides, the whys and the wherefores aren't important. It's the trusting that matters. And I do trust these feelings. Even when they're wrong, the fault's usually mine – misunderstanding, doubting, failing to accept things as they are.' She closed her eyes as if gathering courage. 'Don't ask me to be specific, Allyn, but something *has* happened . . . or is happening. Something bad.'

Despite the grimness in her voice, the atmosphere between them had become very relaxed.

'If I can't ask you anything specific about it, then that leaves us with quite a problem, doesn't it?' Vredech said. 'Namely, what is it that's happened, and what can we do about it?'

Nertha smiled apologetically. 'Just watch and listen, I suppose,' she said. 'Like you've already decided to do.'

They finished the rest of their journey in silence, neither feeling the need or the urge to speak.

Vredech held his own service in the early evening. As if fired by Cassraw's rhetoric, he laid passionate emphasis on those parts of the Santyth that counselled tolerance and compassion, that pointed to the similarities between all peoples rather than their differences, and that, above all, declared each individual to be responsible and accountable for his own deeds. He concluded with the faintly ominous quotation he had given the youth who accosted him at the gates to the Haven Meeting House: ' "Follow no prophets, for I shall send ye none",' but this time he gave it a massive and threatening ring.

'Splendid stuff,' Nertha commented afterwards. 'You sounded almost as if you were drawing up battle lines. What a pity there were so few present to hear it.'

'My fault, that. I've not been at my best these past few weeks. I'll start doing some repair work tomorrow. And yes, I think I was drawing up battle lines. I can't preach personal responsibility and then ignore it when I see something happen that shouldn't.'

'Meaning?'

'Meaning that no matter why he did it, Cassraw was wrong to preach as he did today and I must convince Mueran to make a stand or it'll happen again. Like you, I'm far from happy about where such a thing might lead. There are a great many gullible people about who could be hurt as a consequence of such ranting.'

Then he and Nertha, in contrast to the companionable silence they had maintained on the latter part of their walk from the Haven Meeting House, talked long and enthusiastically into the early hours of the morning. They reminisced, gossiped, philosophized, argued, and generally brought one another up to date with their respective affairs. It was a good time.

That night Vredech neither dreamed nor entered the dreams of anyone else. Nor did he encounter the Whistler, though he was thinking of him as he slipped into sleep, softly whistling the three haunting notes to himself. He slept peacefully.

He did not wake thus, however. Normally, House roused him gently with a delicate tapping on his door, but today she roused the whole house by slamming the main door as she returned from market.

'Are we on fire?' Vredech asked, sitting bolt upright as, following a single powerful knock and awaiting no invitation, House strode into his room. She hurled a copy of Privv's Sheet on to the bed with the injunction, 'Look at that!' accompanied by: 'And keep the ink off my sheets!'

Chapter 21

Privv's Sheet landed with unusual force on more than Vredech's bed that morning. Serjeant Skynner pored over a copy in his office at the Keeperage. Like Vredech he had attended Cassraw's service anonymously to ensure that he had a true report, and, like Vredech, he had been deeply disturbed by what he had heard.

Cassraw's actual sermon however, was an almost trifling affair compared with the version that appeared in Privv's Sheet. Here was written a call for Canol Madreth to make a stand against the moral and spiritual decay that was to be found throughout Gyronlandt: to begin the battle that would lead to a united Gyronlandt. The report was riddled with martial imagery – the word 'crusade' kept recurring, and there was Canol Madreth 'besieged', the Church 'taking arms against', and so on. Skynner shook his head in disbelief. How many drunken brawls had he seen broken up with the participants singing patriotic songs and bellowing for a united Gyronlandt? The whole notion invariably implied 'dealing with' those countries who were perceived as being the cause of the disunity, and great passions about it were easily roused even though there was no corresponding unity of opinion as to which countries these were. There were also some fairly direct references in the Sheet to the Heindral's hesitancy in dealing with the problem of compensation from the government of Tirfelden for the murdered merchant. Skynner did not even want to think about the prospect of the two ideas being thus linked.

Further, a subtle menace pervaded the text. Not to be With, was to be Against. People should publicly demonstrate – prove – the renewal of their fidelity to the church and its doctrines. It was understated, but it was there beyond a doubt.

It occurred to Skynner, not for the first time, that some restraint should be put on what was presented in the Sheets. Privv's writing was a travesty of the truth which, for mercy's sake, was serious enough in itself and well worthy of accurate reporting. Either Privv was appallingly incompetent or he was being wilfully malicious – though to what end, Skynner could not imagine. In any event, neither incompetence nor malice were acceptable in someone whose vocation was supposed to be that of informing the public of important affairs. It did not help Skynner's peace of mind that it was a brilliant piece of writing, as brilliant as Cassraw's sermon had been.

Still, he was only a Serjeant Keeper and while it suited the Heinders of all parties to allow these people free rein, what could he do about it? It was unlikely that any steps would be taken to curb them until one of the Sheeters turned rabidly on the Heindral itself – and he doubted even Privv was that reckless.

One thing he could do however, was to make sure that his captain at least – when he condescended to turn up – knew the difference between what Cassraw had actually said and Privv's unbridled imaginings. The more people in authority who were aware of the truth, the better.

Skynner left his office and strode towards the Keepers' room where the men were preparing to leave on their daily patrols. There was an almost excited atmosphere in the room as he entered, and he frowned as he saw that several of those present were engrossed in Privv's Sheet.

'Good stuff, Serjeant,' Albor said, waving a copy at him.

'Personally I'd fine anyone who didn't go to the service, like in the old days. There's too many people out there need the fear of Ishryth putting into them.'

There was a general murmur of agreement.

'You were there,' Skynner said coldly. 'I expect my men to be reliable witnesses, to be able to tell the difference between what they've seen and heard with their own eyes and ears, and the kind of gross misrepresentation that's being peddled here.' Angrily, he brushed aside a copy of Privv's Sheet that was lying on his chair. 'And if you do your jobs anything like properly, you'll put the fear of the Law into those who need it before we have to drag Ishryth into things.' He looked at his men grimly, defying any of them to disagree with him. 'As for a united Gyronlandt,' he sneered, as he sat down and motioned his men to do the same. 'Whenever someone starts saying that, it's my experience that we can look forward to having the cells full of broken heads, black eyes and vomiting drunks.' He became avuncular. 'And, when all's said and done, what Brother Cassraw preached is, fortunately, the church's affair, not ours, and doubtless they'll be dealing with it in their own way, as we will continue to deal with our problems, our way.'

The enthusiasm of the men for the Sheet appeared to have vanished for some reason, and no one seemed inclined to argue with their Serjeant's pronouncements.

Skynner turned to Albor. 'Now, anything unusual happen during the night?' Albor handed him the notes that had been left behind by the Serjeant on night duty. Skynner frowned as he read through them. There was the usual list of minor crimes and disturbances, then a report about two Sheeters who had been attacked and robbed during the night. Both had been injured and both had had their printing equipment damaged, resulting in their being unable to prepare their own Sheets for several days to come. Skynner pondered their names. By coincidence they were Privv's main rivals.

Dowinne looked up at her husband and smiled greedily. It was a reflection of Cassraw's own expression as he read Privv's Sheet.

'He's done well,' she said.

'Indeed he has,' Cassraw replied. 'And I'll make a point of telling him so. It's going to take some little effort yet to make him truly one of us, but he's going to be invaluable, I can feel it.' He looked upwards, his face ecstatic. 'His name be praised,' he said. 'It's as He said it would be. So much is turning my way so quickly, it's scarcely believable.'

Dowinne walked over to him and, standing behind him, draped her arms around his neck. 'Believe it, husband,' she said. 'A destiny is unfolding here – a destiny I've felt in you, right from the very beginning. As I sat by helpless that night while you lay silent in the Witness House, I could feel great forces gathering. Forces that would work through you to shape this entire land and beyond.' She tightened her grip. 'Seize your destiny,' she hissed. 'Seize it without fear. You must act always in that knowledge that you're His Chosen One – no hesitations, no doubts. He helps those who help themselves, and never more so than now.'

Cassraw closed his eyes and nodded fervently. Of the many changes that had recently come about, not the least had been in his wife. She had become so strong, such a bulwark. He realized that he had never had a true measure of her worth until these past few weeks. She was a fitting mate for him indeed. Dowinne remained standing behind him, her hands resting on his shoulders.

'When I've spoken to Privv, I must go to the Witness House and see Mueran,' he said. Then he took Dowinne's hand and led her round to sit beside him. Leaning forward, he spoke to her almost in a whisper. 'I must explain to him what I really said and how it was misrepresented by this scurrilous Sheeter. Begin the process of bringing him to the cause.'

Dowinne smiled knowingly. 'Mueran's an echoing vessel,' she said. 'He'll boom out whatever message is put into him. All he needs to be sure of is that he'll look well and that he'll not actually have to decide anything.'

Cassraw chuckled and patted her hand. He made as if to stand up, then hesitated.

Dowinne's eyes narrowed slightly. 'Something's troubling you, isn't it?' she said.

Cassraw frowned. 'Vredech was there yesterday.'

'In the congregation? I didn't see him.'

Her husband's scowl deepened. 'He was there, though – under one of the hoods, I'm sure. I could feel him.'

Dowinne shrugged. 'Strange behaviour for a friend,' she said dismissively. 'But does it really matter?'

'Vredech will oppose me,' Cassraw said flatly. 'I'm sure of it. I've felt it ever since I came down the mountain. His hand will be against me.' Then his face became pained. 'I don't want to have to fight him, Dowinne. We've been friends all our lives.'

A coldness came into Dowinne's eyes momentarily but Cassraw did not see it. 'I don't think it'll be so, Enryc,' she said consolingly. 'Why should he oppose you? Besides, your tongue will show him the rightness of what you're doing.'

Cassraw looked doubtful. 'He's nakedly innocent, and very strong when he feels he needs to be.'

Dowinne's hand twisted in his and tightened about it. 'Whatever part he's been given to play, he'll play,' she said. 'But he hasn't a fraction of your strength, nor a fraction of your gifts. He is not the Chosen One. You'll bring him to your side, I'm sure.'

'And if I can't?' Cassraw asked.

Dowinne released his hand and smiled sympathetically. 'Such compassion,' she said. 'Such concern and loyalty. It

272

wasn't for any small reason that you were chosen. But with that choosing goes responsibilities. The way ahead has been laid for you, all you have to do is follow it. You'll always do what is right, what is necessary, and it will always be for the best, no matter how difficult or distressing it might seem at the time. The power is coming to you. I feel it.'

A glass some way from Cassraw tumbled over. Its contents rushed across the simple white cloth and trickled noisily on to the floor. Cassraw started slightly and looked at his hand, puzzled. Before he could say anything, however, Dowinne, her eyes strangely bright, reached out and picked up the glass.

'Many things are coming to you,' she said, as if there had been no interruption.

Cassraw's doubts flared briefly, then were gone. 'Of course,' he said, standing up. 'Allyn will take some persuading, but he'll be with us in the end.'

Dowinne watched him from the window as he mounted his horse and turned it towards the gates of the Meeting House. As he disappeared from sight, she looked at the glass in her hand. She pressed it, cold, against her cheek and smiled.

'All will be with us in the end, husband,' she said to herself softly. 'Or crushed utterly.'

Toom Drommel looked at the Sheet in amazement. That crazy preacher had done it after all, he thought. Though it had only been a few days previously, he had almost forgotten his interview with Cassraw. In fact, it had so disconcerted him that he had deliberately put it from his mind. And despite having read the Sheet very carefully several times he could still scarcely believe it.

Thank Ishryth the man hadn't mentioned his or the Party's name. Drommel was sorely tempted to read the Sheet yet again just to make sure, but restrained himself.

He had little doubt that Privv's representation of the sermon was inaccurate and exaggerated, but it was the version that would be accepted as the truth no matter how many actual witnesses appeared to deny it.

Gradually his thoughts ordered themselves. The whole business might after all prove quite entertaining. Cassraw had seen fit to bring the Church into politics and it would be interesting to see what the church did to him for his pains. And indeed, the affair might even prove useful. Drommel smiled tightly to himself. Later that day he would be able to raise the matter in the PlasHein, and while cautiously deprecating this intrusion into secular matters by a senior member of the church, he should nonetheless be able to use it to apply further pressure on the Castellans. They were in an almighty stew, he knew, and it was only a matter of time before they retreated from their stated intention of expelling Felden nationals and confiscating Felden assets. Such a conspicuous flight from so strong a declaration, dealing particularly, as it did, with the protection of Madren citizens abroad, would cost them dearly at the next Acclamation and would almost certainly result in his party holding the balance of power.

The future was looking very good. Drommel instinctively straightened up, and laid his hand upon the Sheet as though it were some important document of state as he began to see a portrait of himself ranged with those of all the other great statesmen that lined the entrance hall to the main debating chamber of the PlasHein.

Privv chewed on his thumb as he took up his favourite position, with his feet on his desk and the views of the Ervrin Mallos and the PlasHein within a turn of his head. Not that any profound considerations of his place in the social order were troubling him today. He was simply tired. It had been a long night.

But he had been making money. A great deal of money.

Leck was sprawled out on the windowsill, apparently asleep. Idly he touched the cat's mind. His own filled suddenly with unnerving images of darkness permeated with moving, watching shadows and he withdrew quickly. Something about the cat's sleeping mind unsettled him. He could never escape the feeling that, in some mysterious way, he might be drawn into them: taken somewhere from where he could never escape. He shivered and chewed earnestly at his thumb.

The mood passed eventually. It would take more than a brush with Leck's thoughts to mar today. Part of Privv wanted to sag into his chair and just sleep, but he was too exhilarated. His latest Sheet had been a scintillating piece of writing, full of bounding rhetoric and colourful imagery, and every one of the Sheets that he had printed had been sold. Further, following Cassraw's guarded advice he had printed far more than usual. The public appetite for his work was surprising even him.

He leaned back and stared at the ceiling and once again mentally counted his takings for the night's endeavour. If things carried on like this he was going to have to use even more boys to sell the Sheets further around the town, perhaps even beyond. Already far from poor as a result of his Sheeting, he could see a future ahead that seemed to hold no limit to the wealth he could accumulate. It was good. And well deserved for the service he did the community.

Something intruded into his reverie, making him glance around. He frowned as he strained to catch a noise that was hovering at the edge of his hearing. Someone, somewhere was whistling. Or was it some street musician playing a pipe? They didn't usually play in this area.

Before he could ponder the matter further, he was abruptly overwhelmed by Leck's consciousness, full of urgent reflexes.

'Out, cat!' An angry voice filled his head and he was

leaping desperately, on all fours, to avoid a swinging foot.

The image was gone as suddenly as it had materialized, but he was aware of Leck screaming abusively and tumbling off the windowsill, while he himself was falling off his chair. Still partly linked to the cat, he twisted round and landed on his hands and knees safely, if painfully. The chair fell over on top of him.

'Damn you, cat!' he roared.

Leck spat at him viciously. 'It's not my fault,' she hissed. 'He just didn't like cats, that's all.'

'Who didn't?'

'Him.' Her voice faded awkwardly. 'Him . . . in my mind. Sorry.'

Privv was disentangling himself from the chair. 'Well, think about someone a bit less violent in future if you don't mind,' he grumbled, only partially mollified by Leck's apology.

'It's not my fault,' Leck sulked. 'It was all so real, as though I was actually there. I've never felt anything like that before.'

'Well, don't bother feeling it again,' Privv retorted, still struggling with the chair.

A ringing ended their argument. Leck sniffed the air and her hackles rose slightly. 'It's him,' she said. 'Your benefactor – Cassraw.'

Privv scrambled to his feet and righted the chair as if that single act might bring immediate order to the chaos of his room. He felt Leck sneering. She was back on the windowsill and stretching herself out again. 'It's so funny the way you creatures always grovel around a pack leader,' she said.

'Shut up,' Privv snapped. Quickly he sat down at his desk, swept a mass of papers to one side and began writing purposefully on the piece in front of him. There was a loud knock on the door, and it was pushed open before he could speak. A small, scruffy boy, liberally splattered with ink

276

but seemingly very dirty anyway, stood looking at him insolently.

'It's someone called Brother Crasshole,' he announced, scratching his crotch.

Privv was uttering a silent prayer for the immediate death of the child when Cassraw strode into the room, cuffing the boy on the back of the head as he passed him.

The boy let out a yell of raucous indignation. 'I'm going back to bed. You can answer the door yourself if anyone else comes,' he shouted at Privv and, pausing only to make an obscene gesture at Cassraw's back, he was gone.

Privv gave a weak smile of apology and motioned Cassraw towards a seat. 'He's a good lad really, just a little tired. Last night was hard work.'

'Hard work is the way to salvation,' Cassraw declared tersely, looking in some distaste at the hand with which he had struck the boy.

'Quite,' Privv agreed, offering him a cloth.

Cassraw looked at the cloth with even greater distaste and waved it away. 'You have an even greater facility with words than I'd imagined. I scarcely recognized my sermon in your Sheet.'

Privv could not keep the alarm from his face. He pushed a chair towards Cassraw anxiously.

'But it was well done,' Cassraw continued, declining the chair. 'I see that I chose well in you. Stay true to me, Sheeter, and things will come your way that you dare not even aspire to at the moment.' He looked significantly at Privv, but as he did not seem to expect any reply, Privv remained silent. 'I'm going from here to the Witness House, to explain how my sermon has been misrepresented in your Sheet, and to tell them that I've spoken to you on the matter and received an assurance that, in future, any comments you might see fit to write about my sermons will be more measured in their tone.'

He walked over to the window and looked out at the

Ervrin Mallos, idly stroking Leck as he did so. 'I think it would be a good idea if you went to the PlasHein today. I'm sure that several of the worthy members will have something to say about what I'm alleged to have said.' He turned and stared at Privv. 'You printed more Sheets than usual, as I advised?' he asked.

Privv nodded. 'And sold them all.' Then, keeping his face neutral he looked straight at Cassraw even though he could not see his face clearly against the light from the window. 'It seems that my two main rivals were both attacked and injured last night. And their presses damaged.'

'Careful,' Leck hissed.

Cassraw gave no response other than a slight inclination of his head. 'Robbers, presumably. Such is the penalty of material success. It attracts that kind of attention. Ishryth's ways are strange indeed.'

'Indeed,' Privv echoed.

'You must write something about the declining standards in our society which allows such an important, if new, institution to be thus assailed. Perhaps you could point out the need for our Heinders to set a greater example of stern moral resolution. Where they show weakness, others will follow. And the more conspicuous the weakness, the greater the example. Such conduct is not acceptable.'

Then, with a curt farewell, he was gone.

Privv sat down and breathed out loudly. He picked up the cloth that Cassraw had rejected, and wiped his forehead with it. It left an inky stain.

'*He* did it.' He was whispering even though he was speaking only to Leck. 'He was behind the wrecking of those presses.' Confirmation oozed into him from his companion. 'It was the first thing that occurred to me when I heard about it, but I thought, no, couldn't be, not a Preacher. But I could smell it on him then.' He bared his teeth fearfully. 'I hope he didn't see anything on my face.'

278

'It's safe to assume that he knows you know,' Leck said. 'I was getting all manner of alarming reactions from him.' For an instant Privv was full of primitive, predatory urges – a lust for the chase, the kill, warm flesh, and blood. His mouth watered. Leck tore the images back with painful urgency and an awkward silence hung between them for a moment. Then it filled with her anxiety. 'He's stranger than ever. If we're going to get involved with him, you *must* have a good escape route ready for us. I wouldn't trust him the length of my tail.'

'I'll think about it,' Privv said off-handedly. 'I must admit, it's a very strange feeling to have someone from the church resorting to that kind of thing. Heinders, business-men, yes, but Preachers . . .' His face became thoughtful. 'I wonder what game he's really playing?' he mused.

'A dangerous one,' Leck said. 'I've told you, he's a pack leader. And he's stronger now by far than he was when we first met him. He's not like anyone we've ever dealt with before.'

Privv scowled. 'You worry too much,' he said. 'We've dealt with worse than him in the past. We'll be all right if we keep our wits about us.' He nodded sagely. 'And don't forget, whatever it is he's up to, we've already made a lot of money out of it, and we're likely to make a lot more.' He yawned noisily and stretched himself. 'I'm going to have a sleep, then I think I'll visit my esteemed colleagues and give them my condolences, before I go to the Plas-Hein.'

He swung his feet up on to his desk again and closed his eyes.

He was counting the night's takings yet again as he drifted into sleep.

Vredech entered Mueran's office feeling decidedly uncom-fortable. It had been his intention after hearing Cassraw's sermon to speak to Mueran about it. He could not have done otherwise following such a flagrant flouting of the church's long tradition of not interfering in lay matters. Now however, after reading the version printed in Privv's Sheet, he found himself almost in the position of defending Cassraw.

He was more than a little relieved to see that Morem and Horld were there also, and that a copy of Privv's sheet lay on Mueran's desk. It would be much easier to join in this discussion than start it.

Mueran nodded a cursory greeting and waved Vredech to a seat. 'I can't believe that Brother Cassraw actually said these things, or even implied them,' he was saying.

'Nor I,' Horld said. 'Privv's capable of writing anything, *I* should know that.'

'But there must be some semblance of truth to it,' Morem interjected. 'What else could have prompted this Privv to write such things?'

Horld threw a coin on to the desk. 'Money,' he grunted. 'That's all. These Sheets are being sold all over the place. I'd swear he's printed about twice as many as usual.'

'I'm afraid there is some truth to it,' Vredech announced. 'I was there – I heard Cassraw's sermon.'

At any other time, the idea of one preacher attending another's sermon would have provoked some good-natured banter, but the atmosphere in the room was too fraught for that. All eyes turned to him. 'I'd heard he was going to talk about the murder,' Vredech explained, rather self-consciously. 'I was concerned, so I went cloaked just to hear for myself.'

Mueran was waving his hand. 'The reasons aren't important,' he said. 'I'm sure they were sincerely judged. Thanks be that you were there. Tell us what you heard, then perhaps we can decide what to do next.'

Vredech gave them the gist of Cassraw's sermon. When he had finished, his small audience was looking both relieved and distressed.

Mueran was shaking his head. 'It was a reckless thing for Brother Cassraw to do,' he said. 'Well meant, I'm sure, but reckless.' He tapped the Sheet in front of him. 'As these consequences show.'

He put his hands to his head. 'I'm at a loss to know what to do for the best,' he told them. 'We should really ask Brother Cassraw to account for his actions before the assembled Chapter, but in view of this travesty that's been so widely published, I feel we should also be defending him. It's really very—'

A knock interrupted him and a head appeared round the door. He looked up irritably.

'Brother Cassraw's here, Brother Mueran,' the head said. 'He'd like to see you.'

'Show him in,' Mueran said, raising a beckoning hand. The head disappeared. 'I think we should sort out as much of this as possible, informally and between ourselves, before we make any public announcements.'

There was no time for anyone to respond, however, for Cassraw was already striding into the room. His expression was one of both pain and contrition but the authority of his presence filled the room. Mueran and the others seemed momentarily overawed but, to his horror, Vredech felt a violent antagonism rising unbidden within him. He drove his fingernails brutally into his palms in an attempt to stop it.

Cassraw held out a copy of Privv's Sheet. 'My friends – what can I say about this? To be thus traduced. The shame of it.' He clenched his fist. 'I have spoken to the man this very morning and given him the measure of my reproach. I trusted him in this matter and he has betrayed me.'

'And will again,' Horld declared. 'The man corrodes all he touches. He's free of all restraint. I thought it was unwise of you to allow him into the Witness House after your . . . brief illness, but I'd not taken you to be so naive as to actually trust him.'

Cassraw lowered his head.

281

'It's fortunate we have a true witness to your sermon, Brother, or our meeting now could have been a far more serious affair.' Mueran had recovered his composure and was gathering confidence as he saw Cassraw apparently yielding before Horld's reproach. 'However, we're still faced with your blatant disregard for the ways of the church in bringing lay matters to the pulpit. I am sure you must realize that some form of rebuke is inevitable.'

'I understand,' Cassraw said.

Mueran's confidence was gathering now with each word. 'I'm sure that your motives were well-intentioned and that you realize now the error you made.' He nodded his head paternally. 'We've all done foolish things in our younger days – it's one of the ways we acquire wisdom. And the church, being older than all of us, is wiser, too, and that is why its ways should not be set aside, no matter how urgent or tragic the needs of the moment might seem.'

Cassraw looked up slowly. 'I understand,' he said again. 'I'm humbled by your understanding, and grateful. With your permission, I shall go to one of the chapels and give thanks that I am so supported in my time of pain.'

Later, as Vredech rode slowly down from the Witness House, his thoughts were uncharitable. Cassraw's presence at the meeting seemed to have overwhelmed everyone. His regrets, his gratitude, had somehow deflected all four of his listeners from an objective approach to what had happened.

Now, swaying gently through the warm afternoon, Vredech was viewing the matter differently. Mueran's concern about how the church should respond to the problem of Privv had dominated the meeting, and Cassraw had not even been questioned about his true offence – his ranting sermon about the vision of a Gyronlandt united under the Church.

Despite himself, Vredech suspected that the whole affair had been engineered with that in mind. Thoughts of the Whistler and his strange message began to return to him in the mountain silence.

'He's one of you. A priest.'

And then there was Jarry's fearful claim about the return of Ahmral. Try as he might, Vredech could not set all this aside with a smile at his own folly. Thank Ishryth that Nertha was here. Her acid touch would dissolve his problems.

Or etch them into a stark contrast.

Later still, Toom Drommel gave a rousing speech in the PlasHein, rebuking the Ploughers for persisting in their foolish plan, with all the harm it would do to the workers of Canol Madreth, and rebuking the Castellans for their hesitancy in implementing their plan when his party had agreed to support it. The leaders of the Castellan Party were perspiring freely when he had finished and, in the gallery above, Privv was smiling broadly and turning over some robust phrases of his own.

That night, further damage was done to the property of the two Sheeters who had been attacked previously.

And another young man was brutally murdered.

283

Chapter 22

Privv banged the table furiously. 'You can't do this!' he shouted. 'Dragging me here as though I were some common brawler.'

Skynner's jawline tightened. 'I can and I have,' he said, ominously quietly. 'And you haven't been dragged anywhere, you've been officially escorted here because you were interfering with my men when they were trying to do their jobs.'

'*Their* jobs! What about mine? That's all *I* was doing – trying to find out what had happened so that I could let the people know,' Privv persisted.

It had been a grim day so far, with every prospect of it becoming worse, and Skynner's patience suddenly ran out. He was fingering his baton dangerously as he stood up and towered over the protesting Sheeter. 'What the hell's this got to do with the people, whoever they are!' he thundered.

Privv quailed. He was not unused to people trying to intimidate him, but Skynner was large and powerful, and he had genuinely lost his temper. Further, it was an oft-reported fact that Keepers were not above delivering summary justice to some of their customers in the quiet of the Keeperage. Whether it was true or not, Privv had no idea, but he had certainly reported it often enough. Further still, and as he knew for certain, Skynner, being an empowered public official, had an ample supply of minor statutes and by-laws with which he could quite legitimately make life very difficult should he choose. The Sheeter decided not to make any attempt to answer Skynner's question.

The Serjeant was still fingering his baton as he continued: 'It's got to do with the friends and relatives of the poor devil who's been murdered. And it's got to do with *us* because it's our job to make sure that we catch the other person it has something to do with, namely the man who did it.'

Despite himself Privv risked a word: 'The people need to know so they can protect themselves while this lunatic's at large.'

It was a mistake.

Skynner's eyes narrowed and he spoke with great deliberateness. 'All anyone has to do to protect themselves, as far as we can tell at the moment, is to avoid going down dark alleys with prostitutes. But it may not have escaped your eagle Sheeter's eye that since the first murder, almost every man in Troidmallos is sporting a cudgel, or a knife, or even a sword!' He shouted the last word.

'That's no crime,' Privv blundered on.

'I'm well aware of that!' Skynner blasted. 'Nor is it remotely necessary. Now, every other routine drunken squabble my men have to deal with is three times more dangerous than before. And I'll wager that there are more than a few women walking around with knives about their person where once there'd been some ladies' flim-flam.'

Privv looked at him sullenly and returned to his original argument. 'Well, that's nothing to do with me,' he whined. 'People are still entitled to protect themselves and to know what's going on. And running a Sheet is a right.'

Skynner bared his teeth in a scornful sneer. 'Oh yes? One of our most ancient rights, is it? At least fifteen, twenty years old, eh? Those who wanted to know used to

285

be able to find out everything they needed by looking at the posting boards. And don't talk to me about your rights. Any right carries a corresponding responsibility. I've never noticed you being quite as anxious to exercise the one as the other.'

But Privv was not going to let go. 'Don't lecture me, Keeper, until you're looking to your own responsibilities a bit more – such as being out hunting for that murderer instead of harassing honest citizens going about their legitimate business.'

For a moment Skynner looked as though he were debating not whether he should use his baton on Privv, but merely how hard and how long. Then, suddenly, he smiled and sat down again. 'You're absolutely right, Sheeter Privv,' he said politely. 'And I'm sure that we can rely on your cooperation.'

He opened a drawer in his desk and after rooting round for a moment, produced a sheaf of papers. He began thumbing through them diligently, finally selecting one which he proceeded to read with great care. Once or twice he looked up at Privv, as if checking something, then nodded his head and returned to the paper.

Eventually he put it down, though he kept glancing at it from time to time as he spoke. Privv craned forward as much as he dared in an attempt to read it, but Skynner absently laid a hand across it. 'You'll understand, I'm sure,' he said, 'that dealing with such an horrific incident is very disturbing for my men. It takes a toll of them. I have to protect them as much as I can. I get quite . . . fatherly . . . about it.' He leaned forward confidentially. 'They see sights that really shouldn't be seen, and the last thing they need is someone coming round asking all manner of questions that they can't begin to answer. I'd ask you therefore, as a good citizen, to stay away from my men, and of course from the scene of the murder, until they've had time to complete their very unpleasant tasks.'

Privv looked at him suspiciously, far more disturbed by this measured appeal than he had been by the previous ranting. 'For their sake, you understand,' Skynner concluded. Then he became affable. 'If you're interested in knowing how the young man died, then from my own cursory examination it seems that his assailant stabbed him . . .'

There followed a short but extremely unpleasant list of stab wounds and their locations, followed by a list of mutilations and a description of the internal organs exposed to view as a consequence. Skynner's matter-of-fact delivery served merely to heighten the horrors of this information. Privv clenched his fists and his stomach and glanced at the door.

'Would you like to sit down?' Skynner said after a moment, his face concerned.

Privv accepted the offer. 'It was worse than the other one, then?' he managed, hoarsely.

Skynner nodded, then his face brightened. 'If you like, I can take you to the buriers. The body should be there by now. And I've asked the Town Physician to examine it this time. I've nothing like his experience, of course. I've probably missed a lot, there was so much damage. It's amazing what he can unearth from a corpse with a good knife, a saw, and a bit of effort.' He pulled his clenched fists apart as if tearing something. 'I'm sure you'd find his work very interesting. You might even like to write about it.' He stood up and held out his arm as if motioning Privv to the door, but his visitor showed little inclination to leave his seat.

'I don't think so. No, thank you. Perhaps some other time,' he said weakly.

Skynner sat down again, nodding understandingly. 'As you wish, though I doubt you'll get another chance as good as this one. Still, it's up to you. I didn't want you to go away with the idea that I was unwilling to discuss our work with you.' He smiled beatifically. There was a brief silence.

'I'll be leaving then, if you've finished with me,' Privv said, struggling to lever himself up from his chair.

'Actually, there is one thing, while you're here,' Skynner said, looking down at the paper again. 'I wonder if you can help me with another matter? Fortunately it's not as unpleasant as this latest happening, but it is serious and I'm particularly anxious to get to the bottom of it.'

Something in his tone expedited Privv's recovery. 'What is it?' he asked, his voice sharper than he had intended.

Skynner looked at him squarely. 'You've probably heard already that the night before last, two of your fellow Sheeters – your main rivals, as I understand it – were attacked and injured. Also their property, including their printing presses, was badly damaged. So badly in fact that neither of them was able to produce a Sheet today.' He shrugged resignedly. 'This kind of thing happens from time to time, as you know. Robbers entering houses, doing violence and damage. But it's not all that common, and for two such attacks to occur on the same night and to the same kind of people, makes it . . . very unusual.'

Privv held Skynner's gaze. He went on: 'What you've probably not heard yet is that the robbers returned again last night and did further, more extensive damage, particularly to the printing presses. I don't fully understand these things, but it seems that your colleagues will be unable to pursue their livelihoods for quite some time as a consequence.'

Privv was tempted to mouth some platitude at this point, but he remained silent.

'Now I know that there's a great deal of rivalry between Sheeters,' Skynner said, in a speculative tone. 'Friendly, I'm sure. But, as you yourself have had cause to write about in the past, business rivalries can sometimes get

288

quite seriously . . . out of hand. "The love of money is Ahmral's gift," as the Santyth says. And as these attacks bear all the hallmarks of such over-enthusiastic rivalry, I was wondering if there was anything untoward happening in your little community that might throw some light on events?'

Unpleasant knots began to form in Privv's stomach. He pulled a massively thoughtful face for fear that anything else should show on it. 'No,' he said after a moment. 'I've heard of nothing. We Sheeters are thinkers, men of ideas and words, not market-traders. We're not naturally inclined to violence.'

Skynner's face was impassive. 'Nothing, then?' he said slowly.

Privv shook his head. 'I'm sorry I can't help you. I've no idea who'd do such a thing.' He improvised. 'You don't think I might be in any danger, do you?' he said, looking appropriately alarmed.

'To be honest, until I find out more about what's happening, I think it would be foolish of me to reassure you,' Skynner said. 'It would probably be advisable for you to check how solid your doors and windows are, and to be careful to whom you open the door.'

Privv nodded earnestly. 'I'll do as you suggest, straight away. Is there anything else you want from me?'

'No, I don't think so,' Skynner replied. And he allowed Privv to get halfway to the door before he said: 'Oh, there was one other thing.' He clicked his tongue in self-reproach. 'I nearly forgot, it's been such a busy day.' He rooted through his desk again and pulled out another piece of paper. 'Could you tell me where you were last night and the night before.' He poised a pen over the paper.

Privv walked towards him slowly. Skynner answered his question before he asked it. 'I'll tell my superiors what you've said, but in the meantime they've asked me to find out what all the Sheeters were doing when these attacks

289

happened. Don't be offended.' He smiled. 'It's just that we have to be quite painstaking in our investigations.' He was quite pleased that he managed to keep a heavy emphasis off the word 'our'.

Privv briefly considered arguing the point but decided against it. This encounter with the forceful reality of the law had unsettled him and he was more than a little anxious to be away from Skynner's intimidating presence.

'I was working almost all night,' he said. 'Both nights. Printing. You can ask my imp, or my neighbours. They're usually only too willing to complain about the noise.'

Skynner nodded and wrote something on the paper. 'Do you normally work all through the night?' he asked, looking surprised.

'No. I was printing a lot more copies than usual.'

Skynner continued writing. 'Why?' he asked, without looking up.

Privv hesitated. 'I'd a feeling that my account of Brother Cassraw's sermon would attract a lot of attention,' he replied. 'I wanted to be ready. I took a chance.'

Skynner smiled. 'A lucky feeling,' he said. 'I thought there were more copies than usual being sold. You must have made quite a lot of money. Let's hope the people who robbed your colleagues haven't thought the same, eh?'

Privv smiled weakly.

Skynner finished his writing then leaned forward on the desk and said briskly, 'Thank you for your cooperation, Privv.'

Privv almost jumped. 'Is that all?' he heard himself asking.

'Not unless there's anything you've remembered about your colleagues' business affairs,' Skynner said cordially. 'Or unless you've changed your mind and want to come down to the buriers with me and watch the physician examining the corpse.'

Privv shook his head hastily, and with a mumbled farewell, he left.

Skynner stared at the door through which the Sheeter had gone. His genial expression faded and became one of distaste. 'Thinkers, men of ideas,' he said contemptuously. 'You greedy, misbegotten little worm. You're involved in this business up to your inky little neck, and I'll wring it for you before we're finished.'

He ended this soliloquy with a grunt. He had long thought that Sheeters were able to make too much money for too little effort, and their consistent lack of restraint worried him deeply, but nothing was to be served here by rehearsing his own arguments. He was no bully, but he knew how to use his authority and it had been quite enjoyable watching it begin to take the knees from under Privv – quite a difference between your paper words and real life, isn't there? he thought with some relish. Now however, this welcome interlude over, the stark reality of his own profession returned to him as, with considerable reluctance, he switched his mind again toward the carnage he had had to inspect this morning.

This time the body had been identified by one of his men, and almost within the hour he had discovered a series of events that exactly paralleled those that preceded the first murder. A young man looking for a woman, seemingly finding one, and then being brutally stabbed to death and robbed in an alleyway. The only substantial difference from the first murder was the mutilation of the body. Skynner tried not to dwell on the images that he had so gleefully recited to Privv. It took him a few moments to set aside his emotion and bring his mind to the problem.

Of course it was the same murderer, he thought. Apart from the similar circumstances, there had been the same awful expression on the victim's face. He gazed hard into the memory of it to inure himself. It was not easy.

Nor did he find it easy to accept the thought that there

might be two people involved – a woman as lure, and a man who did the killing. If this were so, it somehow made the murders many times worse. And he would be looking now not for a single lunatic who struck at random, but two, who schemed and plotted. It was a chilling thought, not least because, despite considerable efforts, no progress had yet been made towards solving the first killing. A leaden sensation in his stomach told him that none would be made with this, either. He had bemoaned the carrying of personal weapons to Privv, but he could not avoid the feeling that the murderer would only be brought to justice when he met someone faster with a knife than he was. It was not a conclusion that Skynner relished.

Over the next few days, the citizens of Troidmallos were regaled with an increasing number of Privv's Sheets. These dwelt on the latest murder and the lack of any progress towards catching the culprit, though out of a newly heightened sense of self-preservation, Privv took trouble to present the Keepers as uniformly conscientious and hard-working. His articles also reported on the debates in the PlasHein, which were becoming increasingly heated and acrimonious and which, unusually, were attracting a large number of noisy spectators – predominantly young men.

Privv's reports did not reveal the fact that he had visited his two fellow Sheeters, neither of whom had any idea why they had been thus attacked, nor who their assailants were, except that by their general demeanour, they were all young men. Finding them both so seriously distressed, physically and financially, Privv had generously offered to employ them until they could get back on their feet. It was not by any means an unconditional offer, but despite some half-hearted haggling, in the end he had effectively eliminated his two major rivals and more than doubled the market for his own Sheets. Such time as he was not actually working, which admittedly was very little, he now spent gloating.

Underlying all Privv's writings were subtle references to Cassraw's sermon, on the assumption that having set his foot on this road and not been publicly reprimanded by the church, Cassraw would continue down it towards whatever goal he had in mind.

Cassraw himself made no public utterances following his return from the Witness House, but had Privv chosen to study his activities, he would have seen him, accompanied by Dowinne, tirelessly visiting the Preaching Brothers responsible for the various parishes of Troidmallos and even those in nearby towns and villages.

He did not visit Vredech, however. Instead, Vredech visited him. He had told Nertha of the meeting with Mueran and the others and how Cassraw had somehow succeeded in diverting all reproaches away from himself. She had been as concerned as he was, but had little to offer other than a regretful reproach of her own. 'But you said nothing yourself, did you?'

It had been uttered as a simple statement of fact, and quite devoid of malice, but it had hurt. He had not embarrassed either of them by protesting that he was simply a Chapter Member and that the matter had been one on which Mueran, as Covenant Member, should have acted, or at least passed to the full Chapter.

'Straight to the wound, physician?' he said, painfully meeting her gaze.

'Sorry,' she replied genuinely.

Thus it was that Vredech found himself being shown into Cassraw's private quarters at the Haven Meeting House. He was a little puzzled. Normally he would have met Cassraw in his office where, ironically, both of them would have felt more at ease, surrounded as they were by the various administrative trappings of their profession.

'He'll be along in a moment,' the servant said as she was

leaving. 'He's just got some people with him.'

Vredech smiled and nodded. Quite a lot of people, he decided. There had been several horses tethered outside and three or four carriages, and the house bumped and shook with footsteps in the way that houses do when strange people are wandering about.

Unashamedly curious, he went to a window in the corner of the room. It gave him a partial view of the front of the Meeting House and as he reached it he saw two or three Preaching Brothers whom he knew, walking away. They looked excited, and were discussing something heatedly. There was a little more bumping and shaking, and he craned forward to see who would be leaving next.

'Allyn.'

He jumped and turned round guiltily. It was Dowinne. She laughed. 'I'm sorry if I startled you,' she said, walking towards him and holding out her hand. 'I didn't realize you were so engrossed in our garden.'

Vredech took the hand. It was cool, and the grip, though still feminine, was surprisingly purposeful. A tension and a lingering touch in it, coupled with a look in her eyes that he could not identify, unsettled him. For no reason that he could fathom, he confessed. 'I'm afraid I was looking at your other visitors,' he said.

Dowinne smiled and motioned him to a chair. As though she were appointing him as her interrogator, she sat opposite him with the light full on her face. 'Enryc works too hard,' she said, folding her hands in her lap. 'There are people coming and going all the time.'

A slight shadow fell across her face and Vredech was aware of footsteps going past the window at his back. As Dowinne made a slight acknowledging gesture to someone behind him, Vredech forced himself not to turn round.

'That's the last for the moment, I think,' she said confidently. 'Enryc will be along shortly.'

There was a brief silence. Various commonplaces came

294

into Vredech's mind to fill the void but he gave voice to none of them. Dowinne, too, seemed content to remain silent. Vredech looked at her discreetly. Despite the slight heaviness about her jawline, he still found her attractive, beautiful even, and it was not easy to still the faint stirrings of desire that rose within him: reminders of times gone. Yet she had changed, he decided. There had always been a reserve about her but now she seemed more distant than ever, yet more confident, more assured. As with her handshake and her glance, the contradiction unsettled him. It was as if some of Cassraw's strange new magnetism had infected her. He started inwardly at the word 'infected', but had no time to pursue this unexpected word as Cassraw entered, or rather *blew* into the room. For Vredech felt as if he had been struck by a gale of wind as his old friend flopped ungraciously down on to a large bench seat and sagged into it with a loud sigh.

He held out his hands towards Vredech in a distant greeting embrace. 'I'm glad you're here, Vred,' he said. 'I've been meaning to visit you, but I've been so busy. We need to talk.' He did not wait for any acknowledgement on Vredech's part. 'I suppose you've come to shout at me because of my sermon,' he went on.

Vredech opened his mouth.

'And quite rightly too,' Cassraw said, before he could speak. He leaned forward and took Dowinne's arm. 'Something to drink, my dear, if you wouldn't mind. I seem to have been talking constantly since I got up this morning.' He glanced up at Vredech and smiled. 'And I've no doubt I'll have to do a great deal more before Vred goes.'

He leaned back. Like Dowinne he was sitting facing the light. As if he's deliberately trying to tell me that he's nothing to hide, Vredech thought. Yet where better to hide some things than in full view of everyone? Then he set both thoughts aside; neither served any purpose. All he could do was put one foot in front of the other and see where they led.

'It was you who came and listened to my sermon, wasn't it?' Cassraw said, raising a mocking finger of reproach.

As he had with Dowinne, Vredech confessed. 'I'm afraid so,' he began. 'I . . .' He faltered awkwardly.

Cassraw laughed, filling the room. 'Don't be afraid, Vred,' he said. 'I'm sure you were there out of concern for what my recklessness might lead me into. I'm just glad someone was able to tell Mueran the truth after what Privv wrote.'

'You seem very relaxed about it all,' Vredech said, taken aback slightly by Cassraw's joviality. 'You could've been in serious trouble. Suppose Mueran had called a Chapter Meeting to discipline you?'

Cassraw shrugged resignedly. 'But he didn't,' he said. '*You* were there to tell the truth. Horld was there, who more than anyone knows Privv for the liar he is. Morem was there, who's not happy about punishing anyone for anything.'

'You were lucky,' Vredech exclaimed with some force. 'What possessed you to preach a sermon like that?' He thought he caught a momentary flash in Cassraw's eyes, but it was gone before he could decide what it was.

Cassraw stared at him intently, his face suddenly serious. 'There was no luck involved, Vred,' he said. 'He guards me. And He guides me when I speak.'

Vredech felt as he had when he remonstrated with Cassraw before he had stormed up the Ervrin Mallos and into the darkness. He grimaced. 'Don't say such things, Brother,' he implored 'Even in jest. You've behaved so recklessly lately. You only escaped discipline after your last escapade because you were unwell and because you made a handsome apology to the Chapter. Mueran may be the Covenant Member, but he remembers slights and bears grudges. If you keep chipping away at him like this, you'll find he'll fall on your head eventually.'

'Vred, Vred,' Cassraw remonstrated, his voice at once

intimate and powerful. 'You were there. You heard my sermon, but did you *listen*? Everything was as I said it was, the vision that came to me out of the darkness on the mountain.' The intensity of his gaze seemed to redouble. Vredech felt as though his very soul was being searched. 'You, too, were touched by His presence in the cloud, I know,' Cassraw went on. 'I can feel it in you.' He struck his chest. 'It's been your inability to accept the new truth, your clinging to the old ways, that's given you such pain ever since.'

Vredech suddenly found himself wanting to embrace his old friend and pour out the tale of all that had happened to him since that fateful day. He wanted to stand by him and move into this future that Cassraw had been shown, wanted to share this great clarity, this great certainty that had been granted him.

Cassraw's eyes widened in expectation. His arms came out again, beckoning. Vredech's desire grew. Here was the road that he must follow. He put his hands on the arms of his chair.

Yet even as he did so, the memory returned of the darkness that had enveloped him on the mountain, a darkness full of rejoicing for a hope reborn, a fate avoided. An awful, primitive rejoicing that had chilled him horribly. And the Whistler's words returned to him also, overlapping and echoing.

'He was weak . . . holding on like a failing climber, clinging desperately.

'He's one of you . . . a priest . . . plotting, thinking, deceiving . . . sowing disorder and discontent . . .'

The first remarks might well be nothing more than an inner re-telling of what he had felt on the mountain, but whatever the Whistler was, the latter remarks had been spoken *before* Cassraw's sermon. Vredech's whole agonizing debate about the true reality of the Whistler threatened to overwhelm him again.

The hands that had been levering him up relaxed and he dropped back into the chair. 'The only thing that touched me that day was concern for you,' he said, opting without hesitation for a lie.

Cassraw's eyes narrowed. 'You're not telling me the truth,' he said bluntly. 'You are some part of all this, I know. You have a role to play.'

Vredech was suddenly very nervous. 'Perhaps I'm playing it now,' he said, struggling to keep his voice steady. To his relief, Dowinne returned at that moment carrying a tray of glasses. She offered him one, gave one to Cassraw and then, taking the last one herself, sat down opposite Vredech where she had sat before. Vredech felt the scrutiny of the two observers pinioning him.

Cassraw relaxed and smiled. 'Perhaps indeed,' he said. 'Well, all will be revealed in due course. Events are in train which nothing will stop, or even deflect.'

'What do you mean?' Vredech asked.

'I told you in my sermon,' Cassraw replied.

Intimidated by the two watchers, Vredech could find no alternative than to speak out. 'We're going in circles, Cassraw,' he said. 'I don't doubt your sincerity, and I don't doubt that something happened to you on the mountain, but you can't seriously expect me, or anyone else, to believe that Ishryth himself spoke to you, manifested himself, and chose you for some holy crusade. Theological arguments aside, can't you hear how it sounds when I say it? You escaped Mueran's anger yesterday like you did before, by good luck and judicious contrition.' He shook his head in dismay and looked at Dowinne. 'I'm sorry to talk like this in front of you, Dowinne, but this is serious. All that Cassraw and you have achieved,' he waved a hand around the room, 'this place, his position in the Chapter – all this could be lost if he carries on like this. Surely you must see that?'

Dowinne cast a glance at her husband, and smiled. 'I

understand what you're saying, Allyn,' she said, 'but your concern's misplaced. The problem is that *you* don't understand what Enryc's saying. You don't understand what's happened to him. He saw what he saw. Heard what he heard. The Lord in His greatness touched him.'

'A great evil has arisen in the lands far to the north. Beyond the mountains.'

Vredech started at the sound of Cassraw's voice, so full of passion and anger, but as he turned towards him he saw that his face and manner were calm. 'If it is not opposed then the whole world will fall under its shadow. This land, Canol Madreth, has been chosen to become the heart of this opposition, a great citadel from which armies will march forth to spread His word.'

Even as he was registering this pronouncement, Vredech's mind was echoing again with the Whistler's words, full of revelation and hope. 'He has met a terrible foe. He is weak. He is weak.' Then his final terrifying command. 'Find Him. Kill Him.'

All the doubts about his sanity that Vredech had so carefully ordered and balanced over the past weeks came crashing down upon him and his hands began to shake. For a time that he could not measure, he was at once with the Whistler, lying on an unknown hillside in the dying evening light, and sitting in Cassraw's private quarters in the Haven Meeting House. Then he was deep inside the maelstrom of his own whirling thoughts. Beyond, he could see a tiny storm beginning to stir the contents of his glass. The liquid swayed and jiggled and then began to ride recklessly up the side of the glass as if trying to escape a fearful confinement. He was aware, too, somewhere at the end of a rushing, roaring tunnel, of Cassraw and Dowinne watching him. Such movements as they were making were slow and laboured, in stark contrast to his own inner world which was mirroring the growing frenzy in his glass, as thoughts careened

299

to and fro with an uncontrollable momentum.

Like a drowning man clutching at driftwood, he snatched at random fragments of normality as they hurtled past him.

His hand.

He must stop his hand from shaking. Banal social consequences suddenly obsessed him. The fruit juice would stain his clothes, the chair, the carpet. Excuses for the mess he was about to make ran ahead of him, leaving him embarrassed and awkward before his old friends. He would be like a boy who, a little too old for such things now, had wet the bed. All would be understood and 'forgotten', but the deed would linger for ever . . .

He must not give way.

Whatever it cost him, he must cling on to some semblance of sanity until he could get away from this place, these people, and—

And what?

And think.

And breathe.

He was suffocating!

The needs of his body asserted themselves, marshalling his rational mind as it was unable to do for itself. His free hand wrapped itself around his shaking wrist and tightened pitilessly, pressing it into his knee to still it absolutely. His chest expanded to draw in a cold, tight and massive breath through his nose.

'What are you talking about?'

He heard his voice echoing and hollow. The reality that was Cassraw's room solidified a little. Vredech drove his thumbnail into his wrist, using the pain to anchor the change before it could slither away again.

'Are you all right?' Both Cassraw and Dowinne were speaking.

Vredech twisted his thumbnail harder. The dementia

receded further, leaving him at the centre of a small pool of stillness. He felt like a solitary soldier, separated from his comrades but being ignored for the moment by the enemy. The two-voiced question arced towards him like falling spears. He had not now the resources to lie.

'I'm not sure,' he said, forcing his tight face into an uncertain smile, but unable to keep a mixture of anger and disdain from his voice. 'I'm not sure I'm hearing correctly. What are you talking about? A great evil to the north – Canol Madreth a citadel! Armies!'

Each word fastened him more securely into the present. But everything was changed. It was indeed as though he had slipped from a sane world into an insane one peopled with identical figures.

Cassraw blinked as though he had been struck. 'Take care, Vred,' he said, with some menace. 'Events are happening here which will not be opposed.'

Vredech released his wrist and put his hand to his forehead. 'I'm opposing nothing, Cassraw,' he said. 'I just don't understand what you're saying. What's happened to you? Can't you hear how such words will sound to your flock, to the Chapter?'

Cassraw seemed to lose patience. 'My flock will follow,' he said starkly. 'Indeed, as it follows, so will it grow. And the church, too, will follow.' He stood up.

Vredech was too uncertain of his legs to try standing, but he finally found his voice. 'Cassraw, I came here to talk to you about your sermon, to find out what was troubling you so that I could be your true friend, should need arise. But this is beyond me.' He forced himself to stand. 'I shall say nothing about this meeting, but you must know that if you speak like this in public, then no one will be able to do anything for you.'

Cassraw glanced down for a moment. When he looked up, he was smiling. It was a warm, understanding expression, quite free from the glinting self-aware certainty of

the deranged. Vredech looked at him unhappily, his
doubts about himself seeping back. Cassraw took his arm.
'You're quite right, Vred,' he said. 'I see that my new
knowledge is too heady even for you, who knows me. I
would not, in any event, have expressed myself so freely in
public. But you are my old friend. You were on the
mountain with me, and, despite your protestations, I feel
that you, too, were touched, albeit less so than me. Like
me, you have been chosen.'

He looked directly at Vredech, his black eyes piercing, then nodded to himself before continuing. 'I have
much to do before I can speak thus to my flock and the
church, but . . .' His face became both serious and sad.
'Those who oppose what is to happen will be swept aside
– perhaps cruelly so. You must be with me, Vred, or
you'll be one such and I won't be able to save you.'

'Cassraw, for pity's sake listen to yourself,' Vredech said
softly.

Cassraw raised a finger gently to his lips for silence.
'You must be shown more than has been shown to the
others,' he said, almost whispering.

Vredech searched his face.

'Your drink is good?' Cassraw said abruptly, smiling
again.

'Yes, it . . . it is. Very good. As ever,' Vredech stammered, caught unawares, but glad to grasp a simple
commonplace again, not least because it was genuine
praise. He nodded and smiled at Dowinne, who smiled
back at him.

'Look at it,' Cassraw said. Vredech held up the glass,
still half-full of Dowinne's dark red fruit drink and
reflecting the light from the window. Cassraw touched the
glass lightly with his fingertips.

There was no sound, but Vredech felt his skin crawl as
though he had just drawn a fingernail down a window-
pane. And though nothing was to be seen, he felt too, the

302

presence of something foul moving around him, something that did not belong.

The word 'abomination' formed in his mind, but he had no time to speak, for even as he watched it, the liquid in the glass seemed to boil and then it was no longer red, but clear.

His hand began to shake again. Cassraw gripped his wrist.

'Drink it,' he said.

Chapter 23

'Party tricks!' Nertha was almost spitting with rage. 'The charlatan! And how could you be taken in like that?'

'It was water!' Vredech shouted, both embarrassed and indignant. 'I don't know what happened, but I'm not a child, for pity's sake. I was taken in by nothing. I had the glass in my hand all the time. I'd drunk half the stuff. And don't tell me I can't recognize one of Dowinne's drinks. He barely touched the outside of the glass and it changed as I was watching it.' He held his hand near to his face. 'It was this far away.'

'I've seen street clowns in Tirfelden do more mysterious things,' Nertha sneered.

Vredech rounded on her furiously. 'Damn it, Nertha! Shut up if you've nothing to say.' Nertha's jaw came out and she clenched her fists menacingly, but Vredech pressed on. 'You weren't there. You didn't see what happened. And you didn't feel what was happening. And you didn't see them. He's carrying Dowinne with him, somehow.'

At the mention of Dowinne, Nertha curled her lip. 'I wish I had been,' she said viciously. 'He wouldn't have tried anything like that with me there.'

Vredech winced. 'Nertha, please,' he said, suddenly quiet. 'I'm barely clinging on to my sanity, don't fight me.'

Nertha put her arm around his shoulder. Her face was

still grim and angry but her manner was softer. 'There's nothing wrong with your sanity,' she said. 'I'm sorry I lost my temper. I can see the pain you're in. It's just difficult to stand by and listen to all this calmly. I'm not the physician I thought I was, it seems.'

'Let's get out of here,' Vredech said, almost desperately. 'Let's just ride around the town . . . talk . . . think. I don't want to be confined by anything.'

Within minutes they were mounted and walking their horses out into the bright sunshine. Vredech let out a great breath, as though he had been holding it since his return from Cassraw's.

'Do you feel any easier?' Nertha asked after a while.

'Freer, but no easier,' Vredech answered.

Nertha frowned. 'What do you mean?'

Vredech looked up into the bright blue sky. A few white clouds were floating leisurely by. 'It's barely two months since those clouds came out of the north,' he reflected. 'Two months since Cassraw . . . and me, too, I suppose . . . had our strange visitations, but I can hardly remember what life was like before. So much has happened.' He looked at Nertha. 'Am I going mad, Nertha? Have I gone mad? Are you really there? Or am I somewhere else, someone else, dreaming all this?'

Nertha looked distressed. She reached over and took his hand. 'We've had this conversation before,' she said. 'I've told you there's nothing wrong with your mind, not while you've wit enough to know those questions can't be answered. And they can't, can they? I could put on my physician's manner and reassure you that all will be well, that of course you're you, and you're here. But nothing can stand that kind of scrutiny. It's like a child asking, "Why?" after everything you say.' She smiled enticingly. 'The question is not whether you exist, but whether such a question can exist if it can have no answer.'

Vredech did not respond to her gentle provocation, so

305

she shook him. 'Not answerable, Allyn,' she said force-fully. 'So don't ask. And don't fret. You've no alternative but to accept what you see, here and now, as real, and to do what you've already decided to do; watch and listen. Something in that cloud affected both you and Cassraw. For the first time in your life you're dreaming . . .' She waved her extended hand in front of him as he turned to her sharply. 'Or not, as the case may be,' she added quickly. 'Maybe you're going into other people's dreams, maybe visiting strange other realities. It's not important. It's all un-answerable. But whatever's happened to Cass-raw, he's playing some wildly dangerous game that's likely to cost him his career.'

Vredech looked straight ahead. 'The Whistler said that this ancient enemy of his was a priest, sowing disorder and discontent. That was *before* I heard Cassraw's sermon. He also said that this man had met a terrible foe, who had weakened him. Cassraw said that a great evil had arisen.' He turned to Nertha. 'And that was no trick for children,' he said. 'One of Dowinne's drinks was turned to water – but it wasn't just that which affected me. I told you. It was what I felt – as if something foul had suddenly been released into the room.'

Nertha held his gaze. 'Don't look to me for any answers, Allyn. All I can do is what I've just done: remind you of your own solution, to watch and listen. In a couple of days, Cassraw will be giving another sermon. I think perhaps the two of us should go and listen to him together, don't you?'

Vredech nodded slightly, then clicked his horse forward into a trot. Nertha responded and they rode in silence for some time. Then she asked again, 'Do you feel any easier now?'

'Yes,' Vredech replied, almost reluctantly. He looked at her earnestly. 'I don't know what providence brought you here, Nertha, but I'd have been lost without you.'

Nertha's brow furrowed and her mouth tightened into a prim line. 'For pity's sake, Allyn, don't go solemn on me. I don't think I could cope with *that*.'

Vredech smiled at the sight. 'No, I don't suppose you could,' he said. 'But it's true all the same.'

'It was House's letter that brought me,' Nertha insisted tartly. 'Don't get all theological about it. That's what's got you in this mess.' She pursed her lips and looked at him shrewdly. 'I think I will play the physician for a moment. I don't want to hear any more about this business, not until after Cassraw's next sermon. I want to wander about the town with you, see what's changed, what's the same. Persecute one or two old friends with reminiscences. And if this weather lasts we can ride out into the country, get into the silence, right away from Privv's hysteria and Cassraw's dementia, right away from sterile debates and the smell of well-worn pews. Can we do that?'

'How could I refuse such an alluring prospect?' Vredech replied. He took her hand. 'It's really . . .'

Nertha snatched her hand free and raised it warningly. 'No solemnity, Allyn, I warn you, or I'll be tempted to take my crop to you.'

Before Vredech could reply, Nertha reined her horse to a halt. 'What's that?' she said.

Vredech halted his own horse and as soon as the clatter of hooves faded, another noise became apparent. It was faint, but quite definite. 'Sounds like shouting,' he said.

'A lot of shouting,' Nertha confirmed. 'Come on.' She turned her horse towards the sound and urged it into a trot.

'This is taking us further into town,' Vredech called out, as he caught up with her.

'I do know where we're going. I've not been away *that* long,' she shouted in reply.

'I meant it'll be busy.'

'I wonder what it is?' Nertha said, waving him silent

and craning forward as if that would help her make out the noise above the sound of the horses. Then she pulled her mount into a narrow, unevenly cobbled street. Tall terraced houses on either side threw the street into the shade and its steepness obliged the two riders to slow to a careful walk. Both were concentrating on their riding and neither spoke; the sole sound in the street was that of slithering, iron-shod hooves. The few people who were out and about paid them scant heed, although one or two of the older ones bowed respectfully when they saw that Vredech was a priest.

About halfway down, the street turned sharply, bringing them into the sunlight once again and affording them a view over a large part of the town. The sound of the shouting seemed to be much closer now, trapped in some way by the chasm walls that the houses formed. There were several groups of residents standing about obviously discussing it, and as Vredech and Nertha passed, more people were emerging from their houses and beginning to drift down the hill. At the bottom, the street opened out to join a wide road that led directly to the centre of the town. Although the sound of the shouting was fainter here, there were more people, both on foot and on horseback, and the small trickle of folk who had acted as flank guards to the two riders spread out and dispersed into the general throng that was moving towards the source of the noise.

Vredech and Nertha were tempted to trot their horses again, but the number of other riders and scurrying pedestrians prevented this. A rider pulled alongside Vredech and, made familiar by the unusual circumstance, asked, 'What is it?'

'I've no idea,' Vredech replied. He waved a hand vaguely upwards. 'We heard it from up on the top and—'

'I think it's coming from the PlasHein Square,' Nertha interrupted him. She was pointing. They had come to a large junction from which led several roads, one of them in the direction of the PlasHein Square. It was not a wide one, the PlasHein being in one of the oldest parts of Troidmallos, and the crowd, arriving now from many directions and gathering speed as curiosity grew in proportion to the increasing noise, effectively filled it.

For a moment, Vredech felt disorientated. Large gatherings were unusual in Troidmallos and some instinct was tugging at him to retreat.

Unexpectedly, Nertha confirmed it. 'This is not good,' she said. 'We mustn't get too close, there's going to be trouble.'

Vredech frowned and, following a contrary whim, opposed her. 'Nonsense,' he said. 'These people are Madren, not loud-mouthed Felden. Come on.' And urged his horse forward.

Nertha muttered something under her breath, and snatched at his arm as she caught up with him. 'This is a mistake,' she said angrily. As she was leaning over to him her horse shied a little, nearly unseating her. There were cries of alarm from the people immediately around her as the animal jigged sideways while she recovered control. 'Look,' she shouted at Vredech, her face flushed. 'My horse has got more sense than you. Let's get back while we can. I've been in crowds like this before.'

Vredech, bending forward to quieten his own horse, looked around. Apart from those who had been startled by Nertha's horse, the crowd seemed to be good-humoured, if a little excited, and dominated by curiosity. As was he. There was no harm here, surely? And in any event he was a Preaching Brother and that carried its own protection.

'Don't be silly, what can possibly happen?' he was saying when the noise coming from the PlasHein Square ahead suddenly rose in volume, drowning his words. He felt the whole crowd falter, and his horse began to tremble. He patted it and made soothing noises, then stood in his stirrups to see if he could identify the cause of the hubbub, which was continuing and growing noticeably angry.

'What's happening, Brother?' came various requests from around him.

'It looks as if the square's completely full,' he shouted. 'But I've no idea why.'

The high-pitched sound of a child's voice crying fearfully cut through him. Looking round, he could not see who it was, but he noticed a small eddy in the crowd nearby and had a brief glimpse of a woman's face, white with determination and anxiety, as she began moving against the direction of the crowd.

There was another loud roar from the end of the street, and another ripple of movement through the mass of people. It was as though the crowd was no longer a collection of individuals, but had acquired a will of its own, quite separate from, and unaffected by, the will of those who formed it. Vredech shivered and glanced round at Nertha. Her face was white and strained, and her eyes pleaded with him to leave this place.

For a moment he hesitated, unwilling to appear fearful in the face of danger, especially in front of a woman. This reaction startled him. Not since he had been a youth had he felt foolishness like that – at least, not so strongly. It was followed by a surge of embarrassment and then one of alarm. If such long-hidden follies were being brought to the fore in him by this unusual coming together of so many people, what others were surfacing around him? Because it would be these, primitive and deep, that determined the will of the mass, not the more stabilizing attributes of adulthood.

His mouth went dry.

Well, at least he'd go no further forward, he decided, gritting his teeth and reining his horse to a stop. The people around him were now virtually motionless, and the noise that had lured them all there had also fallen. He looked ahead. The crowd resembled a field of dark corn, rippling to a breeze unfelt by the watcher. Here and there, other riders and one or two carriages stood tall and isolated, like strange weeds.

'We must get out,' Nertha whispered urgently, then glanced behind her and swore. Vredech was shocked by this unexpected profanity, but he soon saw the cause. While those around and ahead of them had stopped moving, others were still entering the narrow street and the crowd behind was now almost as large and as dense as that in front. And it was still growing. It would not be possible for either of them to turn or back their horses. Nertha's fear leaked into him, and from him into his horse, which began to shift its feet restlessly. Cries of dismay and one or two protective blows from the immediate vicinity did little to quieten the animal and Vredech found himself trying to soothe both his neighbours and his horse.

Mounted high above the assembly, just as he was when he preached, he did not hesitate to use his priestly authority. 'Be quiet!' he said, not too loudly, but slowly and with great force. 'If you frighten the horses, we will not be able to control them and someone will be badly hurt. Start moving back out of the street, now. All of you.' As he spoke he turned in his saddle and made a broad gesture to indicate his instruction to those who were out of earshot. 'Whatever's going on here, it seems to have stopped, and we'll all find out about it sooner or later.' Sternly he added some reproach: 'Go home, go about your proper business.'

It was not in the nature of most Madren to argue with their Preaching Brothers and as his message passed along, so it was obeyed, albeit slowly.

Scarcely had Vredech spoken, however, than the noise from the square rose again. This time it was an unmistakable mixture of fear and anger. Hastily he stood in his

311

stirrups to see what the cause was. He thought he had a fleeting glance of Keepers' uniforms milling about urgently in the square ahead but any consideration of that was swept aside by what appeared to be a wave moving through the crowd towards him.

It took him a moment to realize that it was the people at the front of the crowd turning and trying to flee back down the street. And a new noise was added to that coming from the square. It was the sound of screaming. Vredech froze as the consequences of this sudden flight dawned upon him, but his horse had no such future judgement to burden it and it reared instantly in an attempt to free itself from the obstacles that were impairing its own flight. Vredech was a reasonable horseman, so he managed to retain his seat though he could do little to prevent his horse from colliding with those immediately around him. As he struggled to control it he had a vivid impression of many things happening simultaneously. A tide of wide staring eyes, gaping mouths and flailing arms, was surging down the street towards him. He saw Nertha wrestling with her own mount. Remorse and guilt flooded through him, but he had no time to dwell on it for the full impact of the flight from the square struck him at that very instant. His horse staggered sideways, frantically scrabbling to keep its feet on the cobbled street. He could feel the awful impact of bodies being crushed and buffeted by it. Then, like a tree being slowly uprooted by a swollen torrent, it sank, almost gracefully, into the surging mass of fleeing people.

Vredech just managed to clear the stirrups and swing his leg away as the horse toppled on to its side, but he had no chance of keeping his balance. Closing his eyes, wrapping his arms protectively about his head and rolling himself up tightly, he tumbled helplessly under the feet of the crowd. For a time he knew nothing except the fear that was consuming him. Blows pounded him from every direction and his ears were filled with a terrible, continuous scream-ing. Then a particularly violent impact burst his grip open. His hands touched something hard, then his face was pressed roughly against it. The touch, gritty and slightly warm from the day's sun, brought some sem-blance of awareness back to him. He opened his eyes. He had been thrown to the edge of the crowd and was being pressed against a wall. The movement of the crowd rolled him along it a little way, but also gave him the impetus to recover his balance. As he did so, someone crashed into him and fortuitously thrust him into a shallow doorway. Gasping with effort, he seized a stout wooden door handle as an anchor and thrust out a leg to wedge himself between the reveals of the doorway.

Looking round, he saw a horror far worse than anything he had encountered or imagined over the last few weeks. A horror that lay not in fantastic manifestations of super-natural mysteries or primitive evil, but in the very ordi-nariness of the people who were fighting and screaming to flee the street. People, some of whom he recognized, seemed to have lost every trait that they would have claimed marked them as civilized. They were punching, clambering over and crushing underfoot anyone whom they could not hurl aside in their desperation to be out of this suffocating mêlée.

The horror was made even worse for Vredech by the certain knowledge that the awful will of the crowd was possessing him also. But for the pure chance that had thrown him to one side and allowed him to rise, he knew that he, too, could well have been at the centre of that striving mass.

'Stop! Stop! For mercy's sake,' he shouted, but his voice was just one more drop contributing to the flood of sound filling the street. Something bumped into him. He almost lashed out at it but, looking down, he saw a child, its face tear-stained and bloody. Quickly he seized it by the collar and thrust it alongside him, placing himself between it and the press of the crowd as well as he could.

'Stay there, you'll be all right,' he bellowed. The child clung to his leg.

Nertha! Where was Nertha?

The thought struck him as windingly as a well-aimed fist and he almost lost his grip on the doorway. He looked down the street but could see nothing above the heaving confusion of bodies. Anger and desperate shame filled him. Nertha was no fragile blossom, but if she had gone down under this . . .

She had come back to support him in his hour of need and he had led her into this crushing turmoil with his foolishness. The thought was insupportable.

'No!' he roared. He felt the child's arms tighten about his leg, but could not risk releasing his own grip to comfort it.

Then, almost as suddenly as it had started, the stampede was over.

People who had been clamouring and fighting were suddenly free of each other.

There was a brief, disbelieving silence, then new sounds rose to fill it: the sound of the painful return of individual consciousness to those who had just been mindless elements in the fleeing herd. Sobbing reached Vredech first, then a gradual chorus of awful noises like a ghastly descant: ranting, frantic cursing, shrieking, and a terrible litany of shouted names as people began to search for children and spouses, and whoever else had been with them when they ventured into this awful, narrow chasm.

And Vredech found himself the focus of many eyes.

'Brother . . .'

'Brother . . .'

From all around.

Arms stretched out to him in appeal.

Nertha, in the name of pity, where are you? he called

silently, his heart rebelling against these demands.

'Brother . . .'

The voice came from the child, still clinging to his leg. As he glanced down he looked straight into the child's frightened eyes, and into the fearful hearts of its parents, wherever they might be. His own grief was overwhelmed. He was a Preaching Brother. He took the respect that these people offered his kind, he guided them where he could and he stood as a personification of the will of Ishryth as proclaimed by the church. Now, above all, his personal concerns must be set aside until those of his flock had been attended to.

He bent down and gently prised the child's hands free, then lifted it up.

'Don't be frightened any more,' he said. 'It's all over now. Put your arms around my neck, you're heavy.'

Then he stepped out of his tiny stronghold.

Standing in the PlasHein Square, Skynner looked about him in disbelief. Faintly, his mind was turning over the consequences that must surely flow from this event, but these thoughts could make no headway through the struggle he was having just to bring himself to believe what had actually happened.

He pointed a shaking hand towards a line of young men who were sitting cowed, sullen and manacled at the foot of the small grassy ramp that sloped up toward the PlasHein.

'Put them in the PlasHein cells for now,' he said, his face tense with restrained fury. 'We'll deal with them later.'

Someone began a small protest. 'The PlasHein cells aren't really suitable for—'

He stopped as Skynner's gaze fell on him. 'Lock them up,' the serjeant said, with grinding slowness. 'And get back here at the double. We need everyone we've got to sort this out.'

Then, like Vredech, the momentum of a lifetime's dedication to duty made him dash aside all his personal reactions and plunge into practicalities. He gave his felled Captain a cursory look, then, satisfied that he was only unconscious, stepped over him and began striding through the remains of the crowd in search of his scattered men. Father, physician and judge in one, he supported the failing, fired the weary, and cured the lame with such alacrity that within minutes he had gathered together all of his men who were capable of standing and brought them to some semblance of order.

'You – Town Physician and fast. Just tell him what's happened and do as he tells you. You – Keeperage, straight to the Chief. Stop for no one. I want every available man here five minutes ago. The rest of you, in groups. Do what you can for the injured. And get this crowd under control. If anyone's not looking for someone specific, pack them off home on pain of arrest. If they are, get a name and bring it here. And if any of them are up to helping, send them here as well. Albor, you see to that, will you?'

Albor was leaning heavily on a colleague. 'I'm not sure I can,' he said feebly.

Skynner scowled at him. '*I'm* sure,' he said brutally. 'Get on with it. You can fall over later. I've got someone I want to see.'

He did not wait for any remonstrance, but turned and strode off through the crowd towards the gates of the PlasHein. Reaching them, he found the manacled youths standing in a bedraggled line while the Keeper into whose charge he had given them was arguing with a man who appeared to be the leader of a group of uniformed men who were currently lined up across the gateway, long axe-headed pikes held determinedly in front of them.

Though quite old, this individual carried himself with the arrogant posture of a man well used to the wielding of petty power. He wore a uniform like that worn by the men at his back, but his was smarter and more ornate. It was similar in many ways to the Keepers', except that it was marginally more colourful – a narrow red sash here, an emblem there, a touch of golden tracery, and it was tailored from generally superior material. These men were the GardHein, official guards to the PlasHein. Constitutionally they were a very ancient group, existing long before Canol Madreth had been known by that name and even throwing mythical roots back to the time of the final worldly confrontation of Ishryth and Ahmral. Then they were said to have stood shoulder to shoulder, ringed around their unarmed lord, who was rapt in deep concentration, fighting his own unseen battle against Ahmral, while Ahmral's great army broke like waves against their shields and pikes. It was one of the great epic tales of the Santyth. Now, the GardHein was, in effect, an hereditary sinecure, a ceremonial group whose charge of protecting the PlasHein and the Heindral was largely unnecessary. Apart from the need to restrain the occasional over-excited Heinder or agitated petitioner, there was little for them to do other than perform their formal patrols about the building and its grounds.

Skynner wasted no time in determining the niceties of the dispute between the Keeper and the GardHein officer. 'I told you to get this lot locked up, didn't I? What's the delay?' he demanded.

Before the Keeper could speak, the officer replied. 'The PlasHein cells can't be used for street brawlers,' he said haughtily. 'I'm surprised you even suggested it, Serjeant. I'm sure you've got perfectly adequate cells of your own at the Keeperage.'

Skynner clamped his teeth together tightly to still his immediate reaction to the officer's tone, but it was impossible. 'I have indeed, sir,' he said, his voice low and ominous. 'Unfortunately there is a slight problem in the square here, and in the surrounding streets, which needs all the men that I have left and more. Might I respectfully suggest that as your men caused this, the least they can do is stop hindering *my* men in the performance of their duties.'

The officer stiffened and his face reddened with anger. 'Do you know who you're talking to, *Serjeant*?' he said, with heavy emphasis on Skynner's rank.

'I know exactly who I'm talking to,' Skynner thundered. 'I'm talking to the jackass whose orders caused this, and I'm not going to waste any more time. People are lying injured out there. Now stand aside and let my man get these louts locked up or, better still, have one of your own men do it.' He drew his baton as he was speaking. One of the guards stepped forward slightly as if to come to the defence of his officer. Skynner flicked his baton into his left hand then, stepping around the head of the pike, seized the shaft with his right. The move was unhurried but fast, and a sudden jerk unbalanced the guard and brought him to his knees with an incongruous, 'Ooh!' A further jerk pulled the pike free from his failing grip and Skynner swung it up and dropped it heavily on top of the line of now-wavering pikes. The sudden weight disrupted the line completely and several pikes were dropped. Skynner meanwhile had dragged the fallen guard to his feet. 'Get these people locked up,' he said, speaking inches from the man's face. 'Then take yourself over to my man there and start helping him sort this mess out.' Skynner's grip on the throat of the man's tunic prevented him from even glancing at his officer. He nodded shakily and croaked something. Skynner released him and pushing the officer to one side turned to the others. 'The same applies to you, too. Get out there and help.'

'I protest!' the officer began, his face now scarlet with indignation. 'You've no authority to—'

'Shut up,' Skynner said quietly, placing the end of his

baton on the officer's chest. Then he turned and walked away from him.

From a wide recessed window on the second floor of one of the PlasHein towers, Privv stood amid a group of Heinders and PlasHein officials watching the scene at the gate as he had watched the whole affair. While his face showed dismay, his true reaction was one of unalloyed pleasure.

'This is magnificent,' he said silently to Leck. 'Look at those bodies. There must be dozens injured. Children as well.'

'There's some dead,' came the reply, uncomfortably.

'Better and better. This could sell my Sheets all over the country, let alone in Troidmallos. These are good times, Leck. Good times.'

'Unless you're one of the crowd,' Leck replied darkly.

'Where are you now?' Privv asked.

'On one of the balcony windows in the Debating Hall,' she replied. 'There's still a lot of members here, including Drommel if you want to talk to him.'

Privv thought for a moment. Looking over the square, slowly being organized by Skynner and the other Keepers, it seemed unlikely that anything else of significance was likely to happen. Drommel, on the other hand, might prove extremely interesting.

'I'm coming down,' he said. 'Keep your eye on him.'

Thus as Drommel emerged from the debating chamber, leading a wedge of other Witness Party members, his first sight was of Privv bearing down on him. He held out a hand to ward him off. 'I can't talk now, Privv,' he announced urgently. 'I've only just heard what's happened outside. It's dreadful.'

Privv nodded understandingly. 'The youths who started the disturbance in the viewing balcony were part of the crowd that came here to support your cause,' he said,

319

matching the tall man's stride and fending off the others who were obviously unhappy at seeing their leader thus accosted.

'It's to be hoped that the Castellans will take due note of the support for our cause among the people, but behaviour such as occurred in the viewing balcony is not acceptable.' Quickly, he added, 'I'm sure it was not the wish of those people who came to support us, although I can understand the frustration of people at having to stand by and watch a government dithering as the Castellans are doing, about the protection of our citizens abroad.'

'You'll be asking for a Special Assize so that those responsible can be brought to account?'

Drommel looked flustered. 'Possibly,' he said. 'But . . .'

Then his fellow party members finally succeeded in coming between him and Privv and he was swept away through the main doors of the PlasHein while Privv found himself stranded in the entrance hall. It did not matter. He could weave more than enough around Drommel's few words. He walked slowly to the door and looked out across the devastation that had been wrought by the panicking crowd. Momentarily he lapsed into genuine curiosity. 'Did you see exactly what happened?' he asked Leck.

'I certainly did,' Leck replied. 'And it was very interesting.'

Privv was taken by her tone. 'Interesting?'

'It was almost as though the whole thing had been organized.'

'That's hardly a revelation, is it?' Privv declared. 'The Witness Party have been squeezing this Tirfelden business for all it's worth. They're not going to get another chance like this for years. Their efforts and my Sheets were bound to draw a big crowd today.'

'I didn't mean that,' Leck retorted impatiently. 'I meant

the disturbance inside the PlasHein and the trouble at the gate.'

'Explain,' Privv said, intrigued.

'Did you see who started the fight inside?' Leck asked.

'No,' Privv admitted. 'There was just a lot of shouting and abuse, then uproar – struggling bodies everywhere.'

'As if it might have started in two or three places at once?'

Privv pondered for a moment. 'I suppose so,' he said eventually.

'Well, when the GardHein were bundling them all out into the square, they ran straight into a hail of stones. Stones, Privv. Where do you find stones around here unless you bring them with you?'

'Go on.'

'Then people began pushing through the crowd to join those who'd just been thrown out, and there was a great scramble in the gateway. It really did look as though the crowd were trying to storm the place.'

'And the GardHein captain panicked and ordered his men to lower pikes and charge?'

Denial filled him. As did Leck's memory of the event, so engrossed was she in recalling it to develop her argument. 'No, that's the point. He wasn't even there. His men managed to get the gate clear, then they lined up to block the gate and began picking up their pikes. But they didn't charge.'

The scene unfolded in Privv's mind and he watched it as Leck described it.

'As if someone had given an order, the men who'd been doing the fighting suddenly all turned and ran into the crowd, shouting, "They're charging. They're charging." The rest was inevitable. Skynner's men couldn't do anything. They were too few, too scattered, and taken completely by surprise.'

321

Privv was silent for some time. 'Now, that *is* interesting,' he said. 'But who'd want to do such a thing? Not the Witness Party, for sure. Nor any of the others. I can't see any benefit to be gained.'

'There's more,' Leck said quietly.

'Don't just stand there, man. Help!'

Immersed in his inner conversation with Leck, the voice made Privv start violently. Absently he had walked down the steps of the PlasHein and was standing in the gateway. The person addressing him was a weary-looking Keeper who was just gently laying an injured woman down on the grassy slope. Privv pulled himself together quickly and bent down to help him. 'I'm sorry, Keeper,' he said. 'I'm having some difficulty in believing what I'm seeing.'

The Keeper nodded and gave him a look full of grim understanding, then turned and walked back into the crowded square.

Privv returned to his silent conversation. 'Go on,' he said, abandoning the woman and moving away from the gate.

'When the panic began, the men who started it walked quietly away.'

Atypically, Privv was lost for words. Leck's observations had added layer upon layer to what was already, beyond doubt, the best story he had ever had. He needed to think about everything carefully and at his leisure to see how he might best profit from it. In the meantime, he realized there were yet more opportunities for him here.

Looking round, he saw a woman kneeling on the ground, her arms wrapped around a child. There was blood on the child's face and it was very still. The woman was sobbing.

True Sheeter that he was, Privv put a compassionate hand on her shoulder, bent forward and said, 'What do you feel about all this, then?'

322

Chapter 24

Vredech looked at the child in his arms. He was holding it tightly to prevent the trembling that was threatening to overwhelm him.

'Come on, young man, we'd better look for your parents,' he said as comfortingly as he could.

'I'm a girl and I was with my brother,' the child exclaimed, and burst into tears.

Vredech resorted to a vague, 'There, there,' and an affectionate pat. 'Let's find your brother, then,' he said.

But there were other demands being made upon him. Hands clutched at him. All around, wide, shocked eyes appealed to him. He was used to dealing with bereaved relatives and people suffering all manner of personal distress, but this had always been in circumstances of domestic intimacy, secure and sheltering. Here, the very familiarity of the surroundings and the blue summer sky overhead merely intensified the bewildered pain that was turning to him for solace.

Despair filled him, acrid and choking. How could he do anything here? He had no experience of such . . .

He did not complete the thought, for immediately in its wake came the answer: nor has anyone else here.

Ishryth had said, 'I shall burden no soul with more than it can bear.' It was one of the anchors of his faith. But . . .

A hand seized his arm. 'Brother, my husband is hurt. Please . . .'

There is no crowd here, just many individuals, he forced himself to think. Those that I can help, I will. Until things change. He turned to the woman and held out the child to her. 'Show me your husband,' he said quietly but firmly, looking into her eyes. 'And look after this little girl, she's lost her brother.'

The woman faltered briefly, then released his arm and took the child. Vredech followed her to a small circle of people, relatively stationary amid the general confusion. The watchers parted as he reached them. Lying on the rough cobbles was a middle-aged man. He was resting on his elbows, as if fearful of lying down, and one leg was twisted under the other in a manner that needed no medical training on Vredech's part for him to know that it was badly broken. Where are you, Morem? he thought. Nertha? He dashed the thought aside almost in panic. He must concentrate totally on what was in front of him. He shivered.

'Are you all right, Brother?' the injured man asked, grimacing with pain.

'A little disturbed,' Vredech replied, formal politeness containing the surge of conflicting emotions that the injured man's unexpected concern released.

'What happened?' the man asked as Vredech knelt down beside him.

'I've no idea,' Vredech replied. 'I'm going to try to make you comfortable until I can get a physician to help you properly. Lie still, don't try to move. Be patient.' He put his arm around the man's shoulder to support him and laid a hand on his forehead. The watching circle was closing about him again. Glancing around he saw that people, anxious to help, were emerging from the houses and shops that lined the street. He looked at one of the spectators. 'Go to one of those people from the houses and ask for blankets and cushions to support and cover this man.' He turned to another. 'You keep hold of him until your friend gets back. Don't move him.' And to another. 'Go down to the square. I imagine there'll be Keepers there by now. Find out what's happening and come back to me.' Then to the wife of the injured man. 'Be patient. Look after the child for me. I'll not be far away.'

As he stood up, he could see that the small crowd around him had grown. Half a dozen hands reached out to him immediately, and voices became clamorous. He held up his arms. 'Be quiet,' he said sternly and with an authority that he did not feel. 'And be calm. If you're walking, then you've no hurt that won't wait awhile. You must help those less fortunate. Do as I've just done. Make them comfortable. Talk to them, quieten them, until we can find out what's happened and arrange for some proper help.' As he had before, he singled out individuals. 'If you see anyone wandering about lost or obviously distressed and not in control of themselves, bring them . . .' he looked around, '. . . there.' He pointed to the doorway into which he had been pushed. A woman was wandering about helplessly, carrying a chair. From one of the houses, he presumed. He took her arm and pointed her to the same doorway. 'Put it over there,' he said gently. 'And have your neighbours do the same.'

For some time, Vredech was able to use his unexpected healing ministry to keep at bay his fear for Nertha, but eventually it burst through and would not be restrained. With a final delegation of tasks he broke away from his following and started moving back up the street, searching anxiously amongst both the standing and the fallen. He resisted the temptation to add to the noise by calling out her name, but his search was no less frantic than all the others going on around him. He passed a small carriage that was lying on its side, the horse still between its shafts. Its eyes were wide and white, but apart from its heaving flanks, it was motionless, obviously having given up any attempt to right

325

itself. The sight added further to Vredech's anxiety. If the struggling crowd had turned a horse and carriage over, what chance had Nertha had on her mount?

'Nertha, Nertha, where are you?' he whispered softly to himself over and over, like a litany. Terrible reproaches filled him.

If only, if only . . .

His mind was instantly full of both the future and the past. Of her funeral and what could be said of her there. Of raucous argumentative mealtimes under the tolerant stewardship of their parents.

If only, if only . . .

Endless causes and effects.

And darkness.

'Allyn! Allyn!'

It was the tone of the voice rather than the calling of his name that eventually broke through into his crowding thoughts. He looked around, startled. The dreadful images vanished and his life began to re-form itself again.

'Here! Over here!'

At first he did not recognize her. Her long hair had been hastily snatched back and bound with a kerchief, her sleeves were rolled up and her face was streaked with blood. The manner however, was unmistakable: she was beckoning him urgently and her face was angry. He smiled.

'Allyn, get over here, will you,' she shouted.

Vredech pushed his way through the crowd. 'Thank Ishryth you're all right,' he said, kneeling down beside her.

She looked at him briefly, reached out and touched his face, as if for reassurance, then said, 'There's a green bottle in my saddlebag, Allyn. Get it, this one's in a bad way.'

Only then did Vredech notice that she was kneeling by an injured man. Badly injured, as she had remarked, for a

326

jagged bone was sticking out of his arm. Vredech felt the blood draining from his face.

'Damn you, Allyn,' Nertha hissed furiously. 'Don't you dare faint on me. Get that bottle – now!'

Vredech nodded, not daring to open his mouth to reply for fear of what he might release. He looked round. Nertha's horse was standing patiently nearby, tethered to a metal grille that both decorated and guarded a basement window. Surreptitiously he steadied himself against the animal as he stood up, then, after some fumbling with the straps, he was rooting through the contents of the saddle-bag. It was full of bottles and small boxes and mysterious instruments, held snugly in several rows of robustly-made pockets.

He could feel Nertha willing him on to hurry, her silence being, as usual, more potent than her commands. Just as he sensed her about to rise to complete the task herself, he found a green bottle.

'Here,' he said, handing it down to her.

She had opened it and was sprinkling the contents on to a kerchief by the time he had knelt down again. A sweet, pungent smell struck him. It did little to improve his stomach, but his relief at finding Nertha steadied him. 'How did you manage to stay on your horse?' he asked.

But she was talking to her patient. 'This will help the pain. Breathe deeply and count to ten.' She placed the kerchief deftly but very firmly over the man's face. He mumbled something, raised his good arm weakly as if to protest, and then went limp. Vredech watched as Nertha's hands moved surely to the man's throat and then to his eyelids. She nodded to herself. 'Watch this and learn,' she said, adding as an afterthought, 'But if you're going to be sick, face the other way.'

There followed a brief interlude during which Vredech stood by, both horrified and fascinated, while Nertha wrestled with the injured man's arm: pulling, twisting, manipulating. Gradually the exposed bone retreated like a nervous animal into its burrow but Nertha's fingers continued poking and prodding, her tongue protruding slightly and her face rapt in concentration. Vredech was reminded of the Whistler's fingers moving purposefully and independently along his black flute. His own fingers were driving their nails into his palms.

Her hands still working, Nertha glanced up at him and grinned ruefully. 'You look awful.'

'I'm fine,' he said defensively.

Nertha's tongue emerged again and her eyes turned skywards as her face contorted in response to the effort being applied by her hands. A sudden click made Vredech start violently. Nertha's face relaxed. 'Got it,' she said, quietly triumphant, dragging her forearm across her brow. 'Let's get him cleaned up and bandaged. He's a lucky man.'

'Lucky?' Vredech was incredulous.

'Unless that wound becomes badly infected, he'll live and he'll probably get the use of his arm back. That's lucky,' Nertha said starkly. 'There's others here with injuries that I can't just shove back into place.' She waved her bloodstained fingers in front of him. 'Internal injuries, head injuries. I hope Troidmallos's Sick-House can cope.' Her voice suddenly became angry. 'What the devil happened, Allyn?'

Vredech looked at her, head bent again, working steadily on the damaged limb while she was talking. He wanted to put his arms around her and hold her safe. The feeling surprised and unsettled him a little and he made no movement. Besides, he knew that such a gesture would be dangerously inappropriate with Nertha in her present mood.

'I don't know,' he said. 'I sent someone to the square to find out and to fetch the Keepers, but . . .' He shrugged helplessly. 'I just tried to get those who weren't hurt organized a little. Make the injured comfortable until someone came who knew what they were doing.'

Nertha had finished. She stood up and gave her patient to the charge of a woman who had been hovering agitatedly about the scene. 'He'll be asleep for some time, and he'll be very uncomfortable when he wakes up, but he should be all right,' she said, very gently. 'Try to keep him still and warm until I can get back.'

She looked at Vredech. 'There's a man with a broken leg up there,' was all that he could think of to say.

'Show me,' she said, unfastening her horse.

'How did you stay mounted through all that?' Vredech asked again, taking her arm as they began to move back through the crowd. 'I was always a better rider than you, but my horse went down almost immediately.'

Nertha patted her horse. 'She's a cavalry mount,' she said. 'And I'm a lot better rider than you now.'

Vredech looked at her inquiringly.

'I knew this cavalryman in Tirfelden,' Nertha said.

Vredech's eyebrows rose. Nertha coloured a little. 'Where's this broken leg, then?' she snapped.

It was late afternoon before the PlasHein Square and the adjacent streets began to revert to something like their normal state. Vredech and Skynner sat side by side on a decorative ledge that protruded from one of the PlasHein's stone gateposts. Nertha had gone with the last of the injured to the Sick-House, her horse tethered behind one of the wagons that had appeared as the citizens of Troidmallos recovered from their initial shock and began undoing the work wrought by their panic.

Soiled, exhausted and shocked, neither spoke for a long time.

Eventually, Vredech lifted his head and gazed slowly around the sunlit square. It was virtually deserted but it looked as it had always looked. It should be different, he thought. Some mark should remain to proclaim what had happened here today. Some subtle change in the inner quality of the stones, the grass, the walls and watching windows. Something which would lie for ever in the heart of everyone who had been here: a lingering darkness. A rider trotted gently by; Vredech watched him. He was looking about him as though surprised to find the square so empty. It was obviously someone pursuing his ordinary business quite unaware of what had happened. Vredech suddenly wanted to scream and shout at him; to make him feel the same desolate wretchedness that he was feeling. Guilt, he diagnosed as the man passed from view and the clatter of the hooves faded. He had seen it often enough in others. Guilt at being alive and unhurt and sitting in the sun, glad of it, when others had been crushed and broken. Guilt at the seeming abandonment of the dead and injured by failing to stop the great momentum of ordinary events dragging him inexorably back into the present and the prosaic.

'They're saying that the GardHein charged the crowd with their pikes,' he said, his voice sounding strange and distant to him.

Skynner started slightly. 'What? Oh yes.' He rubbed his eyes and sat up. 'That's what I thought at first.' He shook his head as if to clear it. 'That was what everyone was shouting when it started. I was just over there.' He pointed. 'But I'm not so sure now. I've precious little time for that stiff-necked old goat of a Captain of theirs, but he's no liar. He says he only arrived as his men were sealing the gate, and that the men who'd just been thrown out, plus several more already waiting, turned around and charged into the crowd.' He looked down. His foot moved forward and began idly pushing a large stone. 'And he said the crowd were throwing stones at his men.' He picked up the stone. Hefting it, he asked the question that Leck had posed to Privv earlier. 'And where do you get stones like this from round here, unless you've brought them with you?'

He was not given time to debate the matter, however, as a group of senior Keeper officers emerged from the gate accompanied by the GardHein Captain and several Plas-Hein officials. Vredech found their smart, clean appearance offensive as he contrasted it with Skynner's and his own, stained, dusty and torn.

'Serjeant,' one of the officers called out, directing the group towards Skynner.

Muttering something under his breath that Vredech did not catch, Skynner stood up wearily. 'Sir,' he responded.

The officer was quite short and he was obliged to bend his head back to look up at Skynner. His expression was unpleasantly officious. Something malevolently angry began to bloom within Vredech.

'Serjeant, the Captain of the GardHein tells me that you've made some extremely serious allegations against his men. Perhaps you'd care to—'

Vredech's anger burst into full flower. He straightened up and stepped forward to confront the officer before Skynner could reply. 'People have been maimed and killed here today, Captain.' He tilted his head on one side, affecting to examine the insignia on the officer's uniform. 'High Captain,' he corrected, in a voice that unmistakably demeaned the rank. '*Maimed and killed*. Serjeant Skynner was almost totally responsible for bringing order to the chaos that was left immediately after the panic. I've no doubt that many people owe their lives to his prompt action. His immediate superior was knocked unconscious and there has been a marked absence of senior officers throughout. Doubtless there will be an explanation of this when a Special Assize is convened to find out exactly what happened here. In the meantime, I'd suggest, High Captain, that any angry words uttered in the heat of the moment, are not worthy of consideration by men who

331

have more important matters to attend to.' He took the stone from an unresisting Skynner and thrust it into the stunned High Captain's white-gloved hand, then bent down and picked up another. 'These were brought here deliberately to be thrown at the GardHein. I understand you have some young men in custody somewhere.' He turned to Skynner inquiringly.

The GardHein Captain, sensing the direction that events were taking, intervened obsequiously with, 'We were happy to make the PlasHein cells available, High Captain. They're not really suitable, but in view of the urgency . . .' He concluded by nodding several times. The High Captain nodded in his turn, glad not to appear totally helpless before the quiet force of Vredech's harangue.

'I'm no expert in such affairs, of course,' Vredech continued. 'But I think it would be a good idea to ask them why. Don't you?'

Vredech's manner did not invite debate however. The High Captain's mouth opened and moved, but it was quite a time before a coherent sound emerged. 'I think . . . yes . . . of course. It . . .' He faltered painfully, but Vredech was not disposed to release him from his black-eyed gaze. Finally his victim resorted to a noisy coughing fit as if to clear his throat. 'Of course, Brother,' he managed hoarsely, at last. 'Due note will be made of Serjeant Skynner's contribution to today's work. He's a greatly valued officer.' He looked at the rock in his hand and wrinkled his nose at the stains it had made on his glove. 'And you may rest assured that the young men responsible for this will be most thoroughly examined. The decision about a Special Assize is, of course, not mine to make.' He clicked his heels, gave Vredech a salute and Skynner a curt nod, then turned and motioned his following back into the PlasHein.

As they disappeared into the building, Skynner chuckled.

'It seems that Brother Cassraw isn't the only one who's determined to drag the church into lay matters.'

'Well!' Vredech almost snarled. 'Standing there all bright and shiny as though he were at a Town function, while everyone else is exhausted and covered in blood and filth.'

Normality beginning to fold itself about him again, Skynner had been toying with another light-hearted comment, but he abandoned it when he heard the deep anger in Vredech's voice. 'He's not too bad really,' he said, unexpectedly conciliatory, and laying a hand on Vredech's shoulder. 'He probably thought he was helping the morale of his men. Keeping up appearances and all that. It's been an evil day. I doubt any of us are thinking straight.'

Vredech closed his eyes and nodded slowly. His anger at the officer faded as quickly as it had grown, in the face of Skynner's plea.

He looked across the empty square again. Unfocused now that the officer had gone, his thoughts wandered. 'Nertha's changed,' he said irrelevantly.

'Been away a long time,' Skynner said, glad of the harmless conversation, but immediately jumping into a spiked pit. 'She's a fine woman. You should've married her instead of letting her go wandering off to foreign parts.'

Vredech's mouth dropped open and his head jerked forward in shocked disbelief. '*What?*' he exclaimed, turning slowly to his impromptu counsellor.

Undeterred, Skynner made to repeat himself. 'I said you should've—'

'I heard you. I heard you!' Vredech blasted back. 'I'm a celibate Preaching Brother, for pity's sake. And she's my *sister.*'

'No, she's not,' Skynner answered, as if surprised that Vredech did not know this. 'She's not related to you at all.

And your celibacy's voluntary.' He pursed his lips knowingly. 'I'd bleach and iron *my* gloves if I thought it'd make her look at me the way she looks at you.'

Just as the High Captain had been minutes earlier, Vredech was completely lost for a reply in the face of this bizarre turn in the conversation. Eventually, he pointed a prodding finger at Skynner. 'You're right, Haron,' he said, his eyes alternately wide and blinking. 'Absolutely right. None of us are thinking straight. Shock, that's what it is. You're delirious. I'm going to look for my horse and go home. No, to the Sick-House. I'm going to the Sick-House to see how my *sister*'s getting on.'

Watching Vredech stalk across the square, Skynner sat down again on the ledge and leaned back against the gatepost. That was a brilliantly handled piece of work, he mused, with some irony. What in Ishryth's name had possessed him to make a remark like that, even if it was true – *especially* as it was true? He let out a small sigh of regret. Still, it was a small thing against the background of today's happenings.

Skynner looked up at the Ervrin Mallos. Part of it was bright and clear, rich in subtle colours in the low afternoon sunshine, while the rest of it, turned towards the pending night, was dark and brooding. He screwed up his eyes, then rubbed them. Fatigue? Dust? Tears? He could not tell what was clouding them, but around the bright summit of the mountain he was sure he could see a dark, shifting haze.

Chapter 25

The consequences of the events in the PlasHein Square rolled back and forth through Troidmallos like a spuming sea wave trapped in an enclosing bay. Privv's Sheet the following day was purple with rhetoric, ill-considered conjecture, and imaginative prose, though, in fairness, even Privv found it hard to exaggerate some of the things he had seen as he walked through the shocked crowds and grim-faced helpers. Unusually, for him, he had been obliged to invent very little.

He should have been exhausted by work and lack of sleep as he laboured through the night to produce more Sheets than ever before and negotiated their sale far beyond Troidmallos, but he was riding on a wave of almost ecstatic exhilaration, no small component of which was the amount of money he was making.

Leck was oddly silent.

The Heindral was in a state of uproar, not only because its proceedings had been thrown into complete disarray by the panic, but because the time was rapidly approaching when the Castellans must either commit themselves irrevocably to their policy of expelling resident Feldens and seizing Felden assets, or abandon it and risk not only jeopardizing their position at the next Acclamation, but bringing it closer, so riven with internal strife were they.

Toom Drommel waited in delight and anticipation, though he was meticulous in hiding this from the public gaze. All his public utterances and appearances were marked by a demeanour that was even stiffer and more unyielding than usual, and by tones so measured as to be almost sepulchral.

Nertha worked through the night and into the following day at the Sick-House, sustained by anger and passionate concern and whatever else it is that sustains a healer in the face of such futile waste.

Vredech was there, too, grateful for any task he could turn his hand to, however menial. With prayer or with plain words, he comforted the injured and the anxious as well as he was able. He fetched and carried, mopped and cleaned. He kept moving. Had he been asked, he would perhaps have said that it was his faith that drove him on, though from time to time he found knots of anger forming inside him, not least when he encountered other Preaching Brothers fluttering about, fearful for their pristine robes or flinching away from blood and pain. The anger distressed him.

Eventually, when all that could be done had been done, whatever had kept fatigue at bay crashed in on both Nertha and Vredech. Rescue came to them in the form of House, who had wakened to find their beds empty and to hear of the events of the day from her neighbours. Distraught, but grimly in control, she had harnessed the Meeting House trap and driven it through the town to the Sick-House.

'I knew you'd be here,' she said, affecting a hearty confidence to hide her wrenching relief as she found her charges leaning on their horses, almost too tired to mount. 'Come on.'

Neither Nertha nor Vredech had any clear recollection of the journey back to the Meeting House, which was perhaps as well, House being a rather intense driver. Several pedestrians and carriage drivers remembered her passing for quite some time.

At the Meeting House, sure in her own domain, she allowed no debate but simply chivvied the two of them to their beds.

At first, though deeply weary, Vredech could not sleep. The time he had spent at the Sick-House had been worse than the time he had spent helping people in the square: there was a leisurely wretchedness about it that had not been apparent in the immediate aftermath of the panic. People had time to think, to burden the pain of the present with the new, uncertain futures that they could see unfolding. And dreadful images crowded in upon him, vying with each other to torment him with their horror. Screams and cries of terror and grief rang in his ears, bloody wounds and white exposed bones floated before him, bodies pressed in upon him suffocatingly, jerking him upright, gasping for breath. Gradually, however, the needs of his body prevailed and, almost in spite of himself, his mind sank into the darkness.

Yet there was no darkness. He was moving. Shapes and colours danced and hovered about him, shifting and changing, growing and shrinking, shattering silently into glittering cascades and jagged streaks, gliding like bright-eyed hunting-birds, rushing and swooping like feeding swallows, flitting frantically to and fro. They merged with and twined around the sounds that were there, too. All manner of sounds. High-pitched shrieking and malevolent cackling carried on moaning winds . . . rumbling, crushing thunders . . . snatches of conversations, now near, now distant . . . laughter . . . sobs . . . strange animal sounds and sounds that could not exist. The whole moved and shifted to an indiscernible rhythm, shot through with fear and hatred, love and joy, hissing fragments of every conceivable emotion.

And at the heart of this turmoil hung a nothingness that was formed of the darkness itself. A nothingness that was diamond-hard and glittering sharp. A nothingness that

337

was the awareness of Allyn Vredech.

Where is this?

I am waiting.

I am lost.

It was not right to be lost here. Something was missing. A guide? The question had no meaning. He was what he was. He was entire, and he was here. This place was his and his alone, surely. He was not afraid. No other could exist here . . .

Yet there *was* a lack. And a paradox. For all that this was his place, many others intruded. This swirling chaos was of their making.

How could he know this with such certainty?

He was changed.

Why was he changed?

How was he changed?

The memory returned of a chilling touch as a dark red liquid had become water. There was the answer, but it told him nothing.

Where is this?

Full circle.

He was drifting.

He was still.

Then he was in the PlasHein Square, confusion and fear pervading him, darkness and noise all around, pressing in, choking, crushing. And again. And again. Over and over. Yet the fear was not his, he was both outside and inside, he was the watcher and the watched.

This was the dream of another, beyond any vestige of doubt!

Indeed, it was the nightmare of another. A tormented soul reliving in sleep the horror it had experienced in the waking daylight. Yet Vredech could not help. It was not in his gift to help; all he could do was observe.

But he could not accept.

'Have no fear,' he thought. Then, for no seeming

338

reason; 'These are but shadows. A great and ancient strength protects you.'

There was a flickering of pain easing, of peace.

And he was drifting again, floating motionless yet hurtling onward. One after the other he touched dream upon dream, passed through fleeting, elusive images, tumbled uncontrolled.

Then, he was held. All was still.

Nothing else had ever been save this stillness.

Here was truth and certainty.

Here was the centre of all things.

Around him was Troidmallos and all its people – and more.

Yet these things were nothing. A collection of artefacts, cunning devices and painted constructs made for his amusement . . .

To break, to rend . . .

Vredech shivered in the coldness of the mind he had become. He should not be here. This place was diseased and awful. Yet he was powerless to flee.

Blood filled him.

Sacrifice.

Endless sacrifice.

That was the true purpose. All was to be laid on the altar, His altar, in blood and terror, so that—

Something tore Vredech away before he could form the scream that he must utter in the presence of what was emerging.

He was wide awake and upright. His hand shot out and struck a small bedside lantern into life, but even before its dawning glimmers had reached into the dark corners of the room, his senses had desperately drawn in the realities of everything around him, and wrapped them about him like a shield wall.

Yet, washing behind him, in the wake of his desperate flight, came the gaping, bloodstained images that reflected the fate of all that had been chosen for . . .

He put his hands to his head in denial as the images beat themselves against him. Then he tore back the sheets, swung himself off the bed and doused the lantern in a single move. The darkness in the room was only momentary, for the daylight immediately made its presence felt even through the drawn curtains. He yanked them open roughly and stood, arms outstretched, in the cleansing light.

Where had he been? Into what abomination had he just stumbled?

He was allowed no time for further thought, however, for even as he stood there, bustling footsteps along the passageway alerted him to another, more benign assault. There was a faint knock on the door, which then opened before he could give a reply.

'Brother Vredech, are you all right? I thought I heard something fall over.'

Vredech turned, thankful that the bright daylight was at his back. 'I'm fine, thank you, House. Surprisingly well-rested. What time is it?'

'A little before noon,' House replied.

Vredech raised a mildly admonitory finger as he saw her preparing more questions. 'I think I'll get changed then,' he said firmly. House looked him up and down, dithered for a moment, then muttering something vaguely apologetic, left.

He moved over to the bed and, sitting, looked down at his hands. They were shaking. And his mind was still full of the images from which he had just fled, their cruel intensity scarcely diminished. He needed to talk to Nertha. But he could not *show* her what he had seen, recount all that he had heard, somehow pass to her his certain knowledge. He could give her only words. She would only see her brother – he stumbled over the word – rambling. Having a recurrence of his 'brain fever'.

340

And perhaps, after all, he was—
No!

Vredech thrust the thought away. While he could judge his conduct to be rational, he would cling to his intention of watching and listening. The ghost of his father would sustain him for quite a while yet. As, too, would his faith.

But these conclusions did not lessen the unease that formed in the pit of his stomach as his hands had stopped trembling. Except for the fundamental doctrines of the church, change was the way of all things, he knew, but too much was happening too quickly and he could not avoid a feeling of pattern, of shape, to events, though what it was, how it had come about, and where it would lead, he could not begin to fathom. So far there had been the crisis in the Heindral looming suddenly out of what was, after all, no more than a tragic drunken brawl in a foreign country; two terrible murders; and now this disaster in the PlasHein Square which had left some people dead and others massively injured, and must surely leave many more scarred and distressed for a long time, perhaps even for the rest of their lives. And twisting through all this upheaval, like the winding robe from an unclean corpse, were the Sheets, particularly Privv's, with their lying, their thoughtless, callous rhetoric, their bigotry and complete disregard for the duty that it was originally claimed they would perform: the informing of the people of events that were occurring in and about Troidmallos. They were a desperately dangerous force, Vredech realized suddenly, spreading ignorance and intolerance where they should spread knowledge and compassion, and spreading them with the peculiar vividness of the printed word. They should be restrained. Their very presence changed the things they wrote about. Such power should not be allowed in the hands of people so blatantly irresponsible.

Yet how could they be restrained, and by whom?

Vredech put his hand to his head. It was just another

thread among the many that were tangling in his mind. And the Sheets were merely on the surface of what was happening, a scrofulous rash caused by a deeper, more serious inner affliction of the body.

His mind swung back to yet another change that had occurred over the last few months: Cassraw. Was his old friend just playing some game of church politics, or was he in reality slipping slowly into insanity? A coldness came over Vredech. There was a third alternative. Perhaps indeed something had possessed Cassraw. Certainly something more profound than the changing of a fruit juice into water had happened yesterday at the Haven Meeting House, though that in itself he still found deeply disturbing, despite Nertha's scornful dismissal. Something had entered that room. Something corrupt and awful, yet enthrallingly powerful. Something that had passed through and over him, awakening . . .

Awakening what?

Perhaps no more than your sluggish wits, he tried to tell himself half-jocularly. But the jibe did nothing.

'I heard Him as I travelled the dreamways. He walks among us again . . . Ahmral.' Jarry's words returned to him. Mad Jarry, driven into drink and violence, yet made suddenly eloquent by whatever it was he had seen, or felt. Was that what *he* was doing now, travelling the dreamways? Or was his mind softening, like Jarry's? Before he could pursue the question, other words came, keen and penetrating: the Whistler's.

'He is evil personified . . .

'Out of the heat of the Great Creation . . .

'He wanders the worlds . . . A predator . . . A parasite, in search of a host . . .'

A host.

Vredech could feel unwelcome thoughts rolling towards him. Thoughts that would lead him into who could say what future. As if to stay their arrival, his body lifted him off the bed and began changing him into his formal day clothes.

'He carries with Him the essence of all that is dark and foul in the human spirit, all that wallows in ignorance.'

The image of the Sheets flitted briefly through Vredech's mind again.

Ahmral does not exist, Vredech forced himself to think. He is merely a representation of the wicked aspects of mankind as a whole: those traits that should be resisted and controlled. But he was on unsure ground, he knew. Ishryth was accepted by the church as a real and sentient force, albeit beyond physical encompassing by any resource in this world. Why not then Ahmral? Could He not be accorded the benefit of the same faith?

Old, old arguments. Arguments that, amongst others, had once been fought over bloodily. Arguments that were not aided by the Santyth, awkwardly ambiguous on the matter. And now the Whistler's scornful words had cleaved through Vredech's ill-judged complacency like a shining axe, cutting into the heart of his world. 'There is nothing supernatural, Priest. There is only the darkness where your ability to measure the natural ends.'

Vredech stepped out of his room. Emerging from a room opposite was Nertha. She looked at him intently. 'You should have slept longer,' she said.

'And you shouldn't?' he retorted as they walked down the broad stairway.

'My job, looking after sick people,' Nertha replied.

'Not like that,' Vredech stated unequivocally.

'I've been involved in the aftermath of some large accidents, but never anything like that, I'll admit,' Nertha conceded. She took Vredech's arm. Her face was concerned. 'It'll linger with you, Allyn,' she said. 'Suddenly you'll be in the middle of it again. That's the way it is with things like that. Don't be afraid. Just tell me if it happens.'

Vredech laid his hand over hers. 'I'm getting well used

to finding myself other than where I think I am,' he said, smiling.

Nertha gave him a sidelong look. 'You don't seem to be too concerned about it any more.'

'I'm trying not to keep gnawing at it, that's all,' he replied. 'But I'm more concerned about what's happening now than I was even yesterday.' He took both her hands. 'Whatever changed Cassraw on the mountain has changed me, too, though I don't know how, or even in what way. I seem to have found a strength from somewhere.' He gripped her hands tightly and held them against his chest. 'But no matter what happens, I'll tell you, Nertha. Trust me in that. I need you and your cruel vision. You must be ruthless in your observations about what I say and do. But conclude nothing until you've debated it with me. And you must open your mind as never before. Will you promise me that?'

'I will,' Nertha replied quietly.

The following day they set out to attend Cassraw's service. The fine, sunny weather continued, and a lively wind had blown up, keeping the streets bright and airy. By contrast, however, Vredech began to feel an oppression about him as he and Nertha neared the Haven Meeting House. He glanced at Nertha riding beside him. She looked uncomfortable.

'The breeze doesn't seem to be helping here, does it?' he said casually. She shook her head but did not speak and they rode on in silence.

As they had two days earlier, they found themselves part of a dense flow of people moving in the same direction. The comparison set Vredech on edge and once or twice he was seriously inclined to turn about and go home. Finally, they rounded the last bend before the climb up to the Meeting House.

'Ye gods!' Nertha exclaimed.

344

Even though it was still some way to the Meeting House, they could see that a huge crowd surrounded it, filling much of the grounds and spilling out to block the street for some distance. And though he could feel the breeze on his face, Vredech felt the oppression increase. Something drew his eye up towards the summit of the Ervrin Mallos. Despite the bright sunlight, there seemed to be a haze hanging about it. He blinked to clear his eyes, but the haze remained.

'Brother Vredech.'

He looked down. A young man wearing a bright red sash and a dark green tunic had taken his horse's bridle. His eyes were alight with fervour, though his manner was quiet and pleasant. 'Brother Cassraw gave orders that you were to be escorted through the crowd,' he said.

Orders? Vredech thought, but he said, 'Thank you, that will be most helpful. I hadn't expected to see so many people.'

'Great is the power of the Lord. Praise Him,' the young man exclaimed.

'I suppose I'm to be escorted, too,' Nertha intruded.

The young man hesitated for a moment before replying, then, 'Of course,' he smiled. 'Follow me, both of you.'

As they moved after him, Nertha brought her horse next to Vredech's. 'Who are these people?' she asked. 'They were everywhere at his last service.'

'They're Cassraw's Knights of Ishryth,' Vredech explained. 'It's some kind of organization that he's started for the young men of the area. It seems to be very popular.'

'Grudging praise,' Nertha observed.

Vredech shrugged a little guiltily. 'Maybe I'm seeing shadows where none exist, but I feel uneasy about them – for no good reason,' he admitted. 'Even Skynner concedes that he seems to have done fine work with one or two particularly disaffected young men.'

345

'They're rather . . . martial,' Nertha commented.

'Indeed,' Vredech agreed. They had reached the edge of the crowd and several other Knights of Ishryth had appeared and were forcing a pathway through it. 'But it's the look on their faces that disconcerts me most.'

'Fanatical,' Nertha said bluntly.

Vredech grimaced. He had not wanted to hear the word, but he could only agree with it. There were a few such individuals in every parish. They were difficult people to deal with and such extreme devotion was discouraged by the church. In fact, part of every Preaching Brother's training included learning how to deal with it gently. If Cassraw was encouraging it, then . . .

He chose not to pursue the idea, but concentrated on keeping a close rein on his horse as it threaded its way through the crowd. Gradually they moved into single file, Nertha moving ahead. For the first time he noticed that she was indeed riding very easily, and was much more relaxed than she used to be. Knew a cavalryman, did you? he thought, but there was a edge to his observation that made him frown.

Then they were passing through the gates. Inside the grounds, the Knights were everywhere, briskly marshalling people into separate areas. Their guide led them to a hastily-rigged tethering rail where they left their horses, in the company of a great many others, before following him towards the Meeting House. Once again the crowd parted before them.

'I'm afraid there are no seats left,' the young man said, his enthusiasm mounting as they walked up the steps to the main door. 'People have been arriving all day. Praise Him. But we've managed to keep some space free at the back for special worshippers such as yourself.'

As they reached the doorway, their guide entered into a brief negotiation with someone just inside that Vredech could not see. Then two red-sashed Knights emerged and, with much apologizing, he and Nertha were ushered into the places they had been occupying.

'Thank you for your help,' Vredech said, as the young man stood to one side to let him squeeze pass.

'You are friends of the Chosen One; to serve is our honour,' came the reply. Vredech was shocked by this bizarre reply, but he was drawn into the building before he could say anything. Inside, the oppression that had been unsettling Vredech was magnified manifold. It struck him like a blast from a furnace. Even Nertha let out a breathy gasp. The Meeting House was indeed completely full. Not only was there not a seat to be seen, but there was virtually nowhere to stand, so crowded were the aisles. People were even sitting and standing in the deep window recesses, thereby making the hall still darker. Instinctively, Vredech put his arm out to protect Nertha. Memories of the stampede returned to him. If this crowd should panic . . .

He felt sweat forming on his brow as he struggled to dismiss the thought, and he glanced over his shoulder to confirm the nearness of the door. Not that that would necessarily avail them much, being as crowded as the rest of the hall.

This is awful, he thought. Meeting Houses by their very construction were usually bitterly cold in winter, but pleasantly cool in this kind of weather.

Yet the airlessness here was not simply due to the heat generated by the crowd. There was something else. Was it his imagination, or was there lingering in the atmosphere here, faint hints of the foulness he had felt on the mountain, and in Cassraw's room as his old friend had worked his petty but chilling miracle?

This was more than awful, he decided. It was ghastly, and frightening. He had come here in the hope of listening to what Cassraw had to say in some semblance of peace and tranquillity so that he could decide what to do next. Now he felt as though he was being bound before the

347

mythical domain of Ahmral as some kind of sacrifice.

The word brought back the final encounter he had had before he had woken the previous day. That cold, blood-lusting dream. He trembled as he recalled it. Whose mind could have formed such a creation? Then he realized that there had been an elusive familiarity about it. His trembling increased. 'Breathe very slowly, very gently.'

It was Nertha. She was looking at him carefully. 'Keep your mind quiet. Relax your shoulders. Relax everything. If you don't, you're going to pass out in this heat.'

Her voice cut into the battle that was beginning to rage in his mind. 'It's like the other day, in the street,' he said, immediately ashamed of the slight tremor in his voice.

'No, it's not,' she said calmly. 'It's worse. The temperature's higher and the crowd's more dense.'

'Some comforter, physician,' Vredech retorted weakly.

Nertha was undeterred. 'There's also much less room in which to move. The pews and the narrow aisles will prevent any mass movement, and at least these Knights of Cassraw's are keeping a watch on things.'

'I still don't like it,' Vredech replied.

'Ah, that's a different matter,' Nertha said. She was grinning slightly, but her face was flushed and Vredech could see alarm in her eyes. The exchange had made him feel calmer, however, which was presumably the object of the exercise. He looked at Nertha surreptitiously. She had always been an interesting, self-sufficient person; but now he was beginning to suspect that she had developed into a truly remarkable woman.

He was given no time to ponder this discovery as the atmosphere in the hall suddenly changed. The muffled hubbub became expectant. Unable to see the front of the hall over the intervening crowd, Vredech presumed that one of Cassraw's lay helpers, or perhaps a novice, had entered to test the congregation. Testing was a relic of the church's most ancient days, when Preaching Brothers had

348

reputedly been warrior princes and lords trying to drag their people out of the ways of war, and when more than one had been treacherously slain as he entered to address his flock. In those days, the tester was said to have been a bodyguard who, dressed as his lord, would pause in the shadow of the doorway before entering the hall. Later, the tester's task became the carrying beneath his robes of a ceremonial sword which he would conspicuously lay upon a table on safely reaching the pulpit. Now, the sword had been replaced by a copy of the Santyth.

A gasp came from the front of the hall. Vredech and Nertha, in common with their immediate neighbours, craned up, but were unable to see what had happened. Then the word 'Sword' hissed through the congregation. Cries of 'Praise Him!' and 'Thus let it be!' rose up from several places as it reached them, and Vredech was aware of considerable agitation about him as people circled their hands about their hearts.

Primitive, he thought, though not in condemnation of those so moved, but as a description of the mood that he felt developing around him. And had Cassraw indeed reverted to the long-abandoned practice of carrying the sword at testing? More noise came from the front of the hall at this point, and suddenly a black form rose up out of the raised pulpit. In common with almost everyone else in the congregation, Vredech caught his breath. For a moment, the figure, hooded and motionless, became one of the shadows that had inhabited the strange twilight world where he had met the Whistler. His mind told him otherwise immediately: told him that it was only Cassraw pursuing whatever design it was that he had chosen to follow, but that did not stop his knees from shaking and his already moist forehead from becoming clammy.

The oppressiveness in the hall grew still further as though it were actually flowing out of Cassraw. It seemed to crush the congregation into silence.

'The time of proving is upon us.' Cassraw's powerful voice rolled sonorously over the silence.

'Let those who doubt that Ahmral's hand is in our midst, turn to their neighbours and ask what befell but two days ago in the PlasHein Square. Let them ask who sapped the moral fibre of our leaders so that the people would be drawn forth in such numbers to make their voices heard in the cause of simple justice.'

Slowly, Cassraw reached up and drew back his hood. As he did so he moved forward and leaned on the edge of the pulpit. The movement itself seemed to crackle through the quivering air. Even at the rear of the hall, Vredech could feel the power of his presence as those gleaming black eyes scanned his audience. 'It is ever the way of Ahmral to use the weak for His ends.'

Silence.

'But so it is ever the way of the Lord to give strength to true believers – to those who are proven – that they might rise up and overthrow those who would lead them astray.'

'Praise Him! Praise Him!'

'And let those who doubt that but look around them, at the numbers that have come here today.'

'Praise Him! Praise Him!'

'And as we are gathered here in witness to His will, so shall all Canol Madreth be brought back to the One True Light, and thence all Gyronlandt, and beyond.'

There was such a roar of approval at this that Cassraw eventually had to silence it by raising his hands.

'But this will be no light task. Ahmral's taint is spread both wide and deep, enmeshing us all. There is no deceit that He will not practice, no lies He will not tell, no treachery to which He will not stoop.' Cassraw leaned further forward. 'Vigilance must be our watchword, my children. Only through vigilance shall we find those who would betray us with their weakness.' His voice became thin and penetrating. 'Seek always for those signs that will show you where Ahmral's taint has been left. Seek even in your loved ones. *Even in yourselves.* For wherever it is found, we must root it out if we are not all to be doomed.'

'Thus let it be!'

'And where the taint is found, however slight, let those who bear it come forward and be purged. Let them show that their faith in the Lord has been proven again. Let them come to me, here. Let them have that awful burden lifted from them. For *I* have been charged with the carrying of that burden unto the place of His coming, unto the place where His new temple shall be built.' Cassraw lifted his hand towards the Ervrin Mallos.

This time there was uproar. Despite the crush of the crowd, people were waving their arms, clapping their hands and crying out, 'Praise Him. Praise Him. Thus let it be.'

This is madness, Vredech wanted to shout, but it was as though an iron band was tightening about his throat.

Cassraw's voice cut through the din. 'But beware, my children. Beware those who would lure you astray with soft words of so-called reason, of compromise with wrong-doers, of doubt about the eternal truths, for their words are as corrosive as Ahmral's spittle. Here is the way. The only way.' He held up the Santyth, and a monstrous passion filled his voice. 'Here are written all things. Go unto those who would seek to rule you and tell them to seek first within these blessed pages for guidance. Let them hear His words before they speak their own. Go unto them and do His work, I command you.'

It seemed to Vredech that Cassraw's voice came no longer from the front of the hall but had become a great solid mass that was pressing down upon him from all directions, pounding itself into him. A blackness started to flow over him. Somewhere in the distance he heard his name being called. The words twinkled through the darkness like stars, but he could not reach out and take them.

The blackness closed over him.

Chapter 26

Darke and Tirec stared up at the Ervrin Mallos. Both seemed distressed, but it was Tirec who spoke first.

'As we've moved further from home, communities seem to have grown more primitive, more ignorant, superstitious,' he said, though his voice contained no judgement. 'I thought this just more of the same, but it isn't, is it?'

Darke did not reply for some time. 'I'm sorry,' he said eventually. 'I'm finding it hard to accept what I'm feeling.'

'You think it's Him, don't you?' Tirec forced the words out.

Darke closed his eyes and tightened his mouth, then he nodded slowly. 'I fear it's something to do with Him, certainly.'

'No,' Tirec said. 'Face it squarely, like you've always taught me. You think it's Him, returned.'

'Too hasty a judgement,' Darke said, too quickly. 'We were there when He was destroyed.'

'We were there when His form in this world was destroyed,' Tirec corrected.

'Elders' talk. I don't know what that means,' Darke said, his tone suddenly angry. 'And nor do you.' Then a look of self-reproach replaced the anger, and he sagged a little and laid an apologetic hand on Tirec's arm. 'We should both have listened to them more, I suppose. Made an effort to learn.' He straightened up. 'Well, let's do what

352

we're good at, what we were sent out to do: discover, learn.'

Tirec opened his mouth as if to reply, but made no sound.

'It's all we can do,' Darke said. 'Though my every instinct's telling me that we've precious little time.'

Then he shivered violently.

'What do you mean, none of this is real?' said a vaguely familiar voice. 'I thought we'd agreed not to debate that any more.'

Vredech opened his eyes. The draining heat of the Meeting Hall was gone and in its place was a gentle evening coolness. In the distance he could see a sky reddened by the vanished sun. A figure moved to one side and with a cry, Vredech struggled to his feet. The figure hopped away from him in some alarm.

'I see that my instruction to kill our friend has offended your priestly sensibilities,' it exclaimed affectedly.

The voice, or rather, the sound, was unmistakable this time. The Whistler was speaking across the mouth-hole of his flute. And they were on the hillside where he had last seen him before waking to the anxious ministrations of House and Skynner.

'What am I doing here?' Vredech shouted.

The Whistler arched his body backwards as though under the impact of the words. 'Not again,' he said. 'Please. Play the game properly.'

Vredech clamped his hands to his head, his thoughts reeling. 'No,' he snarled. 'I won't have this. I'm in the Haven Meeting House, listening to Cassraw's ranting sermon, not standing on some dark hillside with . . . a figment of my imagination. I've fainted with the heat, that's all.'

He fell silent and screwed his eyes tight shut in the hope that when he opened them he would be back standing by

Nertha, but he could still hear the Whistler humming thoughtfully in the darkness. There was a slight scuffling which prompted Vredech to open his eyes again. The lean face of the Whistler appeared, scarcely a hand's span away. His wide, mobile eyes were searching intently. A light had blossomed from something in the palm of his upheld hand – a small lantern, Vredech presumed. Its light was gentle, but almost like daylight in its clarity, for he could see every detail of the Whistler's face. He resisted the temptation to reach up and touch him to satisfy himself that he was indeed truly there.

'You're a strange one, Allyn Vredech,' the Whistler said. 'Here we are, talking like civilized people about matters of great import: about the souls of men, and the roots of things evil, even about the flawed fabric of all things, and you start screaming and blathering.'

Vredech's hands shot out to seize the broad lapel of the Whistler's tunic.

He heard a soft, 'Don't!' then had a fleeting impression of the black flute appearing between his outstretched arms and, suddenly, though he felt no impact, he was briefly on his knees and then rolling on the grass.

As he righted himself he saw that the Whistler was crouching some way away, watching him as though nothing had happened.

'You've a deal of violence in you for a priest,' he said. 'I'm beginning to suspect you've chosen the wrong vocation.'

'What do you mean?' Vredech asked, adding hastily, 'No, no! I don't want to talk about it. I don't want to get involved in another debate with myself. I'm not here. This isn't happening. It's at least two weeks since I left this place.'

'Left?' the Whistler said. He was sitting now, playing softly on his flute. The light was dangling from his hand and bobbing happily. 'What do you mean, left?'

Vredech stood up and walked over to him. Whatever was happening he had to get away from this place, get back to the real world, to the Haven Meeting House, and Nertha, and Cassraw.

'Two weeks,' he said, looking down at the cross-legged figure, strangely mobile in the flitting light. 'Two whole weeks since I was here. People have died in a terrible accident in Troidmallos. The government's somehow managed to turn a small problem into one large enough to bring it down with who knows what consequences. Another young man's been murdered. And Cassraw seems to be going quite mad. *Will you stop playing that damn thing!*' He reached forward angrily to seize the flute. It hovered momentarily in front of his hand then slipped away before he could grasp it. Drawn inexorably after it, Vredech eventually staggered several paces sideways before he regained his balance. He almost swore.

'Definitely the wrong vocation,' the Whistler said over the mouth-hole. He stopped playing and, like an unfolding plant, stood straight up. He held the light out towards Vredech who stared at him uncertainly. 'You're a warrior, Allyn,' he said. 'Not a priest. Did you know that? You resort to violence very easily.' His tone was mocking.

'No, I don't. Look – I'm not going to discuss it,' Vredech said, unnerved by the Whistler's observation.

'Don't worry about it,' the Whistler said. 'You're not the first. And there's not a great deal of difference between a priest and a true warrior. You both care about people after your fashion. Come on.' He threw the small lantern into the air and, twisting round and round, ran after it as it arced through the darkness. He blew an incongruous trill on the flute with one hand as he caught the lantern with the other.

'Where?' Vredech demanded, in spite of himself.

'There's a cave over here. Nice and dry. And warm when we get a fire going.'

355

'But . . .'

'Come on.'

Vredech looked towards the horizon, where a dull purple marked the resting place of the sun. His gaze moved upwards. The sky was full of stars, clear and brilliant – but the patterns they formed were unfamiliar. And there were so many. They were not the stars that shone over Troidmallos.

He stared, at once spellbound and deeply afraid.

'Come on!' The Whistler's voice was distant now. Vredech tore his gaze from the sky and peered into the darkness. The only sign of the Whistler was a light in the distance, jigging to and fro and occasionally soaring into the air.

'Wait!' he shouted as he started running after it. The light paused and became brighter. As he ran towards it he recalled the old Madren tales of benighted travellers drawn into the marshes by malevolent sprites with their flaming lanterns.

He was breathing heavily by the time he reached the Whistler.

'You'll need to be fitter than that when you take up your new vocation,' he said.

Vredech ignored the remark. He was fighting back panic and forcing himself to adjust to the reality of this mysterious place once again. It was no dream, of that he was certain. For now he knew that he had touched the dreams of others; had been both himself and the dreamer. And dreams had an insubstantial quality at their heart, like reflections in water. Their realities, however vivid, were shifting and ephemeral. They had no hold on him, no control, for he was not truly there. Here, on the contrary, everything was solid and true – the grass under his feet, the scented evening cool becoming the night's coldness under the sharp clear sky, his panting breath as he strode out to keep up with the Whistler's rangy gait.

Then they were walking amongst trees. The touch of the lantern-light turned the leaves and branches overhead into domed ceilings, and the trunks into solid columns. It was as though they were walking through a great cellar.

'Here we are.' The Whistler broke into his reverie. A slight slope had carried them up to the entrance to a cave in a rock face that rose sharply out of the ground to mark the end of the trees. He stepped inside and Vredech followed him. The rock walls had a reddish tint to them, and here and there, tiny polished facets bounced the lantern's light back in greeting. The cave was dry and fresh smelling, as if the warm day was still trapped there.

The Whistler took in a deep breath and smacked his stomach vigorously. 'In such simple things lies true wealth,' he said. Vredech looked at him sourly. The Whistler returned the gaze, his expression enigmatic. 'Just a moment,' he said, 'and I'll find some wood for a fire. I won't be long. I'll leave the lantern.'

'I'm not some child, afraid of the dark,' Vredech snapped.

'You're not?' the Whistler said quietly. 'I'll leave it, anyway.'

Vredech sat down and leaned back against the rock. I'm in the Haven Meeting House, he kept forcing himself to think, over and over, as if repetition would make it so. The hard rock against his head and back, the lantern-light etching out the lines of the cave, and the distant sound of the Whistler, now playing, now talking to himself, denied this assertion.

Then he was back and, very soon, smoke was crackling from a small heap of twigs at the mouth of the cave. Vredech watched indifferently as the Whistler's long hands coaxed the smoke into flames and then began to build a fire.

As it flared up, he sat down, apparently satisfied, and motioned Vredech to sit opposite. Vredech did not move.

'You're suddenly troubled, night eyes,' the Whistler said. 'In the blink of an eye you changed. One moment you were assured and coherent, the next, wild and rambling, even resorting to violence. Markedly more primitive. Interesting, but quite startling.' He stared into the fire and then up at the smoke rising from it. An solitary spark drifted skywards. He raised the flute to his eye and peered along it at the dwindling speck. 'I'm intrigued to hear what's happened. Do you know? Or am I talking to myself after all?'

Vredech looked at him intently. 'You must tell me something I don't know,' he said. 'So that I can test your reality when I return to . . . my own world.'

The Whistler's brow furrowed in puzzlement, then he shook his head. 'If you hesitate about your own world, how much more so must I?' he said starkly. 'I don't know where it is – indeed, "where", like "when", means little to me now. And, of course, I don't even know *if* it is, or even if you *are*, so how can I answer such a question?'

Vredech gritted his teeth. 'Then, tell me what He will do. This spirit of evil of yours,' he said, in some exasperation.

The Whistler's fingers twitched along his flute and he lifted it slightly, then changed his mind. 'Tell me first why you're suddenly different,' he said. 'You frighten me.'

Vredech raised his eyebrows in surprise. '*I* frighten *you*? That seems unlikely. You didn't have any problem with my violence, as you call it.'

The Whistler made a dismissive gesture. 'A detail. I took your actions to a consequence different from the one you intended, that's all. You frighten me because your strangeness, your unsettling complexity, makes me doubt my sanity.' His eyes narrowed menacingly. 'It's occurred to me before that wherever I'm lying asleep, I'm mad. Maybe that's why I've locked myself here, like a child cowering under the blankets. Because here I can be sane.

Moving from world to world of my own making, able to reason and think. But since you came, my control of events seems to have slipped away from me. I'm plunged into strange places . . . places that are between the worlds. And you, black-orbed, haunted and haunting, now rational, now demented, come probing into the very heart of my dream. Bringing your plausibility, your bewildering complexity to twist and bend my thoughts. And bringing Him with you, damn you. All control goes when He comes.' He levelled a quivering finger at Vredech. 'If you are real, then what am I? And if you're not, then why should I have Him return and use such a creation as you to be His harbinger? Why should I test myself so? And if I stare into this boiling pit, if I judge myself mad here as well as mad wherever I truly am, then what is the point of all this?' He waved an all-encompassing hand. 'Will it crumble and fall? Will I wake to my true madness? Will I die?'

Vredech flinched away from the pain in the Whistler's voice but he could do no other than reach out and help; the pastoral demand set his own concerns to one side. He snatched at Nertha's words. 'Nothing can withstand that kind of scrutiny, Whistler,' he said. 'It's like a child asking "Why?" after everything you say.' Then, half to himself: 'Even healthy flesh becomes diseased if you pick at it long enough.' He copied the Whistler's own dismissive gesture. 'Play your flute. I'll tell you what happened to me.'

The Whistler moved as if to speak, then turned his gaze back to the fire. Slowly the flute came to his mouth and he began to play the three notes that Vredech had heard at their first meeting. Over and over, each time different, sometimes poignant, lingering, sometimes angry, sometimes full of menacing anticipation. As the Whistler's music filled the cave, Vredech thought that he could hear other sounds, powerful and disturbing, weaving through the simple notes. He listened intently for a moment, then, quite undramatically, told the absorbed Whistler all that had happened since he had found himself back in his room in the Meeting House.

The Whistler seemed to be more at ease when Vredech eventually fell silent. He stopped playing though his head was moving from side to side and he was waving the flute delicately as if he, too, were hearing music other than his own. He looked back into the cave. 'The Sound Carvers lived in caves,' he said. 'Deep, winding, unbelievable caves, full of marvels you could scarcely imagine. I come and play in places like this from time to time, just in case they're here and might want to remember their old pupil. I sometimes think I hear them.'

He gave a pensive sigh. Then his eyes widened lecherously. 'I like the sound of your sister,' he said. 'Quite a woman. I wouldn't mind . . .'

Vredech's fist tightened and his jaw came out. The Whistler's hands rose in rapid surrender. 'Sorry,' he said, his voice full of mock abjectness. And, as suddenly, his manner was earnest and concerned.

'You spin an excellent tale, but I've heard it before. Chaos and confusion in public, blood and terror in private. His hallmarks, night eyes. His hallmarks. Your friend must be a most apt host to have brought this about so quickly.'

Being swept along by the panic-stricken crowd, and learning of the murder of the young men had shaken Vredech, but the implication that Cassraw had something to do with either of them shook him even more.

'No!' he protested heatedly. 'No. You've no right to assume that Cassraw was involved in the murders. Or the panic. You can't possibly think—'

'I can think what I want, Priest,' the Whistler interrupted. There was an unpleasant edge to his voice.

Vredech retreated a little. 'I meant . . .'

'You meant that you knew what I should and should not

360

think,' the Whistler said, suddenly very angry. 'That's the way it is with religions and priests. They give you the authority to walk the easy way, to wallow in ignorance and bigotry and call it divine revelation – anything rather than admit that perhaps everything is not simple, that people might have to make their own judgements, think for themselves, delve into the wonders that are all around us, discover, learn, search out their own destinies, *go to hell in their own way*. You look down from your lofty pinnacles, with your god at your elbow and inflict every conceivable kind of cruelty on anyone who has the temerity to ask, "Are you sure?" ' He kicked the fire savagely, sending up a spiralling cloud of sparks. 'Ye gods, I hate the lot of you.'

So vitriolic was the outburst that Vredech was stunned into silence. A flood of indignant replies piled up so chaotically in his mind that he could not give them voice.

'That's unjust,' he managed after a long silence, and with a softness that surprised him.

The Whistler made no acknowledgement, but began playing again: a bitter, hard-edged marching tune with a driving rhythm which he tapped out with one foot so hard that Vredech could feel the vibration through the ground beneath his own feet. It rose into a shriek and stopped without resolution, though the Whistler's foot continued tapping, and a vague echo of the tune pulsed softly out of his pursed lips.

'And all this business in your . . . Troidmallos . . . happened, between this and this.' He snapped his fingers twice as he spoke.

Vredech was taken aback by the sudden return to their previous conversation. Despite the gentleness of his first response, he was still burning with a desire to engage in angry debate about his religion, but a certain regret in the Whistler's manner prevented him. He could not resist one shaft, however.

361

'You wanted to know, seeker after knowledge,' he said icily. 'And I told you. So spare me any more of your scorn.'

The Whistler's foot stopped tapping and he slouched forward. Vredech deduced that that was as close to an argument as he was going to get and he remained silent.

When the Whistler spoke, his voice was quite calm. 'Do as I told you a few minutes,' he gave a rueful smile, 'or a few weeks ago, as you'd have it. Go to this friend of yours, this Cassraw, and kill him. Do it now, while you still can, and before any more innocent blood is spilt.'

'Don't be ridiculous,' Vredech replied viciously. 'Canol Madreth is a civilized country. We have laws about such minor matters as random murder, not to mention procedures for properly determining guilt. And anyway, we don't execute people no matter what their crime. And, not least, there's the fact that I couldn't even contemplate such an act.' The unspent anger at the assault on his vocation spilled out a little. 'If you can't say anything sensible, *shut up*.'

The Whistler did not respond to Vredech's anger. Instead, his voice remained calm. 'That's still the most sensible advice I can give you, though I can see it's unlikely to be accepted. One of the problems for so-called civilized peoples is that they've usually forgotten the darkness from which they came, and have little or no resistance to it when others, less civilized, bring it down upon them. Barbarians have swept away golden temples and glittering cities, time after time after time. And the ignorant have yoked the learnèd, time after time after time.' He picked up a few pieces of wood and began repairing the damage his kick had done to the fire. 'You know what the dominant response is, of people so conquered?' He raised a quizzical eyebrow and, for the first time since his diatribe about religion, he looked at Vredech.

Vredech shook his head hesitantly, his anger fading and uncertain now.

'Astonishment,' the Whistler said, turning back to the fire. 'It's bubbling under the surface in you, right now.'

There was a long silence. Atypically, the Whistler sat very still, his flute lying idle across his knees. Vredech watched him. The scene, with its soft lanternlight and gently moving firelight, looked like a picture in a book. For a moment, he felt that if he reached out, he would turn over a page and find himself reading some old tale.

Vaguely, he felt powers about him, contending for him, trying to draw him away. But he needed to speak further with this strange individual.

'Answer my first question then,' he said quietly. 'What will happen? What will this evil spirit of yours do?'

The Whistler did not seem to hear, then, as Vredech was about to repeat the question, he said: 'What will happen is up to you, I suspect. No – I *know* it will be up to you. You are near the heart. You're a pivot. A tiny thing about which great things will turn.' He looked sharply at Vredech, angular and alert again. 'These things I've seen. As to when, or where . . .' he shrugged, then pursed his lips and began whistling.

The sound filled the cave instantly, sharp-edged and penetrating. Vredech felt it wrapping around him, cutting through him. Without being aware of any transition he was standing on a high vantage. There was a naturalness about the change that left him unsurprised, but it took him a moment to realize what he was looking at. It was a town, though bigger by far than Troidmallos, spreading out in every direction as far as he could see. Bigger even than one of the Tirfelden cities that his father had once taken him to as a child. And, also unlike Troidmallos, with its winding sloping streets and rows of stepped houses, it was flat. Born and reared amongst mountains, Vredech found the perspective unsettling. Far more unsettling though, was the realization that the whole city seemed to have been destroyed. The view immediately around him was jagged with shattered walls and blackened timbers and, in the distance, great fires raged, hurling flames and dense black smoke into a mocking blue sky.

Then, from whatever eyrie he was perched in, Vredech began to make out movement in the streets below. He needed no telling to identify it, it was hanging in the Whistler's eerie music that was still all about him. The movement was that of people, fleeing. Women, children, old men – the young and the less young were already dead, the music told him. Then there was more movement. Horsemen! A surging tide of them flowing black and relentless in pursuit through the crowded streets, riding over the panic-stricken survivors, crushing them, hacking them down. But this was no battle. That had already been won. This was a hunting, a revelling sport, part of the reward for that winning. The music continued, twining together laughter and screams in an unholy harmony, telling him that of those who did not die here, some would be kept for further, more leisurely sport later, others would be bound and broken in slavery, while the seemingly most lucky, those who would escape, would serve as the bearers of hideous tales to begin the destruction of the next city even before the enemy had set spur towards it. He tried to turn his head away, but it was held firm. Nor would his eyes close. For a brief, terrible instant he was sucked down into the crowd to become once again part of a suffocating, screaming throng, though this time the cries around him were foreign and strange. The terror, however, needed no language.

Then blood filled his vision. Filled his world. Choking . . .

The Whistler was looking at him inquiringly. 'There are many such songs,' he said.

Vredech drew in an agonizing breath. He held out a hand, at once restraining and denying. 'It cannot be,' he gasped. 'Not in Canol Madreth.'

364

The Whistler was playing his flute again, the angry march he had played before, though now it was soft and distant. 'I told you: astonishment. You'll be gaping in disbelief at the sword that kills you, thinking, "this cannot be".' He levelled the flute at him. The sudden silence in the cave was more startling than if there had been a thunderclap. 'Everywhere. Anywhere. Such a fate is always waiting for those who forget the darkness in their nature,' the Whistler intoned. 'Learn it now, or you'll be taught it again.'

'What can I do?' Vredech asked.

'I've told you once and you won't do it.'

His body still reacting to the scenes he had just witnessed, and his mind reacting to the manner in which he had witnessed them, Vredech could not give voice to his returned anger. He shook his head despairingly and snatched at a thread of reasoning for support. 'Your advice aside, Whistler, allow me a moment. If you are a figment of my imagination then perhaps I'm on the way to madness. But if I murder my friend at your suggesting, then I am truly insane, isn't that so?'

The Whistler made no reply for a moment, then he said, 'And if you are a figment of *my* imagination, I'd still like to know why I'm taxing myself with such a problematic individual, with his inconvenient moral dilemmas.'

Vredech's thoughts started to reel as once again he groped for some anchor that would hold sufficiently for him to determine the reality of what was happening. Something inspired him. 'Perhaps you value our debate,' he said.

The Whistler laughed. The sound echoed joyously around the cave but it jarred on Vredech's ears. 'You may well be right, in some perverse fashion,' the Whistler said. 'But I'm afraid I've no advice for you, other than what I've already given you.' He became serious again. 'If you choose not to follow it, then . . .' He shrugged. 'But if you want to stop Him rising once again to power, and devastating your land and its people, then His death is the only thing that will achieve this.' He turned away sharply, and Vredech felt a great wave of sadness pass over him. 'If you kill Him now, then perhaps it will go badly for you. But if you kill Him later, it will have already gone badly for many others.' He paused. 'I'm afraid it's usually so.'

'But—'

'You have your answer, Priest. If you won't kill Him, then you'll have to watch events unfold and respond accordingly. Public chaos and death, you say, has already begun. Private blood-letting and terror you have, too.' He drew in a hissing breath and his hands curled painfully about the flute, as if he had accidentally struck a newly-healed sore. 'They are related, trust me. And be warned. You defend your friend, understandably, I suppose, but he's not your friend any more. He is His. Body and what's left of his soul. I've told you, he's an apt vessel – very apt. The events you'll be watching may well move with great speed. Disbelief and astonishment are luxuries you haven't the time to afford.' He became suddenly pensive. 'Apt,' he murmured to himself, as if the word had set unexpected thoughts in train. 'There's a quality about these things, like . . .' He frowned as he struggled for the words, then lifted the flute and began playing random notes, very slowly, with his head cocked on one side, listening intently. 'Like this,' he said eventually, blowing a single note. As he lowered the flute, the note returned out of the darkness at the back of the cave and hovered briefly before fading. 'An echoing, a resonance. There's a quality in some of this rock that's in deep harmony with this note. It responds when touched in the right way.' He played the note again, and held up a hand for silence as it returned once more. 'So it is with Him. But infinitely more subtle.' He pressed his thumb and forefinger together. 'Who responds just so to His song, builds a way

366

for Him. Large or small, wide or narrow, it will be His way. And He will not relinquish it. He builds ever. And there are many ways in which He can come. Ways of the mind, the spirit, the heart, the flesh.' He snapped his fingers and pointed at Vredech. 'Don't let this friend of yours build anything,' he said urgently. 'No monuments, no palaces. Nothing.'

Vredech made to speak, but the Whistler was continuing. 'Right place, right moment, right . . . qualities . . . prayer, adulation, terror – and such a place can draw Him down on you like lightning down a tree, and the consequences of that bear no thinking about.'

The awful conviction in the Whistler's voice made Vredech shiver. As if in response, the wood that the Whistler had thrown on the fire suddenly burst into flames. The surge of warmth struck him full in the face.

'Allyn! Allyn!'

Nertha's anxious voice pierced the clinging heat as several arms seized him and held him upright.

'Are you all right?'

'Yes, I'm just—'

A roar rose from the congregation, its awful weight crushing him once more. For a moment he was fully in two places. Sitting in the Whistler's cave torn with doubt, and standing in the Haven Meeting House, sustained by unknown hands and full of fear.

Nertha's emphatic voice was saying, 'No you're not.' Then she was shouting, her voice cutting through even Cassraw's frantic rhetoric: 'Clear a way at the back, sick man coming through.' And before Vredech could speak, he was twisting and turning, being passed from hand to hand through the crowd that stood between him and the door, Nertha controlling the proceedings like a sheep dog herding her flock.

Then the short, buffeting journey was over. The stifling heat and gloom of the Meeting House gave way to the warmth and light of the summer sun. The supporting hands became an arm wrapped about his shoulders and a single hand firmly grasping his elbow.

'I'm not doing too well lately, am I?' Vredech said weakly as Nertha led him around to the side of the Meeting House, away from the crowd momentarily distracted from Cassraw's sermon.

'Hush,' she said, at once gentle and businesslike. 'Sit down here in the shade and rest a moment.' Even as she was speaking, she was skilfully manoeuvring him on to the base of a wide recess in the wall. Then she was looking into his face, prising his eyelids back. He pushed her hand away.

'I'm all right,' he insisted. 'It was just the heat.'

Nertha was shaking her head. 'No, it wasn't,' she said. 'I thought it was at first. It was the obvious thing.' Her hands avoided his and touched his face and forehead, then the pulse in his neck. 'You're agitated, but you don't feel like someone who was just about to faint. And you've recovered too quickly.'

'Do you need any help?' The question came from one of a pair of Cassraw's Knights who had helped open the crowd for Nertha; they had followed in her determined wake as she had led Vredech away.

'No, thank you,' she said. 'I am a physician. It's nothing serious.'

'It's the power of Brother Cassraw's great message,' the young man confided. 'It moves people in many different ways.'

'I'm sure,' Nertha replied caustically, though the sarcasm was lost on the listeners.

She turned and dismissed them with a smile of reassurance, then bent forward and gazed intently into Vredech's eyes. Her hands came up to examine them again. 'Stop that,' he said, seizing her wrists. 'There's nothing wrong with my eyes, Nertha. I can see perfectly.' He pointed.

'Look, there's the Ervrin Mallos.'

Nertha was patient. 'Being able to see a mountain doesn't really constitute a test of good eyesight, Brother brother,' she said, smiling slightly at his indignation as he glowered back at her.

He pointed again. 'Then there's the gate to Cassraw's private garden, and Dowinne's precious fruit trees. There's a street lantern that someone's forgotten to turn off. There's those yellow flowers, what're they called?' He snapped his fingers.

'Sun's eyes.' Nertha completed the sentence for him. 'All right, your eyesight's fine, then.' But she was still looking into his eyes. 'It just seemed to me that they looked very strange as you began to lose consciousness just now. Almost as if their entire orbs . . . went black.' She hesitated, then said rather awkwardly: 'Or rather, filled with darkness. It gave me quite a fright.'

Night eyes, night eyes. The Whistler's words rang in Vredech's ears. And he remembered, too, the brief impression he had had when he looked in the mirror after his first encounter with the Whistler. The same fear possessed him now as it had then, but under Nertha's searching gaze he kept his face immobile. 'It was dark and crowded in there,' he said flatly. 'Lots of shadows.'

He saw Nertha controlling her own face as a shrewd-eyed look of suspicion rapidly came and went.

'Dark,' he confirmed. 'And confused. And you'd be shocked, seeing me passing out like that.'

Now the indignation was Nertha's. 'I'm not shocked at the sight of people falling over,' she said, her brow furrowing. 'I'll have you know, I've seen—' She stopped as Vredech smiled up at her. Then he found he was looking at her mouth. His hand moved of its own volition, wanting to reach out and touch. And his chest tightened. Nertha's eyes seemed to widen and she moved her face a little closer to his.

Vredech forced his hand to be still and, stiff-faced, yanked his eyes away. 'Anyway, whatever happened in there, I'm fine now,' he said briskly, though he felt himself colouring. 'Perhaps I'm still a little tired from being awake all the other night. Let's get away from here. We've more serious things to talk about now than my feeling a little dizzy in that crowd.'

Uncharacteristically, Nertha stammered slightly. 'Yes . . . yes. You seem to be well enough now.' She looked around. Even from where she was standing, she could see the edge of the crowd which was gathered at the front of the Meeting House. And she could hear the hubbub inside. She shivered.

'Goose walking over your grave?' Vredech said, standing up.

Nertha grimaced. 'No,' she said simply. 'Just Cassraw. Let's get away from here.'

They left through Cassraw's private garden to avoid the crowd, and rode for some time without speaking. To Vredech, the implications of Cassraw's wild sermon left so many questions that it seemed impossible to start a rational conversation. And his mind was filling again with frantic thoughts about his mysterious transportation to the Whistler and his world, and all that that implied for his sanity.

Nertha had no such problems. She was silent partly because she could see that Vredech needed a little time to recover himself, but mainly because she was thinking. It puzzled her that, though he had unquestionably been on the verge of fainting, Vredech had subsequently shown none of the symptoms of someone overcome by the heat. And the memory of his eyes disturbed her. It had only been a fleeting glance, but she had seen what she had seen, surely?

'Tell me what happened back there, Allyn,' she said bluntly.

'Nothing,' Vredech said vaguely, after a long hesitation.

Nertha glanced at him. 'It was only yesterday you said you'd tell me about everything that happened to you. You volunteered it, I didn't wring it out of you. And you promised. "Keep an open mind – as never before" I think you said. And I said I would. So don't give me "nothing".' She weighted the words with full family reproach.

'You'll think I'm truly mad if I tell you,' Vredech said eventually, and very uncomfortably.

Nertha's reaction was unexpected and tangential, as the Whistler's had been in response to a similar remark. 'Never mind what you think I'll think,' she said with brutal sharpness. 'And don't ever presume to know *what* I'm thinking. Just concern yourself with what I say and do, and I'll give you the same courtesy.'

The abruptness and power of the response jerked Vredech out of his own circling anxieties, and he gaped at her.

'Well?' she concluded forcefully.

Vredech still hesitated. Then he looked up at the Ervrin Mallos. 'What can you see at the top of the mountain?' he asked.

Nertha's expression was impatient, but she followed his gaze. After staring for a moment, she screwed up her eyes and craned forward a little. 'There seems to be some kind of heat haze, I suppose,' she said, settling back into her saddle.

'It's no heat haze,' Vredech said with some certainty. 'It's not the kind of day for a heat haze, and have you ever seen one isolated at the top of a mountain?'

Nertha looked up again and shrugged. 'If it's not a heat haze then it's something else to do with the weather,' she said indifferently. 'But whatever it is, it's not hazy enough to prevent me from seeing what you're up to, so just tell me what happened to you in the Meeting Hall.'

Vredech looked openly relieved. 'I'm glad you can see it, though,' he said. 'I think it's been there for some time now.' Then, before Nertha could speak again, he began

371

telling her of his encounter with the Whistler.

She was silent when he finished. 'I said you'd think I was mad,' he said, watching her carefully.

'And I told you not to worry about what I was thinking,' Nertha replied tartly. 'You wanted me to keep an open mind, and I will, no matter how hard it is.' She looked at him, her face confused yet determined. 'I can do it while I'm sure you're telling everything that's happening. We must trust one other. And in that context, I'll be honest. I'd think you were mad indeed if you'd suddenly awoken with the intention of killing Cassraw.'

Vredech looked at her helplessly. 'What's happening, Nertha? What can I do?'

Nertha replied instantly. 'I've no idea,' she said. 'But whoever and wherever the Whistler is, whether he's something your mind's made up for some reason, or whether he truly does lie in some strange other world, he's doing you no harm so far. Cling to that, Allyn. Cling to that. He's doing you no harm. And while you talk about him, I don't think he will.'

She reined her horse to a halt and stared around, her hands tapping the horse's neck in frustration. 'I know it seems a lifetime now, but a couple of days ago, if you recall, we said we'd ride and talk. I'd tell you how the old place has changed. We'd go out into the country.' Her eyes drifted towards the summit of the Ervrin Mallos, just visible above the rooftops. 'I think we should do that now,' she said, suddenly determined. 'Let's weary ourselves with good honest exercise and go to the heart of this business at the same time.' Her eyes were alive and challenging. 'Are you with me?' she asked, as if they had been children daring one another into mischief again. 'Let's take this devil by the tail. There's time before night. Up to the top of the mountain.'

Before Vredech could answer, she had swung her horse about and was galloping away.

Chapter 27

Vredech found the pace trying. He had always been a better rider than Nertha, and the sight of her moving not merely ahead of him but getting steadily further away, revived sensations that he had not experienced since his youth.

'Come on, nag, move,' he growled furiously to his mount, urging it forward, but to no avail. He caught up with Nertha only when she stopped, and by then he was red-faced and breathless.

'You should try letting the horse do the running,' she said, laughing.

'It wasn't fair, it was uphill,' he said fatuously, spluttering into laughter himself as he realized what he had said.

Nertha swung down from her horse. 'We'll walk them awhile – let them cool down. I doubt your horse has had any exercise since you bought it.'

Vredech affected a dignified silence.

Their gallop had carried them to a little-used road high above the town. Below them lay the familiar jumble of winding streets and grey-roofed houses tumbling down towards the larger buildings at the centre of the town, and thence to the towers of the PlasHein. Had they searched, they would have been able to see the roof of the Haven Meeting House, but neither of them did.

Looking round, Vredech remembered the vision that the Whistler had shown him, of a vast, strangely flat city devastated by a cruel enemy. He remembered, too, his denial, and felt it again here. Not in Canol Madreth. It wasn't possible – was it?

'It's not cavalry country, is it?'

Nertha's remark struck him like a blow.

'What?' he exclaimed fiercely.

She looked at him wide-eyed, startled by his response. 'I said it's not cavalry country,' she repeated. 'It's better suited to light infantry.'

'What are you talking about, girl? What do you know about cavalry and infantry?' He was almost shouting.

'Don't call me girl,' Nertha blasted back. 'You know I hate it. And what are you shouting at me for?'

Vredech's mouth opened wide, then closed again unhappily. 'I'm sorry,' he said, wilting. 'I was just thinking about what the Whistler showed me – that ruined city and riders swarming through the streets, killing people, just for fun.' He folded his arms about himself protectively.

Nertha watched him closely. 'Vivid?' she said.

His face twisted with the pain of the memory. 'Yes. There was so much in his music that I can't find words for. I don't want to think about it.'

Nertha looked out across the valley. 'Strange,' she said. 'I'm half-envious of you and your strange new friend.'

They stood silent for a little time, then Vredech said, quite simply, 'Don't be,' and started walking away. Nertha followed him.

There was no more solemnity as they continued on their journey, now walking, now riding, trotting, galloping until they reached the Witness House. They gave their horses to a groom there and continued on foot. Vredech strode out strongly until they were out of sight of the Witness House then he slowed.

'I suppose you did that because I rode faster than you,' Nertha panted as she caught up with him.

Vredech chuckled. 'As a matter of fact, no,' he replied. 'But only because I forgot. I just wanted to be away from the Witness House because I think I'm going to be living up here over the next few days, discussing what's happened.' He pulled a wry face. 'I wonder what else Cassraw said while we were outside?'

'Forget it, and get up that mountain, or go and see Mueran right now,' Nertha insisted. 'I'm not having you looking over your shoulder every two minutes. It's one or the other – I'll do whatever you want.'

'Very well, father,' Vredech said piously. He turned and looked at the steep grassy slope ahead. 'Let's see how fit your legs are after so long away from any proper hills.' Nertha curled her lip at him and motioned him upwards with an sharp inclination of her head.

Vredech made no effort to race, however. He had given up that kind of folly many years ago, as time had given him a little more awareness of his own vulnerability. And besides, he was far from certain that he could outstrip Nertha, for all his bluster. Thus they walked more or less side by side, moving steadily upwards until they came at last to Ishryth's lawn. They paused there, as did most people, and rested for a little while in the silence and the sunlight. Neither spoke.

Then they began the final ascent towards the summit. Nertha kept pace with him easily and Vredech made a quiet resolution to do more walking when all this was over.

When all *what* was over?

His own question jolted all his concerns back on to him. As if sensing it, Nertha turned and issued a brisk, 'Come on. We'll stop at the next skyline,' and then moved off smartly. It was sufficient to release him for the moment, but Vredech knew that some of the magic of the impromptu journey was irreplaceably lost. Nevertheless he was still content to be where he was, concentrating on placing one foot in front of the other and moving quietly upward through the clear mountain air.

When he reached the skyline he found Nertha, a little red-faced and breathless, staring curiously at the summit which, for the first time since they had started up the mountain proper, was now in view.

The strangeness about the summit which Nertha had casually identified as heat haze, was there still, an uneasy distortion which made the summit appear to be shifting and changing, although when any one part of it was examined, it seemed quite still.

'I'm not even sure I'm seeing what I'm seeing,' Nertha said, rubbing her eyes then squinting up at the peak. 'Can you see it? Moving and not moving.'

Vredech nodded. It was as good a description as any.

'What do you think it is?' Nertha asked.

Vredech felt something stirring deep inside him. Not so much an anger as a combination of hatred and a predator's lust for its prey. 'I've no idea. Let's do as you said. Take the devil by the tail.' He bared his clenched teeth. 'And *twist* it,' he said, his hand miming the deed. Nertha glanced at him uncertainly and then squeezed his arm.

As they began clambering up the final rocky slope, Vredech felt far less assured than he seemed outwardly. Despite his best efforts he found himself thinking of the many legends that hung about the mountain: about how it had been torn from a land far away by Ishryth to crush a terrible foe, or how it had been driven upwards from deep below to escape the awful cries of a king imprisoned by Ishryth, and too, how the Watchers of Ishryth looked over it from their great palaces in the clouds. A whole gamut of stories were wound about the mountain, from holy texts in the Santyth to children's tales and dancing rhymes. Most of the tales in the Santyth were either allegorical in character or had obvious historical derivations and, of course, as he kept saying to himself, none of the more fanciful myths were to be taken seriously. But the Ervrin

Mallos dominated not only the land of Canol Madreth, it also loomed large in the hearts and minds of its inhabitants, and no one was absolutely free of some superstition about the place. That it had become the site for the heart of their religion testified to that.

It took Vredech far more mental effort than he would have imagined to hold his growing anxiety at bay. He found it comforting simply watching Nertha clambering agilely over the rocks and looking about her constantly, eyes prying into the faint haziness about the summit. She seemed in some way to be invulnerable, while fear was hovering increasingly at the edge of his mind. Fear of the darkness that had hung over the mountain when he had been here last, and of the deeper darkness that had enveloped him, and, not least, of the strange barbarous paean of rejoicing he had heard, and the terrible, interrogating coldness that it had presaged.

He looked up at the sky. Bright blue and littered with small white clouds, it was the very antithesis of that day. Yet though the sun's warmth more than compensated for the cool breeze that was beginning to blow as they neared the summit, he began to feel a chill deep inside – a tiny, ice-cold knot. They must have moved into the region of the haziness by now, yet there was no sign of any disturbance in the air.

'Nertha, wait!' he called out.

She stopped and looked back at him. 'What's the matter?'

All he could think of to say was, 'Be alert.' He moved quickly to her side and took her arm. 'Be aware.'

Her face filled with questions but she asked none of them. They continued upwards. The chill inside Vredech began to grow. It was not the chill of the mountains, nor was it the chill of fear, or the clammy iciness of death. Rather it was the cold of complete absence. Coldness of the heart from the absence of love, coldness of the mind from the absence of doubt, coldness of the spirit from the absence of awe at anything beyond itself. Coldness that was the very negation of life, that was the very opposite of the great heat from which all things were said to have come.

And he recognized it. It was the coldness that had held him, searched him . . .

Dismissed him!

Anger welled up inside him as the memory returned of the judgement that had found his inadequacy, his worthlessness, so total. Left him nothing but fist-waving fury by way of rebuttal. Yet, in truth, why should he want the approval of such a fearful judge?

'You're looking grim.' Nertha brought him back to the present.

'Just remembering,' he said.

Nertha looked at him closely. 'Are you all right?' she asked.

He smiled faintly. 'I'm beginning to know your physician's manner,' he said, then, 'Why do you ask?'

Nertha's nose curled. She was about to say, 'No special reason,' but instead she told the truth. 'There's an . . . unpleasantness about this place.'

Vredech borrowed a phrase of their father's. 'Be specific,' he said. They smiled at the old memory, but only briefly, as if such light-heartedness were too alien a bloom to flourish in this place.

Nertha looked troubled. She put a hand to her face. 'I can feel the breeze blowing, and yet I can't. There's a terrible stillness about this place.'

Vredech glanced around at the sunlit vista of Canol Madreth laid out before him. There was still no shifting haze that he could see. All was clear and bright. Yet something was amiss. Here, on a day like this, he should feel deeply relaxed, joyous even, many petty perspectives righted by the massive and ancient presence of the mountains and sight of the tiny houses far below. But now, there

378

was nothing. He did not know what he had expected to find up here, but it was not this cold emptiness that forbade all responses.

'Let's go on,' he said, very softly but with a determination that made Nertha frown anxiously.

They did not speak again until they were clambering over the jagged rocks at the very top of the mountain.

Nertha folded her arms about herself and shivered. She looked at Vredech reproachfully. 'It's you and your damned superstitions,' she said, offering an explanation before one was sought.

Vredech shook his head. 'No, it's not,' he said gently. 'It's whatever's attached to this place. You feel it, too, don't you, but you don't want to talk about it because it makes no sense. Something's reaching into you and laying a cold hand over . . .' he paused '. . . over everything in you that's human. Perhaps even everything that's living.'

Nertha turned her head from side to side, as if trying to free herself from something. Then she grimaced and let out an almost animal growl. 'Everything has a rational explanation. Nothing is to be feared, it is only to be understood.'

'There is only the darkness where my ability to measure ends,' Vredech said.

Nertha's angry expression changed to one of surprise. 'Yes,' she said.

Vredech met her gaze and extended a slow embracing arm across the craggy summit. 'Then there is great darkness up here, for both of us,' he said. 'You can't explain what you're feeling, but you're feeling it nonetheless, aren't you?'

'Hush!' Nertha said sharply. 'I need to think.' Holding out a hand as if to keep him at bay, she sat down and leaned back against a sloping rock, then closed her eyes. Vredech sat down nearby and rested his chin in his hand. *He* did not close his eyes. The last thing he wanted now

379

was to be confined in his own darkness. He wanted to take in the familiar mountains and green valleys billowing away into the distance. He wanted every possible contact with this real familiar world, wanted to embed every least part of it into him as protection against the cold alien presence that was pervading the mountain.

But it would not be enough, he knew. What hung here, what was somehow seeping into Canol Madreth through Cassraw was no passive spirit. He remembered again the all-too human triumph in the clamour he had heard during his search for Cassraw. Rampant, savage joy. The kind of joy that danced on the crushed body of an enemy. Devoid of respect, of compassion, of everything save awareness of itself and its insatiable needs.

What hung about this place was merely the aftermath of its touch. The will that had brought it about was gone.

'Who responds to His song builds a way for Him, and He will not relinquish it,' the Whistler had said. 'And there are many ways in which He can come. He builds ever.'

Vredech nodded to himself as he pondered the remark. He found he was staring absently at the motionless form of Nertha. She seemed to be more solid even than the ancient canting stones about him, yet, ironically, she also looked soft and very vulnerable, leaning back against the rock. He was happy that she was here with him.

Not cavalry country. The thought came from nowhere and made him smile. What in the world could Nertha know about such things? But in its wake, as if suddenly released, came other, more sobering, martial images: Cassraw's first sermon with its talk of armies – multitudes marching forth, united under His banner; the Whistler showing him the awful sacking of that alien city; then, almost prosaically, the faint menace of real conflict with Tirfelden that was hovering silently around the edges of the political mayhem in the Heindral. A spasm of terrible fear suddenly shook him at the prospect and he clenched his hands together in the manner of earnest prayer. In the name of pity, let none of this be, he thought desperately, as the images persisted. Then, atypically, and not without a touch of guilt, he asked of his god: 'Reach out and stop it, Lord. Reach out, I beg You.'

Bridgehead.

The word came out of his rambling war-filled thoughts with an almost physical vividness. It seemed to be important and he scrabbled after it as if it might suddenly be snatched back. In common with most Madren, he knew nothing of war save such of Canol Madreth's early history as he had been obliged to learn at school, and such as could be gleaned from various dramatic passages in the Lesser Books of the Santyth. Yet, as he turned over the word 'bridgehead', memories began to return from the time when, as a child, his father had read him a tale of a single warrior who had held an entire army at bay while his companions demolished the very bridge he was standing on. The idea and the manner of the telling had thrilled him enormously, and he had spent many exciting daydreams holding one of the local bridges against unspecified but overwhelming odds for a long time afterwards. To his surprise, some of the excitement lingered yet, his palms tingling slightly with the feel of the grip of his long-sheathed and quite imaginary sword that had solved so many problems so invincibly and so simply. He allowed himself a smile of regret at the passage of such childish intensity. And as the word carried him back across the years, so it spanned into the future. Doubts about what was happening fell away from him. Not his intellectual, reasoning doubts, but those ill-formed doubts that prowl the realms of the mind beyond the depths of reason and gnaw at the roots of faith. He shied away from using the name Ahmral, but he could no longer turn away from the inner knowledge that some power was intruding into his life and potentially, the lives of everyone in Canol Madreth. Nor could he turn away from the knowledge that Cassraw was being used by Him. And, just as Cassraw was His, or, being charitable, was becoming His, so He had chosen this place. A bridgehead. An enclave deep inside enemy territory.

Let him build nothing . . .

Many ways . . .

'Nertha,' he said, very softly. She opened her eyes immediately. 'What are you thinking? Tell me right away, however foolish.'

She looked up at the sky and then, as he had been doing, around at the surrounding mountains and valleys. 'I'm thinking that the sky looks different here, and the mountains. I'm thinking that everything feels different, too, as if this place weren't the summit of the Ervrin Mallos any more, but something else – and somewhere else.' She spoke without hesitation and with no sign of embarrassment. Then she stood up and looked at him. Vredech saw that her face was tense with the effort of keeping something under control. The same tension came through in her voice when she spoke again, her words measured and deliberate. 'Yet I feel no different, and I think I'm an experienced enough physician not to allow my affection to cloud my judgement about what's been happening to you too badly. So I must presume that what I feel up here comes from something outside of me, for all it's as though it were coiling round my insides.' The control faltered slightly and she folded her arms and hunched up her shoulders. 'There's something here that's colder than death,' she said. 'Yet it's alive and wilful.'

Vredech frowned. 'You feel an actual presence? A will?' he said, trying to keep the alarm from his voice.

'Yes, I think so,' she replied. 'Faint, but there. Something very old. Something very strange, and frightening.'

Suddenly concerned Vredech reached out and took her

382

hand. 'Perhaps we should leave,' he said urgently.

'It's all right,' she said reassuringly. 'I'm female. By my nature I'm nearer to the truth of things than you are. There's much easier prey available for it than me.' She looked at him pointedly. 'I'm also a devout sceptic and a trained physician. And what I smell here is the onset of a disease. The inconsequential symptoms of a grievous sickness to come. It can be resisted.'

'I feel no presence,' Vredech said, still anxious. 'I did, when we were searching for Cassraw, but not now. I feel only a kind of . . . desolation. A waiting.'

Nertha took his hand. 'Your turn,' she said. 'Tell me what you've been thinking.'

Vredech coughed awkwardly. 'I thought – "bridge-head",' he said. 'Something establishing itself here against a future intention.'

Nertha half-closed her eyes, testing the idea. 'Yes,' she decided. 'That's good.'

Vredech ventured his most fearful question. 'What do you think it could . . .'

Nertha's free hand came up to silence him. 'What or who it is, where it's come from, and why, I can't begin to think. I've precious little logic keeping me afloat as it is. I'm really sailing along on my intuition.'

'It's all we've got, I suspect.' Vredech was not unhappy to abandon his question. 'But it's all right saying nothing is to be feared, only understood. That doesn't necessarily make whatever lies in the darkness beyond where we can measure any less dangerous.'

'Oh, it's dangerous,' Nertha said, her eyes narrowing. 'I can feel that.'

'What can we do, then? We can't just debate and do nothing. But how can we fight something that we can't see?'

A shadow fell across the summit of the mountain, making them both start, but it was only a cloud passing in front of the sun. Nertha pulled free from Vredech's grip with a cry of annoyance at being so foolishly startled. 'I fight things I can't see all the time,' she said angrily, striding away across the rocks. Then she stopped and pointed a determined finger at Vredech. 'You do what *you* can. Say your prayers, speak your blessings, whatever you feel is right.' For a moment Vredech thought she was being sarcastic, then he realized she was quite sincere. 'I'm going to try to cure this place. If there's a disease here, then there's a cause.' The pointing hand became a clenched and angry fist. 'I'm going to look for it like I'd look for any other disease. And if I find it I'm going to root it out.'

As Nertha moved away, Vredech felt the cold inside him intensifying. For a choking moment he thought that he was not going to be able to move, that he would become like one of the great fingerstones that marked the summit.

'Come on.'

The call transported him momentarily back to the night-time hillside where he had met the Whistler only hours earlier. Though he had not felt that his vision was impaired in any way, everything was suddenly in sharp focus, as though a fine veil had been drawn back. And the cold no longer bound him.

'Come on,' Nertha shouted again, waving to him. She was clambering up a small cluster of rocks that marked the highest point of the mountain and that did indeed look as if they had been pushed up from below by some last desperate effort. He walked across and climbed up after her.

Nertha was standing with her hands resting on one of the rocks and her eyes closed. 'Do your praying silently,' she said. 'I need to concentrate.'

Vredech was half-inclined to ask her what she was doing, but the tone of her voice forbade it. He grunted an acquiescence.

384

He did not close his own eyes, however. Instead, as before, he watched Nertha, for fear that, in the stillness of her own darkness, she might be in some kind of danger. Silently, he started to reach for the abundance of prayers and litanies that were a routine part of his religious life. After a moment, he hesitated. They would not be enough, he realized. They would suffice for most people, for most of the normal ills of life, but this was no normal ill. Nor was he an untutored member of a flock to be consoled by a solemn utterance. He was a Preaching Brother, well versed in the origins and inner meanings of the church's rituals and, if he were brutally honest with himself, more than a little hardened to their balm. No form of words, however revered, would aid him here. It came to him that if he was truly to find the strength to oppose this menace, then he must look to the very heart of his faith.

He felt helpless. Nor was he unaware of the dark irony of his position, standing on top of the Ervrin Mallos and looking to find form where generations of scholars had searched and failed. He was given no time to ponder his position, however.

'It's here,' Nertha said, her voice a mixture of triumph and disgust. He looked at her. Her eyes were still closed, but she had removed her hands from the rock and was waving them vaguely in front of her. As she turned, one of her hands struck him and she seized hold of him. 'It's here, Allyn,' she said again. 'Something that doesn't belong. Something that's binding it here.'

'What do you mean?' Vredech asked, bewildered. 'There's me, you, and the rocks, nothing else.'

Nertha's head shook in denial. 'Hush,' she said. 'I'm listening.' She released him and, gently easing him to one side, held out her hands again, searching. She was treading carefully, her feet testing the ground before she placed them down, her hands moving slowly for fear of impact with the rocks that formed this shattered crown of the mountain. For an instant, Vredech felt cackling mirth rise up inside him at the sight; mirth without humour, full of the savage unrestrained cruelty that only a young child can know. He wanted to take hold of her and push her with all his strength from their small eyrie, to end this foolishness here and now and to walk away from everything.

The shock of the thought made him gasp.

'Hush,' Nertha said again, irritably.

This time it was cold fury that filled Vredech and he found himself looking around for a rock suitable for dashing this insolent woman's brains out. He was on the point of bending down before he realized what he was doing.

'Here!' Nertha cried.

'No!'

Nertha's eyes opened and she turned to him sharply, for there had been such rage in his shout. 'What's the matter?' she asked, alarmed, as she met his own wide-eyed stare.

Vredech gaped and shook his head several times before he could release the words. 'I don't know,' he managed. 'Such thoughts, such emotions. Horrible.'

Nertha, her arms extended, was leaning forward, half-sprawled across a flat-topped rock. She was torn between going to him and leaving what she had discovered, as if it might somehow slip away from her. Vredech ran his arm across his forehead. It was clammy with sweat as though he had just completed some massive effort.

Nertha frowned and, still reluctant to move, motioned him toward her. Vredech's head began to spin. He put out a hand to steady himself on one of the rocks. 'I think I'm going to be sick,' he said.

And he was.

Nertha abandoned her discovery immediately and in two long strides was by his side, offering a supporting arm. He brushed it aside. 'I'm all right, I'm all right,' he said.

386

'You don't look it,' Nertha retorted. 'What brought that on all of a sudden? We've both had the same things to eat.'

Vredech was fumbling for a kerchief to clean his mouth. 'Guilt and disgust,' he said, quite clear in his diagnosis. He turned to her. 'I had such appalling thoughts . . . about you. Dreadful, primitive. They came out of nowhere.'

'Tell me,' Nertha said. Vredech shook his head. 'Tell me, damn you, Allyn. Whatever they were, they're gone now. Bring them out into the light for pity's sake if you don't want them to come back.'

The Whistler's words came to him. 'We must remember the darkness in our own natures,' he said softly, speaking more to himself than to Nertha. 'If we forget, we'll be taught again.' He looked at her earnestly. 'I understand that,' he tapped his head, 'as an idea. But when it came like that, possessing the whole of me, visceral . . . unreasoning . . .' He shivered.

'This is your Whistler's advice, is it?' Nertha asked. Vredech nodded. 'Well, he's got more sense than you have,' she said with some appreciation. 'Now just tell me what happened.'

Vredech knew Nertha well enough to accept that he would have to tell her sooner or later, and telling her now was likely to be much easier. He did so. Nertha grimaced, but more because of the pain it was causing him, than from distress at the nature of his thoughts.

'Very interesting,' she said calmly, when he had finished. 'Don't feel bad about it. You should hear some of the things I've heard. They'd *really* make you throw up.'

Vredech was still distressed. 'But—'

Nertha shook him. 'They were nothing, Allyn. Smoke in the wind. They're out and gone now. Gone for good. And you didn't act on them, did you?'

'I nearly did.'

Nertha sneered. 'Nearly, nearly. Nearly's nothing.

Nearly pregnant. Nearly a virgin. The point is, you didn't do anything.' She tugged at his arm. 'Forget it. Come and look at this.'

Nertha's earthy dismissal set Vredech's concerns aside for the moment, but he had the feeling that something within him had been changed for ever.

'I felt it here.' Nertha was back at the flat rock, her hands splayed over it. She closed her eyes. 'It's gone,' she said angrily. 'I've lost it.' She swore at herself. 'I'm not very good at this kind of healing.'

'What was it?' Vredech asked, puzzled by the reference to healing.

Nertha tapped the rock anxiously. 'I can't really explain. If I was dealing with a patient I'd say it was a hurt, a tension – a wrongness.'

She looked at him uneasily, as if expecting him to laugh, but Vredech was watching her carefully. 'And when you'd found such a hurt in someone, what would you do?' he asked intently.

'Look to ease it, obviously,' she replied.

'How?'

Nertha looked flustered. 'It depends, doesn't it? I can't answer a question like that. You have to be there.' She became defensive. 'I told you, I'm not particularly good at this kind of healing. It's an intuitive thing.'

Vredech took her hands. 'I understand,' he said. 'It's like faith. There are no words for it.' He held up a hand for silence as she made to speak. 'Don't say anything else. And don't doubt yourself so much. Go back to where you were before I distracted you.' He laid her hands back on the rock. As he did so he noticed a dark stain in the centre of it. In so far as he had noticed it previously he had assumed it to be residual dampness from rainwater or dew that had collected in a slight hollow. But there had been no rain for some days, and virtually continuous sunshine. Even as he looked at it he felt a sense of unease returning.

Hesitantly he reached out and touched it. The unease pervaded him.

'What's the matter?' Nertha asked.

Vredech replied with another question. 'What's this?'

Wrinkling her nose, Nertha wiped her fingerends across the stain and peered at them intently. Then she closed her eyes and sniffed them.

'It's here,' she said, her eyes opening in horror, her voice low and awe-stricken. 'This is what I felt before. The seat of the hurt, the wrongness.' She hesitated for a moment, and a look of fear and disgust passed briefly over her face. Then it was replaced by the expression that Vredech had seen as he had watched her treating the injured in the PlasHein Square and the Sick-House: a strange mixture of compassion and almost brutal determination.

'What is it?' he asked again.

Nertha bent forward over the stain and ran a finger along a thin line radiating from it. There were several such, Vredech noted. They were splash lines.

'I think it might be blood,' she said softly.

As she spoke the word, Vredech knew the truth of it. Blood and sacrifice. The cold, cruel dream he had touched had come back to him. He felt the oppression about the summit grow in intensity. 'Some injured animal?' he asked faintly, knowing that this was not so even before Nertha shook her head. No animal was going to clamber to the top of the mountain to die from an injury.

'It must have been brought here,' she said quietly. 'And it was brought here as part of all this . . . business. I can feel it again now. It's awful.'

So many questions filled Vredech's mind that he could give voice to none of them. In the end he said, 'We can't leave it. We must do something.'

'I need to think,' Nertha said, a hint of desperation in her voice.

389

Vredech shook his head. 'No,' he said agitatedly. 'Now we must feel. React in the way our hearts and stomachs tell us to, while we're here. You know this. Later, we'll think. I'm going to pray over this. A prayer of purification of some kind, or for the safe passage of the dead, I don't know – whatever comes to me.' His agitation increased. 'You can heal it.'

'I . . .'

'Do it!'

He seized Nertha's hand and placed his free one on the stain. Nertha did the same. Their fingers were touching. Both closed their eyes.

In the darkness, the oppression of which he had been vaguely aware seemed to take an almost solid form about Vredech. And, like Nertha, he began to sense a will behind it. To his considerable alarm however, he found that, try as he might, he could remember none of the prayers that were his stock in trade; prayers that he had recited from memory week in, week out, year in, year out; prayers to which he had turned many times in his own private meditations. His mind filled first with a scrabbling confusion and then fear. He felt Nertha's grip tighten about his hand. It was the only sign that passed between them of their common struggle. It heightened his resolve. He must cling to his faith. But still his prayers eluded him, mocking him with disjointed fragments of long-familiar phrases. His fear began to twist into panic. And into the now almost crushing oppression came hints of scornful amusement. He recognized them as the will that had touched him once before, when he and the others had been searching for Cassraw. He was the merest mote before such awesome power and majesty.

If Your power is so great, why do You use such a feeble vessel as Cassraw?

The thought, stark in its challenge, emerged through

390

the whirling confusion of his mind, its source unknown. Another came.

Whatever else I might be, I am near enough *his* equal. If You need his strength to do Your will here, then know that I will oppose You with a strength no less.

'I need the strength of no mortal. Cassraw is my Chosen. My vessel. My Way.'

The voice that spoke inside Vredech was icy and terrible, but to his horror, the voice that his ears heard, though distorted and distant, was Nertha's.

He could not move, and he dared not open his eyes.

'Why do you seek to persecute me, your Lord?'

Vredech could feel the presence moving through him, searching, testing, learning. Soon, he must surely fall before this terrible possession. Despite the defiance that he had offered, the words of his faith were gone, the heart of his faith was—?

Yet something other than this will held him. As he clung to his sanity, so something clung to him. Literally. In the shapeless darkness and turmoil he felt it, tight and desperate, pressing itself into him with a force that cried out for help.

It formed itself into Nertha's hand, gripping him now with appalling force. Vredech's awareness cleared. As she had supported him so much over these last few days, so now he must support her in whatever pain she was suffering.

Abomination! he shouted silently into the darkness. Whatever else You might be, You are not my Lord. Get Thee hence, demon. Leave us, I command You in the name of Ishryth.

The words rolled back over him, echoing hollowly, empty and futile. They were not enough to warrant even a flicker of attention. They had been like the least of insects riding the uncaring wind to dash themselves to destruction against a great cliff-face.

Vredech's ordered resistance, such as it was, crumbled at the insight. Beneath it was a primeval desperation, full of a burning fury.

'Nertha!' he cried out. 'Nertha, I'm here. Hold on to me. He can do nothing, except twist our thoughts and desires. For all His seeming power, He is weak and feeble. A great enemy has wounded Him sorely. He holds Himself here by the merest of threads. Threads which *we* can break. Hold on. Reach out and heal the hurt that He is.'

But even as he called out, he knew that the hatred and anger that was in him was merely sustenance for the obscenity that was binding him here. He felt it burgeoning, nourished by his own will. Yet he could not relinquish his rage. It poured forth like the vomit that had poured from him only minutes earlier.

Then he was surrounded by a sound like a great rending. Its terrible shrieking tore at him, making him cry out, though he could not hear his own voice. He felt as though he had been lifted into some fearful limbo where nothing existed save the pain and the noise. And Nertha's clinging hand. Still holding on to him, trusting, dependent. Nertha, who could no more bring herself to believe in Ishryth and Ahmral than fly. He seemed to hear the Whistler saying, 'Astonishment, Vredech. Astonishment.'

And that, he realized, was why Nertha had been so easily possessed. She would not have believed what was happening to her.

But he did. He would not be downed by his own inability to accept.

His rage became a determination. Whatever else happened on this desecrated mountain-top, he would save her, even if it cost him his sanity and his soul.

'Hold me, Nertha,' he called out into the tumult. 'As you love me. And I you. Hold me. He can do nothing, but what we allow.'

And, as abruptly as it had begun, like the sudden

closing of the door to a boisterous inn, the noise was gone.

As was the presence.

Vredech slumped forward across the rock. Silence flooded into him.

Silence and horror.

He opened his eyes, fearing to see what he knew he would. Sunlight burst mockingly into them, but nothing could illuminate the darkness that was filling him now.

For the summit was deserted.

Nertha was gone.

Chapter 28

Vredech had no measure of the time he remained at the summit of the Ervrin Mallos, save that it was dark and a bright moon was high in the sky when he finally came to his senses. He was leaning over the rock that had been the focus of all that had happened, gazing into the stain, black now in the moonlight, as if he could see through into wherever Nertha had been transported.

Physical exhaustion racked him, his robe was soiled and torn, as too were his hands. They confirmed the frantic, confused memories that he had of dashing about the summit, desperately searching for Nertha, ridiculously turning over rocks, peering into impossibly small crannies, going repeatedly to the edge of the precipitous face that dropped away from one side of the summit and staring over it, despite the fact that he could see no sign of her on the rocks below. Calling out her name as though for some reason she might be playing one of their childish hiding games. Calling and calling, now angrily, now fearfully, now pathetically. All to keep him from turning to the truth that she was gone.

Then, for a hideous, timeless time, he had curled into the lee of an overhanging rock and sobbed hysterically, gnawing on his fists and driving them into the unyielding rock. Sobbing not only for the loss of Nertha, but for fear that there had been no loss, save that of his sanity. Fear that Nertha had never really been there, that all the mysteries and horrors of the past weeks had never occurred, that he was still on the mountain, searching for a demented Cassraw, separated somehow from Horld and the others and lost himself now. Lost and utterly crazed.

He straightened up painfully. Now, though none of these questions were answered, he was too spent to sustain such agitation. And into this strangely enforced calmness, thoughts began to emerge that grimly demanded order from the churning chaos of his mind. There was little else he could do now, but he was trembling with the effort as he exerted all his will to determine that order.

He spoke out loud through gritted teeth. 'If this is the day of our search for Cassraw, then I've simply become separated from the others – suffered a seizure of some kind. Dreamt all this, for some reason. I don't dream, so perhaps my first would affect me thus.'

The sound of his own voice was unreal and jarring but he forced the words out.

'If it isn't, then all that has happened is true. And Nertha has gone . . .'

The words tore open his burgeoning inner quiet. He slammed his hands down on to the rock and lifted his face to the moonlit sky. 'Where could she go?' he roared at it. 'Where? She was there, then she was gone. *It isn't possible!*' His voice faded. 'It isn't possible.'

'What isn't?'

Vredech spun round with a cry. A tall figure stood a few paces away from him.

'Who was there and then gone?' the figure asked. Then, without waiting for an answer: 'You've not had a young woman up here, have you my man?' The stern righteousness in the voice combined with the tall, thin stature to identify the speaker.

'Horld,' Vredech gasped, his voice awash with relief. 'Horld, thank Ishryth it's you. I thought – I don't know. I . . .' He stumbled into silence.

'Is that Brother Vredech?' Horld said incredulously. 'Allyn, what in pity's name are you doing here? And what was all that noise? I came up to meditate in the silence only to find someone bawling like a market-trader. What—?' But Vredech was staggering across the rocks towards him, a single question dominating him. Horld caught him as he almost fell.

'Where is Cassraw?' Vredech demanded urgently.

Horld looked at him, the moonlight deepening the lines on his worried face. 'I've no idea,' he said. 'Calm yourself, Allyn, please. He's probably down at the Haven Meeting House, haranguing whoever's there – the more gullible members of his flock. Sad to say, some of our own Preaching Brothers.' He curled his lip in distaste. 'And doubtless his precious Knights of Ishryth.'

Vredech tore free from Horld's grip and turned away to hide his face, fearful of what the other might read there. Relief and awful shock filled him equally. Relief that the past weeks had not been some bizarre nightmare, yet shock at this confirmation that they, and thus the last few hours, had actually happened. Where then was Nertha? His insides tightened into a unbearably painful knot.

'I heard you were at Cassraw's circus today. Passed out with the heat, I believe,' Horld said. His bluntness helped Vredech to recover himself a little.

'It was bad,' he said, forcing himself to straighten up and maintain some semblance of a normal conversation. 'I came here to think about it, like you. Were you there?'

Horld shook his head. 'No, I've better things to do on Service Day. Sent a novice, though. Came back babbling and wide-eyed. Had to give him a rare roasting to bring his feet back to earth again. I can't imagine what Cassraw's up to, Allyn. It's almost as if he's—' He stopped.

Vredech turned back to him sharply. 'Possessed?' he said.

Horld seemed reluctant to accept the word now that it

had been spoken, but he could not reject it either. Vredech seized his own courage and risked touching near his concerns. 'When we came out that day, looking for Cassraw, I stumbled, had a brief fainting fit, do you remember?' Horld paused for a moment, then nodded but did not speak. Vredech peered into the dark shadows of his eyes. 'Tell me what you felt as you saw me fall,' he said softly, but with great insistence.

Horld attempted a dismissive shrug, but his manner was uneasy. Vredech pushed. 'Please, Horld,' he insisted. 'It's important.'

Horld coughed awkwardly. Vredech gripped his arms earnestly and abandoned caution. 'You've been troubled ever since that day, haven't you? Or you wouldn't have sent out your novice to listen to Cassraw, nor come trailing up here to meditate. I'm offering you no insult when I say that of the many kinds of Preaching Brother you are, contemplative is not one. Tell me what you felt.'

Horld looked away from him then seemed to reach a decision. 'I thought I saw something, heard something. It's hard to explain. There were shadows moving about, voices clamouring, and something unpleasant seemed to pass by me. I don't know. It was all very fleeting, like blue flames dancing over the coals. In so far as I thought about it at all, I imagined it was just the darkness, concern for Cassraw . . . and for you.' He straightened up and cleared his throat. 'It's all foolishness,' he muttered.

Relief was flooding through Vredech. 'No!' he said urgently. 'Foolishness is the last thing it is. I saw those shadows, too, Horld. Heard those awful voices. Something evil came with those black clouds, something that took possession of Cassraw.'

Once, Horld would have dismissed such a notion out of hand, giving whoever had suggested it the benefit of a memorably caustic rebuttal. That he did not speak at once, and that his posture reflected his uncertainty told

Vredech much. Frantic for allies now, he gave the older man no opportunity to be brought back to comforting normality by the momentum of his everyday thinking.

'After you survived that fire at your forge, you were touched by something, weren't you?' he said. 'Something you couldn't put into words but which was strong enough to make you leave everything you'd ever known and turn to another life. Well something's touched Cassraw also, and is turning *him* to another life. You felt . . . you knew . . . that it was Ishryth touching you after that fire, and I'm more than inclined to call whatever's touched Cassraw, Ahmral. But the name doesn't matter. What does matter is that both you and I felt it, and Cassraw seems to have gone almost insane since he went to the heart of it.' He shook Horld's arm before too many doubts could form around the name Ahmral. 'Think back. Remember what Cassraw was like when he came out of the darkness and took hold of us both. And his strange, arrogant manner until I opposed him at the door of the Debating Hall and he collapsed. Remember! Remember it all!'

'I don't know what to think,' Horld said eventually, his manner agitated. 'Almost every part of me says you're talking nonsense, but the tiny part that doesn't is shouting louder than all the rest put together.' Abruptly, he began walking away. 'I need time to think.'

'You'll reach no conclusions,' Vredech said starkly. 'Ishryth knows, I haven't, and I've been wrestling with it for months now. Just remember Cassraw on that day and since, remember what you felt and, in the name of pity, remember this conversation.' A thought occurred to him. 'And perhaps ask yourself what prompted you to climb the mountain so that we could meet thus.'

Horld turned back and looked at him. Vredech sensed a debate about to start, but he could not afford it. Not only would it be fruitless, for despite Horld's partial acceptance of what he had said, he still could not tell him everything that had happened. Worse, the inner frenzy about what had happened to Nertha, contained so far only by his need to seem calm in front of his colleague, was threatening to take complete possession of him at any moment.

'I've no answers to all this,' he said, barely managing to keep his voice steady. 'But, in any case, what Cassraw's doing is wrong by a score of the church's tenets, you know that. The least we can do is watch him and see that Mueran and the Chapter censure him properly, take steps to stop him.'

Horld relaxed visibly at this simple practical suggestion.

'I've been here longer than I intended,' Vredech said hastily. 'I've a lot to do. I'll leave you to your privacy.' He paused and looked back at the flat-topped rock. The stain dominated his vision, darker by far than all the shadows that lay across the summit. 'Could I ask a favour of you?'

'Of course,' Horld said.

Vredech was about to ask him to say a prayer over the rock, when he remembered the painful futility of his own words as they had rebounded upon him, mocking his shattered faith. 'While you're here, do as I asked you. Think again about what brought you into the church. Set aside your training and your studies, and all the words. Remember that touch which showed you the way.'

Horld looked uncertain.

'Please, Horld. Stay here and do this for me. It's important.' Vredech felt his remaining control slipping. He had to get away. 'You said you came here to meditate. You said you needed to think. I don't know what you're going to find, but where you found Ishryth is the only place to look.'

There was a brief, agonizing silence then Horld said, 'I'll do as you ask, because you ask, Allyn. It'll do me no harm, for sure. But we must talk again, and soon. This is all very—'

399

'Mid-morn tomorrow at my Meeting House,' Vredech interrupted, nodding purposefully. 'We can talk the day into evening if we want.' Then, with a cursory farewell, he began clambering down the rocks, fearful that Horld might attempt to prolong the conversation.

As he looked back he saw that Horld, a shadow amongst the shadows now, was sitting on the rock, one foot pulled up on to it to support his arm and his head; an oddly youthful posture. He was gazing out across the moonlit valley.

As Vredech paused to watch him, some small night-hunting animal scuttled across the rocks nearby, making him start violently. He set off down the mountain again.

Once away from the summit and his friend, his terrible anxieties returned in full suffocating force, this time laden pitilessly with guilt. He had known that great forces were in play, so why had he let Nertha go up to the place where they were actually producing a physical manifestation? Why had he so rashly challenged it with his poor prayers? Why had he pushed Nertha into using her own unsure healing skills to that same end? What had been that terrible noise? And, overriding all, incessant and unyielding in its grip on him: where had Nertha gone?

Such a thing as had happened was not possible!

Yet *he* had been transported bodily to some other world. And even to worlds within *that* world.

Hadn't he?

Fabric's torn, 'fore all was born . . .

For a timeless interval as his body carried him down the mountain towards the Witness House, Vredech's mind teetered at the edge of disintegration. The only thing that prevented it from shattering and scattering into the void in wretched imitation of the stars domed over him, and struggling with the moonlight for supremacy of the heavens, was the knowledge that Horld, too, had been touched

400

by the presence that had invaded the mountain and taken possession of Cassraw.

But even in this, barbed thoughts tore at him. Perhaps his meeting with Horld had been no more than another illusion generated in his failing mind.

And for the span of an eternal heartbeat, darkness closed over him and he was falling . . .

Lost . . .

'There's nothing wrong with your sanity.'

'Nothing can stand that kind of scrutiny.'

'Not answerable. Don't ask.'

'No alternative but to accept what you see – here, now.'

'No alternative . . .'

'No alternative . . .'

Nertha's words wrapped themselves about him, soothing even though they could not heal, holding together what was striving to break, holding him to here, to now.

Holding him . . .

And Horld, heat-scarred and solid, furnace-bronzed and anvil-weighted. He could be nothing but here, now.

Mid-morn tomorrow . . .

A fixed point.

Cold night air rushed through him, like an icy mountain stream, and with it came clear night vision, showing him familiar mountains etched sharp in the moonlight, and the silver-damp roof of the Witness House below him.

It was beautiful.

All about him was beautiful. In the least and the greatest of Ishryth's work there lay beauty. All that was needed was the vision to see it.

Then came an inner knowledge, a realization that whatever had happened at the summit had not been the doing of that invading presence; it had been *his*! Some part of him had moved to protect Nertha. Somewhere, Nertha was safe.

Vredech gazed at the moonlight bouncing brightly off

the roof of the Witness House. A calmness came over him. He tried to resist it. Nertha transported to Ishryth alone knew what limbo by some unknowing act of his, and he was feeling euphoric! It was obscene. He should be frantic, he should be thinking where he could turn to search for her, what books he could consult, what learned scholars, what ancient manuscripts . . .

But still he was calm.

He put a hand to his eyes, for the moonlight was becoming unbearable.

'Too bright,' he said.

'Oh!'

The soft cry, laden with relief, was followed by arms wrapping themselves about him, holding him chokingly tight. 'You're back, you're back. Thank Ishryth.' The voice became reproachful. 'You frightened me half to death. What do you think you were—' The question remained unfinished, and the embrace tightened further.

Vredech gently eased the clenching arms apart and, eyes blinking in the sunlight, reached up. 'Nertha,' he said, touching her face. 'You're all right?'

'Of course I'm all right,' came the reply. Nertha released him and bent forward to look into his face. Her expression was a mixture of deep concern and shrewd penetration. 'And so are you, it seems,' she declared. But the concern dominated. 'What happened? What did you do?'

Vredech reached out and touched her face again. 'I thought I'd lost you,' he said.

Nertha took his hand, kissed it, then pressed it back against her cheek. It was not a sister's kiss. 'And I you,' she said simply, meeting his gaze.

Then the moment was gone, pushed aside by the torrent of questions demanding answers. Vredech clambered to his feet. He was still at the summit, a little way from the stained boulder. And he had with him the calmness that had come to him when he had looked out over the moonlit valley and the glistening roof of the Witness House . . . only moments ago?

'What did you do?' Nertha asked again.

'Do?'

'Yes – do!' Nertha said, a tension in her voice that he had never heard before. 'I was trying to heal that thing,' she waved towards the rock, 'and feeling more than a little foolish, I might add, when something just swept me up. Took possession of me.' Her face twitched and she shuddered violently. 'It was awful. I haven't the words for it. Cold, inhuman – I was nothing to it. A barely adequate tool – a channel. And yet it was viciously cruel at the same time. Delighting in pain, in terror. I could do nothing. Even while it was happening, I couldn't believe it. It wasn't possible. It isn't . . .'

Vredech brought his finger to his lips for silence. 'I understand,' he said. 'I, above all, understand. You know that, don't you? Just tell me what happened. What did I do?'

Nertha looked surprised. 'You called out to me. I heard your voice or felt it full of anger, goading it. Then there was a terrible noise – for want of a better word – and whatever it was that held me was torn away. Torn away completely. When I opened my eyes you were lying there sprawled across the rock, unconscious.'

'And?'

'I didn't know what to do. I was trembling all over – still am. Shock, I suppose.' She shook herself as if sloughing a cumbersome coat. 'You didn't seem to be hurt. It was more as though you were asleep – dreaming. I managed to drag you over here, out of the sun. Checked you again. Paced up and down, like an apprentice nurse on her first night duty.' Her voice was full of self-reproach. Vredech took her hands. 'I didn't want to leave you in case you recovered and had lost your memory, or something.' Her voice faded away weakly.

Vredech wanted to ease her pain, but could find no words that would reach through their deep knowledge of one another. He squeezed her hands gently. 'How long was I unconscious?' he asked.

'Half an hour or so, I think. I was just plucking up courage to leave you and go for help, when you woke up.' She closed her eyes and grimaced.

'Are you all right?'

Nertha suddenly pulled her hands free with an oath. 'No, I'm not,' she shouted. 'Ye gods, I'm not. I've just spent the most wretched half hour of my life.' She struck her chest with her fist. 'Me, a more than adequate physician, even if I shouldn't say it, fretting around, helpless and hopeless, as much use as a nun in a brothel.' Vredech's eyebrows shot up and he raised a tentative priestly hand to stay the onslaught, but Nertha was gathering momentum. 'And I'm a rational being, Allyn. What am I doing up a mountain trying to heal a *rock*?' She kicked the stained boulders. 'And battling with mythical demons that I don't believe in?'

The questions were rhetorical, but he found himself answering them anyway.

'You're doing what rational people do in such circumstances,' he said. 'You're accepting change, new boundaries to your thinking. And you're shouting because, like me, you're scared witless. Remember, nothing is to be feared, it is only to be understood.'

'Don't you quote my quotations back at me, Allyn Vredech.'

'*Your* quotation? I'd say it was more of a fundamental truth, wouldn't you?'

He turned away before she could answer, and laid his hand on the rock. Nertha caught nervously at his elbow, but he shook his head reassuringly. 'It's not the same,' he

404

said. 'It's more distant.' His expression became pained. 'It's still there, though. Waiting. I think we've done something to it.' He put his arm around her shoulder and turned her so that they were both looking out over the valley.

'It's beautiful, isn't it?' he said.

Nertha made to look at him. 'Allyn, how can you—?'

He eased her back to the view. 'Here, now, this is beautiful,' he said. 'The air in your lungs, the sun on your face, these hills ranged about us. All things change. If we value what we have while we have it, then any pain in the change is so much less.'

Nertha made no sign but he felt some of the tension leave her.

They stood for some time, motionless, watching the shadows of the clouds marching across the land. Then Nertha asked, 'What happened to you when you were unconscious?' adding uncertainly, 'Did you meet your Whistler again?'

'No,' Vredech replied. 'Someone else. Come on, let's get back to our horses and go home. There's nothing else we can do here.'

As they descended the mountain, Vredech told of his encounter with Horld, in a world that both was and was not this one. He told her, too, of his near plunge into complete insanity. Nertha, seemingly herself again, stopped and looked at him purposefully. 'We have a test then?' she said, sternly logical despite the unsteadiness creeping into her voice.

'Yes,' Vredech replied flatly. 'And, perhaps, an ally.'

They completed the rest of their journey back to the Witness House in silence. As they were walking up the path towards the main door, it swung open and Horld emerged. He seemed unusually agitated, and started visibly when he saw Vredech.

Vredech walked to the foot of the steps and looked up at

Horld. He took a deep breath. 'Mid-morn tomorrow at my Meeting House?' he said.

Horld unashamedly circled his hand about his heart. 'Who are you?' he said hoarsely, his eyes widening.

'Who I seem to be, old friend,' Vredech replied softly. 'Don't be afraid. I think we need to talk, don't you? Were you about to leave?'

Horld nodded and abruptly began answering questions that had not been asked. 'I fell asleep in the reading room. I don't normally fall asleep in the day. I can't think what . . . I wasn't even tired. I just . . .' He snapped his fingers. 'Then it was night. And I needed to think. To be alone, and quiet.'

Vredech moved up the steps and took his arm. 'Get your horse,' he said, very gently. 'We'll talk as we ride.'

The journey down the mountain through the lengthening shadows of late afternoon was strained and awkward, with Horld struggling hard against what Vredech was saying, his common sense crying out continually that what he was hearing was patently impossible. But his dream, as he had considered it to be, had been too vivid, and lingered too clearly in his mind. And Vredech's knowledge of it was too thorough for him to take refuge in denial. Gradually he found himself obliged to accept that what had seemed to happen, dream or no, had actually happened, and that he and Vredech had held that conversation and made that promise to talk again. Though how or where it could all have been, he could not even begin to conjecture.

'Ishryth's will,' he concluded after a long silence as they reached the wider, less steep part of the path at the foot of the mountain. 'This is hard for a simple iron and coals man like me, Vredech. I can't bring myself to accept that Cassraw's possessed in some way. It's what Laffran said at the outset and he's invariably wrong.'

Vredech leaned over and laid a hand on his arm.

406

'Perhaps he wasn't, this time,' he said. 'More has happened to me than I've told you or that I can tell you at the moment, my friend. But more than once these past months, I've thought myself going insane. Perhaps because you, too, were touched by something in that darkness you were drawn to me in your . . . dream . . . by your concern about what happened to Cassraw that day. Perhaps we're simply tools in a greater scheme, I don't know. But I could wish for no better ally than you with your simple iron and coals vision. And if you can provide me with an explanation full of reason and logic, I'll embrace it heartily, and publicly announce myself as a fool.'

Horld grunted self-consciously. 'Well, be that as it may,' he said gruffly, 'I'll admit that for all the strangeness of what's just happened, I feel easier now than I've felt for some time. It's been as if those black clouds were still hovering over my head. In fact, I'm still getting worrying tales from some of my flock about nightmares and the like which seem to stem from that day.' He gave a dismissive shrug as his common sense drew in its stern rein. 'But I think we'd best keep our own counsel, don't you? There's enough in the way of wild words flying about with Cassraw ranting like a mad thing, and all this business over Tirfelden in the Heindral. And our tale would strain the wits of even the calmest listeners.'

'What are we to do then?' Nertha had been silent for most of the journey. Now she brought a practical voice to the debate that was quite the equal of Horld's.

'We oppose him, my girl,' Horld declaimed unhesitatingly. Nertha bristled and glowered at him, but Vredech discreetly signalled her to remain silent. 'We've not been granted this insight to stand by and watch idly,' Horld continued. 'Ishryth helps those who help themselves.'

'I'd be interested to know what you've got in mind,' Nertha said acidly, though Horld was too preoccupied with his own thoughts to notice the tone.

'Possession or no, we must put a stop to his nonsense before it gets completely out of hand,' he said, suddenly stern. 'The church will have to act.' He looked at Vredech. 'Tonight, I want to think about today and . . . everything. Think about it very hard. But whatever the outcome of that, tomorrow we must see Mueran and have him call a special meeting of the Chapter to bring Cassraw to heel.' He looked suddenly sad. 'It's a great shame,' he said. 'He's a very capable man, but I always felt he'd been brought on too quickly. The Haven Parish is a big responsibility for even an experienced Brother.' He sighed. 'Still, if we can bring him to his senses, I'm sure there'll still be a fine future for him in time.'

Vredech kept his doubts silent.

A little while later they parted.

Vredech looked at Nertha surreptitiously as they rode on. 'I'm all right,' she said defensively, catching the look. Vredech allowed his scepticism to show. 'Well, I'll confess to still being a little . . . bewildered,' Nertha admitted. 'Being calmly objective about your problems is one thing, being sucked up into them is another.'

'Bewildered, eh?' Vredech said. 'The Whistler said that the response of most ostensibly civilized people when they are suddenly overwhelmed by barbaric, primitive forces, is astonishment. "You'll be gaping in disbelief at the sword that kills you," he said. An appropriate comment, do you think?'

Unexpectedly, Nertha's face contorted and for an alarming moment Vredech thought she was going to burst into tears. The spasm passed. 'He's done something to me, Allyn,' she said, through gritted teeth. 'I'm so full of anger and hatred, it's frightening. I don't know where it's coming from.'

'It's coming from inside you,' Vredech said coldly. 'The only thing He did to you was make you aware of your darker nature. Weren't you the one who was telling me not to fret about my dark thoughts only a little while ago?' He waved his hand towards the top of the mountain. 'Don't worry about it, it's a good thing.'

'What? How can this be good?' Nertha made a jagged gesture of self-loathing. 'I've not felt anything like this since—'

'Since you were a child.' Vredech completed the remark. 'Before you became civilized.'

'Damn you! Will you stop presuming to know what I think,' Nertha shouted.

Vredech held up both hands in surrender, but pressed on. 'It's neither good nor bad,' he said. 'It simply *is*. Just like it's always been, except now you've seen it again. Now you know. Now you're wiser. You understand, so you'll not be afraid. You'll have another weapon in your armoury of defence if you choose to use it.' He leaned across to her and added grimly: 'You won't be astonished the next time He tries to use you, will you?'

And where did you get this coldness in your soul from, to harrow the woman so, Priest? came a merciless thought. Vredech reined his horse to a halt and lowered his head, shocked by this new insight into his changing inner landscape. 'I'm sorry,' he said. 'I've no right to talk to you like that. I'm hardly in control of affairs, am I?'

Nertha, girding herself for an argument, faltered. 'It's all right,' she said. 'We *are* probably still shocked after all that's happened to us.' She smiled weakly. 'In fact, I must be in shock, or I wouldn't be trying to diagnose it in myself.'

Vredech looked at her, waiting a little way ahead, and half-turned towards him. Stained with the soil of their journey up the mountain and her face deep-shadowed by the sinking sun, the sight of her nevertheless lightened his heart. It occurred to him that only a few hours ago, there had been some kind of a future ahead of him which, while it might have twisted here and turned there, like the past behind him, ran along a broad and reasonably knowable path. Now there was darkness, doubt, and confusion before his every step. And the changing character of his affection for Nertha was beginning to unsettle him also. Yet the calmness that had come to him in the mysterious world he had drifted into . . . been thrown into? . . . remained with him, though it gave him no easy peace. It was the calmness of a man who knew that he could do no other than turn to face whatever was about to happen, however fearful, and struggle to make right what was wrong.

The Whistler's words echoed in his head. 'There's not a great deal of difference between a priest and a true warrior.' Vredech shook his head. He was no warrior by any definition, he was sure. But he understood.

'Let's just say we're tired,' he said. 'That's simple enough, and probably true. Such a lot has happened over the last couple of days, and tomorrow's going to be very busy. Let's walk slowly home, and let House fuss over us. That'll make three of us happy.'

Albor sat down on the flat-topped wall that fringed a basement stairway, and swore softly. These wretched night patrols around the warehouse district were as boring as they were time-wasting. It was an area that was quiet under normal circumstances after the businesses closed their doors each day, but it was quieter than ever following the two murders. Such few people as were here at night, mainly watchmen and caretakers, were confining their patrols to the insides of their particular properties, making doubly certain that all doors and windows were securely bolted.

He drew out a kerchief and wiped it across his forehead. The boredom he could tolerate; on the whole it had to be

410

better than encountering the lunatic who was committing these crimes. But this heat!

The tall brick and stone walls, having soaked up the sun's warmth throughout the day, were releasing it into the night, and where their presence did not actually still the night breeze that was soothing the rest of the town, it warmed it so that its touch was like that from a suddenly opened oven. Albor wriggled his damp shirt off his back again. Still, doing this duty was probably better than keeping an eye on the crowds that had been swarming all around the Haven Meeting House today, and it was certainly better than doing crowd control duty in the PlasHein Square tomorrow. He frowned. Memories of that crushing, panicking crowd and its aftermath still hung about him, subtly draining him and making him nervous and edgy. He and most of his colleagues had either panicked or simply floundered helplessly when the crowd had started to move. None of them had known what to do. There were no official procedures laid down for dealing with such eventualities. Why should there be? There had never been anything like it before. He shook his head to dismiss the thoughts that were beginning to circle again. He knew that they would only make him frustrated and angry and it was hot enough already. It was not as if he could do anything about it. The Chief and the High Captains and the Captains would doubtless hand down their collective wisdom in due course, without asking his advice, though, with a bit of luck Skynner and the other Serjeants might have the chance to colour it with a little practical experience before it became set in stone.

Dismissing the thoughts yet again, he growled, and laboured himself upright to continue on his patrol. He had scarcely gone ten paces, however, when a noise reached him. Thin, high-pitched and shrill, it bounced from wall to wall, until it surrounded and encased him. He could not begin to identify it, but its tone made the hairs on his neck

411

rise up and he drew his baton as he looked around to try to identify the source.

It stopped.

And started again, coming now in short gasps which were all too recognizable. It was a human voice, and it was terror-stricken. Painfully, it twisted into a mewling, 'Help,' then disintegrated again. As it rose and fell, so it entered deep into Albor, mingling with the scream that he could feel forming within himself as he ran towards where it was loudest. But even as he ran, so the intensity of the scream shifted from place to place.

Over here . . .

Over there . . .

Albor turned round and round in the middle of the street, the sense of panic and failure that had possessed him two days earlier in the PlasHein Square, returning in full force to condemn him for his inability to go to the rescue of the tormented soul that was filling the street with its awful cry.

Then it fell abruptly into a long sobbing whimper and as it faded so did its many echoes until there was only a single thread. Grim-faced and full now of fighting rage, Albor ran through the clinging night warmth towards its source. As it died, so he gathered speed until he found himself tumbling into one of the dark alleyways between the warehouses. The sudden disappearance of even the faint street lighting brought him to a staggering halt. The sound, almost inhuman now in its desperate pleading, was directly ahead of him, but full of fury though he was, his years of experience on the streets exerted themselves. He snatched his lantern from his belt and struck it.

As it hissed gently into light, so another hissing rose to greet it, and something flashed towards him . . .

412

Chapter 29

The sun was rising as Privv dropped into his favourite chair, swung his feet up on to his desk and lifted his hand to his mouth. After a brief, half-hearted chew at his thumb, he let the hand fall to swing idly by his side. Leaning his head back he stared vacantly at the ceiling.

'I'm not going to be able to carry on like this,' he said. 'The responsibility of running this Sheet is getting far too much. I am *exhausted*.'

'Yes,' Leck replied sympathetically. 'Counting money is such a wearisome chore. I really can't imagine how you've managed to get this far without positively collapsing.'

'Do I detect an element of sarcasm in that remark?' Privv said, turning his head slightly to eye the cat.

'Ishryth forbid,' came the reply. 'I stand in true awe of your selfless dedication to the presentation of the truth to the good people of Troidmallos . . .'

'And surrounding shires,' Privv added.

'Oh yes, we mustn't forget the surrounding shires, must we?' Leck waxed. ' "First Sheet in Canol Madreth to reach out into the countryside." Quite an accolade, that. Quite fortuitous, too, that a peasant's coin is as sound as a merchant's.'

'One has to eat,' Privv replied haughtily. 'And a labourer's worthy of his hire.'

'Better not let your new assistants catch wind of that,' Leck said.

413

Privv returned his gaze to the ceiling. 'I can see that you don't truly understand my motives in this endeavour.'

Leck was suddenly sombre. 'Quite possibly,' she said. 'I don't even understand my own. Since all this business started I've been thinking that a gift like ours was intended for more beneficial things. I feel as though something's missing.'

Privv gave a weary sigh. 'Oh spare me the feline philosophy. Just tell me what you've unearthed on your nightly travels.' A wave of deep sadness from the cat passed over him, but before he could react, he felt Leck deliberately withdrawing from him.

'Not a great deal,' she said flatly. 'There's endless comings and goings at the Haven Meeting House – Preaching Brothers – lots of his precious Knights, especially that lout Yanos who seems to have found such favour with the good Brother.' The last trace of Leck's dark mood faded as she extended her claws, clicking against the wooden sill. 'Threw a stone at me, he did – and he's a damned good shot. I'll have his throat open if he's unlucky enough ever to get hold of me.' She became grimly pensive. 'In fact, I've half a mind to find out where he's sleeping and sneak in and lie across his face – nice and heavy, relaxed and warm.' She stretched herself and chuckled malevolently.

Privv was not disposed to pursue the singularly unpleasant images that were drifting into his mind. 'Well, what's it all about then?' he demanded.

'I've no idea,' Leck snapped, angry at this disturbance of her sweet visions of vengeance. 'I couldn't get inside.'

'Why not? You can fawn with the best when you want.'

Leck became defensive. 'I'm not keen on that wife of his. She's as bad as he is if you ask me, if not worse. I didn't want to get near her.'

Privv waved a scornful hand. 'It'll be church politics with the Brothers, I suppose. But what about the

414

Knights?' He sat up and rested his head in his hands. 'I'd dearly like to know what he's up to with those young men.'

'Why don't you do what you normally do then, and make it up?' Leck said acidly.

Privv didn't even hear the sarcasm. 'What, and breach the trust he has in me?' Leck looked out of the window. 'No. He'll tell me when he's ready.'

'Better you know in advance though,' Leck warned. 'I've told you, he's using you, you know.'

'You worry too much,' Privv replied, catching the tone. 'And it's me who's using him, don't forget that. Who's the one who's getting rich, eh? And I *mean* rich,' he said, tapping his chest. Faintly he felt her strange introspection returning. He dismissed it and lay back in his chair again, smug now. 'I shall take a well-earned nap, and then get down to the PlasHein to listen to the great debate.' He rubbed his hands together gleefully and yawned.

Others were making plans too, that day – Toom Drommel for one. He had a splendid speech prepared, one which would see the Castellans suffering appalling political damage as they were at last obliged to retreat from their avowed intention of expelling Felden nationals and seizing Felden assets. The only problem he was having was some stiffness in his back as a result of trying to stand even straighter than he already was, and some discomfort in his throat due to withdrawing his chin further and further as he was speaking, in an attempt to make his voice still more solemn and statesmanlike. Such Heinders who were of both a musical and a frivolous bent had noted that he had lowered his voice by the best part of an octave since the first debate, and were now laying wagers on whether or not he would attempt the full span. Drommel himself was quite oblivious to such levity, however, self-satisfaction and unctuousness filling almost every part of him. Beyond

415

the inevitable retreat of the Castellans today he saw an early Acclamation and a rise in the fortune of his party such as it had not experienced in generations. He would have the support of the church, too, for though he had affected to dismiss Cassraw's patriotic tirade after their meeting, it had struck chords in him that resonated still and which had played no small part in the preparation of his speech. He could already hear his name being spoken of along with the great leaders of the past.

Sitting at his desk as he glanced once again through his speech, he moved one hand here, the other there, inclined his head this way then that, crossed and uncrossed his legs, for the benefit of the official portrait painter who must surely be calling on him within the year.

As Drommel preened himself and larded his present with the glories of his future, Vredech was saddling his horse prior to riding to Horld's Meeting House, and thence to the Witness House. As they had intended, he and Nertha had allowed House to fuss over them on their return the previous day, and when he had finally retired he was relishing the warmth and security that this had brought back to him from his childhood. He relished them all the more because he knew that while they were quite false, they were nonetheless a measure of the selfless affection of another person for him, and as such, protected him in far more subtle ways.

Somehow he was able to let the turmoil of the day pass over and through him. What he could do, he would do now. Even though some mysterious entity, whose true nature lay quite beyond his understanding, might be seeking to gain a foothold in this world, it was seemingly working through only Cassraw and, in the morning, simple practical steps would be taken that would surely put an end to Cassraw's manic progress.

He went to sleep almost immediately and was largely

untroubled as once again he found himself moving through what appeared to be the dreams of others. Even as he drifted uncontrollably between them he had the feeling that here was a gift that he should be able to use for the benefit of others. Memories of the brooding, bloody dream he had encountered as he had slept on his return from the Sick-House came to him to heighten this idea. A dream as full of murderous passion as it was cold indifference to anything other than itself. A dream that could only be the product of a deeply disturbed mind. Yet there was a familiarity about it. If he were able to identify the dreamer, he would perhaps be able to help him. But the familiarity eluded him and he could give his ideas no coherent shape and was soon lost in the blackness of his own sleep.

Now he was both looking forward to and dreading what was to come. Looking forward because it was action, and it was right. Dreading because it felt like treachery to his friend. He was also a little tense because he had clashed with Nertha who had wanted to go to the Witness House with him to give her own account of Cassraw's sermon. There had been a small storm as, thoughtlessly, he had refused outright, though he had eventually managed to mollify her by saying that it was, after all, 'church business' and how would she and her colleagues feel if a Preaching Brother decided to tell them how to go about treating the sick?

As he mounted his horse, he cringed inwardly at the thought of Nertha and Mueran meeting head on.

As if he didn't have enough problems at the moment!

Skynner, too, was planning that day. Or trying to. The rota of Keepers' duties and routines which had served him almost all his professional life, and others before him, was in complete disarray. The first murder had put a strain on it, and the second had more than doubled that strain, but the events in the PlasHein Square had rendered it totally useless. Not only was there more work to be done, but much of it was completely new in character as senior officers flapped and floundered, trying to work out 'procedures' for the controlling of large crowds. They were holding meetings, forming committees, preparing reports, promising this, promising that, promising anything to quieten a plethora of equally ineffectual Heinders howling for action. One thing they were not doing was asking the opinions of those who might have some practical ideas about the matter, but that gave the proceedings an almost refreshing hint of normality.

Added to all this was the fact that several of Skynner's men had been injured trying to cope with the stampede in the square, and all of them were still suffering after-effects in one form or another.

Skynner looked at the paper in front of him. It was the latest offering from above about what was to be done today to deal with the crowd which was anticipated in the PlasHein Square. It required more than twice as many men as he had. He laid it to one side with a resigned sigh, and shook his head. He could not even begin to implement it, nor could he debate it with its author: by the time *he* appeared, the crowd would probably be gathering.

Or, more likely, dispersing, he added as a sour after-thought.

He looked at the list of men he had available. With men off through injury, and others moved to extra night duty to cover the warehouse area, he had precious few, and most of them were tired and dispirited.

Still, that he could cope with. Getting his men motivated was something that he was good at. Skynner picked up a pen and, while his masters fumed and fretted, he sketched out a solution to the day's problem in a few minutes. Not an ideal one, by any means, but adequate.

He would cope. His men would cope.

Thus was the day faced, well-planned and ordered.

Toom Drommel made his booming speech – finally hitting the octave, to the glee of that minority of listeners who set store by such things – and the Castellans, seriously divided amongst themselves and continuing to show the political ineptitude they had demonstrated throughout this affair, retreated from their position, or rather slithered over backwards to crash in total confusion.

Drommel's face looked strained and drawn as his moment of triumph came and, in truth, he was finding it almost unbearably difficult not to laugh and jeer outright. A nervous twitching of his left foot was the sole outward expression of the dance he wanted to perform.

Despite the stiffness in his jaw, he managed to make a formal demand, through the uproar, for the immediate dissolution of the Heindral. The leader of the Castellans gave an equally formal refusal, citing precedent, tradition and the general public good. Salvaging what he could of the débâcle, he managed to imbue his speech with a little surprised indignation that such a thing should even be considered, but all there knew that a train of events had been set in motion that must inevitably lead to an early Acclamation.

There was great excitement.

Inside his stony frame, Toom Drommel glowed as he saw his future unfolding before him like a great, golden sunrise.

Vredech and Horld too, found themselves musing over what had been an unexpectedly successful day as they rode back together from the Witness House, though their mood was in marked contrast to the raucous pandemonium ringing through the rafters of the PlasHein. Neither took either credit for or delight in what had happened.

Mueran had affected surprise when they had presented themselves, though in fact he was highly relieved. Gossip about Cassraw's latest venture had been reaching him from innumerable quarters and, despite the usual stately outward manner that he was maintaining, his indecision and reproach against an unkind destiny that had brought him such troubles had reduced him almost to panic just before they arrived.

He had nodded sagely as they talked, tapped his fingers against his lips thoughtfully, frowned, sighed, shaken his head, given all the impressions of being totally in command of affairs. Then he had listened to their suggestions – Cassraw *must* be called before the Chapter as a matter of urgency, to receive due censure for his actions. For censure there must be now after the things he had said. Sadly, any accounting he might offer could only be in the nature of mitigation. By prior agreement both Horld and Vredech assiduously avoided any conjecture about 'possession' or any other possible cause of Cassraw's wild behaviour, save perhaps overwork.

'This jeopardizes his holding of the Haven Parish, you know,' Mueran had said.

'*He* jeopardizes it, Brother,' Vredech said powerfully, his sense of guilt making his voice strident. 'Not we. There's plenty of freedom to hold differing views within the church, but he shouldn't speak thus. It's not as if it's a gentle touching on secular affairs – it's rabble-rousing politicking such as hasn't been seen even in the Heindral in a dozen generations, let alone the church. I can't think what he's trying to do, but he's master of his tongue and his wits as far as we know. Nothing compels him to behave like that, and he must bear the responsibility for it.'

It was an argument that could not be gainsaid and Mueran, much calmer now that he had someone to shoulder the blame, should the affair take an unexpected direction, had agreed to their proposed action. Notices would be sent out summoning an emergency meeting of the Chapter prior to the next Service Day. It was unlikely that all the Chapter Brothers would be able to attend, but there would be enough to ensure a fair hearing.

'This is a wretched business,' Horld said eventually, breaking the silence that had hung over them since they left the Witness House. 'I know that what we've done is right, but . . .' He shook his head.

Vredech had little consolation to offer. He used the argument that he had employed with Mueran. 'It's none of our doing, Horld. Cassraw behaving like that left us no alternative but to act. However badly we feel now, we'd be feeling far worse if we'd done nothing.'

Horld nodded unhappily. 'I think it's the element of deceit in our actions that's disturbing me.'

Vredech looked at him, puzzled.

'This business about Cassraw being possessed,' Horld went on. 'I've prayed all night in the hope of some guidance, but I'm none the wiser. I don't doubt the sincerity of your belief, Allyn, but I can't accept that Ahmral has taken human form to walk amongst us again. It goes against reason, commonsense – against all current theological thinking.'

'Set the name aside,' Vredech said. 'It's not important. Have you any doubts about the nature of what touched you that day on the mountain? Or about the fact that you and I met and spoke together in the same . . . dream?'

Horld's face was pained, but he shook his head.

'Then cling to your faith in those in silence,' Vredech said. 'All that we've raised with Mueran is what Cassraw's been *saying* – a matter that by now dozens of people can testify to. Plain, simple, everyday reality. Iron and coals. My feeling, and it's growing stronger by the day, is that some evil power – call it what you will – came in that cloud and took possession of Cassraw. Now, something far beyond our understanding of everyday reality is afoot. I'll have that always in my mind, but only to you and to Nertha will I speak of it.' He turned and looked straight at Horld. 'It may be that amongst your own thoughts about this, is one that says I'm raving mad myself.'

Horld looked startled and shifted awkwardly in his saddle.

'It's a fair enough assumption,' Vredech went on, smiling slightly, 'and I take no offence at it. But give me the right we've agreed to give Cassraw: judge me by my actions.'

Horld stammered slightly as he spoke. 'I wouldn't dream of judging you, Allyn,' he said. ' "Judge not, lest *ye* be condemned".'

Vredech smiled at the embarrassment in Horld's voice as he resorted to quoting the Santyth. ' "But by their deeds shall they be measured",' he countered, quoting from the same Dominant Text. 'I give you the right to judge me, Horld. No – I demand it!' He tapped his head briskly. 'I demand the rigour of your mind applied to the judgement of my actions, and to such of my thoughts as I reveal to you.'

Horld was openly embarrassed now. 'You sound like Nertha talking,' he flustered. 'With her logic and her interminable, probing questioning.'

Vredech's smile turned into a laugh. 'She's quieter than when you last seriously crossed swords with her,' he said. 'Different, too. I think perhaps she's found some answers after all.' His manner became distant. 'She's really a most admirable person.'

Horld grunted and gave Vredech a long, curious look.

Vredech abandoned his reverie and spoke earnestly. 'You must do this, Horld,' he said. 'You're my shield against my own folly, as perhaps I am against yours. While we test one another, I doubt we'll do any malice.'

Horld nodded.

They did not speak again until they parted company at the foot of the mountain.

After giving due credit to good fortune, Skynner, too, congratulated himself on a successful day. The public balconies in the PlasHein had been completely filled, but the crowd that had gathered in the square had been much smaller than the one three days previously, doubtless as a result of what had happened then. There were few women present and no children.

When the result of the debate was made known, there was uproar amongst the Heinders, but the watching public had taken it comparatively quietly, seemingly more interested in watching the antics of their representatives in the hall below than encouraging any particularly partisan opinion now that a decision had been reached. Those people in the square dispersed quietly and in good order. With his limited resources, Skynner had made no attempt to marshal the crowd, but had concentrated on identifying any individuals who looked likely to cause trouble, and quietly removed them. There were remarkably few – a point which reinforced Skynner's strengthening opinion that the previous incident had been deliberately engineered, though for what purpose and by whom, he had not had the time to ponder quietly.

And he laid the questions aside once again. Many other voices would have their say about what had happened, in due course, though the Special Assize which had been promised would inevitably be some time away now, with all the current political upheaval. He would continue to interrogate the youths who had been arrested on the day, but he held out little hope of clarification there; they were a mindless lot, and if they were involved at all then it was purely as the unwitting agents of others.

He leaned on the heavy stone surround to the doorway of the Keeperage, and looked up and down the street. Not a bad day, he thought, as he watched the late afternoon traffic pursuing its usual business. In so far as they ever would after the tragedy in the square, things were getting back to normal. He might perhaps get a decent night's sleep tonight.

Thus the day passed for the people of Troidmallos; planned, ordered and for many, successful. Things were, indeed, getting back to normal.

As Skynner turned to go back into the building, a movement caught his eye. A single movement out of all the bustle that filled the street, yet even as he searched to identify it more clearly, the instinct that years of experience had given him was telling him unequivocally that his self-congratulation was premature and that his night's rest was far from assured. As the movement became clearer, so this instinct began to raise deep alarms in him, for even though the approaching figure was still a long way away, it seemed that he could see its mouth gaping and its eyes staring wide with awful shock.

So vivid was this impression that he had walked down the steps to the Keeperage and was moving towards the doom-laden messenger when the man finally arrived. He was a junior Keeper, scarcely out of his training, and he was white-faced and gasping for breath. Skynner took his arm firmly and, without speaking, marched him out of the public gaze into the Keeperage.

'Calm down, Kerna,' he said sternly when they were inside, experience this time giving him a patience that he did not really feel. 'Just breathe easy and tell me what's happened, slowly.'

Somewhat to his surprise, the Keeper took a deep, steadying breath and straightened up. The abrupt recovery heightened Skynner's alarm. Something *really* serious had happened.

'Another murder,' the man said, pointing. 'In the warehouse area again.'

Skynner's heart sank. But there was more, he could tell. 'Albor's dead, as well.'

As the words struck him, Skynner heard himself giving the news to Albor's mother. Struggling to set the thought aside, he felt a myriad tiny clamps suddenly tightening all over his body, holding his hands, his arms, everything, rigid, setting his face, channelling his thoughts, as if any movement, any digression, however slight, would shatter the control over himself, and his men, that he would need now.

He asked a series of simple, terse questions: 'Where? Who's there? Who else knows?' He forbore to ask, 'How?' He would find out soon enough anyway and to ask now would be to cause delay. Within minutes he was on horseback, trotting through the sunlit streets as quickly as the busy citizens would allow, his control still icy and pervading both his horse and Kerna, riding behind him.

A small crowd of men was gathered at the entrance to the alley when he reached his destination. They looked round at the sound of his approach, then parted to let him through. He stared down at them. 'Unless you've anything to say about how this happened, go back to your work right away, gentlemen,' he said. Though his voice was quiet, there was a quality in it that dispersed the group almost immediately.

Skynner paused for a moment. The alley was very narrow and received little light from the blue strip of sky overhead. It was also littered with rubbish. Some way along stood a group of three Keepers. A man was sat huddled near to them, leaning on the wall.

As he wended a careful way towards them, Skynner felt as though he were moving back through time. This was the third occasion he had made such a walk, with lowering walls hemming him in and a circle of uncertain Keepers waiting to greet him. For an agonizing moment, his control slipped and he was flooded with the fear that he would be walking thus for ever, nearing but never reaching, yet always seeing, torn body after torn body, an inevitable and somehow necessary witness to the fulfilment of some great and insatiable need.

He clenched his teeth so tightly that they cracked painfully and he was himself again, facing what had to be faced, doing what had to be done. He stepped around a pool of fresh vomit to be greeted by a fellow Serjeant, a man some years his junior who was also struggling to keep command of himself. 'Young Kerna, I'm afraid,' he said. 'Not that I can blame him. This one's even worse than the others.'

'Where's Albor, Stiel?' Skynner asked bluntly.

Stiel pointed unsteadily to a shape that was almost indistinguishable from the rubbish cluttering the ground. Skynner walked over and squatted beside it. He reached out to pull back the cloak that had been thrown over the body then hesitated, a flicker of anxiety passing over his face.

'As far as I can tell, his neck's been broken,' Stiel said. 'He's not been . . . cut up. Whoever did it had apparently had enough . . . exercise . . . with the other one. He's really bad. It looks as though there's bits been ripped right out of him. There's—'

'All right!' Skynner said sharply, raising a hand to cut off the description. 'All in good time.'

Bracing himself, he pulled back the cloak and looked at his dead friend and colleague. As he took in the familiar face, now pale and empty, and the unnaturally crooked head, a terrible anger and pain filled him. He crushed them both ruthlessly. They would serve him best as a fire in which to temper his resolve, rather than a great flaring of empty words.

His hand trembling a little, he touched Albor's face.

426

'He's been dead for hours,' he said, a question in his voice.

Stiel's glance took in the whole alley. 'No one comes down here, except to dump their rubbish,' he said. 'It was only by chance that that old scavenger found them.' He flicked a thumb in the direction of the man sat on the ground by the Keepers, his head slumped forward and his arms around his knees. Skynner looked down. Into the many thoughts that he was trying to order, came another, loosed by Stiel's remark: there could be other bodies lying undiscovered in this district. It was a truly awful thought and he turned away from it. He looked again at Albor's face.

'He looks surprised,' he said, half to himself.

'The other one's the same as before, but worse,' Stiel said. 'Horribly frightened.' He wiped his forehead. 'I'll be lucky if I can keep him out of my mind tonight.'

'Don't try,' Skynner said starkly. Then, pensively, 'Why would he look surprised?'

He knew the answer even as he was asking the question. Albor had come into the alley to investigate something, seen and *recognized* the murderer, and died before he even knew what was happening. But that begged many other questions. Why surprise and not anger? And who could have killed him so quickly and with such force? Albor was no junior cadet when it came to looking after himself.

Skynner stood up and pushed his fingers into his closed eyes. He felt old and lost; it was a bad feeling. He forced back the pain that was struggling to overwhelm him. 'We're going to have to ask the Chief to levy part of the militia,' he said, clinging to present needs. 'We'll have to search every alley and every disused cellar around here, and we'll have to mount Ishryth knows how many more night patrols to cover the area properly.'

Stiel frowned but nodded. 'I suppose so,' he said. 'But it'll create quite a stir.'

'Not as much as more murders would,' Skynner

427

retorted, turning and walking back along the alley. 'And there will be more and more until this lunatic's caught.'

As he stepped out from the dark alley and into the bright sunlight, it seemed to Skynner that everything about him was tinged blood-red.

Another unexpected incident occurred on that well-planned day.

As is the way with small self-contained communities, the Madren were viewed in many ways by their neighbours. Adjectives such as 'crafty, self-righteous, churlish' and even 'stupid', were a commonplace but, in fairness, were apt to be reciprocated by the Madren, as is also the way with small, self-contained communities.

However, amid this sea of vague and general impressions, fed as it was by rumour and hearsay, and moved by the irresistible gravity of ignorance, some evil currents flowed. For every five that spoke ill of the Madren, one was bred who said that they needed to be taught a lesson, and for every five of these, there was one who said they *should* be taught a lesson.

Not that these populations were fixed. They ebbed and flowed within each individual and throughout communities, in accordance with laws as immutable and as incalculable as those that blow the wind here instead of there. And, in Tirfelden, they had been flowing quite strongly of late.

While the Heinders pushed and jostled amongst themselves, and while Privv worked diligently to increase his personal wealth by embellishing and spreading tales of their activities, the great clatter of rhetoric that arose was heard far beyond Troidmallos. And while the Heinders pushed and jostled, they neglected to notice who else was listening to the garbled and broken echoes of the sounds that they were making.

It was a mistake.

There were laws in Tirfelden that constrained Sheeters to tell the truth, on pain of drastic financial and sometimes physical punishment, and when some of Privv's Sheets began to appear there, sent by anxious Felden living in Canol Madreth, they were read against such a background and the tide of tribal mistrust began to flow very strongly.

Felden officials in Canol Madreth noted the clamour that was being raised about their country while they themselves were not being addressed. They received little reassurance from their counterparts in the Madren bureaucracy as the Castellans, compounding their mishandling of the situation in the heat of their conflict in the Heindral, were either not consulting them or not listening to them. They were regretfully obliged to shrug their shoulders helplessly when asked what the real intentions of the Madren government were.

Consequently, it was not long before the Felden authorities found themselves dealing with large public demonstrations demanding that they 'do something' about the now strident Madren. And being more apt to be led than to lead, they did.

Thus, while Privv was concocting yet another Sheet, while Vredech and Horld were pondering their own strange revelations, while Toom Drommel was awaiting destiny's embrace, and Skynner was quietly mourning his friend, a company of the Tirfelden army marched into Canol Madreth.

Chapter 30

Tirfelden, unlike Canol Madreth, but like every other state in Gyronlandt, had a long history both of internal dissension and of menacing or being menaced by its neighbours in varying degrees. Thus it had always had some form of standing army. There had, however, been quite a long period of internal stability, and no serious aggression for even longer and, of late, the need for such an army had come under question.

The uproar in Canol Madreth, rendered raucously bellicose by distance and telling, and the responses that it provoked within Felden society were thus ideal for those factions which wished to retain the army. Not least amongst these was the military hierarchy itself, some out of genuine patriotic concern, but most out of fear that they might find themselves reduced to hewing and tilling for their bread.

Fortunate enough to be inexperienced in actual combat, the Felden army was no hardened and skilled fighting force. It consisted of a largely ceremonial officer corps drawn from the sons of Tirfelden's richer families, and a markedly rougher element drawn from those members of society who could master no trade – or at least no honest one – or who for other reasons found the freedom and rigours of civilian life too intimidating.

Nevertheless, it was competent enough for one of its companies to march in and take over the village of Bredill that lay on the main route between Tirfelden and Canol Madreth. Once they were established, an official envoy and token escort, resplendent in formal uniforms, galloped to Troidmallos bearing a strongly-worded ultimatum. This told of the action that had taken place and offered it as a demonstration of the Felden government's willingness and ability to take 'reprisals of the utmost severity' should Canol Madreth proceed with its proposals to expel Felden nationals and seize Felden assets.

Unfortunately, when they arrived, it was dark and it was only by asking the way of a bemused Keeper, that they were able to find the relevant government office. It was shut. The escort stood to one side in discreet silence while the envoy pondered. It is rumoured that he was heard to mutter, 'Now, what would mother have done?' but, truth being ever the first casualty of war, this is disputed. However, doubtless in reality fired with patriotic fervour by his senior officers rather than any residual maternal influence, he made his decision and boldly took out the ultimatum to fix it to the closed door. In the absence of hammer and nails he was obliged to fold it rather awkwardly under the iron ring which served as a handle to the door. That done, escort and envoy departed in a splendid echoing clatter of hooves.

Some way from the town they became quite badly lost and had to rouse a local farmer to find out where they were.

The only spectator to this small piece of history was Leck. Attracted by the unusual noise of galloping hooves and the strange scent that the newcomers brought with them, she had sidled over and rubbed herself against the legs of the envoy, startling and unbalancing him as he had tried to fasten the ultimatum under the iron ring with martial sternness.

When he had left, Leck jumped up and clawed the paper free. Dragging it to a nearby lantern she read it.

Then she lay down on it and, eyes closed, let out a silent yell, loud enough to penetrate through whatever Privv was engaged in at the moment.

Within minutes he came racing along the street to examine the paper for himself.

Thus it was that the people of Troidmallos heard of the invasion of their land by Tirfelden. Not from a solemn-voiced official crier, but from a hastily produced and very simply worded Sheet – smaller than usual and its price slightly increased.

While Canol Madreth had no army it nonetheless had a much revered tradition of a civilian militia. Every male save the young and the old was obliged to have 'and maintain' a bow, thirty arrows, a sword, a knife, a 'sturdy' staff, a rope of at least twenty paces in length, plus various other accoutrements which, should need arise, would serve to make him a formidable and self-sufficient mountain soldier. All this was laid out in great detail in the Annex to the Militia Statute – a copy of which he was also supposed to have, together with the Santyth, of course.

Unfortunately, tradition was almost all that was left of the militia now, as apart from the occasional flurry of social conscience, the authorities took little trouble to fulfil their obligations towards the militia in maintaining a programme of levying and training. And men, being men, naturally preferred to talk a war than actually risk fighting one so, apart from a few conscientious enthusiasts, the militia was more a glowing word, similar in character to 'a united Gyronlandt', than a practical reality.

Nevertheless, it was a word that came suddenly into popular usage as Privv's Sheet spread the news through and beyond the town. Many a shed and attic was ransacked that day for 'that old bow' and 'those arrows of mine,' and so on . . .

Eventually, the caretaker, a lowly government official, arrived to open the office to which the ultimatum had been delivered. A fine, sour-faced example of Canol Madreth's janitocracy, he scowled for quite a time at the now-creased and soiled document lying on the step before picking it up and, with an obligatory grumble, pushing it into his pocket unread. It was not, after all, his job to deal with such things. Only when he had performed his morning routine of lighting unnecessary fires in all the rooms, transferring boxes of files to their wrong destinations, and re-distributing the dust – brushing was the only activity he pursued with any vigour – did he deign to hand the document to anyone. The anyone he chose was a junior clerk, who, new to the service and thus rather rash, read it. Seeing confirmed under the Crest and Seal of Tirfelden, what he had fearfully read in the Sheet earlier, he compounded this initial rashness by taking it upon himself to deliver the document personally to the chief adviser to the government rather than commit it to the internal mailing system – that is, to the ultimate charge of the same individual who had just given it to him.

The chief adviser was an educated and cultured man who, 'Never read Privv's Sheet,' so his copy was still concealed in his documents, pending an opportunity arising which would allow him to read it without fear of disturbance. He was thus one of the few people in Troidmallos who did not know what had happened. So he would have remained, had not the junior clerk slammed his own copy of Privv's Sheet in front of him with the observation, 'It's just like it says 'ere. Wot are you goin' to do?'

The chief adviser was not disposed to enter into a debate on the matter. A man not without resource in a crisis, it took him only a moment to realize where his responsibility lay and, with barely a moment's hesitation, he snatched up both the Sheet and the ultimatum and fled with them to his political master, currently in the form of the bemused and rapidly failing leader of the Castellan Party. By coincidence, this worthy was on a like errand. They met in a corridor halfway between their respective offices. It was an internal corridor and thus rather dark, as the caretaker, being too busy lighting the lanterns in other, windowed, corridors, had neglected to light those that hung there. The two men, Sheets in hand and held high, moved towards one another like short-sighted army signallers in the gloaming of second-hand daylight that seeped through from the doors of adjacent offices.

Prior to this momentous meeting however, other events had occurred, inadvertently set in train by Privv who, following some Sheeter's instinct, had personally delivered a copy of his Sheet to the Haven Meeting House. He stood silent as Cassraw read it, Dowinne looking nervously over his arm.

'You've actually seen this ultimatum?' Cassraw asked, turning towards him.

'Of course,' Privv said, risking a little indignation.

Cassraw's face became a mask. 'You were right to bring this to me,' he said. 'Those who follow me will always be rewarded.' Somewhat to his surprise, Privv then found himself ushered quickly out before he could begin to interrogate Cassraw. As he rode away he wondered where he had heard Cassraw's last comment before. It sounded like something out of the Santyth, but it wasn't, he was sure.

When Privv had left, Cassraw went out into the grounds of the Meeting House. Dowinne followed him. He stood motionless for a long time, his gaze fixed on the summit of the Ervrin Mallos. Dowinne did not move either, though her gaze was fixed on her husband.

'I've been uneasy these last few days,' Cassraw said eventually. 'It's been as though His presence about the mountain has been disturbed in some way.' His face became pained. 'I'm striving to the limits of my ability,' he went on. 'The clarity of my vision of the future, my insight into the true meaning of the Santyth, grow daily. As do these strange powers which flow from me.' He looked at his hands. 'And people are flocking to the new way. But . . .' He turned to his wife. 'Could He be abandoning me? Am I failing Him in some way?'

'You will not be abandoned, my love,' she said. 'These doubts are surely nothing but a testing.'

When Cassraw did not reply, Dowinne stepped close and gripped his arm fiercely. 'A testing, Enryc,' she hissed. 'How far have you come these past months? Your old self was a mere shadow to what you are now. But how can you expect to become His arm in this world, to fulfil His great purpose, if you are not constantly tested and re-forged?'

Cassraw nodded slowly. 'Yes,' he said. 'You're right. These doubts are weakness and I must tear all weakness from my soul if I'm to prepare the Way for His Coming.'

'And you must see His hand in all things,' Dowinne urged, her grip still tight about his arm, her look significant. 'Others than you have to be tried and tested if they're to serve truly.'

Cassraw nodded again, then his expression changed to one of urgency. 'His chosen land is assailed by unbelievers,' he said, his voice filling with anger. 'The Felden must be envoys of the Great Evil of which He spoke. It's upon us already, and we're unprepared.' He drove his fist into his hand in frustration. 'This is the fault of those weaklings in the PlasHein,' he fumed. 'Had they held firm yesterday and pursued their original intention, the Felden would not have dared to act thus. And they'll do nothing about them now, except beg and plead with them to go away, wringing their hands and saying that it was all a misunderstanding. Such is the consequence of deviation from His ways. The Madren lie leaderless, like scurrying sheep before the Felden wolves.'

'The Madren lie leaderless at His will,' Dowinne said,

her voice soft and insinuating and her eyes gleaming. 'He's shown them the worth of the leaders so that they may choose others.'

Following their impromptu, paper-waving dance in the twilit corridor, the leader of the Castellan Party and his chief adviser eventually calmed one another down sufficiently to set about putting to rights what had occurred. Obviously the Felden had not heard about the Heindral's decision of the previous day, and informing them of it was a matter of urgency. It should be no great problem to reassure them that it had all been a matter of purely local politics, and that there had never been any serious threat of action being taken against Tirfelden nationals. That done, the Felden would surely withdraw their army, then arrangements could be made for future discussions to resolve this matter sensibly.

Ministers, party leaders and senior officials were hastily gathered to agree an appropriate response and, by noon, liveried government gallopers were leaving Troidmallos for the borders, while official criers were being sent about the town to announce what was under way to the anxious crowds that were already gathering.

His political horizons widened once again beyond the cockpit of the Heindral by this action from outside, the leader of the Castellans demonstrated a little redeeming wisdom by declining to issue an order for the precautionary levying of the militia, on the grounds that it would be both provocative and ineffective. Toom Drommel, however, seeing an opportunity to present himself yet again as a sternly patriotic politician, spoke against this, citing the 'long and proud tradition' of the Madren militia and the need to 'make a stand'. He was ignored. He might have been instrumental in causing the turmoil in the Heindral, but he was still only the leader of a minority party and the Castellans and Ploughers took great delight in making this silently clear to him. His new bass voice eventually rumbled off into a pouting silence.

'Now we can only wait,' the leader of the Castellans said as the gallopers left. He reached into a pocket, unearthed a large flask and took a long drink from it.

The gallopers reached Bredill without mishap, and not all that long after the Felden envoy and his escort had finally found their way back. They were brought before the officer commanding the company, to whom they handed a personal letter from their government together with sealed letters which were to be carried to the Felden authorities. The officer read the letter carefully, then smiled and stood up.

'A storm in a pot then, gentlemen,' he said to the gallopers. 'I can't say I'm unhappy that it's blown itself out before blows were struck. My men and I will have to remain here until I hear from my own government, of course, but I doubt that'll be very long. Then the diplomats can sort it out.' He looked resignedly about the crude tent he was occupying. 'And then we can return to the comparative comfort of our barracks.' He was about to offer the Madren a drink when he remembered that it was the inability of the Madren to cope with Felden liquor that had played no small part in this affair. 'Will you dine with us before you return to Troidmallos?' he offered. 'Only field rations, I'm afraid, but we've lost no one so far.'

But the gallopers were less than enchanted at the prospect of spending the night in what they regarded as the wild outlands of their little country, and took their leave.

'Humourless beggars,' the officer muttered to his aide as they rode off. 'They'd have soured any ale we gave them anyway.'

And that was the end of the negotiations.

Seeing a successful and painless conclusion to their

adventure, the Felden caroused late that night and either feeling no need, or just forgetting, set up no sentries and allowed their fires to sink when they retired.

It was a full and cold moon that rose over the sleeping camp, draining the colour from it and spreading long shadows of unfathomable darkness. Grey wisps of smoke rose secretively up from the dying fires before escaping silently sideways into the night. Slowly, figures began to approach the camp. They were carrying what appeared to be sticks, though here and there, moonlight flickered on polished blades. This was not, however, the approach of skilled soldiers; there was a great deal of whispering and the figures moved with no ordered pattern of mutual protection. Yet they moved with a clear and single intention, and someone amongst them was obviously in charge.

As they approached the Felden tents, the whispering fell away, and all that could be heard was the sound of the sleeping men.

Then a single soft word sped around the group and, shouting and screaming, they fell upon the tents, hacking through guy ropes and clubbing and stabbing anything under the tossing canvases that moved. There were fewer attackers than Felden soldiers but, drowsy with ale and dazed by the surprise and ferocity of the assault, the Felden stood little chance of defending themselves. One of the tents caught fire when a lantern was knocked over, and at the height of the killing it became a ghastly funeral pyre, its flames throwing grotesque dancing shadows through the fearful mêlée.

Suddenly, a figure burst out of the blazing tent, his clothes alight. It was no scream of terror he was uttering, however, but one of battle-crazed rage. Confronted by two attackers, he unexpectedly threw himself to the ground then, maintaining his momentum, he rolled over, simultaneously overturning both of them and dousing his burning

438

clothes. He was on his feet immediately and a single blow lifted another attacker off his feet to drop him dead, with a broken neck, three paces away. Then the man was gone, fleeing into the darkness beyond the flame-lit camp. A figure, one of several hovering about the edges of the scene, watched his flight then circled wide after him.

The man paused only momentarily in his bull-like charge, to look for somewhere where he might evade pursuers. He chose a large stand of trees and reached them without hindrance, for there was no one at his heels; the unexpected resistance and the downing of three of their own so easily, had dampened the killing fervour of such of the attackers as had seen him leave. He crashed a little way into the sheltering darkness of the wood, then stopped and turned to look round at the burning camp. Instinctively, he put his back against a tree. Weals, livid even in the leaf-filtered moonlight, scarred his face, and his clothes were still smouldering. He shook his head violently to clear it, then seemed for a moment to be debating whether he should return to the fray to help his lost comrades. It took him only a little time to realize that he could do nothing except save himself and get back to Tirfelden to spread the news of what had happened.

As he made to move away from the tree, a taunting voice nearby said softly, 'Turn and die, defiler.'

He spun round. Some way from him, fully visible in the moonlight, stood a figure. The man started, not so much at finding someone there as at the fact that the figure's face was blank, save for two lifeless eyes. A mask, he realized almost immediately, though the shock remained with him even as he crouched low, expecting others to emerge and surround him. None came, however. He glanced quickly through the trees towards the still-blazing camp. As far as he could judge through the flailing shadows, the attackers were still concentrated there. This one must have followed him on his own. The Felden soldier's anger returned to brush aside his initial alarm. Well, there'd be one less Madren celebrating this murderous treachery when the daylight came! He took in the waiting figure. Though rendered bulky by a cloak, his challenger was obviously no great size.

Yet there was something unsettling about him. The Felden hesitated.

Then the figure stepped back uncertainly as if to flee. The action drew the Felden forward like a hunting dog and he charged at the figure recklessly. His hands were almost about his victim's throat when he caught a glimpse of a blade emerging from underneath the cloak, and his ears filled with the sound of a deep breath of pleasure being drawn in. He tried to step aside and at the same time swing his arm to deflect the blade, but to no avail; he was moving too quickly. He felt a dragging blow on his arm and, though there was no pain, he knew that the knife had cut through sleeve, flesh and muscle in one stroke, for almost immediately he could not use his fingers.

Very sharp, he thought incongruously. A butcher's edge. He had miscalculated. Yet he felt no fear, only more anger – at himself, at his attacker, the Madren, his officer, at many things. It whirled round the dominant thought that now he faced a journey back to Tirfelden badly wounded. He must finish this assailant quickly and do something to bind this hurt before he started to lose blood seriously.

But his mind blundering into the future left his body leaderless in that Madren wood, staggering under impact after impact as the attacker moved about it, almost leisurely at first, and then with increasing speed, cutting, hacking, then finally and frenziedly, stabbing, until the Felden slumped to his knees then fell forward on to the ground, his terrified mind gone to regions beyond any knowing.

The figure squatted down a short distance away and

waited for all movement in the body to cease. It took a little time. Then, like a carrion-seeking animal, it crawled towards the corpse and, removing its gloves, began running its hands over the open wounds, until they were completely covered in gore.

'Let this be the destiny of all Your enemies, Lord, and let this offering repair the renewing of the Way, so foully desecrated,' it whispered, its voice trembling ecstatically. It held up its moonlit blackened hands as it spoke. There was a brief sound, like a sighing wind, and abruptly the hands were clean again.

The figure stood up and moved off silently into the trees.

Only two men survived the attack on the camp and that was because they were deliberately spared. Surrounded by the masked victors, they stood dazed and shocked, desperately afraid of what was about to befall them. The circle opened and a stocky, well-built figure entered and approached the two men. It was Cassraw, his face alive with exultation, his eyes blazing with zeal. 'On your knees!' he said harshly. 'On your knees and pray.'

One of the men hesitated, but the other dragged him down. Cassraw bent towards them and extended an arm to encompass the destroyed camp. 'Pray thanks to Him that you have been privileged to see the fate of all those who oppose His will and who choose to follow the Great Evil.' His speech was punctuated by an erratic chorus of, 'Thus let it be,' and 'Praise Him,' from the onlookers. 'Pray thanks to Him that you have been spared to carry news of this to His enemies. Tell your people that His coming is nigh, and that Gyronlandt shall once again be united under His banner. Tell them this, and that if they do not return to the paths of righteousness then this night's work shall be writ across your whole land. Tell them that the choice is theirs, and to choose well.'

He took the chin of each in turn in his hand and stared into their eyes.

'Go now. He will speed your flight.'

The two men looked at him uncertainly then clambered to their feet. Cassraw nodded his head and the circle opened to let them through.

They ran, and the circle closed about Cassraw again, waiting. He spoke to them. 'A great and glorious victory, gentlemen,' he said. 'The village of Bredill has been liberated from the followers of the Great Evil by your courage. You are truly His Knights now, sanctified by the blood of his enemies. News of this great battle will ring about Canol Madreth – nay, it will ring about the whole of Gyronlandt – as a clarion call to all who would follow the true Way, and as a knell to those who would oppose His coming.'

Some of the watchers dropped to their knees as Cassraw spoke and were praying fervently. Amongst the others a wide range of responses to their night's work was beginning to appear.

'Why did we allow those two to live, Brother?'

'Why did we have to kill so many, Brother?'

Cassraw gave the same answer to both. 'To spread fear and dismay to His enemies, my children. To begin their destruction before even a sword or arrow is drawn. Soon the very shadow of our coming will bring armies to their knees. By this killing, countless other lives will have been saved, and His true enemies exposed. You have been strong and you have done a wretched task well. Great will be the honour that you receive when He finally calls you to Him.'

He knelt beside the body of the man killed by the fleeing Felden soldier. 'Even now, our comrade Marash will be standing before His throne, hearing His judgement. A judgement in which all previous wrongdoing will have been set to rights by the giving of his life so bravely.

442

To die fighting His enemies is to die a true martyr and to know no punishment in the after-life but to enter immediately into Deryon, the Place of Heroes, where all your wishes will be fulfilled and all that you have denied yourselves in this world will be granted to you. Carry him back to Troidmallos with honour.'

The next day, Privv's Sheet did not appear until much later. It was shorter than ever, and even more expensive, but that passed unnoticed amongst its purchasers, for it contained only two stories. One was an account of the Battle of Bredill, in which the valiant Knights of Ishryth had marched through the night to face and utterly crush several companies of Tirfelden's finest troops in open combat. Several tales of courage and bravado were recounted, but the greatest praise was left for the single casualty, Marash, who had killed no less than six Felden soldiers as he defended a wounded friend, before finally succumbing to a treacherous blow from behind. The other was a blistering diatribe against the government for its weakness in allowing such a situation to arise and for cowering before the 'unprovoked Tirfelden aggression'. It concluded with a call by Cassraw for a service of thanksgiving at this deliverance to be held that night at the summit of the Ervrin Mallos.

'An excellent piece of work,' Cassraw said to Privv as he returned the slightly amended draft to him. 'If you continue thus, there will be a place of high honour for you in the new Canol Madreth.'

After the meeting, Privv was elated. Leck simply said, 'We should get away from here. This is all wrong. We shouldn't be doing it.' Privv's elation was such that he did not even hear the remark.

'I've already started work on my report about tonight's service,' he announced rapturously. 'It'll be even better than the battle report.'

★ ★ ★

Such was the momentum of the events that Cassraw had set in train that little could be done to stop them. Those in authority who read the account in Privv's Sheet were both outraged and horrified but were at a loss to know what to do. The chief adviser to the government hastily sent gallopers to Bredill and Tirfelden to find out exactly what had happened, but both were stopped and held at Bredill by a group of Cassraw's Knights, together with all other travellers between the two countries. He also sent an instruction to the Chief of the Keepers that Cassraw be arrested immediately, only to receive the embarrassed reply, 'For what?' No action could be taken on the strength of a report in a Sheet, and if Cassraw's Knights had indeed defeated an invading enemy, then where was the illegality? More sinisterly, he added in a footnote, his men would not be able to get near Cassraw, such were the crowds gathering about the Haven Meeting House.

Hearing this, the leader of the Castellans took out his flask, drained it, and sent for another. The leader of the Ploughers, a harmless idealist by disposition, fluttered pathetically, listing in great detail what the government had done to bring this about, and what they should have done, and how they, the Ploughers, could accept no responsibility for it, and what they would have done, had they been given the opportunity, and if . . .

'. . . there weren't any such thing as sin,' muttered the chief adviser as he left him, only just managing not to slam the door.

Toom Drommel however, was struck as though by a blinding light when he read of what had happened. The lingering memory of his meeting with Cassraw and the power of the man suddenly washed over him and swept him away. This could be *his* moment, even more so than his triumph of the other day. Cassraw was a man who was beyond a doubt going to change Canol Madreth, and those

444

who did not follow him would be left to wither by the wayside. He called for a carriage to take him to the Haven Meeting House.

Vredech actually staggered when he read the news, and had to sit down. For a brief moment, all the doubts and torments he had suffered since the day of Cassraw's strange conversion, piled up like a monstrous, mocking wave, as black and ominous as the clouds that day, and threatened to break over him and sweep him into true insanity. But even as this was happening the Whistler's voice came back to him.

'Astonishment,' it said. 'You'll be gaping in disbelief at the sword that kills you.' Then, 'If you kill Him now, perhaps it will go badly for you. But if you kill Him later, it will have already gone badly for many others.'

The memory both quieted and chilled him. Although more at ease with himself following his mysterious encounter with Horld, he still could not think about the Whistler calmly. Yet whether the Whistler were real, or some bizarre figment of his imagination, his words were disturbingly prophetic. How much more of what he had said might yet come to pass? But as he looked about his familiar room with its memories echoing back through the years, Vredech could not even begin to school himself to the idea of simply walking up to Cassraw and killing him. No, it was absurd. Almost certainly, Privv's Sheet would be inaccurate. It was inconceivable that a group of youths could annihilate a company of the Tirfelden army. Doubtless the government would even now be trying to find out exactly what had happened. His resolution cleared. Whatever anyone else was doing, he at least could get up to the Witness House and put some fire into Mueran's belly with a view to taking immediate action against Cassraw. He paused as he walked from his quarters to the stables as another reason for his determination surfaced, albeit unclearly: the prospect of Cassraw's call for a public

445

service to be held at the summit of the Ervrin Mallos struck notes of alarm so deep within him that they shook his entire frame. He shivered violently.

Late in the afternoon, a solitary figure clambered up the rocks that topped the Ervrin Mallos. It was wrapped in a stained travelling cloak and wore a mask that identified it as one of the Knights of Ishryth who had been at the Bredill slaughter. It knelt before the stained rock that Nertha had declared to be the focus of all the ill that hung about the mountain and, head bowed, embraced it.

Then it drew off its gloves and held its hands high. The air about the summit seemed to quiver lustfully and the hands were suddenly covered in blood. Then the figure was wringing them slowly, as if washing. The blood began to drip from them to splash on to the boulder, slowly at first and then in a steady stream until it had filled the shallow hollow at the centre of the rock and was spreading over its flat top. Then it was spilling over the edges and running down the sides.

The figure was speaking. 'Blood and terror I bring you again, Lord, to renew the Way. Your power grows within me and there shall be no end to it. Your Will be done.'

Then all about the summit was deathly still. The figure, its hands clean, bent forward and embraced the boulder again, then quickly, though without any signs of haste, clambered down the rocks and slipped away.

A long, moaning sigh filled the summit.

446

Chapter 31

Vredech was so preoccupied with his concerns about Cassraw that he barely noticed the agitation that was pervading the Witness House when he reached it. The groom who took his horse muttered something rhetorical about, 'where was he supposed to put this one?' – but Vredech had reached the top of the steps before he registered the complaint and was in no mood to take the man to task.

As he closed the main door behind him, he paused at the sight of twenty or thirty novices of various degrees milling about the high-domed entrance hall, all talking agitatedly. Years of stern hierarchical habit overrode his immediate concerns.

'What is the meaning of this?' he shouted over the noise. 'This is the Witness House of the Church of Ishrythan, not a market-place. Get to your quarters. Turn the energy of this unseemly display to your studies.'

The clamour fell immediately but the agitation remained.

'But Brother Vredech, what's going to happen? Half the Chapter is here and there's uproar in the Debating Hall,' someone asked.

'What's going to happen is what's going to happen,' Vredech announced, unrelenting. 'And all of you here are a considerable way from needing to worry about what the Chapter is debating or in what manner. Nor are you likely to come any nearer, frittering your time away here.'

He concluded with a massive gesture of dismissal that scattered the gathering like a wind scattering autumn leaves. The unrest remained, however, though now it was his, for voices still echoed around the entrance hall. Voices which must presumably be coming from the Debating Hall, judging by their direction. Ignoring any attempt at seemliness himself, Vredech took the stairs two and three steps at a time and then ran along the passageway towards the source.

As he drew nearer, the anger which had been kindled by the sight of the novices filling the entrance hall flared up, for the door of the Debating Hall was half-open, and the din escaping through it put their noise to shame.

Grim-faced, Vredech entered silently and watched what was happening for a few moments. As the novice had told him, almost half the Chapter was assembled, but disorder appeared to be reigning. Mueran was seated at the head of the table and periodically slapped it, trying to be heard. He did not look well. On one side of him sat Horld, his face clouded and ominous, and on the other sat Morem, patently distressed. Of the others, nearly all seemed to be talking at the same time, some to each other, some to everyone else. Four of them were standing and gesticulating towards Mueran, whose table-slapping was having no effect whatsoever.

Vredech's anger tilted momentarily toward despair as he saw the leaders of his church in such disarray. Like any group of people who shared responsibility for the running of an institution, they suffered from internecine quarrels from time to time, sometimes difficult and unpleasant, but this . . .

His anger returned, redoubled.

Opening the door wide, he slammed it violently. The sound filled the room and brought all eyes round to him. He strode forward. 'In the name of mercy,' he said furiously, 'the sound of your squabbling is filling the entire building. I've just rebuked half our novices for making a tenth the clamour that's being raised here.'

Before anyone could reply, he turned to Mueran.

'My apologies, Brother Mueran,' he said. 'I shouldn't have spoken thus, but . . .' He shrugged.

Mueran nodded and motioned him to his chair, atypically allowing his gratitude to show in his expression. Vredech's intervention had given him the respite he needed to restore his authority. 'We've all been badly shaken by what's happened, Brother,' he said, raising a hand to silence two would-be speakers and firmly indicating that those who were standing should sit. He turned his remarks towards the gathering in general. 'A little confusion in our proceedings is perhaps inevitable. However,' he was completely in control again now, 'Brother Vredech's reproach was both timely and correct. Nothing is to be served by our bellowing at one another.'

A figure at the far end of the table jumped to its feet. 'But Brother Mueran, I insist—'

'SIT DOWN AND BE SILENT!' Mueran's voice made even Vredech start, reminding him that this vacillating and hypocritical man had reputedly once been quite ruthless in his ambition, a much-feared figure within the Church. 'This meeting may have been called in unusual circumstances, but it will be conducted correctly.' He turned over some papers in front of him though Vredech noticed that his eyes were not looking at them. 'Two days ago . . .' Briefly the true man broke through. 'Was it only two days?' he said softly, shaking his head in disbelief. Then he was the Covenant Member again. 'Two days ago it was put to me that a Chapter Meeting be called to examine the deplorable conduct of Brother Cassraw . . .'

'No!' several voices cried out.

'Be silent!' Mueran shouted. 'Or this meeting will turn its attention to your own disruptive behaviour. This is *not* a debate!' His authority held, but only just. 'It needs no great study of our church canons to know that Brother Cassraw has preached two outrageous and quite unacceptable sermons of late. He has wilfully strayed into secular areas that—'

The opposition broke out again, several voices speaking at once.

'No! Secular and spiritual are one. To speak otherwise is heresy.'

'Brother Cassraw has been chosen to renew the church, to root out hypocrites and hair-splitting theologians who seek only after their own aggrandisement.'

'He has been shown the truths in the Santyth!'

'He has been given powers.'

'He and his Knights have already saved the country!'

Mueran's hand was dithering over the table, this time not even having the decisiveness to slap it. He looked utterly lost. The brief resurgence of the younger, stronger man was gone. Unexpectedly, Vredech felt a wave of compassion for Mueran, watching his life's ambitions and struggles turning to dross before him. He felt torn. He could intervene as he had before and take control of the meeting. Horld and Morem would support him, he was sure – Horld himself, he could see, was on the verge of doing something anyway. But that would effectively destroy Mueran's position, and what would be the consequences of that?

Yet to allow this riot to continue would be worse. Looking at the clamouring faces he saw what had happened. Mueran had been able to call only those Brothers with parishes in and around Troidmallos – the very ones that Cassraw must have been most assiduously working on.

He was preparing himself to bellow through the turmoil, when he noticed the door opening. A head emerged round it sheepishly. It caught Vredech's eye.

He released his bellow. 'Yes, what is it?'

As before, his voice silenced the gathering and drew all eyes first to himself, and then to the novice who was hovering at the door.

'I'm sorry to disturb you, Brothers,' quavered the novice, 'but I think you should see what's happening outside.'

Both Vredech and Horld stood up immediately, Vredech mouthing to Mueran that he should suspend the meeting and motioning him to follow them. As the Chapter moved through the building following their unexpected guide, it collected most of the novices that Vredech had dismissed earlier. Some of these were in a state of high excitement. Vredech glanced at Mueran in the hope that he might enforce his own earlier command, but it needed no great skill in the reading of character to see that Mueran was capable only of following events now.

At the gate of the Witness House grounds the assembled Brothers found themselves witness to a ragged procession of people trailing up the mountain. For a moment they stood and gaped in silence, then Vredech stepped forward.

'Where are you going?' he demanded loudly.

One of the passers-by turned and smiled at him, but his eyes were distant. 'To the summit, Brother. To Brother Cassraw's service of thanksgiving for the saving of our land from the Great Evil.'

'And to worship at the place where Ishryth appeared to Brother Cassraw and chose him as His voice in this world,' said another.

'Thus let it be.' The voice came from behind Vredech. As he turned, one of the Chapter Brothers pushed past him. 'Praise be,' he said. 'I shall walk with you, my children. To the One True Light.'

Two others joined him. Cries of 'Praise be, praise be,' rang out from the passing crowd. Then something seized Vredech's arm. He was so angry and fearful at what he was watching, that his clenched fist was raised as he whirled round to see what it was. He found himself staring into Mueran's gasping face, then he was supporting him as he collapsed.

'Stand back, stand back. Lay him down gently.' Morem had moved to Vredech's side and was helping to lower the sagging frame of the Covenant Brother on to the stone pathway. His face was concerned as he began loosening the garments about Mueran's neck.

'What's the matter?' Vredech asked anxiously.

Morem, his head bent against Mueran's chest, beckoned for silence. 'I don't know,' he said. 'It might be his heart, or perhaps blood to the head, I can't tell.'

'It's the will of Ishryth,' said one of the Brothers, his eyes wide and fearful. 'He has been struck down because of his denial of the truth of Brother Cassraw's revelation.' He made to push by the group around Mueran's prostrate form with a view to joining the crowd. As he did so, Vredech seized hold of the front of his cassock, swung him round and struck him a powerful blow on the chin. The man went sprawling out of the gate and into the crowd, knocking two people over and scattering several others. He was quickly hoisted to his feet, but was staggering badly as the crowd carried him along.

Vredech looked down at his hand, his face alight with bewilderment and horror. 'What have I done?' he stammered, gripping his bruised fist and raising it to his mouth in dismay.

An arm closed gently about his shoulder. It was Horld. 'We must tend to Mueran,' he urged, but Vredech was too shocked to respond. He shook himself free and gazed around – at the passing crowd, at the Witness House, at the fallen form of Mueran with Morem bent over him. Only one thought occupied his mind however. What had possessed him to strike his fellow Chapter Brother, he who had never struck anyone in his entire life, and who himself had been rarely struck, even as a child? The horror and shame of it rang about his head like the tolling of a great bell. It seemed to him that the crowd was emerging from and disappearing into a long echoing tunnel, and that Mueran and Horld and the others, too, were far, far away.

'More a warrior than a preacher.'

Denial rose within him as the Whistler's words echoed through his mind. But other things the Whistler had said came, too, and the memory of the sacked city and its massacred inhabitants. 'Such a fate is always waiting for those who forget the darkness in their nature. Learn it now or you'll be taught it again.'

The darkness in their nature?

The darkness in *my* nature, he thought.

No!

'Learn it or you'll be taught it again.'

'Allyn, snap out of it, we must tend to Mueran.' Horld's voice broke through his turmoil, jerking him back giddyingly to the gates of the Witness House. A residual flurry of regret and apology washed at the edges of his mind for the violence he had committed, but he ignored them. Somewhere their importance had been diminished.

'What can we do, Morem?' he asked unsteadily, looking down at Mueran's livid face. 'Shouldn't we take him inside?'

Morem shook his head. 'I don't think so,' he said unhappily. 'It's something serious, and I don't think we should risk moving him. We need a proper physician – someone will have to go down and fetch one quickly. All we can do here is get blankets to cover him with, keep him warm.'

'Let me through.'

Purposeful hands pushed an opening in the gathering around Mueran. They belonged to Nertha. Vredech was at once relieved, surprised and ashamed to see her, but she knelt down by Mueran's side without even acknowledging him. Her initial examination was swift and expert, but Vredech read her conclusion from her posture even before she finally stood up.

'I'm sorry,' she said. 'I'm afraid he's dead.'

There were gasps of dismay and disbelief and several of the Brothers, Horld included, circled their hands about their hearts. Morem's hands went to his mouth in a curiously feminine gesture. 'There was nothing you could have done,' Nertha said to him, laying a hand on his arm.

'Why?' someone asked rhetorically. 'Why now? Why here?'

For an instant, Vredech half-expected some caustic comment from Nertha about the questioner being better placed to answer that than she was, but she merely shook her head, causing Vredech more self-reproach. It whirled round him jagged with guilt and anger and helplessness.

'We must take him inside,' he heard Horld saying, his voice strained. 'Away from this . . . this . . .' He gave up. 'Cover his face. Lift him gently.'

Vredech turned towards the passing crowd. They were paying no heed to what had just happened. He wanted to shout and scream at them, curse them for their blasphemous folly in what they were doing, for their callous passing by, but he merely gaped.

Then Nertha was in front of him, staring at him intently. 'Allyn, look at me. Look at me!' She took hold of his chin and turned his head until his eyes met hers. They were shining with half-formed tears, but her voice was steady. 'I'm truly sorry about Mueran. There was nothing anyone could have done.' Her look became almost imploring. 'But what's happening here? Why did you hit that man?'

Vredech barely took in her words. 'What are you doing here?' he asked.

'House told me about the crowds coming here,' she replied impatiently. 'I had a bad feeling.' She gave a self-conscious shrug and turned away from him. 'I thought I should be with you. I was afraid.'

'Afraid of what?' he asked.

'All of a sudden, of everything.' She was almost shouting. 'So many awful things happening so quickly. I can't really believe it.' She glanced over her shoulder at the crowd still trudging relentlessly by.

'Disbelief and astonishment are luxuries we haven't the time to afford,' Vredech said, speaking the Whistler's words as they also returned to him. Resolve was forming in him in the wake of his violent outburst and the shock of Mueran's death. 'We must accept reality as we find it, however unbelievable, however unpleasant.' He took her arm and began moving after the impromptu cortège bearing away Mueran's body. As he reached it he took hold of Horld with his other hand.

'We must try to stop Cassraw holding this service,' he said urgently.

Horld made no effort to conceal his anger. 'I think we've more important things than Cassraw's foolishness to deal with at the moment, don't you?'

Horld's anger stirred Vredech's own. 'No, I don't,' he replied bluntly. 'Mueran's gone, Ishryth speed him, but Cassraw right now is leading hundreds of people to the very place where he encountered whatever it is that's possessed him. He's also done something that could start a war with Tirfelden, and, for what it's worth against those two items, he's the Haven Parish incumbent and by tradition, the new Covenant Member until elections are held!'

Horld faltered under the impact of this brief but portentous list. The others continued into the Witness House. His face became stern and unreadable and after a long pause he murmured, 'Better *me* as Covenant Member than Cassraw.'

They paused only to allow Horld to announce their

intention to Morem and the others then the three of them set off to join the crowds heading towards the summit. As they were passing through the gate to the Witness House, they were joined by Skynner, brought here by a mixture of curiosity and deep concern about what was happening. Instinctively uneasy about Cassraw's intention of holding a service on the summit of the Ervrin Mallos he had set off in the hope that someone at the Witness House would be able to tell him whether it was legal or not. As he had made his way through the crowd he had largely abandoned any idea of attempting to stop it on the grounds of simple practicality, but on hearing of Mueran's death he renewed his intention.

The mood of the crowd was strange. For the most part it was good-natured, but for every face that was smiling or excited, Vredech saw two that were darkened by a grim earnestness, or lit by an unreasoning zeal.

'Not in Canol Madreth,' he had said to the Whistler after his vision of the devastated city.

'Anywhere. Everywhere,' had been the reply.

He began to feel afraid. He found himself softly whistling the Whistler's three notes in elaborate cross-rhythms to that of his plodding footsteps. The way was steep and all four were too preoccupied with their own thoughts for conversation, but Vredech was relieved to have them by him.

When they reached the gulley that led up to Ishryth's lawn, Skynner used the authority of his uniform to push a way through to the front of the crowd that had accumulated there. He used it again to lead his party through the people lingering on the lawn's grassy turf prior to beginning the final ascent.

Before they began this last part of the climb, Skynner looked at the sky. Clouds were gathering – not the black ominous ones that had marked the fateful day of Cassraw's transformation – but dark and ominous enough to say that they carried a good deal of water and that the growing crowd could look forward to a wetting and a premature evening.

'This is going to turn into a nightmare,' Skynner muttered. 'Saving your cloth, Brothers, but I'm beginning to think that Brother Cassraw has gone raving mad. If we don't get two score injuries out of this lot on the way down in the dark and the pouring rain, I'll eat my baton.'

Vredech and Horld exchanged glances. 'We'll try to talk him out of it before it gets too dark,' Vredech said half-heartedly.

Horld however was uncompromising. He used Vredech's own reference. 'A man who's reputedly set about starting a war with our nearest neighbour is unlikely to be concerned about a few cracked heads and sprained ankles.'

Vredech let the matter lie and concentrated on where he was putting his feet. Nertha remained silent throughout, her long legs keeping her a little way ahead of the group, seemingly effortlessly.

Then they were at the summit. There was already a large crowd there but it parted to let them through. 'More your uniform than mine this time, I think,' Skynner said quietly to Vredech and Horld as they walked along the aisle that had been formed.

Nertha whispered to Vredech: 'It's much worse than it was the other day. Something's happened up here since then.'

Vredech nodded. The presence that he had sensed and ultimately opposed a few days earlier was all around him again, but many times stronger. He glanced at Nertha. She was pale and her face was tense. 'We must be very careful,' he said. She did not seem to be listening. He shook her arm, making her start. 'Now you know, He can't take possession of you again.' He shook her once more. 'Do you understand?' he hissed.

Nertha nodded agitatedly. 'Yes, yes.'

'Well, cling to it,' Vredech said urgently. 'Cling to it above all else. We stood against Him once almost by accident. The two of us prepared can do it again if need arises.'

'I don't know how,' she stammered.

'Just remember who you are, who we both are.'

'It's much stronger.'

'So are we.'

'What are you doing here?' Skynner's commanding tone ended the whispered exchange. He was addressing a group of Cassraw's Knights who were apparently guarding the cluster of rocks that marked the summit. They were masked.

'Brother Cassraw told us—'

'Take that thing off your face when you talk to me, lad,' Skynner said impatiently.

The Knight waxed indignant. 'These are the masks we wore at the Battle of Bredill. They are badges of honour. They—'

'No honourable man hides his face before the law,' Skynner said, real anger seeping into his tone. 'Take them off, all of you. As for what you did at Bredill, that'll doubtless be a matter for an Assize in due course. Now do as you're told, or do I have to do it for you?'

There was a moment of hesitation in which the Knight took in Skynner's lowering bulk, and the hand resting on his baton, then with a markedly ill grace he pulled off his mask and motioned the others to do the same.

As the surly features of the young men emerged, Skynner nodded. 'That's better,' he said. 'Now I know who I'm talking to – Troidmallos's finest, part of Yanos's little band of heroes. I wonder if Brother Cassraw really knows who's getting into his precious Knights?'

'They're all exhausted,' Nertha whispered to Vredech as she took in their sunken eyes and drawn features.

'They're all leaving,' Skynner said, catching part of

Nertha's remark. 'Go on, clear off. Get back to your homes and present yourselves at the Keeperage first thing tomorrow morning. There's a deal of questions to be asked of you and your friends.'

Without waiting to see if his command was being obeyed, he clambered on to the stained rock. It began to rain as he addressed the growing crowd. 'Listen to me, all of you,' he shouted. 'Go back to your homes right away. It's too dangerous to have so many of you up here. The light's failing, the weather turning, and many of you could be hurt descending. Go now while you can, and go carefully.'

Voices were raised in argument.

'The Chosen One is coming.'

'We've come to see where He revealed Himself to the Chosen One.'

'We've come to give thanks for the saving of our land from the Felden devils.'

'Go home!' Skynner thundered through the mounting din. 'Go home now.' He took a chance. 'No service can be held here. This place has not been proven by the church.'

'This place needs no proving by the hand of man, Serjeant.'

The voice over-topped Skynner's. It was Cassraw.

All eyes turned towards him. 'This is His most holy place,' he went on, stepping forward. 'To here He will return and from here will His renewal of the world begin.' Cries of 'Thus let it be' and 'Praise Him' rose from the crowd.

Vredech and Horld looked at Cassraw aghast. He was dressed in the formal black cassock of the church, but across it ran the red sash of his Knights of Ishryth, and draped over one arm was one of the faceless masks that the Knights had worn at Bredill. Around his head he wore what appeared to be a silver circlet; it rose to a point at the front and culminated in a single star-shaped jewel. Behind

459

him stood Dowinne, dressed in a long undecorated black robe. On either side of him stood a rank of his Knights, and behind Dowinne another group of Knights were bearing a stretcher over which was draped the Madren flag.

'This is a mockery,' Horld burst out. 'Your words and your appearance are sacrilegious.'

'I forgive you your intemperance, Brother Horld,' Cassraw said, though his eyes were far from forgiving. 'I have just heard of the sudden and tragic death of our beloved Covenant Brother, Mueran, and your distress is understandable. But while my heart grieves for the loss of a dear friend and counsellor, his sceptre falls to me by tradition and, with all humility, I will take it and carry it forward as he would have wished, striving ever for the good of our church. Mysterious are His ways, and not for us to question.'

Horld stepped forward, eyes blazing, but Vredech caught hold of him. At the same time, the Knights flanking Cassraw moved close about him.

'There's nothing we can do,' Vredech whispered to Horld, desperately fearful that the once blacksmith was about to resort to violence. And indeed, he felt the man's considerable strength trembling against his grip before it finally relaxed. 'He's right. He does have tradition on his side at the moment, not to mention those thugs and this crowd. But we have time and the lay authority, and tradition, too, which demands a proper election of the Covenant Member within fifteen days.'

Cassraw and his entourage advanced towards the rocks and Horld and the others stood aside. As Cassraw passed, Vredech caught his gaze. 'Turn away from this path, Enryc, I beg you,' he said, very quietly. 'Whatever touched you that dark day, it was not Ishryth, it was some ancient evil. Only horror lies before you. Some part of you must know that. Look deep into yourself and find again your true nature before you destroy both yourself and countless others.'

Cassraw stopped and doubt flickered briefly in his eyes. But it was like the flare of a candle caught in the howl of a gale, and was gone before it could illuminate anything.

'Follow me or . . .' He faltered. 'Follow me, Allyn. Follow me. There is no other way. All has been revealed to me.'

He turned away quickly and stared up at Skynner, still standing on the rock. 'You are defiling His most holy place,' he said, his voice menacing.

Skynner crouched down and looked at him squarely. 'I'm standing on a rock, Brother Cassraw. I'm not going to trade theology with you, though as I recall the Santyth, when Ishryth was asked should a temple be built for him, said that all places are his temple and should be respected equally.'

Cassraw almost snarled, 'Your interpretation of the Santyth is flawed, Keeper, as is that of many others. *I* shall disclose the truth of His words as they have been and as they will be revealed to me. Now remove yourself.'

Skynner ignored the strident tone of the last remark and tried appealing to reason. 'Brother Cassraw,' he began. 'Look at these people, look at this weather. This is neither the time nor the place for a service. People are going to be hurt.'

'Hurt!' Cassraw hissed, his voice low despite its power. He turned towards the stretcher being carried by the Knights. '*This* is hurt. Young Marash here suffered the supreme hurt, perishing at the hands of the servants of evil as he defended his motherland while those who should have been doing it, squabbled like children. I will not ask you again, Serjeant: remove yourself from this sacred stone!'

Skynner bent forward and brought his face very close to Cassraw's so that only he could hear what was being said.

'I didn't care for the "or else" in that last remark, Brother. Let me remind you that you are disobeying a lawfully-given order from an officer of the state, which, as you know full well, will not be countenanced by the church authority when all this, and whatever comes of it, is accounted for – which will be soon, I guarantee you.' His voice fell even lower and, though as if in spite of himself, Cassraw leaned forward to hear. 'If perchance you're thinking of further aggravating matters by having these louts of yours lay hands on me, not only will that, too, have to be accounted for, but you should be quite clear in your mind about whose head will be cracked open first.'

Cassraw's entire body began to quiver perceptibly at this implacable opposition, and his face went first white, then red. Before he could speak, however, Dowinne took his arm. He turned to her sharply, and Vredech noticed her grip tightening powerfully. He caught no hint of any exchange between them other than eye contact, but Cassraw's manner slowly softened. When he turned back to Skynner, he wore a conciliatory smile. Skynner's eyes narrowed suspiciously.

'I'll not debate this further with you, Serjeant,' Cassraw said. 'Your ignorance is excusable, this time, but it is not fitting that I, the Chosen, should allow it to distract me from my mission here. I offer you no reproach. There are many in this land who are ignorant and who await the One True Light, to bring them the truth.' He placed his hands on the boulder. 'See though, how He weeps at your obduracy.' He looked pointedly at Skynner's feet. Skynner could do no other than follow his gaze.

The rain had been falling in a fine drizzle throughout this confrontation and the rock upon which Skynner was crouching had been thoroughly wetted, a small pool forming in the dip at its centre. Suddenly the water gathered there swirled forward and splashed angrily around Skynner's boots, tiny waves at the foot of an

462

obdurate cliff. At the same time, a flurry of rain struck him in the face, making him raise his hand in protection. Neither event was conspicuous or violent, but the rain in Skynner's face disturbed him, and the strange movement of the water around his feet startled him and the two together caused him to slither incongruously off the rock.

Cassraw laughed. It was an unpleasant sound, full more of triumph and malice than humour. The crowd followed his cue. Vredech stepped forward and helped Skynner to his feet. The action was virtually a reflex, however, as he had felt himself almost physically assaulted when the water on the boulder had started to move. His skin was crawling exactly as it had when Cassraw had transformed Dowinne's simple drink into water, and Cassraw's laughter was twisting about him like a choking noose. Again the word *abomination* came to him in response to the presence he felt about him; the presence he had also felt invading Nertha and trying to possess him at this same place only three days ago. As then, he could find no response to what was happening other than rage, although the rainwater that was still splashing unnaturally about Skynner's feet fell away suddenly as though touched by his anger.

'Are you all right?' he asked Skynner.

'No, I'm not,' Skynner replied fiercely with an oath. He made to move towards Cassraw, but this time it was Nertha's hand that stayed him.

'Leave it,' she said simply. 'Only harm will come of resisting him here. You've done all you can.'

Skynner looked from her to Cassraw and back again, then yielded to her will. 'Very well,' he conceded. 'But as I'm here, I'll stay, so there's at least one accurate witness to what's going on.'

'There'll be four,' Nertha said, wiping the rain from her forehead and glancing at Vredech and Horld.

Cassraw was now on the far side of the boulder, his arms extended. Dowinne stood beside him, and the Knights

463

bearing the body of Marash were ranked behind him.

'His blessing be upon you,' Cassraw intoned.

'Thus let it be,' the crowd chanted back as one.

'My children.' Cassraw's voice was unnaturally loud. 'I have brought you here that you might know the place where He revealed Himself to me.' He laid his hand on the boulder. 'Here, but months ago, as I sat alone and desolate with a fearful darkness all about me, a voice spoke to me in the midst of my prayers. His voice, my children. His voice. He told me that such wickedness was abroad that once again it was necessary for Him to venture forth into this world.' Cassraw's voice grew gradually louder and a pulsing, driving rhythm began to permeate his speech. 'He harrowed my whole being, my children. Showed me such things as would chill your souls to know. But He held me firm and gave me the strength that I would need, for He told me also that I was the vessel that He had chosen to set in train the righting of this world, the undoing of the work of His enemy. And as He chose me, so I choose you, to be the flame that will rekindle the true faith in this godless land.'

Excited cries were rising from the crowd in response to Cassraw's own mounting passion. His voice dropped suddenly and he leaned forward. The crowd fell silent immediately. 'But great will be that task, my children, let me not deceive you. For His enemy has laboured long and silently to corrode His truth.' He turned and laid a hand on the body of Marash.

The rain was falling more heavily now. Vredech felt his hair plastering flat over his head. He wiped his eyes as Cassraw continued.

'The price for some may appear high – a price that your most inner thoughts whisper is too high; something that you could not do.' His voice began to rise again. 'But fear not, for this seeming loss is but a moment's discomfort. For those who perish in this world in battle against His enemies, will know no punishment for their sins and will be judged, not by His terrible Watchers, but by Him and Him alone, and they will be found fit to enter into Deryon. Deryon, that place beyond imagining, that place which is as this world but where all is perfection, and where there is neither labour, nor pain of any kind and where all that can be desired is to be won by the mere asking. There, even as I speak to you, the spirit of our murdered Brother Marash will be rejoicing.'

'This is as grotesque and primitive as it is heretical,' Horld murmured, his eyes wide with disbelief at what he was hearing. Vredech nodded but signalled silence. He could feel the rain beginning to reach through to his back, shivering cold.

Cassraw looked straight at him. 'Many of you have heard me speak and have understood. Great is the wisdom and vision of those who are unclouded by learning. But there are others – even those who have seen His hand at work before their eyes – who doubt yet. These lost souls are more deserving of our pity than our anger, my children, so blind are they. But only thus far can their blindness be forgiven, for it is in truth a wilful pride that turns them away from the Way when it has been so plainly shown to them. How great is such a pride, my children, that tells them they can deny His truth?' He paused significantly. 'Well, just so great is His mercy, for He has given me the power to bring to such doubters a sign.' The crowd was very silent. 'Let those among you so weak in faith as to need a sign, look upon this, and question it if you dare!'

As his last words boomed out over the crowd, he stood up, threw his head back to face the falling rain, and extended his arms wide.

Vredech drew in an agonizing breath as he felt all that he had felt before in the presence of one of Cassraw's 'miracles' but this time, immeasurably worse. For a

465

moment he thought he was going to lapse into unconsciousness, and indeed, in the darkness behind his briefly closed eyes, he thought he saw the Whistler looking at him curiously, his head on one side and his flute seemingly paused on its way to his mouth. The image was gone the instant he opened his eyes, but he heard himself softly whistling the familiar three notes.

There was agitation all about him, and cries of wonder coming from the crowd. Simultaneously he heard Nertha gasp, Skynner swear, and Horld cry out. As he looked around he realized that the rain had suddenly stopped. But as he looked further, he saw that beyond the crowd in every direction it seemed to be still falling. Then he discovered what had so startled his companions. His flattened hair, his previously sodden clothes, the rocks under his feet and all about him, were completely dry.

Chapter 32

Vredech looked at Nertha anxiously. 'Are you all right?' he asked.

They were sitting by the fire in Vredech's private quarters. Two lanterns, turned well down, added a little light to that thrown by the fire. It should have been a moment of quiet indulgence as they both luxuriated in the soft light and the after-glow of changing from cold, sodden clothes into dry ones. House had anticipated their condition and was fully armed to deal with it when they eventually returned. But no amount of physical comfort could assuage the tension they felt, though by silent consent they had kept it from House.

Vredech repeated his question, and Nertha nodded unconvincingly.

Following Cassraw's eerie demonstration of his power, there had been an uproar which ended only when most of the crowd had sunk to their knees. Cassraw gazed triumphantly at the four for whom it was primarily intended, but said nothing to them.

Instead, he had addressed the crowd.

'Such is the least of the powers that have been granted to me. Daily I am given more. Tell this to all who doubt. Tell them what you have seen, what you have felt, at this holy place. Spread the word. Seek out the doubters and convince them. Especially blessed are you, for you needed no sign, but *all* must be with us. The proving is begun.'

Then his voice had swelled again. 'Two things you are charged with. Firstly, you must levy the militia and prepare for battle. Wait for no instructions from above, other than those I give you now, for you are led by weaklings and cowards. I will send forth His Knights to your homes with the ordering of your ranks. And lastly,' his voice was soft again, but full of a menace that was made all the more frightening by the ecstasy that veined through it, 'you shall hold this place most holy and walk no more upon it, for a great temple is to be built here. A temple of such wonders that all Gyronlandt will turn towards it and know His power.'

For the rest, Vredech had only a kaleidoscope of memories: the silent return to the Witness House, the hasty empowering of such of his fellow Chapter Brothers as still remained, to deal with the temporary running of the Witness House and, not last, the arrangements for the removal of Mueran's body. Then, finally, the strained, almost unreal journey through the now-returned rain back to the familiar anchor of House's hospitality.

Throughout all this, his dominant concern had been for Nertha. Among them she seemed to be the most affected by Cassraw's demonstration. Skynner had left them at the gates of the Witness House. He had said nothing about the 'miracle', apparently shutting it from his mind, but had seized on Cassraw's call for the levying of the militia. Perhaps the holding of a service on the summit of the Ervrin was a legal act, perhaps not, he announced, and while Cassraw's assumption of the office of Covenant Member seemed suspicious to him, he was unfamiliar with such matters and, in any event, it was purely a church affair. But setting himself up as a levying officer for the militia was indisputably illegal. The whole point of a citizen militia was that it could *not* be levied at the whim of any individual, save in extreme emergency. It could be levied only on the order of the Heindral, and there was an established and well-defined procedure for the issuing of that order.

And while Cassraw's actions had driven Skynner to take refuge in familiar practicalities, it had, ironically, convinced Horld utterly of the rightness of Vredech's interpretation of events. 'I felt it. Horrible, horrible. I felt it. Just as on that day, but worse,' he said many times on the journey down the mountain, shivering far more than the cold demanded. When they parted at the gates, he apologized to the others. 'I'm sorry,' he said. 'I'm rambling. I need to think, to pray, to seek some guidance. When I'm quieter in my mind, I'll come to your Meeting House.' He half-turned away, then with a grimace, turned back. 'No. I'll come whether I'm settled or not. I'll come.'

Vredech had watched him go with some unease, but took comfort in the fact that Horld was above all an 'iron and coals' man, well-rooted in reality.

Reality?

Safely home now, the word floated to him on the Whistler's tune, taunting him. Where and how had he met Horld that moonlit evening on the mountain? Who was the Whistler? Did he exist? What he had said was coming to pass, but . . . And from whence did this awful power come, that had so possessed Cassraw? With a cold resolution that surprised him, Vredech set all these questions aside and brought his attention back to Nertha. She had been silent since Cassraw so mysteriously stopped the rain, and though she had seemed to be listening to Horld's spasmodic outbursts, and Skynner's desperate legalizing, Vredech knew that her mind had been elsewhere.

'Nertha, you're frightening me,' he said finally. 'Did He . . . it . . . try to possess you again? Speak to me, please.'

Then she turned to him and for the briefest of moments he saw into her unbelieving soul and understood. He saw that the reason and logic which dominated her thinking

469

and informed her attitudes, were not the tight choking circle that he had always imagined. They were tools with which all things could be examined and, perhaps, understood. They were tools that removed the darkness and shed light along a magical road of learning and discovery that went on for ever.

For ever.

And awe and wonder were not lessened by what they revealed; they were enhanced.

And now she was frightened – desperately frightened. Not that these tools might fail her, he could see, but that she, with her human frailty, might fail herself in the use of them. And now *he* was afraid, because she must surely bring her will to bear on what was happening. She was a physician, a healer, her very nature would not allow her to turn away from something that could bring such horror and pain without attempting to right it – or excise it!

He dropped to his knees and put his arms around her. After a while, her arms folded about him and though she made no sound, he felt her weeping. They were no longer brother and sister. Then she said the words.

'Allyn, I'm so afraid.'

The reply was difficult.

'So am I,' he said eventually.

The worst was past.

He held her tighter, until eventually the weeping faded away, and her body became awkward and stiff. He let her go as she began wriggling to take a kerchief from her pocket. Wiping her streaky face and blowing her nose she made no apology for her tears and Vredech made no mention of them.

'Where can we start?' she said, clearing her throat.

Vredech looked at her quizzically.

'We have to do something, Allyn,' she said, with some impatience. 'Cassraw's got to be stopped. This . . . thing . . . that's taken over him is corrupting him totally.

Whatever anyone else thinks, *we* know this. And these powers he's developed.' She shook her head. 'Unbelievable.' Unexpectedly, she smiled, and Vredech felt the room brighten. 'A salutary lesson re-learned, Preacher,' she said. 'I should know by now not to allow the limits of my sorry imagination to dictate what is and is not possible.'

Then, fleetingly and in contradiction to his previous fears, Vredech was afraid that she would *not* venture forth to do battle by his side, but would sink into the familiar warmth of the room and the fire and the spell that House had woven for them, like a tiny field creature unaware of the approaching armies coming to trample over it. House's magic, he knew now, should be valued for what it was, not what it seemed to be. But Nertha dispelled this concern.

'Still,' she said, 'believable or not, it was as real as a broken leg.' She gave Vredech an apologetic look. 'And it was no party trick either. I'm sorry.'

Vredech gave a dismissive wave then laboured himself up off his knees and sat down on his chair again. Nertha reached out and took his bruised hand. He winced as she manipulated his fingers then, satisfied that no serious harm had been done by the punch he had thrown, she gave a guilty chuckle and clicked her tongue. 'Fisticuffs between the Brothers, eh? How Father would have laughed.' There was more sadness than humour in her manner, however, and she returned his hand to him gently. Then, quite soberly, as though she were speaking to a normally conscientious student who had just made a careless mistake, she said, 'If you're going to hit someone in the face, use your open hand, not your fist. You might have been permanently crippled.' She demonstrated as she spoke.

Vredech gaped at this unexpected advice, but before he could respond, Nertha had leaned back, her face

471

thoughtful. 'It would help if we knew what it was that's taken over Cassraw,' she said.

Vredech raised an eyebrow. It was the kind of obvious question that would probably never have occurred to him.

'I suppose it would,' he said vaguely. 'But I don't know—'

A violent knocking on the Witness House door made both of them start. It went on long enough for Vredech to rise and move to the door of the room in some concern. As he opened it he heard House's voice raised in indignation, then the knocking ceased. He paused, listening. Almost immediately House cried out. Vredech ran through into the hallway. House was standing by the open doorway while sprawled across the threshold was a man wearing the uniform of Cassraw's Knights of Ishryth. Another man, short and strong-looking, and a tradesman judging by his clothes, was bending over him, trying to rouse him.

'What's going on?' Vredech demanded sternly, thinking that the fallen man was drunk.

'Please help me get him up, Brother,' the kneeling man implored. 'Please! I couldn't think of anywhere else to come. I'm sorry. Please help.'

'You're Yan-Elter, aren't you?' Vredech said, recalling the man's name.

'What's happening? . . . Oh!'

The exclamation came from Nertha, who had been drawn inexorably after Vredech. She knelt down by the fallen man, gently motioning Yan-Elter away. Vredech gave the man a reassuring nod. The sight of Nertha kneeling over the prone figure brought back the memory of Mueran, and Vredech found himself holding his breath. This time however, there was no resigned slump of the shoulders as she stood up.

'Pick him up and bring him through here,' she said authoritatively.

Vredech and Yan-Elter lifted the unconscious figure

472

and manhandled him awkwardly into Vredech's room, House following, wringing her hands anxiously. At Nertha's further instruction they laid him on a long couch and she began to examine him. The man's uniform was torn and soiled and his face was begrimed and bloody. 'House, could you get me something to clean this young man up with, please, and some blankets?' Nertha asked as she turned up the lanterns and lit another one.

Vredech repeated his initial question to Yan-Elter as House left. 'What's going on, Yan?' he asked.

'Is he going to be all right?' Yan-Elter asked Nertha, ignoring Vredech. Nertha waved a hand for silence and continued her examination. Her manner brooked no interference and the man turned to Vredech.

'Give her a moment,' Vredech said, his manner softening. Catching Nertha's eye for confirmation, he added, 'I'm sure he'll be fine.' Then House entered carrying a bowl of water and some towels and the two men retreated before the subsequent bustle of female activity that eventually restored the unconscious man to some state of cleanliness.

'He's got bruises and abrasions, mainly to his arms and legs, and his ankle's swelling up badly, although it doesn't seem to be broken,' Nertha concluded eventually, wiping her hands. 'I'm not getting any signs of serious internal injury, but we'll have to wait until he wakes up before I can check that properly.' She directed an unexpectedly stern gaze on Yan-Elter and asked Vredech's question again. 'What's been happening here?' she demanded. 'As far as I can tell, the main thing that's wrong with him is that he's absolutely exhausted.' She turned to Vredech. 'Those Knights of Cassraw's looked the same.'

Vredech rescued the man, pointing him towards a chair by the fire. He had barely sat down when the figure on the couch began to thrash about violently, throwing off the blanket that had been placed over him and only narrowly avoiding knocking over House's water bowl. Nertha moved to his side and took hold of his flailing arms. Then slowly, from the depths, a great cry of pain and horror rose out of the man. 'Hold his feet! Gently!' Nertha cried out to Vredech as she began to use her weight to reduce the man's spasms.

Yan-Elter moved to the man's head. 'He's been like this all the time. And crying too,' he said. Then, to the sick man: 'Iryn, it's me. You're safe now. You're back. Everything will be all right.'

But the man's agitation only increased, as did his cries, and for a little while all three were fully occupied in restraining him. Suddenly he began to gasp for breath. Nertha sat up and sniffed, then, her jawline stiffening, she gave him a mighty slap across the face. The man's eyes flew wide open.

'You're all right now, Iryn,' Nertha smiled into them winningly. 'You're safe here. Rest back.' Then, to Vredech, with a poke of her elbow that gave the command an urgency which she kept out of her voice: 'Get my bag. And some water for him.'

When the bag appeared, Nertha delved into it expertly and produced a small bottle. She measured a few drops into the water.

'Drink this,' she said to the still-bewildered Iryn. 'It'll help.'

Iryn seized the glass in both hands and gulped the contents down without question. Nertha watched him carefully. 'Dehydrated as well as exhausted,' she said. 'Go to sleep now, you're very tired. Go to sleep. We'll talk later.'

Even as she was talking, the man's eyes were closing.

Nertha looked at Yan-Elter more sympathetically than before. 'You don't look all that much better than your friend,' she said.

'He's my brother,' Yan-Elter said.

Nertha shrugged. 'Then you don't look much better than your brother. He'll be asleep for some time now, which is what he needs. Sit down. House will bring you something to eat and drink, and then you can tell us what's been going on.'

Yan-Elter sagged and moved back to the chair while Vredech went to deliver Nertha's request to House. Nertha remained on the edge of the couch by her patient.

When Vredech returned he sat down opposite Yan-Elter and looked at him expectantly.

Yan-Elter became suddenly animated. 'It's that mādman, Cassraw,' he burst out. 'Saving your cloth, Brother, but some things can't be left unsaid. He's not right in the head.'

Vredech raised a hand to calm him. 'I understand,' he said. 'You can say anything you want here without fear of reproach, but please try to stay calm, and take whatever time you need. What's Cassraw got to do with your brother being in this state?'

Yan-Elter pressed his hands to his temples as if trying to still his thoughts. 'He's got everything to do with it!' He pointed towards his sleeping brother. 'He was at that Bredill business,' he said vehemently. 'I still can't believe it was only yesterday.' Vredech and Nertha waited until he composed himself again. 'Yesterday, one of his cronies from these Knights of Cassraw's came for him. "Captain Yanos's orders," he says. "Come right away. Very important. Going to see the Felden off".' Yan-Elter looked at Vredech. 'Now, Iryn's not the wisest of souls, but he's not totally stupid. For his sins, he's a mite too keen to use his fists in an argument, but he wouldn't want to get involved in fighting real soldiers. So, he asks what's going on. Then, this Knight . . .' his voice was snarling with contempt '. . . simply says, "Come now, it's an order, you don't have any choice". Iryn's still not happy and says so, whereupon the Knight says, "Come *now* or take the consequences of breaking your holy oath". Very slowly he says it, full of menace. And Iryn just . . .' he shrugged '. . . went quiet and left with him.'

'Didn't you try to help him?' Nertha asked.

'I wasn't there!' Yan-Elter exclaimed reproachfully. 'I got the story off our mother when I came home from work. She was really frightened.' His tone changed to one of anger. 'This Knight was a nasty piece of work, she said.' He drove his fist into his hand. 'I'll make a piece of work of him if I catch him. And that lunatic Cassraw.'

Vredech let the threats pass.

'The next thing I hear, there's all this blather in the Sheets about a battle at Bredill and the Felden army being defeated. I had to leave the job I was on and go home. I knew Mother would be really frantic now.' He clenched his hands together and gritted his teeth as if to force the next words out. 'She'd already been to the place where these . . . Knights . . . meet. There were a lot of them there – in bad shape, she said – but they just told her to—' He hesitated. 'To go away,' he said uncomfortably, 'before they threw her out.' He lowered his voice. 'There was a lot of abuse. Then one of them said Iryn must have got separated on the way back. Quite a few had, apparently. He'd probably turn up later.'

'So you went and found him?' Vredech said, cutting through the rest of the tale.

Yan-Elter nodded. 'More by good luck than anything else,' he said. 'Just caught sight of his precious red sash in the gorse some way off the road.' He looked at his two listeners. 'He could've died for all they cared. He must have just wandered off exhausted, and collapsed.' He shook his head in disbelief. 'It's beyond me. Whatever kind of a crowd they are, you look after your own, don't you? You don't need to be a Preaching Brother to know that. You don't just abandon people when there's trouble.' He fell silent.

'Has he told you what happened?' Nertha asked.

Yan-Elter shook his head. 'I managed to wake him up, but he was rambling. Shouting and moaning. And thrashing about – like just now. I don't know how I got him here.'

'Why did you bring him here?' Vredech asked. 'Why didn't you take him to a physician?'

'Have you told your mother he's safe?' Nertha asked, leaning forward and gesturing Vredech's question aside urgently.

Yan-Elter looked rapidly from one to the other. 'No,' he stammered guiltily to Nertha, then to Vredech, 'He didn't seem to be hurt badly. He could walk, but he kept . . . sitting down, as if he just wanted to lie there and give up. I asked him if he wanted to go to Cassraw's but he started throwing a fit again, really badly. You were all I could think of, Brother Vredech. I know I'm no service-goer, but . . .'

Nertha, momentarily deflected by this tale, recovered herself and pointed to the door. 'Get home to your mother, now, right away,' she said indignantly. 'Tell her your brother's safe, and where he is, and make sure she's all right before you come back.'

'Bit fierce with him, weren't you?' Vredech said when Yan-Elter had left.

'Well, for mercy's sake,' she said impatiently. 'The poor woman'll be demented while he's sitting here, gossiping.'

Vredech changed the subject. 'What do you make of it?' he said.

Nertha looked at the sleeping figure, then at Vredech. 'We'll have to wait for him to wake up before we can get the answer to that,' she said simply.

'How long will that be?'

Nertha took Iryn's pulse then shook her head. 'The draught I gave him should keep him asleep for a couple of hours or so, but he's very agitated. His mind's fighting it.'

477

She grimaced. 'I doubt his dreams are helping him rest.' She stood up and lowered the lanterns again, restoring the relaxing glow that had pervaded the room before Yan-Elter's interruption. 'I think we're in for a long night,' she said. 'You make yourself comfortable in that chair and have a sleep while you can. I'll keep an eye on our patient.'

Vredech tried to protest, but Nertha pushed him back into his chair and thrust a cushion under his head. 'Don't argue,' she said quietly, stroking his cheek. 'I'm used to this kind of thing, you aren't. This is the waiting time. What can be done, has been done. All we can do is float in the time between that and whatever's to follow. Besides, I think you're going to have plenty to do when he wakes up.'

The practical note reassured Vredech and he relaxed as he had been instructed, though with the clear intention of not actually sleeping. Very shortly, though, the warmth of the fire and the soft lights weighed down his eyelids and when Nertha looked at him again, he was fast asleep. She smiled. That was one less to worry about for the time being.

Maelstrom.

Sounds and patterns swirled about and through him. He was moving yet still; here and not here. The consciousness that was Vredech knew he was at the place that he came to before being hurled recklessly from dream to dream. How strange, he thought, that he had become used to this bizarre phenomenon. The why? and the how? of such a thing should torment him, so far was it from the reality of everyday affairs. Perhaps he had absorbed Nertha's attitude: not allowing the limits of his sorry imagination to dictate what was and was not possible – especially when he could do nothing about it. But there was a deeper change – a rightness about what was happening – no sense of anything unnatural, still less of evil. Yet too, there was a sense of incompleteness about it. The feeling that something was missing, that he needed guidance, knowledge and, oddly, that *he should not be alone here*.

Then he was out of the chaos and into a dream. This was the way it always was – never the slightest sense of change. And again he was both in the dream and aloof from it, feeling the dreamer's emotions but unaffected by them – though those that swept over him now were profoundly disturbing. Delight at a goal having been reached, at fear having been overcome, at the sense of unity with his fellows in a venture from which only glory could come. And a deep, visceral response – ecstatic, almost. He *liked* hitting people. Liked it a lot. And here you could hit and hit without restraint, without reproach, because you'd been told to by those in the highest authority and because those you were hitting were lesser, contaminated creatures who were not the Chosen, were not fit to live, and who would do the same to you if they got the chance.

And so he hit. Oh, how he hit. His weighted cudgel balanced and easy in his hand, all fatigue gone, he could do this for ever without tiring, so joyous was it.

Noises wrapped comfortingly around him. Vicious taunting jeers from his fellows, strange gasps and moans from the enemy, struggling under their downed canvases. Then one of the sounds tore through the others to become a high-pitched and terrified voice, sobbing and pleading.

'Please. No more. Please.'

And a face filled his vision. A young man's face. He saw the trembling, begging mouth, black in the moonlight. The voice streaming from it became a solid thing, moving to seize and bind him. It held him immobile, while the voice skewered into him agonizingly.

'Please!'

And then, more horrible by far, he saw into the eyes. Eyes that showed him the true depths of terror. Eyes that cried many times louder than the voice: 'Let me go! Let

me run away! Leave me be! Let me live.' Young eyes . . .
. . . like his own!

Forgotten emotions began to stir inside him. The face's primitive terror reached into him and found his own cowering soul.

He mustn't . . .

But the revelation added its own frantic fury to the irresistible killing momentum, and the weighted club with its sweet whistling song rose unbidden to erase this ghastly discord.

Yet its last blow struck down not only the face with its drivelling terror, but also himself as it shattered his own sense of the rightness of events. The sound it made, dull and awful now, echoed through and through him, bringing to full wakefulness those burgeoning restraints and reproaches that had been too late and too feeble to prevent the deed.

The club slipped from his hand and a cry formed within him. A cry that he tried not to utter for fear of those about him. But the cry struggled and fought. It was a live thing. He seized it and pressed down on it with his whole weight, his heart pounding. But a whimper slipped around his grip. It sounded through the flickering flamelight like a clarion. And all was suddenly silent. In his weakness, he had revealed himself as the enemy. Black, red-sashed shadows paused from their threshing, and their unseen eyes focused on him, seeing into his true self. They began to close upon him.

He shrank and shrank until he became the gaping mouth and terrified eyes that he had just crushed . . .

Vredech was torn into wakefulness by the sudden ending of the dream. He gasped as he awoke, but the sound that filled his ears was of a despairing cry. Through his sleep-blurred eyes he saw Nertha bending forward over Iryn, talking, comforting. Vredech made to rise. He had to tell Nertha what had just happened.

But something turned the soft-lit image of Nertha and her charge into a stillness, like a distant picture, subject unknown, painter unknown. He blinked as he looked at it. When his eyes opened they were filled with a bright, flickering light. He closed them again quickly, bringing his hand up for protection. Then he re-opened them slowly, allowing them to adjust to the light.

He was standing in a forest. It was a bright sunny day, but a strong wind was buffeting the treetops, turning them into an iridescent shimmer. Rich forest scents assailed him, borne on that part of the wind that was exploring the lower reaches of the trees. He looked down at his hands, turning them over and touching his arms with them to confirm what he already knew: once again he was in two places at the same time. He was both asleep by the fire in his Meeting House, and here, wherever that might be. He stepped forward. Long fallen twigs cracked under his feet.

As he moved away from the tree under which he was standing, he saw a familiar figure sitting on a log. He was apparently asleep, his head drooping and his arms folded across his flute as he leaned back against a tree trunk.

Vredech waited.

There was no sound, but the breath of the wind and the forest.

Slowly, the Whistler looked up at him.

Chapter 33

After leaving Vredech and the others, Skynner had galloped to the Keeperage. Years as a Keeper had given him a cold and sceptical eye, and he had seen more than a few tricksters in his time effecting 'miracles' that, in the end, usually only effected a miraculous emptying of the pockets, or coffers on occasions, of anyone foolish enough to believe them.

What Cassraw had done at the summit must be yet another piece of trickery . . . surely? In common with most people, Skynner accepted without question such miracles as the turn of the seasons, the rising and setting of the sun, the growing of seed into tree and flower, even the arbitrary comings and goings of the wind and the rain. These were 'natural'. But all else, he knew, was determined by an inexorable and conspicuous law of cause and effect. What cause Cassraw had evoked to create that particular effect was beyond him, but that was no doubt Cassraw's intention and he, Serjeant Keeper, was not going to waste time being distracted by it. The artifice would come to light sooner or later and, in any event, was irrelevant. He had a duty to cut through to the heart of Cassraw's intentions, or as nearly as he could, because even though he could not see what they were, he could see enough to know that they were not in the interests of the public safety and the peace. And whatever game he was playing at, Cassraw's call for the levying of the militia was unequivocally illegal. Skynner would have been within his rights to arrest him there and then, but it needed no great sensitivity to the mood of the crowd to realize that that would have been a foolish, potentially fatal thing to attempt. He would have to advise his superiors and let them choose the time for taking a step as serious as arresting a Chapter Brother of the church.

The duty Serjeant looked up in surprise as Skynner strode noisily into the Keeperage, but reading Skynner's expression, he bit back the jocular remark he was about to make, and simply pointed straight up with the comradely warning, 'Careful, Chief's in.'

'Good,' Skynner said grimly and headed for the stairs.

As he drew near to the Chief Keeper's office, he reached the carpeted area of the building and the change in the sound of his footfalls set in motion long-imbued habits of discipline. He flattened his hair, straightened out his tunic, and began to marshal his words. Going straight to the Chief instead of through his Captain and High Captain was not something to be done lightly, but it *was* urgent, and as the Chief fortuitously happened to be there . . .

Two or three paces gave him a handful of excuses for his directness. Once he had made those he'd have no trouble holding the Chief's attention. He gave his uniform a final twitch outside the door, then knocked briskly.

'Come in.'

There was a middle-of-the-day wakefulness in the voice that made Skynner pause. As he reached for the door handle, he asked himself for the first time what had happened to bring the Chief in at this time of night.

He opened the door quickly and stepped into the office.

Someone else was there as well as the Chief Keeper. Someone sitting not across the desk from him, but in one of the comfortable chairs by the fireplace. The Chief Keeper was sitting opposite him and lying dolefully between them was a dull red and grey fire.

Skynner recognized the Chief's companion immediately as Toom Drommel. So that's why he's here, he thought. Want the old beggar on a Keeper matter and he's nowhere to be found. Let some politician snap his fingers and he abandons home and hearth in the middle of the night to make reassuring noises.

Well, this politician's business could wait.

'I'm sorry for disturbing you, sir,' he said, 'but an extremely serious matter's come to light. I need to—' he was about to say discuss but changed it quickly '—*report* it immediately.'

The Chief pointed to a chair. 'Bring that over here and sit down, Haron,' he said.

Skynner's every instinct leapt on to the defensive. The Chief using his given name like that was *not* a good sign. Something difficult was about to be brought up. Nevertheless, and trying not to look as tense as he felt, he did as he was told.

The Chief addressed Drommel as Skynner sat down stiffly between them. 'This is Haron Skynner,' he said. 'Our most senior Serjeant.' He became avuncular. 'Should be a Captain by rights, but he insists he prefers footwork to paperwork and he's not to be persuaded to higher ambitions.' He nodded sagely. 'I think perhaps he's wiser than we know. I must confess, there's been many a time when I've sat here and wished devoutly that I could be out there with my men, doing what we're trained for, and best at.'

With commendable restraint Skynner remained silent, confining himself to a self-deprecating but knowing smile.

'I've seen Serjeant Skynner many a time on duty at the PlasHein,' Drommel said, endeavouring to ape the Chief's informality but still having a little difficulty with his statesman's voice. He nodded creakily towards Skynner then gave the Chief a significant look.

The Chief nodded. 'Serjeant Skynner's one of my best

men, if not *the* best. There's nothing I'd not trust him with, and he's very sound in practical matters. A street Keeper to his boots.'

If only that didn't sound like an insult, Skynner thought.

'And what we have to deal with is nothing if not practical, is it?'

Skynner was watching the two men carefully, waiting for an opportunity to commence his account of Cassraw's actions. Gradually, however, he became aware of an undertow of excitement between them.

The word 'conspiracy' came to him unbidden.

Drommel gave a sign of acquiescence. 'I trust your judgement implicitly, Chief,' he said. 'I can see it will be important that the Serjeant and his colleagues be aware of what's going to happen and why.'

The Chief nodded briskly and stood up. Skynner made to rise, but the Chief waved him airily back down on to his seat. He took up an authoritative stance with his back to the fire and his legs planted solid and wide. 'Serjeant,' he began, as though addressing a parade. 'You know that, as Keepers, we avoid getting involved in politics. We're executive officers of the state and it's our job to do as the law-makers decree, not decide what should and should not be the law. We advise occasionally, of course, but purely to lay before them the benefits of our experience for their guidance.' Skynner began to feel uneasy. The Chief rocked forward. 'However, it needs no great political insight to realize that, for various reasons, the country's currently facing serious difficulties. Difficulties that will need a strong head and a strong hand to see us through.'

Skynner nodded tentatively, as the Chief seemed to be awaiting some response, though he was feeling increasingly uncomfortable.

'The situation is this, Skynner. The Castellan Party is in complete disarray. They've no one else of the calibre of

485

their present leader and he, frankly, is . . . unwell.' He made a drinking gesture. 'I have it on good authority that he'll probably resign very shortly. That'll leave us with the Ploughers in charge.' He puffed out his cheeks in dismay. 'They, unfortunately, are almost as disunited as the Castellans. And in any case, they've always been more theoretical in their thinking than practical, and under their present leader – a worthy soul as you know but hardly a driving force – they're not remotely capable of standing firm in the face of what's likely to happen after the routing of the Felden army. Frankly, I can't see this present Heindral lasting the week. Then we'll be facing an Acclamation. An Acclamation, Skynner. Two months leaderless with Tirfelden undoubtedly preparing to send another army against us.' He shook his head. 'Suicide, man. National suicide.'

Skynner was uncertain how to respond. He was about to tell the Chief that the situation was even worse than he envisaged, and that Cassraw was arbitrarily levying the militia, when the Chief forestalled him. 'Fortunately, we have at least two strong men in positions of responsibility who can act to save us from this predicament. One is Heinder Drommel here, who has consistently tried to embolden the Heindral to take firm action against Tirfelden. The other is Brother Cassraw, who for months now has been decrying the moral decay in the country and who, with his Knights of Ishryth, has saved us from the first thrust of the Felden assault while our ostensible leaders dithered and appeased.'

Skynner had faced many difficult situations in his time and had considerable skill in separating his inner reactions from his outward responses. It was strained to the limit by this revelation of the Chief's thinking, however. All that saved him from denouncing the remarks as ridiculous, was the realization that what had been said about the Heindral and the country's position was correct. Further, he began

486

to realize, if the Chief and Drommel and perhaps Cassraw were playing some political game together, then *others* would be involved. Others whose names, whose power and influence, he did not know. It behoved him, he reminded himself, to remember that he was only a Serjeant, and whatever he thought about what was happening, such power as he had to affect it could be removed from him with little more than a snap of the fingers by the man addressing him. Nevertheless, he could not stay silent.

'Brother Cassraw is a remarkable man, beyond doubt, sir,' he said carefully. 'But he's causing great controversy within the Church, which may see him losing the Haven Parish. And I'll confess I'm uncomfortable about members of the Church becoming involved in lay matters. It confuses people. And I'm afraid that some of the young men he's recruited for his Knights of Ishryth are not exactly desirable – a bunch of thugs and louts with whom we're all too familiar. And his own behaviour is unusual, to say the least. He almost started a riot at the summit of the Ervrin Mallos with a trick he played there, and the consequences could have been serious. That's one of the things I came to see you about.'

He was aware of the two men watching him very closely – judging him.

'We know,' the Chief said. 'But no actual harm was done, was it? You see, Brother Cassraw has a true gift for handling people.' He leaned forward and Skynner felt the scrutiny intensifying. 'And I think there's little doubt that he has indeed been chosen for some great mission.'

Still Skynner managed to give no outward sign of the shock he felt at this further revelation, but inwardly he was reeling. The Chief's words resounded in his head like tolling funeral bells. They had had someone on the mountain! They knew what had happened! The ranting sermon, the trick with the rain, the call to levy the militia . . . and they were content to do nothing about it! Frighteningly, the conclusion formed that they might actually have been party to it.

And that the Chief should think Cassraw was some kind of chosen prophet . . .

He did not want to pursue that idea.

The Chief was continuing. Skynner dragged his scattering thoughts together. 'Apart from the many other signs we've been shown, Serjeant, is it not strange that poor Brother Mueran should pass on so suddenly and unexpectedly, thereby elevating Brother Cassraw to the position of Covenant Member?' He leaned back on his heels and pontificated. 'It's not for the likes of us to question the ways of Ishryth's providence, but to see where our duty to Him and the people lies, and to act accordingly.'

Skynner made a final cautious attempt at resistance. 'As you say, sir. Not my province at all. But I'm uncertain about the legality of Brother Cassraw levying the militia, sir. It should properly be done through the Heindral.'

The Chief nodded understandingly. 'We have no Heindral, Serjeant, except in name,' he said forcefully. 'And it's uncertainty and fretting about niceties that's brought us to this.' He became comradely again. 'I could go out of here and consult a dozen different lawyers on our constitutional position and come up with two dozen different opinions – as you know yourself. The fact is, there's never been a situation like this before. There are no precedents to guide us – nothing. So, humble servants of the state like you and me must put our faith in our duty to protect the people, and encourage them to protect themselves.'

'I couldn't argue with that, sir,' Skynner said, determined now simply to watch events, and move as they dictated. A little humility wouldn't go amiss, he decided. 'But, as you said, sir, I'm just a simple street Keeper. I'm not quite sure what part I have to play in these affairs. I just do my job and follow orders.'

The Chief and Drommel exchanged a satisfied glance and the Chief, though still holding his position in front of the dying fire, relaxed noticeably. 'Heinder Drommel has been in consultation with Brother Cassraw today, as have I, many times of late. I find him most . . . impressive. We both knew of his intention to call for a levying of the militia and we agreed with it, even though, technically, its legality is arguable. The exigencies of the times will acquit us, should it prove we've been over-zealous.' His face became sombre. 'Tomorrow, Heinder Drommel will put a motion before the Heindral calling for its dissolution and the institution of an emergency militia government pending the holding of an Acclamation.'

Skynner's brow furrowed as his mind stumbled back through the years to his basic training and the cursory instruction he had received then in constitutional law. A rote-learned definition slowly emerged. 'The vesting of all authority in the hands of a few appointed ministers and officials under a—' He clicked his fingers.

'High Commander,' Drommel said, as Skynner struggled to remember the title.

Skynner nodded his thanks. 'But it's never actually been done, has it?' he said. 'Isn't it a relic of the days of the Court of the Provers and earlier?'

'That's true,' the Chief said. 'But the provision is still there within our laws. And again, who can say what providence allowed it to remain there, for it's precisely what we need to deal with the situation we now find ourselves facing.'

The look of concern on Skynner's face was genuine, but he wilfully added confusion to it for the benefit of his watchers. 'And my part in this?' he asked, reverting to his previous question.

'Under militia government, the responsibilities of the Keepers are greatly increased, as are their powers. This is necessary because, sadly, not everyone has our sense of duty. Many will view the prospect of defending their country with sufficient distaste to take active steps towards avoiding it. Such individuals must be dealt with swiftly and severely by way of example before their actions spread resentment and opposition. Further, the requirements of a fully levied militia will disrupt normal social and business life greatly, and in such circumstances there are more opportunities than ever for the criminals amongst us to ply their various trades. Men of your experience will be essential for the efficient running of the state until such time as normal government can be restored.'

Under an impassive demeanour, Skynner was still struggling to come to terms with all that he had heard during the last few minutes. Having only dealt directly with the Chief a few times in the past, he had no way of accurately assessing his mood and temperament. The man was known to have political ambitions, but these were always regarded as a joke amongst the men. And what he had said was both accurate and appropriate. Though it took him an effort to form the words, Skynner accepted that the country was indeed 'at war' with Tirfelden. Perhaps diplomacy might resolve it, but perhaps not. If not, the consequences would be truly awful and strong leadership was essential. Yet there was a stridency in the Chief's tone which Skynner found deeply unsettling. He needed time to think.

But he posed a question instead. 'I accept what you say, sir, but with respect, what if the Heindral doesn't pass Heinder Drommel's motion, and chooses to bumble on as before?'

The Chief smiled knowingly. 'As I told you, Heinder, a solid practical man,' he said to Drommel before answering Skynner's question. 'Don't concern yourself about that, Serjeant,' he said, reaching forward and patting Skynner's shoulder, fatherly now. 'That's politicians' work. And you can rest assured that a great deal more has been happening behind the scenes than I'm at liberty to discuss, even with a fellow Keeper.' Skynner managed to smile appreciatively. 'What Heinder Drommel and I need to know now, Serjeant, is are you with us in this?'

Drommel twitched slightly at this clumsy conclusion to the Chief's peroration, and Skynner noted the movement with some satisfaction. It seemed to make the Chief a familiar figure again. But that was only a temporary verbal stumble in the presence of an individual who really did not matter all that much. The realities of what had been said would be unaffected by it. Skynner resorted to his own rhetoric. 'I'm a Keeper, sir. Keeping the peace and protecting ordinary folk from those who'd harm them is what I'm good at. I'll do whatever I have to do. You can rely on me.'

A little later, alone in a narrow alley at the back of the Keeperage, where he had come to clear his head with cold night air, Skynner had a vision of Canol Madreth at war and under the heel of Cassraw and Drommel and the likes of his Chief. He was violently sick.

The Whistler frowned. 'You're a grim sight to mar such a day, night eyes,' he said, raising his flute and squinting along it. A sudden breeze gusted around the two men, sending leaves pirouetting about their feet. The Whistler's eyes widened in delight and he held out the flute, moving it, twisting it, turning it, until a faint sound came from it. His long, bony finger danced along the holes and the sound became a brief, jigging tune. The Whistler smiled as it faded away and then looked at his hand strangely. 'Thus blows the forest, thus walk my fingers. It seems they're content to see you.' He wiggled his fingers. 'I wonder why they didn't play you a dirge? That would've been *my* reaction on seeing you again.' He threw his head back and sniffed. 'You've got *Him* about you, stronger than ever. Damn you to hell.'

He stood up and took three jerking steps towards Vredech, keeping the same foot forward. 'What do you want, Allyn Vredech, priest of Ishrythan?' he said, hopping from one foot to the other, his manner incongruously at odds with the darkness in his voice. 'Why do you disturb my dream again? I'd thought to have been rid of you a hundred years ago.' His eyes moved to the left. 'Or was it yesterday?' They moved to the right. 'Or perhaps tomorrow.' Then straight forward, into Vredech's. 'I can't remember. Are you a memory of the future, Priest? A shadow cast by the light of a time to come?'

Vredech lifted a hand, appealing for silence. Whether the Whistler was his own creation, or something else, he had no time for him now. He had to get away from here, return to the Meeting House.

'Where are we?' he heard himself asking.

The Whistler danced away, his manner now impatient. 'We're here, Allyn Vredech. Where else could we be?' Then he blew a piercing whistle and Vredech found himself assailed by a roaring din, and unfamiliar but not unpleasant odours. He blinked, not so much to bring the scene before him into focus as to make it recognizable. He was by a huge lake. So huge in fact that he could not see the far side, although he could make out two or three islands in the distance – if islands they were, for they seemed to be moving. A trick of the light, he presumed, for the edge of the lake was alive with motion. Waves, bigger than any he had ever seen, spuming white in the sunlight, were swelling and over-topping themselves, then washing up the sandy shore towards him, spreading themselves thinner and thinner before retreating to oppose the next advancing rank.

This was no lake, he realized slowly.

'It's the sea,' he said, his voice full of wonder. He had never seen the sea.

492

'And *we* are here,' the Whistler said. 'Just as we are here.'

There was another whistle, sharp and jagged this time.

In the distance, over rolling fields, Vredech saw a great castle set between two mountains and glinting like a precious stone. Its ramping towers and turrets glowed golden in the dawn light. For a moment, as he took in the scene and breathed in the still morning air, all his concerns fell away from him. 'This is a beautiful place,' he said softly. 'Such peace.' He turned to the Whistler, half-expecting some barbed comment, but the lanky figure was frowning. A fluttering sound nearby made him turn again. A large black bird, sitting on the branch of a tree, was flapping its wings and looking at them, its head tilted to one side. One of its legs looked strange, Vredech noted. Before he could say anything, however, he felt the Whistler's hand on his shoulder.

Urgently, he tried to pull away.

He did not want to leave this place!

But even as the thought came to him, the Whistler's tune had borne them both away again. Borne them to a place which could hardly have been a greater contrast, for though a bright summer sun beat down on them, the air was filled with such a din that Vredech's hands went immediately to his ears. There were the screams of men and animals, mingling with the thudding of hooves, and clashing of arms. Some distance away across the green, undulating turf but close enough to terrify, row upon row of men were locked in savage combat. Vredech backed away, seizing the Whistler's arm like a fearful child. The battle spread as far as he could see, a dark mass of striving men, wavering pennants, galloping horsemen. As he watched, a black cloud leapt high into the air and fell back again. Only when the sound reached him did he identify it. Arrows! Hundreds of them. And again. And again. He shuddered as the sounds of their landing reached him also.

A movement away from the battle caught his eye. He turned and saw an old man running. He was looking about him, bewildered and fearful as though he was being pursued. But again, before he could speak, Vredech saw the Whistler lifting his hand to his mouth.

As the sound he made folded around the scene and bore them away, Vredech thought that he heard wolves howling.

Yet there was nothing but the rustling of the trees in the forest.

'Whistler! Enough!' Vredech shouted angrily. 'Let me go. Let me get back to my own time and place, to my reality where—' He stopped.

The Whistler was uncharacteristically still, though his jaw was working slightly as if he were actually chewing his thoughts. He was looking at Vredech strangely. 'Everything goes amiss when you appear, Preacher,' he said. 'I'm carried to places I've never known. The song becomes infinitely subtle.' He held out his hand, his thumb and forefinger pressing together tightly. 'The least change here . . .' he whistled two notes then his eyes opened wide and he flicked his hands open, spinning the flute around one of them '. . . and such changes there. Such changes – very strange. Never known the like. Who are you, Preacher?'

'Enough, Whistler!' Vredech shouted. Then with a cry of frustration he began driving his fingernails into his forearm in the vague hope that perhaps the pain might rouse him or in some way restore him to the Meeting House. Nothing happened. The Whistler watched him narrowly.

'You haven't killed Him then?' he said, his voice matter-of-fact.

Vredech abandoned his attempt to rouse himself and glared at the Whistler.

'You're a dark sight, Priest,' the Whistler said, suddenly

angry. 'Standing there with your doomsday-black robe and your eyes like pits into who knows what purgatory, fouling the forest with the stink of *Him*!' Then the anger seemed suddenly to drain out of him and he gave a resigned shrug. 'Tell me what's happened then,' he said.

'Go to hell!' Vredech snapped.

'I probably will if I follow you and your like,' the Whistler retorted viciously. 'Now tell me what's happened.'

For a moment, Vredech felt a rage such as he had never known. He found himself about to rush forward and attack his tormentor, but even as his body stiffened, the Whistler moved slightly and bringing the flute to his mouth played the familiar three notes, long and plaintive. The movement and the sound seemed to scatter Vredech's intention.

'Tell me, Allyn,' the Whistler said.

Vredech felt his knees buckling, as if unable to sustain his confusion, and he sat down before he fell. 'Let me go back,' he pleaded. 'I've nightmares enough in the real world – or whatever it is – without this. I need to be there. There's no other true place for me.'

The Whistler approached cautiously and crouched down in front of him. 'Tell me,' he said again, very softly.

Vredech slumped, and without looking up told all that had happened since they had last met. It did not take long. Throughout, the Whistler blew gently across the mouthhole of his flute, with a sound like the wind blowing over a bleak and distant plain.

There was a long silence after Vredech had finished.

'You frighten me, Allyn Vredech, with your monstrous Cassraw,' the Whistler said eventually. 'But it's Him that brings the changes, not you. I'm sorry. He distorts the fabric of everything with His lust!' His final word drifted away into the soft sigh of the wind.

When Vredech looked up, he was staring at Nertha,

sitting on the edge of the couch by her patient, her head bowed slightly and her profile lit by the firelight. How strange that he'd never before noticed how beautiful she was, nor how precious she was to him. The strange serenity he had felt as he had stared at the distant castle in the dawn light but moments before returned to him, calming him.

'Are you awake, Allyn?' Nertha asked quietly.

He nodded and turned back to her. 'Yes,' he said. 'How long was I asleep?'

Nertha smiled. 'Not long. Yan-Elter's not back yet.'

Vredech stretched luxuriously. 'How's Iryn?' he asked.

'He's sleeping normally now, but he's still disturbed,' Nertha replied.

The words brought back the memory of the dream he had entered before he had been drawn again to the Whistler. It had been so powerful, so vivid. And he had never before remained in one dream for so long. It must have been Iryn's, he realized. Perhaps because they were so close physically, perhaps because Iryn's dream was so compellingly awful or, it occurred to him, perhaps he was still changing – in some way becoming more controlled, more sensitive. Like the Whistler's tunes.

'I know why,' he said.

Nertha looked at him.

'He's dreaming about Bredill,' Vredech said, prising himself out of the chair and moving to the couch. 'I've been inside his dream.' So much had happened that day that, despite her training and experience, Nertha could not keep the distress from her face at this remark. Vredech knew the cause and pressed on to the cure without pause. Gently he motioned her away from the sleeping Iryn, then very quickly, almost whispering, he told her about the dream. 'It was no glorious battle,' he concluded. 'It was a treacherous and bloody ambush. A slaughter of sleeping men.'

Nertha took his arm. 'But—'

'Wake him and ask him,' Vredech instructed.

Nertha hesitated.

'Wake him!'

Then he stepped past her, smoothing down his hair, ruffled from his brief sleep, and fastening his clerical robe. He sat on the edge of the couch by Iryn and gently shook him. Gradually the young man awoke, blinking and rubbing his eyes in the soft lantern-light. Vredech gave him no opportunity to speak.

'You're safe now, Iryn,' he said quietly but with a preacher's ring to his voice. Nertha watched him carefully. 'I'm Brother Vredech and this is my sis . . . Nertha, a physician. Your brother rescued you and brought you here, after your friends had deserted you. He'll be back soon. He's gone to tell your mother that you're well. She's been desperately worried about you since you went off to Bredill.'

At the mention of Bredill, Iryn's face began to contort. Vredech laid a restraining hand on him. 'I can feel your pain, my son,' he said. 'And I can help you with it.' Iryn put his hands over his face and uttered a muffled, 'No.' Vredech pulled the hands away. '*Yes*,' he said. 'I know you're no service-attender, but that's of no great consequence. The true heart of the church doesn't lie in buildings and rites and practices, it lies in people's hearts. Ishryth might be a stern god, but He always sustains those who turn to Him. He will not burden you with more than you can bear, but you must speak of that burden if you wish it to be lightened.' He leaned forward. 'Speak it now. Speak out what it was that you and the others did at Bredill which is giving you such pain that it's almost crushing you. Speak out so that you can start on the path towards reparation and forgiveness.'

Iryn screwed his eyes tight shut and, gritting his teeth, shook his head violently from side to side.

497

Vredech's preaching tone was relentless in its authority. 'There is *no other way*,' he declared. 'Speak it and let us help you, or be burdened with it for ever.' He leaned still further forward, 'For ever, Iryn. For the rest of your life – and beyond.' Though both his look and his voice were full of compassion, his tone was a cruelly judged goad.

Nertha caught his arm, but he shook her off.

All of a sudden Iryn began to utter a high-pitched squeal. He clamped his hands over his face again, driving his fingernails into his forehead. Vredech took hold of them, but made no effort to move them other than to prevent Iryn from injuring himself.

The squealing rose to a climax and then began to break up into sobs. Eventually, gasping and disjointed, and punctuated by inarticulate bursts of remorse, the tale of the glorious Battle of Bredill emerged. Vredech nodded and encouraged the confession, but his eyes kept moving to Nertha, who was now sitting by the patient's head. Towards the end, Yan-Elter returned. Vredech motioned him urgently to silence as he came into the room.

When it was finished, Nertha had heard the account that Vredech had given her repeated in every particular, save that there was more, for Iryn's account told also of Cassraw and Yanos's murderous driven march across the countryside to bring their force to Bredill and then to return it to Troidmallos. Encouragement had taken many forms, but predominantly it had consisted of vicious abuse, and later blows and kicks. There were hints in the telling that others than he had simply been abandoned, both going and returning, but Vredech did not press for details. Nor did he press for an account of other things that Cassraw apparently did to keep his warriors moving, as the existence of these seemed to lie in sudden silences, and they obviously inspired a fear in Iryn that was far deeper than any remorse.

'Bravely told, Iryn,' Vredech said when all was apparently finished. 'These were awful deeds, but your feet are on a truer path now. I want you to stay here and rest, and we'll talk again in the morning. There are things to be done which will help undo some of this harm.'

'It's not going to bring anyone back to life, is it?' Iryn said, his hands moving towards his face again, but stopping.

Vredech shook his head. 'No,' he said quietly. 'But we can try to stop others from being killed. A great many others.'

'What's happened?' Yan-Elter demanded as Vredech finally stood up.

'Your mother's all right?' Vredech said, authoritative again.

'Yes, but—'

'I'll tell you what's happened later. Nertha and I have a lot to talk about now. What I want you to do is sit by your brother. Just be there where he can see you. Let him sleep, let him talk, whatever he wants. But *no* questions, do you understand? No questions. Everything will keep until the morning.'

Nertha was looking at him strangely as they sat down again by the fire and she pulled their chairs closer so that they could talk privately.

'I don't know whether I'm more or less frightened after hearing that,' she confessed. 'You really did go into his dream, didn't you?'

'I'll answer your question for you,' Vredech said. 'You're less frightened, because now you don't have to be quite so fearful for my sanity. You're also *more* frightened, because you've never known or heard the like before, and you don't know what's happening or how.'

'All I need is your Whistler to come through the door,' Nertha said, self-mocking.

Vredech smiled and shook his head. 'No, I don't think

499

so,' he said. 'You'd be wondering then whether you, too, had gone insane.'

Nertha reflected his smile then gently admonished him. 'Enough,' she whispered. 'We shouldn't be talking like this after what we've just heard.'

Vredech turned towards Iryn and Yan-Elter. Just as he and Nertha were engaged in a subdued conversation, so were the two brothers.

'An idle street lout,' he said. 'The family misfit. Slipped through caring hands – or jumped, perhaps. Destined for some twilight life at the fringes of our society, and probably prison in the end. But now a murderer under Cassraw's tutelage. As clear a measure of Cassraw's corruption as my telling of his dream was of my own strange . . . ability.' He looked back to Nertha. 'You prefer things to be hard-edged, don't you?' he said.

Nertha met his gaze. 'I'd prefer some things never to be,' she said. 'But yes, given that they are, the more signs point the way, the happier I feel about the direction I'm travelling.'

Vredech took up the analogy. 'Have you thought about what direction we're travelling?' he asked.

'Towards war and horror,' Nertha replied simply. 'It'll take the Felden some time to gather their army together, but when they do they'll come for revenge, I'm sure. And if Cassraw can fire the militia as he fired these Knights of his, then whatever the outcome, there'll be blood spilt and hatred ignited that'll go down through the ages even when the original cause has been long forgotten. Children unborn are already dying of it.'

Vredech shivered at this cruel analysis.

'And where does that leave us?' he asked. 'You and me? The people who know.'

Nertha looked at him for a long time. 'Other than being desperately afraid of what's going to happen and the speed

500

of what's actually happening, I don't know.' She did not carry helplessness well.

'Yes,' Vredech whispered very softly. Then he stood up and walked over to a sideboard. He opened a drawer and after a clumsy search in the comparative darkness, found what he was looking for. He returned to Nertha and gave it to her.

'I've a small medical problem I'd like your help with,' he said.

'It's Father's militia knife,' she said, smiling as she recognized it. She took the knife from its sheath and tested the edge. 'Good as ever. He'd shave with this sometimes just to show off and give us all a fright, do you remember?' Her smile faded and she looked at Vredech anxiously. 'What do you mean, a small medical problem? And what have you got this out for?'

Vredech glanced at Yan-Elter and Iryn, then took the knife from Nertha's unresisting hand. He spoke softly but very deliberately. 'I'm as responsible for those deaths at Bredill as that lad over there. I'm going to take some advice I was given a little time ago but which in my priestly wisdom I chose to ignore. I'll listen to yours, however, and follow it carefully.'

He looked down at the knife, its blade glinting in the firelight. 'I need to know, Physician, the quickest and most effective way of using this to kill Cassraw.'

Chapter 34

It was raining again the following day, a fine vertical drizzle that soaked only a little more slowly than a summer downpour. Grey clouds descended to obscure the mountain tops and to sustain the soft mists that were greying everything else.

But for all the dampness in the air, Troidmallos was alive with activity. Privv's Sheets were everywhere, proclaiming the Chosen One, waxing rapturously about the miracle that had been shown to the assembled throng, announcing the call for the levying of the militia, and eulogizing both Mueran and Marash as martyrs to the new Canol Madreth that was imminent, and was to be the heart of a united Gyronlandt. They even risked suggesting that in the wake of the Chosen One, there might be the Second Coming of Ishryth himself.

'I don't think there's anything even in the wilder reaches of the Santyth about that,' Leck offered tentatively when Privv, riding high on creative hyperbole, had mooted this. She stretched herself. Privv pondered long and hard about her observation, this being so serious a matter, but by the time Leck had finished stretching, he had decided to include it. It was, after all, quite consistent with his normal policy of never allowing facts to stand in the way of his deathless prose.

Needless to say, Privv himself had not actually been present at Cassraw's service – there were limits even to *his*

502

sense of duty towards seeking out the truth, and climbing the Ervrin Mallos was one. Besides, the mounting burdens of his vocation were leaving him ever more exhausted.

In addition to his rhetoric about Cassraw, he also inveighed against the weakness and confusion in the Heindral, and made strident demands for strong and resolute leadership. Atypically, he had allowed Toom Drommel to assist him with that. Drommel had an excellent range of determined adjectives.

The whole, of course, had passed Cassraw's scrutiny and been found good.

The Sheets fed acid into the streams of gossip that were corroding the town. Where there had been indifference, the Sheets turned it into concern, where concern, fear – and where fear, near panic.

Not that everyone was in agreement with the way in which developing events should be handled, but following the Felden invasion and the Battle of Bredill, none could gainsay the need to levy the militia, and under this unanimity there developed an insidious reluctance to raise any voice in dissent.

Throughout Troidmallos and its immediate neighbours, such individuals who had not already been galvanized by the mounting tension were now drawn in. Few darkened corners escaped scrutiny in the search for long-forgotten weaponry and equipment. Fletchers and bowyers were suddenly inundated with work, as were blacksmiths and all other tradesmen whose goods were to be found listed in the Annex to the Militia Statute.

Not that these activities carried any frisson of excitement or celebration. As the dark clouds had infected Cassraw, so now his actions spread a subtler darkness. The atmosphere pervading the town was one of fear. And growing out of the fear, vigorous and strong, came unreason and mindless anger. Skynner was obliged to redeploy many of his men to guard the premises of

503

companies who traded with Tirfelden, as the dregs of Madren society began to cling together and rise to the surface, their ignorance and general ineptitude reforged into raucous self-righteousness. Such Keepers as were not involved in this sudden awakening of social conscience were occupied in dealing with innumerable domestic squabbles and public altercations – not least in the premises of the tradesmen who found themselves so suddenly in demand.

Though harassed, however, Skynner was almost relieved at this activity as it kept his mind from dwelling on the implications of his meeting with the Chief and Toom Drommel. He was uncertain which boded the worst: their assumption that they could use Cassraw to play some game of their own, or their actually believing in him. Not that he could keep such thoughts at bay all the time, and whenever they returned to him, he found himself glancing up towards the summit of the Ervrin Mallos. It was shrouded in mist, but he sensed that had he been able to see it, the strange haze that had grown there and then had briefly faded, would be present again, probably more pronounced than ever. For the first time in many years he began to get stomach-ache.

Thoughts of Albor, too, would emerge unexpectedly in the middle of the day's turmoil. These disturbed him even more than his concerns about the Chief and his intentions, and they were less easily set aside, there being so many small reminders of his friend and colleague about the Keeperage. And with the memories of Albor came thoughts about the murderer. Grim, fearful thoughts, like a deep, unheard note underlying the cacophony of all that was happening around him. That many more innocent people now fretting through their ordinary lives might be within weeks, perhaps even days, of death, when they might reasonably have expected years, did not lessen his anger and frustration at these random murders. It unsettled him profoundly that all his experience and his knowledge of Troidmallos and its people had yielded nothing in his investigations. Somewhere, possibly with an accomplice, a monstrous creature wearing the appearance of an ordinary person was still walking the town.

Walking, watching, waiting, for the opportunity to kill again.

And he, Serjeant Keeper, guardian of the law and the people, was lost and floundering. He could do nothing – except fail in his most fundamental duty, doomed to await the next killing and hope that something, someone, might be seen, or some clue be left to which he could cling and which might bring him to the killer. All he had learned so far was that the murderer was physically powerful. He must be, to have defeated Albor man to man . . .

And before his thoughts could begin to circle fruitlessly, Skynner would turn again to the more pressing needs of the day.

Vredech wrapped his cloak about him. It was sodden, but it was still keeping the rain from him. After spending the remainder of the night sleeping fitfully in his chair, he had risen silently at dawn and managed to leave the Meeting House without disturbing anyone. He needed to be alone and to think.

Nertha had greeted the declaration of his intention to kill Cassraw with a confusion of emotions, not the least of which had been disbelief. They had conducted a bizarre, whispered dispute for fear of waking the dozing Yan-Elter. As the seriousness of Vredech's intention eventually emerged, Nertha had fallen silent and stared at him intently, her eyes searching his face.

'I'm no more mad than I was before,' Vredech said, reading her look. 'You're the logical one. Find me an alternative.'

505

'It's not a matter of logic,' Nertha said.

Once, such an admission would have given Vredech the opportunity for an ironic rejoinder, but his mood could admit no humour.

'Isn't it?' he said coldly. 'I could pray, I suppose.' Nertha looked distressed at the cynicism in his voice, but Vredech went on, 'Oddly enough, my prayers mean more now than they've ever meant. After thinking I had lost you the other day, and then finding you and standing by you, looking out across the valleys – so beautiful – I think I understand Ishrythan more than ever before. My faith seems to be changing. I don't seem to need Ishryth Himself so much. It's strange. Cassraw says his . . . mentor . . . reveals the inner truths of the Santyth to him. Well, I think I've found them for myself. I suppose I should be grateful for that.' He paused, as his thoughts swung back to matters practical. 'But more than ever I know that what part of our destiny lies in our hands, we are responsible for, completely.' Nertha tried to intervene, but he silenced her. 'You and I have been shown what's happening. And Horld – maybe even Skynner. They will do what they must do, in their own judgements. And I will do what I must do in mine. I'll be able to get close to him—'

Nertha burst in: 'Allyn, stop talking like that, you're frightening me. You're no more a murderer than I am. You're physically incapable of killing anyone. You killed a bird with a catapult once then cried yourself to sleep for two nights. Do you think you can kill Cassraw, an old friend, whom you've known all your life, even allowing for what he's turned into?' Then something seemed to snap inside her and she almost snarled, 'And you don't know what you're talking about, for mercy's sake. Look!' Before Vredech could prevent her, she had snatched the knife from him, unsheathed it and, thrusting the handle into his hand, drawn it towards herself so that the point was almost

506

touching her throat. 'Here's where you'd do it. Like this,' she said savagely, showing him. 'You're right. You'd probably be able to get near enough to him to do it, but could you push this blade in?' She drew it nearer to her throat, forcing Vredech to pull back in alarm. 'And if you do, shall I tell you what'll happen?' Vredech stared at her, wide-eyed. 'It won't be like cutting yourself shaving. There'll be blood spouting everywhere as his heart bursts itself trying to stop the wound, from here to that wall – and splattering across it. And there'll be noises that'll ring in your ears for ever. Not to mention the look on his face.' She held his gaze fiercely for a long moment, then her hands went suddenly limp. The knife slipped out of Vredech's grip and fell with a thud to the floor.

'Are you all right?' Yan-Elter's sleepy voice made them both start.

Nertha recovered first. 'Yes,' she said hoarsely. 'How's Iryn?'

'He seems quieter.'

'Good. Go back to sleep. We've done everything we can for him. We'll have to see what the morning brings.'

Yan-Elter nodded and drifted off to sleep again. Vredech picked up the knife.

'Promise me you won't do anything foolish,' Nertha said, taking his arm. She was not sobbing, but tears were running down her face. 'There's another way somewhere.' Vredech made to stand up but her grip was too strong. 'Promise!' she demanded. 'We'll think of something if we give it a little time.'

'Time?' Vredech exclaimed. He brought his face close to hers. 'It's scarcely ten days since Cassraw's first sermon, Nertha. Ten days! It feels as though it were some other age, but . . .' He was going to mention the Whistler's remarks about events moving with great speed but he stopped himself. 'We probably don't have any time left. Who can say what'll have happened in another ten days?'

507

Nertha just said simply, 'Promise me you'll do nothing foolish.'

Vredech looked at her thoughtfully, then nodded. 'Very well,' he said, pushing the knife into his belt. 'I'll do nothing foolish.'

Nor will I, he thought, as the murmured but frantic debate came back to him yet again. He was shivering. Not with the dampness of the day which, oddly enough, he welcomed; the obliteration of the mountains and the greying of all else seemed to leave his mind free to roam unhindered by things familiar. He was shivering because he was afraid. He would do nothing foolish, true, he had promised. But killing Cassraw was not an act of folly, it was one of wisdom and necessity. People had died already because of his neglect, though he took some solace in the knowledge that he could not possibly have followed the Whistler's advice when it had first been given to him. That certainly would not have been rational. But now? Although, as he had said, only a few days had passed since Cassraw's first demented sermon, it was indeed a different age now. So very different. For a moment, Vredech began again to doubt the reality of all that was happening. After all, had he not been drawn into a world that was still Canol Madreth when he had met Horld on the mountain? Perhaps somewhere he was walking through a rain-shrouded park in a world where he could return to his Meeting House to sit in its comforting warmth and talk with Nertha and look to a future that was once again knowable. A world in which Cassraw was his old friendly argumentative self, untainted by whatever had lured him into the darkness.

The idea brought a lump to Vredech's throat and tears to his eyes but he pushed them away. There was no alternative but to do what he was going to do.

Nertha's savage exposition about how to use the knife had been cruelly effective, deeply unmanning him, and the images she had conjured kept returning to taunt him. But he was no longer the child who had cried himself to sleep for the gratuitous slaying of a bird. The killing of Cassraw might perhaps cost him his sanity, maybe even his life, but he had been shown, or had imagined, it mattered not, the ravages that would come to countless thousands if Cassraw's dark and primitive view of Ishrythan were to spread. Reality might well be underlain by beauty and simplicity, but in its workings, in the many combinings of this simplicity, it was complex and subtle, full of shifting needs and decisions that required continuously the weaving, learning, skills of Ishryth's second greatest gift, the mind, to judge any course of action. No book, not even the Santyth, for all the wisdom it contained, could hold such knowledge. Still less, could one man. And any man who claimed such knowledge and would seek to impose it, seek to constrain the incalculable spirit of a people into the suffocating limits of his own ignorance and fear, could bring only destruction.

As he was already doing.

Vredech sat down on a bench beneath a broad canopied tree. The bench and the grass about him were still dry. He was calmer now. His thoughts had run so many courses so often that they had finally fallen silent. He reached inside his cloak and laid his hand on the knife.

What are you doing, Priest, even thinking of taking life? he asked himself again. But the question no longer meant anything. Nor did he listen to Nertha's plea that some other way could be found. Instead he clung to Iryn's nightmare. He was prepared to take that upon himself if it saved others having to suffer it. That *was* a priestly duty.

And now he must await events. Confine himself to simple practical matters, such as where he might find Cassraw. Would he be at the Haven Meeting House, or was he already assuming his role of Covenant Member and establishing himself at the Witness House?

All he had to do was ask.

But he'd sit here a little longer, in the grey stillness. Think about the sunset he had seen from the hillside with the Whistler playing his meandering flute, and the view across the valleys as he had stood by Nertha. Appreciate what you have while you have it, then the pain of parting from it would be less.

It was true.

But still he did not want to part from it, nor confront the pain of what he had to do.

His concerns slowly left him as he looked at the shadows of the trees in the misting rain and listened to the steady hiss of its fall and the occasional spluttering rattle as a solitary drop would cause a leaf to shed its tiny load on to the leaves below, and thence to more leaves until finally a cascade of many drops splashed to the ground.

He leaned back against the tree. As he did so, he noticed a movement in the distance. It took him a moment to bring two figures into focus.

They were walking slowly towards him.

Chapter 35

Vredech felt a small twinge of irritation at this disturbance of his contemplation. Still, he thought, they'll probably pass on their way. It was unlikely that anyone would be abroad today other than on some necessary errand. He watched them idly. Both were cloaked and hooded. One, he judged, was about his height and build, while the other was a little shorter but more heavily built.

As they drew nearer, it seemed that they would indeed walk past, but one of them glanced casually at him then stopped and held out a hand to detain his partner. There was a brief conversation then they walked directly towards him. Vredech's irritation increased but he managed to keep it from his face.

'Good day,' the shorter one said courteously. Vredech noted the speaker's foreign accent with surprise.

'Good day,' he replied automatically, standing up.

The stranger bowed slightly. 'Please forgive me accosting you like this,' he said, 'but I notice from your dress that you are a priest in the local religion.'

Local religion! Vredech felt mildly demeaned, but he replied that yes, he was.

The stranger held out his hand. 'My name is Darke.' He emphasized the last syllable. 'And this is my friend Tirec. We're travellers . . . scholars. May we talk to you, or are we disturbing you?'

The man's gentle assuredness transformed the remainder of Vredech's annoyance into self-reproach. He ventured a small joke by way of reparation. 'Not at all,' he smiled, extending his hand towards the bench. 'Please join me in my office.' For a little while at least, he would be able to put aside thoughts about what he had to do. He introduced himself. On hearing his name, Darke looked pleasantly surprised.

'We've heard of you,' he said. 'And are honoured to meet you. You're highly thought of by such as we've spoken to.'

Unskilled in receiving compliments, Vredech coughed awkwardly and changed the subject. 'Sadly, you've chosen an evil time to visit our country,' he said as he sat down. 'It grieves me to have to say this, but I'm afraid, being foreigners, you may even be at some risk. There is a great deal of confusion about.'

'Yes,' Darke nodded. 'Though the confusion, as you call it, is mainly around Troidmallos, and directed towards those from the west – the Felden?' Vredech nodded. 'The further reaches of your land are less troubled and so far all your countrymen have been most obliging to us.'

'If a little distant?' Vredech inquired, noting a hesitation.

The man gave a slight shrug.

'We are apt to be reserved with strangers,' Vredech explained, smiling again. 'It's a national trait, I'm afraid, and one I take no pride in admitting. I hope you've not been offended by our seeming coldness?'

Darke shook his head. 'We've travelled through many countries and have learned to accept the different ways of many peoples. We've also learned that apparently major differences between communities are often little deeper than the various costumes they wear. Underneath, people are very much the same everywhere.'

Vredech, suddenly feeling very parochial, found himself

wholly absorbed in what Darke was saying. It was Tirec who spoke next, however. From his face Vredech took him to be about his own age though, like Darke, who was perhaps nearer World's age, his mannerisms were those of a younger man. 'To be honest, we're quite content not to have been attacked in the street after reading this,' he said, pulling out a neatly folded copy of Privv's Sheet.

Vredech's nose wrinkled in distaste. 'You treat it with more respect than it deserves,' he said. 'Screw it up and use it to light your camp fire, or put it to some other simple practical use when you're away from the comforts of civilization. I beg you, don't judge us by that.'

Tirec grinned, but Darke's manner was more sober. 'We treat it with the respect that all dangerous things warrant: fires, floods, sharpened edges.'

Vredech's grim preoccupations returned at this last remark, and without thinking, he patted the knife in his belt. 'Don't you have Sheets in your own country?' he asked.

'We have the printed word and many books, and many ways of carrying the news of events, but nothing like this.'

'Not when we left, anyway,' Tirec added.

'True,' Darke conceded.

'Consider yourselves fortunate,' Vredech said warmly.

Darke looked at the Sheet. 'We have several of them to take with us for study,' he said. 'They seem like a worthwhile idea.'

Vredech gave a heartfelt sigh. 'They *are* a worthwhile idea,' he agreed. 'But Privv . . .' He hesitated. 'Privv's an undisciplined scoundrel with a gift for words and he seems to be getting worse by the day.'

'We were coming to that conclusion ourselves,' Darke said. 'Though why anyone should wish to embellish the truth so, defies me. Can't he be restrained in any way?'

'It's too complicated to explain,' Vredech replied. 'And of little value to you to know, I suspect. If you wish these things to be let loose on your own land, then learn from what you've seen here. Whatever lawmakers you have, have them oblige a writer of Sheets to confine himself to the truth.'

'I'll remember your advice,' Darke said.

Vredech suddenly had the feeling that he had been tested in some way, and that these two strangers needed no advice on the running of a Sheet. Darke looked at him intently. 'May I ask you something delicate?' he said.

'Of course,' Vredech replied, as much out of curiosity as from priestly habit.

'I think this man, Privv, has done your community great harm,' Darke said. 'More perhaps than you know. Please tell me to hold my peace if I offend you – just attribute it to a rash foreigner's ignorance – but it seems to us that even greater harm is coming from the heart of your own religion.' Vredech bridled slightly, but it was more a reflex than a true response. 'This Brother Cassraw seems to be . . .' Darke searched for the words he needed '. . . unusually naive in his preaching, and rather at odds with what, in my limited understanding, I take to be the main tenets of your religion as set out in your Santyth.'

Vredech looked at him closely. 'You've studied the Santyth?' he asked.

'I've read it,' Darke said. 'Not studied it.'

'What are you scholars of?' Vredech asked.

Darke smiled broadly. 'Everything, Brother Vredech. We put reins only on our conduct, not our minds. There are so many wonders to be seen, to be learned about, to stand in awe before, to celebrate.' He reached down, plucked a tiny white flower and brought it close to his face. 'Even though a lifetime of such journeying may not even tell us all there is to know about this single, solitary flower. For then, I suspect, we would know everything.'

'How strange,' Vredech said, genuinely moved by

Darke's manner. 'I was thinking similar thoughts myself only a moment ago.'

Darke looked at him intently again, then seemed to reach a decision. 'This is hardly a cheering day,' he said, looking around. 'Would I be right in assuming that you're sitting here in the stillness and silence because of your concern about the conduct of your colleague?'

Briefly, Vredech was disposed to be indignant about this question, but it was too accurate. It hurt, however, and the pain came through in his answer. 'Yes,' he replied simply. 'Though I don't see what business it is of yours.'

Darke laid a hand on his arm. 'I apologize for the hurt of the remark, Brother Vredech,' he said, 'but I had a reason for asking the question.'

'Where are you from?' Vredech asked bluntly, reluctant to return to the topic of his own worries. 'You speak our language well, but I can't place your accent at all.'

'We're from the north,' Darke said, adding as Vredech started to shake his head: 'From beyond the mountains. Our home is far, far away.'

Where Vredech had felt parochial at unexpectedly meeting these foreigners, he now felt small and insignificant. Beyond the mountains was tantamount to being on the moon for most of the people of Gyronlandt, and he was no exception. He had heard that occasionally, travellers from the lands to the north would come through the mountains to some of the countries along the northern boundary of Gyronlandt, but to actually meet such people . . .

It tore open the tight cocoon of his own concerns and for a moment he felt disorientated as this brief insight into a larger world sank in.

'Are you all right?' he heard Darke asking.

'Yes, yes,' Vredech replied, a little embarrassed. 'I'm sorry. You surprised me.' Then, his cocoon seeking to make itself whole again, he asked sharply, 'Why are you here? There's precious few people in Gyronlandt bother to come to Canol Madreth. Why should such as you, from so far away? There are richer, more exciting states in Gyronlandt to lure travellers.'

Darke did not reply at once, but his hand twitched nervously. As did Tirec's.

Vredech's emotions, still unsteady, swung to suspicion. 'You said you knew of me. Have you sought me out on purpose?' he demanded.

Darke smiled broadly and shook his head. 'No,' he replied. 'We came to Troidmallos on purpose, but finding you here, now, was . . .' He shrugged. 'Fate, destiny, whatever you choose to call it. Personally I'm quite happy to settle for chance. I think, however, that we would have sought you out in due course.'

Vredech allowed his suspicions to show. 'Why have you come to Troidmallos, then? And why would you want to see me?' he asked. Darke's smile faded and a slight spasm of pain passed over his face. He reached up and massaged his shoulder. This time it was Vredech who inquired, 'Are you all right?'

'Yes,' Darke replied. 'I hurt it falling off a horse once. It gets a little stiff sometimes.' He gave his shoulder a final shake. 'And I can't answer your question, not directly. As much as anything, we've been *drawn* here.'

'Drawn?'

Darke glanced at his companion, as if for advice.

'Ask him, he'll understand. He's the one we need to speak to,' Tirec said, answering the unspoken question. He gave an urgent nod of encouragement. 'This place is frightening me to death. We need to know.'

Vredech frowned at this enigmatic remark. Darke fumbled with the copy of the Sheet, then placed it carefully in his pocket.

'Brother Vredech,' he said. 'Bear with me, please. I'll tell you what I can, but I need your help first.' He did not wait for a reply. 'We've learned many things since we came here, just by listening to gossip and asking the occasional question. Please tell me if I'm inaccurate in any particulars.' Vredech's frown deepened, but Darke continued. 'Several months ago, a darkness came over this land. Your colleague, Cassraw, stormed up into this darkness in a great rage. When he returned, he believed he had been chosen by your deity, Ishryth, to bring about some great "purifying" of the land, for want of a better word. And since that time, your country has begun a seemingly unstoppable plunge into decay and disorder.' He watched Vredech carefully. 'We've heard, too, that he's been given certain powers. Powers that he used the other night to control the rain. Is this a reasonable gathering of what's happened?'

'It is,' Vredech said. 'But—'

Darke brought his finger to his lips for silence, at once apologetic and authoritative. 'We've heard also that you, and a Brother . . . Horld, I think was the name . . . went after Cassraw on that day, and we know that you've been gently striving to oppose what he's been doing since his return.' His gaze allowed Vredech no escape. 'Although I'm a complete stranger to you, Brother Vredech, I'll ask you to trust me,' he said. 'I'll ask you to tell me what happened to *you* when you went up into that darkness after Cassraw, and what you think has happened to *him*.'

Vredech opened his mouth to speak, but his throat was dry. 'Who are you?' was all he could manage.

'We are who we say we are,' Darke replied. 'Travellers and scholars. And I'll tell you what I can in a moment, as I promised, but please, tell me what happened to you that day. And since.'

Vredech looked away from Darke and caught Tirec's eye. Though the younger man was striving to hide it, there was fear in his eyes, and Tirec did not give the impression of a man who frightened easily. Slowly, Vredech lowered his head and closed his eyes.

'In your travels, have you ever heard of a man called the Whistler?' he asked into the darkness. 'A legend – a story, perhaps?'

He was aware of Darke shifting awkwardly beside him. 'I've heard all manner of tales about pipers, flute-players, whistlers, in different places. In some he walks in dreams, in others he walks strange worlds, worlds like this but in some way beyond, his tunes building the bridges between, or binding them together. Some say he's mad, some say he's a great righter of wrongs, a fighter of evil. Some tell of him as a man trapped in his own dream.'

'Are there worlds beyond this, Traveller?' Vredech asked. 'Worlds around us that are here, yet not here?'

There was a long silence.

'I've heard it said so, and by people wiser than me by far,' Darke replied eventually. 'It's a disturbing thought, enough to shake any man's sanity. Why do you ask?'

Vredech did not reply, but let out a long breath. Then he opened his eyes and looked up. A small flurry of raindrops cascaded from the leaves above. Most fell on the grass at his feet, twinkling momentarily despite the dullness, but a few fell cold on his hair. He ran his hand over them.

It occurred to him that he had slipped into another world again and that the two men were of his own creating. But did it matter? he thought. No harm had come to him previously from such excursions. Indeed, on the last occasion it had perhaps saved Nertha from some dreadful fate and, in involving Horld, much good had come of it. He could see now that, each time, he had come away a little wiser. Suddenly, it was as though a keystone had fallen into place, locking together disparate and unstable parts into a solid whole. He was in the world he had always known. And he would know in future when it was otherwise, though he could not have defined the source of this new certainty.

Then, without preamble, he told Darke and Tirec what had happened on the mountain and since. He made no mention of his own pain or of his meetings with the Whistler, and he spoke in unconscious imitation of Darke, simply and straightforwardly.

As he talked, he saw the fear in Tirec's eyes grow, and pain appear in Darke's. When he had finished, they both remained silent.

'I've thought myself mad on more than one occasion these past months,' Vredech admitted, 'battling endlessly with screaming doubts.' Then, slowly, he asked, 'What does this mean to you?'

Neither replied for some time, then Tirec stood up and began pacing to and fro. He spoke to Darke in his own language, though the strangeness of it could not disguise the fear-driven anger that filled it.

Darke looked at him then very gently said, 'Of course it's true. We've known it all along.' He rubbed his shoulder again. 'We've just not had the courage to accept it.'

Tirec seemed disposed to argue the point, but Darke motioned him to sit. 'And speak Madren in front of Brother Vredech,' he said, with a hint of sternness. Tirec sat down heavily.

Vredech waited. He was about to repeat his question when Darke began to speak. 'In our land, we know of the one you call Ishryth,' he said.

Vredech could not contain his surprise. 'You worship as we do?' he asked.

Darke smiled, rather sadly Vredech thought, and shook his head. 'No, we accord all things respect, in so far as we are able, but we worship nothing and no one.'

'But—'

Darke held up his hand for silence.

'This may be hard for you,' he said, 'but it's known that from the Great Heat at the beginning of this world, Ishryth and his three companions – the Watchers, I think you call them – emerged and, through a time that we cannot measure, shaped the world as we know it, and all that's in it.'

' "Known"?' Vredech queried, briefly a theologian again. 'Believed, surely.'

Darke shook his head. 'Known,' he confirmed. 'As certainly as anything past can be known. There are unbroken lines of recorded thought back through the ages to the time when he walked amongst men.'

Vredech was suddenly alarmed. Was he dealing with people whose religious beliefs were as primitive and simplistic as those to which Cassraw was reverting?

'I see your doubts,' Darke went on, 'and I understand them. Just accept what I say for the time being. There's a body of knowledge available which will withstand your finest scholarship, believe me. We're a clear-sighted and inquiring people.' He waved a dismissive hand. 'But that's by the by. Suffice it that Ishryth and his companions existed and did what they did. So also did the creature you call Ahmral. It's said that He, too, came from the same Great Heat, but even Ishryth did not know this. What He did is touched on in your Santyth. He took on human form – or perhaps already possessed it – and destroyed Ishryth's work wherever He could, the focus of His greatest endeavours always being the destruction of life. Men were His most apt pupils, His greatest allies.'

'And in the Last Battle He ventured forth amid the pitiless slaughter of men by men, seeking to slay Ishryth, unarmed and at prayer. But around their lord stood a circle of his Chosen, barbed sharp with spear and sword, and seeing it, Ahmral faltered and was brought low. And with the passing of His body so was His spirit scattered. Yet His teachings lingered.'

Darke nodded in response to Vredech's quotation from the Santyth. 'That is from what you call the Lesser Books, is it not?' he said.

'Yes,' Vredech replied. 'Its origins are uncertain and it's read as an allegory.'

'It's no allegory,' Darke said starkly. 'It's substantially accurate.'

Vredech frowned. Darke cut through his thinking. 'I appreciate you've no way of knowing this, but I'm neither simpleton, madman nor jester, Brother Vredech,' he said, with unexpected authority. 'I am, however, a long way from home and the people I need to speak to about what's happening here – the same people who could show you the truth of what I'm going to tell you. And, like Tirec here, I'm also desperately afraid about what we're discovering.'

'I don't know what to say,' Vredech said.

'Say nothing for the moment, just listen,' Darke replied. As if he could no longer contain it, strain showed suddenly on his face. 'Ask whatever questions you wish when I've finished.'

'Very well,' Vredech said, though with some reluctance.

Darke began. 'Several years ago, through a combination of evil chances and, sadly, our neglect, Ahmral rose again. Took mortal form again.' Vredech's eyes widened but he managed to stay silent. 'And too, His ancient lieutenants – those you call the Uleryn – were roused. They were out in the world raising armies to free Him from the bleak land where we unwittingly surrounded Him, before it was discovered what had happened.' He paused before continuing, though whether to marshal his thoughts or to contain some powerful emotion, Vredech could not tell. 'I'll spare you the details, but in the end, like a faint echo of earlier times, an alliance was formed and battles were fought and He and His Uleryn were destroyed.' Then in a tone that cut through Vredech in its pain; 'As we thought.'

Vredech wanted to be able to laugh out loud into the

silence that followed, to dismiss this rambling nonsense out of hand, to declare these two strangers obviously deranged. But Darke's telling had wrapped about him like a damp, clinging sheet, binding him, chilling him, with an awful certainty.

'He's come again,' he heard himself saying. It was not a question.

'His hand is here, for sure,' Darke said. 'I can offer no stern logic for this, but my every instinct tells me that dreadful events are in the offing. Your Cassraw does His will. And there is a strangeness lingering visibly about the summit of your holy mountain the like of which I've never seen before. Nor Tirec, and he was born to mountains.'

'Bridgehead,' Vredech said softly.

Darke's brow furrowed quizzically.

'A foothold in enemy territory,' Vredech continued. 'To it, He will come, and through it pass amongst us. He waits only for the temple that Cassraw will build, then . . .' He left the conclusion unspoken.

Darke and Tirec glanced at one another.

'What makes you say that?' Tirec asked.

'Who slew Him?' Vredech asked, ignoring the question. The two men looked at him uncertainly. 'Who slew Him?' he said again with some force. 'Ahmral! You said He was destroyed. Who destroyed Him? Who wielded the sword? Did you see Him slain? Did you see His body?'

'We were . . . nearby,' Darke said after some hesitation. 'But no man slew Him. He destroyed Himself.'

'Be specific,' Vredech said coldly, his father's voice echoing through his head as he spoke. It was a command that his two listeners seemed to appreciate.

'This will not be easy,' Darke said.

Vredech gave a grim laugh. 'This was never going to be an easy day,' he said. 'Just tell me your tale.'

'As you wish,' Darke replied, though again, his face was pained. 'He was destroyed because He believed that a

522

flickering remnant of Ishryth's conscious spirit was in fact Ishryth re-born, as He had been. In His rage – or terror – He unleashed such power that His human frame could not contain it and was destroyed utterly, as was the great citadel that He had built.'

But Vredech scarcely heard the tale. 'What do you mean, a flickering remnant?' he exclaimed. 'Ishryth is the Source and Creator of all things – this world, the stars, the whole universe. He is Supreme . . .'

Darke cut across his outburst. 'Ishryth came from the beginning of this world, and formed it thus. What was before, no one knows. What he is, or was, no one knows: save that for a time he took human form. But he did not create this world, still less the stars. If there is a Supreme Being, it is not Ishryth. And how could *we* frame such a creature in our puny minds? Two things Ishryth said as he faded from the final conflict. That he was amongst us all now, and that both he and Ahmral were aberrations of the Great Heat from which they came. Make of that what you will.'

Fabric's torn, 'fore all was born . . .

Vredech felt as though he had been suddenly plunged into freezing water. He began to gasp for breath. As he had in the strange night meeting with Horld on the Ervrin Mallos, he felt his mind lurching into darkness, all points of familiarity, of anchorage, gone. What were these two men? Were they indeed creations of his own? Was the Whistler? Were they Ahmral's demons taunting him?

But no sooner did these thoughts appear than they vanished, and the certainty that had formed about him earlier returned. He could not test Darke's story, subject it to any theological rigour, but it was as if it had reached below his thinking mind and shone a light into the doubts and hesitations he had fearfully stored there over the years. He felt the death of many things that he had accepted as articles of faith, but there was no true pain, no sense of loss. He had been given more questions than answers, but they were wise questions and asked in a wider, more wondrous world. He had told Nertha that his faith was changing but now, at the touch of this story, he saw that, as a dried and shrivelled seed becomes a flower, or a caterpillar a butterfly, so his faith had been transformed into something far greater than it had ever been.

He was who he was and he was where he was. And still he must do what he had set out to do, though it cost him his life. But now, there was hope. Now he was no longer pitted against a supernatural evil rooted in the essence of creation, but against the all-too-human evil he had heard exulting as it took possession of Cassraw on the Ervrin Mallos.

He looked at Darke. The man's face was full of pain and guilt. 'Don't reproach yourself,' Vredech said. 'The truth is always to be preferred to ignorance, however painful. And I'm in your debt more than I could begin to explain to you. Tell me now why you're here.'

Darke looked as though he wanted to pursue further the hurt he might have done, but Vredech's manner gave him no opportunity.

'Ahmral returned because of our negligence and our ignorance,' he said uncomfortably. 'Now many of us are travelling the world. Some to seek out enemies who fled after the battle and who must be brought to account, others . . .' He indicated Tirec and himself '. . . to learn more of the world beyond our own self-satisfied boundaries. And to see how far and how deeply His teachings had spread.'

'And now you've found Him whom you'd thought destroyed?'

'It would seem so. We heard and felt both His death scream and the destruction of His citadel. They were not things to be either misunderstood or forgotten. And those skilled in such matters pronounced Him gone. Yet . . .'

'Yet the stink of Him is all around you?'

Darke nodded. 'An apt phrase,' he said.

'I heard it from someone else who knows Him,' Vredech said. Darke's eyes widened, but before he could speak, Vredech asked, 'What will you do?'

Darke shook his head. 'I don't know. We could try to destroy Cassraw, I suppose, but I doubt we'd get close enough from what we've seen of him so far. And we know from experience that people who have gained such powers are often armoured in ways we cannot understand. But what did you mean by "someone else who knows him"?'

'You must return to your own people,' Vredech said. 'Tell them everything you've heard and seen.' He leaned forward earnestly. 'And tell them this. It's important. There *are* worlds beyond this. I cannot say how and why, but I've been drawn to them of late, and it's shaken my sanity to the core. But they are there as surely as we are here. And somewhere, spread through and between them, distorting, twisting, His spirit exists still. He's done hurt in other places than this. Perhaps it's there He must be sought, I don't know. And tell your people, too, that though He is still strong by our lights, He was grievously weakened by what you did to Him.' He held Darke's gaze. 'Will you tell them this?'

Darke's eyes were searching. 'Yes, I will,' he said. 'But . . .'

'As for Cassraw,' Vredech went on, allowing no interruption, 'you were correct – you'll not even be able to get near him. But he's my friend, my Brother in the church, my responsibility. *I* will kill him.'

Darke started at this last pronouncement, then Vredech could see him calculating. He felt no resentment.

'You're a priest,' Darke said eventually. 'A priest in what, for all its ignorance, is at heart a humane and compassionate church. You couldn't do it.'

Vredech drew the knife from under his robe. He heard a

slight hiss from Tirec but before he knew what was happening, Darke had seized his hand and twisted the knife from it. He gasped as he found himself powerless in a grip that scarcely seemed to he holding him. Darke handed the knife to Tirec. 'Sorry,' he said to Vredech, though there was little apology in his voice. 'You startled me. Old reflexes, I'm afraid.'

Tirec was examining the knife. 'Not bad,' he said. 'Bit rough, but robust and practical. Quite a good edge, too.' Darke inclined his head and Tirec handed the knife back to Vredech who took it with a shaking hand.

'You were going to show me something with it?' Darke said.

Vredech put the knife back in its sheath clumsily. 'Yes,' he said, then, using his hand he offered it to Darke's throat. 'Like this, I was told,' he said, demonstrating what Nertha had shown him. 'It'll make . . . a mess . . . I believe.'

Darke nodded unhappily and as he looked up Vredech saw tears in his eyes. 'Yes, it will indeed,' he said hoarsely. 'But it's as good a way as any. My heart tells me I should dissuade you, but I can see you'd come to this of your own free will before you met us, and all I can do is to wish you luck.' He looked away for a moment, then said 'It *is* the right thing to do, I fear, but if I may counsel you briefly, clear your mind of all doubts before you come close. All doubts. And come close before you draw the weapon. Then don't hesitate, not for even the blink of an eye. It's the only way. For both of you.'

'I understand,' Vredech said.

'I think perhaps you do,' Darke nodded.

'What will you do now?' Vredech asked, anxious not to pursue the matter further.

'Perhaps stay a little longer. Learn a little more,' Darke replied.

Vredech looked nervous. 'I will act today,' he said.

526

'While I have the resolve and before Cassraw grows even stronger. I'd be more settled in my mind if I knew you were carrying news of these happenings to someone who can understand them.'

Darke stood up. 'Then we'll burden you no further,' he said. 'We'll leave immediately.'

Vredech, too, stood up and extended his hand. Darke took it. 'I'll counsel you again, Brother Vredech,' he said, 'for I can see death in your eyes. The death of the wrong person – you.' His grip tightened. 'You're at war, Priest. There's no law for you now except survival, and you *must* look to survive or you'll die for sure. Don't be afraid to look to tomorrow. There'll be one, and you'll have much to do in it. There are no endings or beginnings. Remember.'

Vredech did not know how to reply. 'So many questions,' he said.

Darke smiled a little. 'Always,' he replied.

Tirec reached out and took Vredech's hand in both of his. He was more openly concerned than was Darke, but his voice was steady when he spoke. 'Thank you,' he said simply. 'Live well, and light be with you.'

Vredech stood watching them as they walked away. Before they faded into the mist, they turned and waved to him.

Then they were gone.

Chapter 36

Vredech sat for a while after the two men had left and pondered the strange meeting. What was it Darke had said? 'Fate, destiny, whatever you choose to call it. Personally I'm quite happy to settle for chance.'

Chance . . .

Travellers from a far distant land. And bringing such tidings.

But 'drawn here', Darke had said. Vredech moved his shoulder as if to ease it, mimicking Darke's movement. Strange word, 'drawn', he thought. Like hunters after prey.

Yet they were hunters of a kind those two, for all their quiet words, he decided. They communicated with one another in silence, and Darke had taken the knife from him with breathless ease. And how strange, too, that he should feel more kinship with them than with almost anyone he'd ever known. Perhaps that was what happened to people who had been touched by Him. A deep awareness of a common and awful foe.

And what of his faith? Darke's revelations should perhaps have shattered it, yet, he felt more whole than ever before.

It surprised him that he was accepting such changes so easily.

What forces were moving beneath the surface here?

He looked down at his hand then lifted and lowered it.

He had his free will, as far as he could tell. The question was thus not only unanswerable, it was irrelevant.

'You're a warrior, not a priest,' the Whistler had said. 'You resort to violence very easily.' Vredech laid a hand on the knife. 'You both care about people after your own fashion.' That remark he understood now. And its deep irony. For true warriors honed their dark skills so that by understanding violence they could better dedicate themselves to avoiding it. He smiled sadly. Turning *easily* to violence was the prerogative of intemperate priests, and others who were loath to accept the violence inherent in their own natures.

So many questions.

Always.

He walked slowly back to his Meeting House.

He found Nertha absent and House in a fluster. 'Those two men have gone,' House announced. Vredech had to pause for a moment before he recalled Yan-Elter and Iryn. 'The young man seemed much quieter,' House said, before he began to feel guilty about this neglect. 'His brother said they'd come back later to talk.'

'And Nertha?'

'She's looking for you, young man.' Vredech wilted under the reproach and House rubbed it in. 'She seemed worried.'

Vredech suddenly felt chilled to his heart. The return to familiar surroundings and House's concerns had temporarily made him forget the deed he had set himself to do that day. Now it was on him again in all its horror.

'I didn't want to wake her,' he mumbled, moving past House into his office. 'I have to go out again in a few minutes. Tell her to wait here when she comes back. Tell her not to worry.'

'What about *my* worries, Brother Vredech?' House exclaimed. 'You coming in wringing wet then going out again straight away. Nertha wandering the town with all this trouble going on, and her wearing those Felden clothes of hers.'

Vredech stiffened angrily, but managed to think before he spoke. 'It's only my cloak that's wet,' he said, not entirely succeeding in keeping the effort out of his voice. 'And I doubt anyone's going to see Nertha's clothes under hers. Please don't concern yourself.'

'Easy to say,' House retorted, 'but there'll be some scenes today, you mark my words, what with Brother Cassraw speaking in the Heindral and all. I'll not rest until she's safe.'

'Where did you hear that?' Vredech asked, suddenly urgent.

House waved an airy hand. 'Everyone's talking about it.'

Vredech frowned as he pondered this news.

'He's the new Covenant Member, they say,' House added. 'Poor Brother Mueran. So sudden.'

'Yes, of course,' Vredech said, as reassuringly as he could. It was an old tradition that a newly-appointed Covenant Member address the Heindral, but for Vredech it was a further measure of the change in Cassraw that he had dismissed such a trifling detail as his election by the Chapter – a matter which was by no means a formality. Far worse than that however, was the prospect of Cassraw having the attention of the Heindral. Almost certainly, every Heinder would be present, and there would be a substantial public crowd as well. And while it was also a tradition that such a speech be bland and uncontroversial, he knew that for Cassraw this was simply an opportunity to subject an important audience to his powerful binding oratory. Undoubtedly, too, he would perform some 'miracle' to convince any waverers of the truth of his claim to be Ishryth's Chosen One. Rational debate and discussion would not be able to make itself heard over his ranting emotion.

Vredech became very calm. Now at least he did not have to look for Cassraw. And his assessment of what was likely to happen had made his planned assassination even more imperative.

'I'll get your other cloak if you're going out again.' House's injured tone interrupted his reverie, and with a hasty thanks, Vredech retreated into his office.

He leaned back against the closed door and surveyed the room. Desk, books, furniture, pictures. All so familiar, resonating back into the past. Changed yet unchanged. And, by the window, a large copy of the Santyth on a lectern. He walked over and laid his hand gently on it. It seemed smaller somehow, yet the wisdom that it held and which had guided him for so long, remained. When this was over, he must read it again, with his new vision.

His fingers clawed up into a fist, scraping over the carved leather cover, as the thought came to him.

'You *must* look to survive,' Darke had said. 'Don't be afraid to look to tomorrow.'

He was right, of course. Slaying Cassraw was essential, but he must seek to survive so that afterwards he could explain – or great harm could still come to pass. Yet, try as he might, Vredech could not see beyond the deed. All roads led him to that point and ended there.

'There are no endings or beginnings.'

That, too, was true, but of no value to him right now.

He was so afraid.

Gripping the edges of the book, he closed his eyes and bowed his head. 'Ishryth, if this cannot be taken from he, give me the strength to do it.'

Silence.

No revelations came. No guiding quotation from the Santyth. No Whistler. Nothing. Just a black, all-enveloping cloud of fear, fringed about with swirls of bitter anger and resentment that he should be thus burdened.

He moved to his desk and spent a few minutes writing a letter. He laid it first on top of the desk, then changed his mind and placed it conspicuously in the central drawer. It would be found there eventually, and he certainly did not want Nertha to find it too soon. For a moment, thoughts of her almost overwhelmed him. Like so much else, his feelings for her had changed with a totality and suddenness that he could scarcely believe. Why should he not succumb to them? The two of them could flee now, ride away from Canol Madreth before Cassraw's insanity possessed it completely. She was a skilled physician, he was . . . not beyond changing. They could find a quiet and useful life together in one of the other states of Gyronlandt. Nertha above all, would understand.

But even as the thoughts swept about him, racking him, tempting him, he remembered Darke and Tirec, figures in the mist, drawn here from a country far away. Their presence told him that neither time nor distance offered protection against the power that he called Ahmral, and that Gyronlandt itself was but a small part of a greater world. And, too, he knew that Ahmral existed even in those mysterious worlds Beyond – the worlds that were both here and not here, the worlds that should perhaps be inaccessible to mere mortals such as he.

There was no place where he could hide and not expect this evil to reach him eventually. And there was no place he could find quiet, knowing that he had turned away from the task that had fallen to him.

He closed the drawer gently and stood up. Then, with a final look around his room, he left.

Debate in the Heindral was nominally controlled by the leader of the majority party, though he was heavily constrained by precedent to ensure that each party was allowed time or speakers roughly in proportion to the number of seats they held. It was a system that worked adequately enough, though not infrequently a great deal of noise and acrimony was generated by it. On occasions such as this, however, when a respected member of the community was to address the Heindral on some formal or ceremonial matter, the Heinders could be quite impressively orderly. They would fall silent as the leader rose to his feet, and would listen attentively – or at least quietly – to the honoured speaker. Then they would generously applaud him and there would be fulsome speeches of appreciation from representatives of each party. It was the smug self-satisfaction of these occasions that the Heinders used to convince themselves that their normal behaviour was acceptable, its raucousness invariably attributed to the Heinders belonging to other parties.

Vredech arrived quite early at the PlasHein. As Cassraw's haste had wrought havoc with the protocol of the proceedings and thrown the PlasHein officers responsible for organizing such affairs into disarray, Vredech needed only the authority of his cloth to gain access. The chairs which lined the walls of the Debating Hall at the Witness House had been brought down during the night and placed in front of, but with their backs to, the podium from which Cassraw was to speak. This, at least, the officers had remembered, but only when carts began to appear bearing the chairs. The chairs were arranged thus so that the Covenant Member's words, passing over the heads of the Chapter Members, were deemed to be those of the whole church.

Vredech took a seat to one side of the podium so that he would be able to stand up and move to the lectern where Cassraw would be standing, in a straight, unhindered line. He went through his proposed intention over and over. There were three steps up to the podium. From where he was sitting it was perhaps four paces to the lectern.

One, two, three, four . . .

One, two, three, four . . .

Over and over.

Darke's advice stuck horribly in his mind.

Clear your mind of all doubts before you come close.

Come close before you draw the weapon.

Don't hesitate – not for the blink of an eye.

It's the only way – for both of you.

Over and over.

Could he do it? How could he *not* do it? Cassraw was not Cassraw any more. He was a creature of Ahmral's – a vessel, a harbinger, come to prepare the way for His coming. This was not a matter where he had any choice.

But . . .?

The word hung about him like a pleading child, clawing at him, bringing back to him long-forgotten memories – of growing up, of his time as a novice, of the time when he had supported Cassraw's promotion. And, most cruelly, came thoughts of Nertha, his sister who was not a sister. Who was now . . .

Somehow he put the longing aside. It was not easy.

Don't be afraid to look to tomorrow.

But . . .

He looked around at the people arriving. The public galleries were filling, rumbling footsteps echoing along the wooden floors overhead and mixing with the confused babble of voices. Heinders were drifting in and manoeuvring with practised familiarity for places on the long tiered benches. And Preaching Brothers were arriving also. Many of them Vredech knew, but he gave only the most cursory acknowledgement of such greetings as he received. The merest glance at their faces told him of the church already riven. There were smiles, frowns, looks of distress, of anxiety, of ambition, of conspiratorial neutrality. Studying them would serve no useful purpose. Very soon all these concerns would be changed.

One, two, three, four . . .

He did not know whether to be surprised or not that he

534

could see no sign of Horld or Morem and others whom he would have expected to stand against Cassraw. Perhaps they had not heard of what was happening. After all, he had only heard by chance, and there had been no time for formal notification. It was appropriate, he mused. When ignorance and bigotry superseded reason, then gossip was as accurate a medium for its transmission as anything else. He gave their absence no serious thought. On the whole he was quite relieved when the seats beside and in front of him were filled with people he either did not know, or knew only casually. He wanted no debate with close colleagues now. He wanted Cassraw to arrive so that this horror could be ended. But more than that he wanted to be through to the other side of the awful fear that was consuming him. Through the darkness and into the light, whatever it revealed.

Then the place was full.

As he had surmised earlier, almost every Heinder was present and the public galleries were packed with curious spectators. From snatches of overheard conversation he learned that, despite the continuing rain, a large crowd was also occupying the square. Many people were wearing their militia uniforms underneath their cloaks, and he could see that almost everyone was armed in some way. It's your hearts and heads you'll need armed today, he thought, not your bodies. Then he laid his hand on the knife again.

The atmosphere quivered with a mixture of agitation and expectation. The government was teetering, the militia was being levied to face a belligerent neighbour, and a new spirit was spreading through Troidmallos which must surely spread across the whole of Canol Madreth and then beyond: the words 'United Gyronlandt', with their special magic, were frequently to be heard. And, above all, strong men were emerging from unexpected sources in this time of need. Toom Drommel from the Witness Party, of all places, and this powerful Preaching Brother who had suddenly risen to become a Covenant Member and who was seemingly possessed of *miraculous powers*.

Ishryth sided with the righteous.

It was good.

Vredech felt sick.

Then, in response to some unheard signal, the eyes of the crowd turned to the far end of the chamber and the hubbub fell through a cascade of hissing shushes to a low, buzzing murmur.

Vredech had to force himself to breathe.

Silently, the Heinders stood. The Preaching Brothers remained seated.

Vredech found his vision shrinking so that the aisle along the centre of the chamber seemed to taper into a vast distance. Along it, moving towards him with painful slowness, he saw various officers of the PlasHein, resplendent in ancient liveries full of great constitutional significance. Then down each side of the aisle came two lines of the Knights of Ishryth, their faces covered with the blank masks that had been worn at Bredill, and their red sashes garishly counterpointing the more sober splendour of the PlasHein officers. They lent an alien menace to the scene.

Then Cassraw was there, dressed as he had been the previous evening – was it truly such a short time ago? – with Dowinne walking a few paces behind him. For Vredech, Cassraw was at once distant and very close, completely filling his intensely-focused vision. He began to tremble uncontrollably.

Strangely, this involuntary movement of his body released him from the hypnotic effect of the slow procession approaching him. In an effort to still himself, he forced his calves hard against the legs of his chair, and pressed his elbows down on to the arms until he was in pain. The action further cleared his vision. Now there

536

were just men moving towards him, performing their kind of ritual as he had often performed his. Soon it would be over and Cassraw would be at the lectern.

One, two, three, four . . .

Suddenly he panicked at the thought that his trembling legs would not carry him so far; that he might simply go sprawling across the floor, the knife clattering guiltily from his hands to come to rest at Cassraw's feet.

He must walk slowly, deliberately. With an insight that frightened him a little in its coldness, he realized that a slow approach towards his victim would, in any event, be less likely to provoke a hasty response from Cassraw or anyone around him, than some reckless dash.

Yes, he would walk carefully, deliberately.

And do it without hesitation.

It was the only way – for both of them . . .

Strange, snarling emotions began to filter into his mind. Cassraw looked ridiculous in that crown thing he was wearing. What was it supposed to mean, for pity's sake? And he'd always been an ambitious bastard, more interested in his own aggrandisement than serving the church or his flock. What's more, his grasp of theological principles had always been weak; no wonder his beliefs had lapsed into a crude, not to say, grotesque ingenuousness.

These thoughts disturbed Vredech. It was as though part of him was trying to lessen the significance of what he was about to do, justifying it by reducing the victim to something akin to an irritating, perhaps loathsome nuisance. But the wrongness of it offended him. The thoughts were both petty and untrue. And it was not necessary that Cassraw be demeaned in order for Vredech to do what he had to do. Indeed, it was essential that in so far as such a deed could be honourable and done with dignity, then this should be. To kill Cassraw in meanness and spleen was a true obscenity. The act must be one of . . .

Of?

Love.

The word jolted him.

But it was correct. He must kill Cassraw for a good that transcended them both. For the good of the people of Canol Madreth and who could say how many others across Gyronlandt and beyond? And he must kill him for the sake of the true Cassraw that surely lay bound and blind within the heart of what he had become.

He felt sick again.

Cassraw walked to the lectern. Dowinne stood behind him and a little to one side. The Knights were ranged in an arc behind them both. Vredech turned and looked again at the route he was to follow.

One, two, three, four . . .

The trembling that had possessed him seemed to have moved from his limbs and become a shimmering force radiating through him.

Cassraw looked slowly around at the public galleries, then at the Heinders, then he closed his eyes and lowered his head as though he were praying. After a moment he looked up again. His eyes were bright with a fearful intensity. Slowly he extended his arms as if to embrace the entire chamber.

'My flock,' he said. The words echoed through the chamber as a thunderclap rolls across a stormy sky. Vredech felt the hairs on his arms stirring; there was such power in Cassraw's voice. He had always been a fine, commanding preacher, but the hypnotic quality of these two simple words was tinged with an unnaturalness that jarred as much as it thrilled.

'We are faced with dark times. The beloved leader of our church has been taken prematurely from us. The army of the unbelievers of Tirfelden will soon be turned against us in reckless aggression. Evil forces have conspired to weaken our government, leaving the people without guidance in worldly matters.'

538

Vredech watched the audience as he listened. Such was the power in Cassraw's voice that each word was having an effect. And with each further word, more and more of those present would fall under his spell. The trembling within Vredech was growing relentlessly. It was as though his planning for this moment had gathered a momentum that could not now be stopped, and would destroy him if he did not move with it.

'But, my children, I bring you good news. I bring you news of the light that will shine through this darkness. The light that will blind and scatter your enemies. The light that will show you the true Way. His Way. The light that is the One True Light . . .'

Enough!

Vredech did not know whether this inner cry was at the physical distress he was suffering or at Cassraw's mounting rhetoric. He became aware that he was standing up. Then, slowly, he was mounting the podium steps and moving towards Cassraw.

One, two . . .

He was aware of the eyes of Cassraw's guardian Knights, uncertain and looking from one to the other for guidance behind their blank-faced masks. But none were moving.

Three, four . . .

Vredech's hand closed about the knife.

Don't hesitate – not for the blink of an eye.

As Vredech's grip tightened about the knife, Cassraw turned towards him. Their eyes met.

Vredech hesitated.

'Allyn,' Cassraw said softly, with a slight smile. 'I'm so glad you've come to stand by me.'

Vredech found himself looking into the familiar face of his old friend.

'You must kill him! Now!' cried out voices within him, desperately.

KILL HIM!

But his hand would not move.

Cassraw turned back to his audience. 'My friends,' he said, his voice less powerful but filled with emotion, 'you must forgive me if I am suddenly a little unmanned, but Brother Vredech has rightly sought to question the revelation I have received, and question it sternly. To have him by my side now moves me . . . more than I can say.' He paused then held out his arms again. 'And Brother Vredech's public reconciliation is yet further testimony to the guiding presence of His hand—'

'NO!'

The cry, high and shrill, and loaded with frenzied desperation, filled the chamber, crackling through the tension that Cassraw had built and shattering it. There was not one person present who did not start at the sound.

Then all was confusion as everyone sought to see who had cried out. It was not immediately apparent, but Vredech was amongst the first to see who it was as his eye lit on a commotion in the public gallery at the end near the podium.

A figure was clambering over the balustrade.

'No! No!' the cry continued frantically.

Vredech recognized the figure. It was Mad Jarry. With a nimbleness that belied his size and his normal lumbering gait, he dropped on to the tiered seats beneath the gallery and began scrambling over them, heedless of the bewildered Heinders in his way.

He was moving towards the podium and Vredech knew his intention even before he heard Jarry's new cry.

'No! No! You mustn't listen! He's Ahmral! He's possessed! He came in the darkness! I've seen His dreams! I've seen His dreams!'

Then he saw that Jarry was wielding a large knife.

At the same time he became aware of Cassraw's Knights recovering themselves and beginning to move forward to intercept this unexpected threat. To little avail, however. Drawn from Troidmallos's more troublesome youths, secretly schooled by Yanos at Cassraw's behest, and hardened at Bredill, they were not unused to violence, but few could have withstood Jarry's demented charge. Those who came within reach of his massive flailing fists were dashed brutally to one side. A couple managed to seize hold of him, but he paid no heed to them, dragging them along like paper streamers. Another stood directly in front of him only to be lifted bodily and hurled into a group who were running to help him.

And all the time Jarry was crying out.

'Ahmral! Ahmral! I've seen His dreams!'

Vredech, his body trembling again and his mind numb from his failure to strike Cassraw down, watched the whole scene as though it were being performed by street players as a mockingly slow ballet. He saw Cassraw's mouth dropping open at the sight of this approaching nemesis. He saw Dowinne's hands rising protectively and he heard her begin to scream. For no reason that he could have analysed, he reached out and seized her, dragging her roughly away from Cassraw and placing himself between her and Jarry.

He heard the words, 'No, Jarry,' forming in his throat, but even as the sounds began to emerge he saw Jarry reach Cassraw and drive the knife into him. At the same time Jarry disappeared under a writhing mass of figures, stabbing and beating. Glittering blades, red sashes and bloody gashes began to blur, mingling with the nightmare cacophony of screams and groans, panic-stricken cries and grunts of appalling effort. And the trembling that was shaking his body threatened to master him completely.

Then one sound dominated the others and he became aware of a powerful hand turning him round. His entire vision was filled with Dowinne's face. Yet it was scarcely recognizable, so contorted with fury was it. Raking through him, he heard, shrieking and awful: 'Damn you to hell, Allyn. What have you done?'

He gazed at her, shocked and helpless, but almost before he had a chance to register what she was saying, a blow shook his entire body and plunged him into gasping darkness.

Chapter 37

In the hasty preparations for the ceremony at the Plas-Hein, Skynner had been only too willing to agree to Cassraw's Knights forming the honour guard for their leader. His own men had more than enough to do at the moment and he personally wanted to keep as far away from Cassraw as he could. Thus he was present with only a few Keepers, forming in effect a small honour guard of their own for the Chief Keeper and other senior officers seated in the public gallery.

On seeing Jarry's reckless descent from the balcony, Skynner's long-instilled sense of duty had swept aside his misgivings about Cassraw and he dashed immediately for the stairs, a single command bringing his men close behind him. In the few seconds it took them to reach the Debating Chamber, however, Jarry had stabbed Cassraw and been brought down himself. The place was in uproar, with everyone shouting or screaming, half those present trying to flee the chamber while the other half was struggling towards the podium to see what had happened. He had a vivid, kaleidoscopic impression of people being crushed against walls and the fixed furniture, and being trampled underfoot. Even as he watched, he saw bodies tumbling from the public galleries on to the Heinders milling about below. For a moment he was paralysed as memories of the panic in the PlasHein Square flooded back to him. Then the deep fear and anger that he had been nursing since his interview with the Chief and Toom Drommel burst out, releasing him. He could do nothing about the crowd, but he could get to the podium and take charge of whatever was happening there.

This was no easy task, and even though he was not gentle about the matter, it took him and his men some time to shoulder their way through the clamouring onlookers. In the course of this advance, several political worthies received baton blows that took the edge off their curiosity, not the least of these being Toom Drommel, who 'accidentally' received a backswinging elbow just below the arch of his ribcage.

Skynner's satisfaction at this however, was dampened by the sight that greeted him as he reached the podium. Cassraw, covered in blood, lay on his back. He was not moving. Across him sprawled the equally motionless body of Jarry, his rough tunic covered with blood-streaked rents and gashes. Nearby lay Vredech. Several of the Knights, under the frantic command of Dowinne, were struggling to lift Jarry's body off that of his victim, while others were just milling around.

As the labouring group finally succeeded and Jarry's great frame rolled over on to its back with a thud, Skynner grimaced. He had been terribly injured.

Dowinne, seemingly in a state of shock, knelt by her husband and began nursing his head. Skynner reached down and gently took her arm. There was no quiet yielding, however. Dowinne swung round, her free hand lifted with the obvious intention of striking him. Reflexes brought his own arm up to block the blow but immediately the other hand attacked him. Without ceremony, he grasped both her arms and yanked her roughly to her feet.

'That's enough!' he shouted. 'Remember who you are. This is doing no—'

Before he could finish, a hand had gripped his shoulder and spun him round. He found himself facing the blank

544

mask of one of the Knights. 'Keep your hands to yourself, unbeliever. No one may touch the Chosen One's wife. Go down on your knees for forgiveness before her.' The Knight's voice was quivering with passion; he held a bloodied knife in his hand.

Skynner recognized the voice and, still in the mood for settling long unfinished business, he seized the hand and twisted it violently. The Knight arched up on to his toes with an incongruous cry then, equally rapidly, began to sink down in response to the agonizing pressure on his wrist. As he did so, Skynner wrenched the mask from his face, and in one swing took the baton from his belt and brought it down on his captive. It was a pitiless blow and Yanos's body shook the floor as it landed. 'You keep *your* hands to yourself, young man,' Skynner snarled. 'You're under arrest for threatening a Keeper with a weapon.'

Some of the Knights moved as if to intervene, but a swift flurry of blows sent three of them reeling back crying out in pain and nursing elbows and wrists. The remainder lost interest in defending their fallen leader. Skynner pressed home his advantage. 'And if it proves we're under militia rule at the moment, then you know what the punishment for attacking a Keeper is, don't you?'

They didn't. Nor did Skynner for that matter, but there was too much menace in his voice for debate. 'Take those stupid masks off, drop those knives and get over there out of my way.' Although the Keepers were outnumbered, Skynner's authority and his grim-faced companions, watching them, batons drawn, ensured acquiescence, reducing the sinister masked Knights to a group of surly young men.

Skynner turned back to Dowinne, who had stood transfixed as these events took place. What he saw almost unnerved him. It was as though he were looking into the eyes of a wild and cornered animal. Something deep stirred within him. 'Kill this or flee,' it said, but habit held him there and he simply took his eyes from hers.

'Let's look at your husband, lady,' he said, kneeling down by Cassraw. At the same time he motioned one of his men to go to Vredech. Jarry, he could see, was dead. Before he could begin examining Cassraw, however, he was interrupted by an angry female voice.

'Let me through, damn you.'

Looking up, he saw Nertha pushing her way through the crowd. He snapped his fingers and two of his men went to help her. When she reached the podium, she stepped over Cassraw's body without a glance, and went straight to Vredech. Dowinne made to move towards her, but Skynner discreetly detained her.

'Where was he hit?' Nertha demanded of no one in particular as she examined Vredech.

'He wasn't hit,' one of the Knights volunteered. 'He just fell over.'

Nertha carefully lifted one of Vredech's eyelids, then quickly released it and stood up. 'He's just unconscious,' she said, though Skynner sensed an awkwardness about her. 'Keep away from him, please. Give him air.'

She looked sadly at Jarry's body then moved to Cassraw. At first her examination was almost off-hand. Then she became alert. 'He's alive!' she said, her voice soft and urgent. She looked around. 'Get these people out of here and get me some proper light.' She began unfastening Cassraw's robe.

Dowinne stepped forward. 'No,' she said forcefully.

Nertha looked at her with a mixture of anger and amazement. 'He'll be bleeding like a pig under this lot,' she said brutally. 'Looking at where he was stabbed he's lucky to be alive, but he won't stay that way unless—'

'The Chosen One will lose no blood,' Dowinne said stiffly. She signalled to the Knights. 'Take him up and bring him to the summit of the Holy Mountain.'

'What?' Nertha exclaimed, eyes wide with disbelief.

'Are you mad?' She turned to Skynner. 'You can't let her do this. She's insane, for pity's sake. He's liable to die if we try to move him to the Sick House, let alone up the Ervrin Mallos.'

Skynner looked at her. 'Best for everyone if he did,' she read in his eyes, and for a moment she faltered, understanding Skynner's stern and practical compassion for what might follow if Cassraw survived, and remembering again all that happened over the last few days.

But still she could not let him die if some effort on her part might save him.

'Serjeant.' Dowinne's voice interrupted the silent exchange. 'See that he's taken as I've commanded. Immediately.' She turned to Nertha and inclined her head towards Vredech. 'You look to your . . . brother,' she said, a sneer breaking through her cold haughtiness.

Nertha's eyes narrowed and her jaw tautened but she said only, 'He'll die if you move him.'

'No,' Dowinne said, cold still and categorical. She turned to the Knights with a commanding air. Skynner nodded, and they moved forward and picked up Cassraw's body. Nertha winced at the action and looked again at Skynner, her eyes anxious.

'Leave it,' he said simply. 'Tend to Allyn.' She was about to remonstrate with him further, when he turned her round gently and said: 'Look.'

With Dowinne leading the way, Cassraw's body was being borne on the shoulders of his Knights down the central aisle of the Debating Chamber. Without any command the crowd had fallen silent and opened a way for the slow procession. Many were circling their hands over their hearts and, as the body passed, they fell in behind it, heads bowed.

'Like worshippers,' Skynner said, suddenly afraid.

The diamond-hard nothingness that was Allyn Vredech's

547

awareness hovered amid the flickering lights and shapes that were there and not there, and which danced to the endless gibbering chorus of sounds that could and could not be heard.

It was no longer unfamiliar, but still it disturbed. *Between the dreams*, he thought.

Timelessly he waited.

Then into the awareness came memories of the Plas-Hein. Of his own failure, of Jarry demented, of blood and confusion, of Cassraw falling, Dowinne raging . . .

Why was he here?

Was it all over? Was Cassraw dead? Had poor simple Jarry with his clear, tormented vision succeeded where he, with his self-indulgent agonizing, had failed?

Futile questions, he knew. However he had come here, he was helpless and, as always, he felt incomplete. Something was missing – something that would guide him.

Then he sensed danger somewhere in this lost, dimensionless world. Terrible danger. The lights and shapes swirling about him became agitated and jagged, slicing and glinting like a myriad tumbling knife-blades. And a swollen redness rose to taint everything. Fear threatened to overwhelm him, but he could do nothing: could not move, could not scream. And soon, in so far as time meant anything here, for this was all that had ever been, he would be tumbling through this fearful, menacing chaos . . .

A presence stirred.

Vredech was filled with sensations utterly alien to him, strange, overwhelming scents, each bearing its own message, and sounds that should be beyond hearing, acutely heard. And overlying all, a musky lethargy shot through with lusts and greed.

This was not his, yet it would suffice.

The sudden knowledge came from deep within, and though it made no sense to him, yet it was true.

548

'What are you?' he asked into the presence.

The question echoed back through him.

'I am Allyn Vredech,' he replied and, though the words merely flickered over the surface of the true meaning: 'You are my Guide.'

There was bewilderment and denial. 'I'm Leck. I'm Privv's. This can't be.'

Vredech was suddenly angry, as if he were being defied. 'This *is*,' he said brutally. 'Do what you have to do. Guide me, guard me.'

Realization flooded through him – Leck's realization. This was how it should be. This was her true task. Briefly a surge of regret for things done, time wasted, soured the knowledge, then, though Vredech felt no movement, she was leading him down, through, along, the tangled dreamways of which he was now a part. The bond between them, new-formed though it was, would lead the cat to the place where they were needed.

There was no time to ponder the many thoughts floundering in the wake of this journey.

And, without any sense of change, he was there. He was Cassraw, standing motionless, staring at the summit of the Ervrin Mallos. It moved uneasily within a shifting haze. Vredech had stood in the dreams of others before, albeit briefly, and felt their emotions and thoughts while remaining aloof from them, but here such unbridled desire pulsated that nothing could have protected him from its impact!

Cassraw turned from the summit and looked out across the land. Before him lay the whole of Gyronlandt, subdued and compliant. Armies of his Knights held sway over all the land while 'for the greater good' hooded Judges of the Court of the Provers relentlessly sought out and 'brought to the light' those lost souls whose faith was inadequate, or whose thoughts deviated from the True Word. Rivers ran red with the blood of doubters and unbelievers, and glinted in the light of their living funeral pyres. And he himself, with his hand upon the Santyth, which he alone could interpret, stood at the pinnacle of all power, the Judge of Judges. With the least of his gestures, towns and cities were put to the sword. He bore the cries and screams of the slaughtered with stoic fortitude and accepted the adulation that washed across the land to sustain him in his ecstasy.

Chilled to his core by this vision and consumed with guilt at his failure to slay its architect, Vredech remained very still.

Cassraw turned back to the wavering summit.

'Here is the gift I shall bring You, Lord,' he intoned. 'Show me Thy will and that, too, I shall bring to pass.'

As he watched, the summit began to change. Sometimes rapidly and erratically, sometimes slowly and with a strange grace, towers and spires and ramping walls began to rise from it. They shifted and changed as their creator tested them and found them wanting. And as they grew, so Cassraw saw them all simultaneously, from every vantage point at the foot of the mountain, from high above as though cloud-borne, from far horizons and from immediately beneath the sheer walls looking up at the giddying perspective looming above. Inexorably the building rose high into the sky, glistening menacingly against the gathering black clouds, like a blessed hand reaching out to bring forth the Lord.

But where Cassraw saw a fulfilment, a culmination, Vredech saw the work of a dreadful and inhuman intelligence. He felt its every spire impaling him with its awfulness. Its clawing points and edges tore through the fabric of what was and brought together those things which should be kept apart. It was a monstrous creation that would draw through to this world a darkness and horror that even Cassraw's mind had not yet encompassed.

And as if in confirmation, as the towers rose ever

550

higher, so he received a vision of labyrinthine tunnels and shafts and dank passageways burrowing deep into the heart of the mountain and yet further below, like sapping roots drawing sustenance from the world.

Then, worse by far, came the knowledge that this impossible structure was to be built by men. That the blood and terror of Cassraw's campaigns across Gyronlandt were merely to supply what was needed in people, materials and skills. That its awful image would be branded in the hearts of all. That the pain and horror involved in its creation were an integral part of it – indeed, they were its bloody heart.

Vredech felt himself reaching out to touch Leck's consciousness for reassurance. The cat was nearly demented with fear, but she would hold her ground, he knew. The gift that made her what she was, and had brought her to him in his moment of need, carried deep obligations, heightened now by her deep sense of past regret. Yet her fear sharpened his own awareness, and he began to sense a presence in the dream other than himself and Leck. The dream was strained, distorted. It was more than a dream. It reached beyond the dreamways.

This could not be . . .

He felt Leck's fear tearing at him but he ignored it.

Then he knew that the terrible crown growing from the top of the mountain was not of Cassraw's creating. It was being created for him. Through that part of the dream which was not a dream was coming the Will that was forming this monstrosity, embedding its every detail into Cassraw's mind.

Vredech could do no other.

'No,' he said.

The dream moved, and the scene before him became like a faded picture in an old book.

And he was no longer Cassraw. He was himself. And, for some reason, terrifyingly, Leck was gone, although he was faintly aware of her scratching and screaming in some place unknowable. Somewhere she was hunting for her lost charge more ferociously even than she would have defended her own young. But he was alone. Inside and outside the dream. Standing before a portal, he sensed, though neither sight nor sound informed him.

Some of the Knights shifted their feet uneasily. They were at the foot of the road which led up to the Witness House and Dowinne had stopped, almost as if she had heard a command, and called them to a halt. Since then she had stood silent, her hand resting on Cassraw's chest as he lay on the makeshift stretcher hastily rigged from PlasHein pikes and curtains.

It was still raining.

A little way away stood Skynner with Stiel and Kerna. The Serjeant had quickly superintended the removal of Jarry's body and the safe transporting of Nertha and the unconscious Vredech to their home, then he had set off in discreet pursuit of Dowinne with his two colleagues. Ostensibly, it was to ensure that the new Covenant Member came to no harm through neglect, but his real motives were an unsteady mixture of curiosity, suspicion and alarm at unfolding events.

In this timeless place, Vredech waited. Then, seeping slowly about him he felt again the Will that had touched him when he had stood in the darkness on the Ervrin Mallos as he and the other Chapter Brothers had searched for Cassraw.

It curled through him, searching, testing. But where before it had dismissed him scornfully, now it paused.

A long sigh of comprehension passed through him.

He reached out in fearful appeal towards Leck's frantic clawing. 'Help me,' he cried out. But Leck was not of this place.

Dowinne's eyes opened suddenly and she stiffened. Her movement was copied by the tired Knights still supporting their injured master's body, expecting an instruction to continue their journey.

'I hear, Lord,' she said. Then before any of the Knights could react, she drew a long knife from beneath her robe and plunged it twice into Cassraw's chest. For a moment the Knights gaped then, as she raised the knife to strike again they let the stretcher fall, tumbling Cassraw on to the wet ground. Some of them leapt away while others made to wrest the knife from her. The first who came near died on a single rapid thrust while the second was cut from shoulder to hip by a whistling slash. The others retreated immediately, forming a ragged, uncertain circle about her and the bloodied heap that had been her husband. Then she stabbed Cassraw again, and plunged her hand into the wound.

Skynner, gasping from his sudden frantic charge to reach the group on seeing what was happening, pushed his way roughly through the men to stand facing Dowinne. Stiel and Kerna were close behind him. Dowinne was a grim sight, her eyes wide and crazed, her nostrils flaring and her teeth bared like a cornered animal. As she moved the knife slowly to and fro in front of her, she was hissing.

Skynner drew his baton.

All was roaring chaos about Vredech. It was as though he had been caught in an avalanche. Great forces had swept out of nothingness to beat about him, to draw him inexorably into . . .

What?

Instincts he did not even know he possessed rose to tell him of an appalling danger and that he must escape while he could. But no guidance came with this knowledge. All that sustained him in his terror was the faint, hysterical scrabbling of Leck trying to reach him: a slender, failing thread weaving through the turmoil.

A soft, kindly voice spoke to him. *'Do not oppose what must be, Allyn Vredech. Follow your true destiny.'* And it seemed to Vredech that a great roadway was opening before him, one which would lead him calmly from this fearful maelstrom.

Leck's distant frenzy redoubled itself. It stirred something deep within Vredech, and even as he was about to step forth on the road before him, the knowledge rose to the surface, scorching in its urgency.

'You are in the dream of a dead man. Flee!'

It was primitive and irresistible, like the force that powers the struggles of a drowning man.

'Allyn . . .' repeated the voice, still honeyed and alluring, but now Vredech saw to its corrupted heart and he shouted.

'To me, Leck! To me! I hear you!'

And suddenly the clawing, slashing presence of the cat was all about him and he was tumbling over and over; caught up in its killing fury.

Then he was free of the dreadful lure and crashing through into wakefulness. But even as he did, to his horror, he felt Leck's heart bursting.

'Too ignorant. Didn't know,' the cat gasped feebly. 'All my life. Didn't know. Sorry. And not truly yours. There is a companion for you somewhere. Learn what you are, Allyn Vredech. This isn't finished yet.'

And spiralling, dwindling, into a never-attainable distance, she was gone.

'No!' Vredech cried.

He lurched forward.

Skynner felt the hairs on his neck stand on end as he looked at Dowinne, her crazed eyes staring at him, the bloodstained knife extended in front of her and her gore-covered hand beckoning him forward. Dealing with women who tipped over into violence was always particularly frightening because of their almost suicidal lack of restraint in such circumstances. And dealing with someone wielding a knife had its own special terrors. But it was not simply the combination of these two fears that was disturbing him. It was something else. Something namelessly awful.

Then Dowinne canted her head as if she was listening to someone and her eyes rolled upwards, replacing their manic stare with a dead whiteness. But Skynner could still feel her gaze on him.

'As You will, Lord,' she said.

Her eyes closed and she sank to the ground.

Chapter 38

Vredech scrambled rapidly to his feet and looked around wildly. He was at the summit of the Ervrin Mallos. Rain was drizzling down and all about was greyness.

'Allyn!' The cry was accompanied by a vigorous shaking of his arm. Terrified, he snatched himself free and spun round poised to defend himself, only to see Nertha, her eyes wide with fear. 'For pity's sake, what's happened? Where are we?'

Without thinking he put his arms around her and held her tightly. He wanted to say, 'Don't be afraid,' but he couldn't. There had always been truth between them, and it held even now. 'I don't know,' he said. 'Just stand by me. And be aware.'

'Allyn, how can this be?' Nertha burst out. 'Tell me I'm dreaming.'

Vredech shook her. 'Listen,' he shouted. 'You're *not* dreaming. I don't know how or why we're here, but as you love me, stand by me.' He closed his eyes. He was different. Something within him had been awakened by his mysterious contact with Leck. 'We are here,' he said softly. 'And we are in the Witness House also. I can feel it.' His voice was full of awe, then a hint of irony came into it. 'Asleep to anyone who sees us.'

Nertha looked at him, still fearful. 'This is madness,' she said. 'I *am* dreaming.'

'No,' Vredech said. 'This place *is* as surely as Troid-mallos is. Whether it should be or whether we should be

556

in it, I don't know. I've no answers to any of your questions, but trust your senses, and be alert. Something dreadful's happened. I think Cassraw's dead.'

Nertha clutched at his hand, her grip desperate. She was taking slow deep breaths, her mind demanding control over her shaking body. 'We can't be in two places at once, it's not possible,' she muttered, as if she needed to hear the words spoken out loud before she could continue.

'This is the darkness where your ability to measure ends,' Vredech said. 'You're not afraid of the dark, are you?'

'Not at noon,' Nertha retorted immediately.

A smile formed inside Vredech at this hint of recovery, but it barely reached his face, so strained did he feel.

' "Fabric's torn 'fore all was born",' he quoted.

'I *wondered* who would come to this dismal place in such weather.'

The voice made both of them start, for all that Vredech recognized it. The Whistler emerged from behind a rock. He looked at Vredech thoughtfully. 'I was going to call you "night eyes", but I see you're not any more.' He flicked the flute to his eye and squinted along it. 'It's a marked improvement,' he said. 'You look almost human.' Then, before Vredech could reply, the Whistler turned his attention to Nertha. His eyes gleamed, at once mocking and lustful. 'Ah, you must be the sister who isn't a sister. The wonderful Nertha.' He held out his hand. 'My dear, you're as lovely as I'd imagined. Quite the kind of dream I prefer. I can see why my man here is so taken with you.'

Nertha's eyes narrowed, but out of a mixture of courtesy and curiosity, she took the offered hand, at the same time tightening her grip on Vredech's. Vredech looked on darkly. 'Allow me to introduce myself,' the Whistler said. He carried the hand to his mouth and kissed it with a flourish. 'I am your . . .' he paused '. . . your maker, I suppose.'

Vredech leaned forward and placed a significant forefinger on the Whistler's chest. 'Truce, Whistler,' he said. 'Who's dreaming whom no longer matters. We need to be back in our own world, something bad's afoot.'

The Whistler looked down at the finger. 'Martial as ever eh, Priest?' he said, releasing Nertha's hand lingeringly and smiling massively at her. Then he shrugged. 'My dreams pursue their own course, Allyn, you know that,' he said, but suddenly there was pain in his eyes. 'He's here, isn't He? All around us. Stinking the air.'

Vredech felt Nertha's grip on his hand tightening again. He had been so preoccupied with tending to her distress at their mysterious arrival in this place that he had not noticed but, as the Whistler said, the presence of the spirit that had infected Cassraw was permeating everything.

'Damn you, Priest,' the Whistler burst out angrily. 'Must it always come to this? Must I always have to face Him myself? Why didn't you kill Him like I told you to?'

'Cassraw is dead,' Vredech shouted back at him. 'I was in his dream as he died. He nearly took me with him.' Then, furiously, 'Why don't you play your damned flute and whistle off to some other place if you don't like this one? Leave us alone! We'll get back somehow.'

Unexpectedly, the Whistler sagged and looked down at his flute. 'I daren't,' he said uncomfortably. 'It's too . . . sensitive. It always is when He comes too close. I daren't play it. Everything's too fragile – so many worlds come together. The least note opens so many, and I've not the skill to separate them. No control.' He leaned forward confidentially, and spoke softly. 'I'm frightened, Allyn. I think perhaps I'm on the verge of waking when it's like this, but what's waiting for me when I wake? Am I some sick lunatic bound in a cell for my own good? Or a miserable labouring peasant languishing in a hovel? Then, perhaps again, I'm about to die. But in either case, where will *you* be when I abandon you?' He gazed up into the greyness about them, waving his hand, fingers twitching. 'You'll be nothing. Gone. All of my creations, gone.'

Torn between compassion for the Whistler's patent distress and fury at his own confusion and helplessness, Vredech could only stare at him.

Then, Nertha reached forward and took the Whistler's arm. 'Help us, please,' she said.

The Whistler looked at her, his eyes full of pain. Then he gazed at Vredech.

'I've made such fine people,' he said. He pursed his lips and screwed his eyes tight shut. When he opened them they were wide and full of manic mischief. 'I was always susceptible to beautiful women. And we should live our dreams with a little flare, don't you think, Allyn? Let's raise the devil.' He lifted the flute to his lips and looked at Nertha. 'For you, my dear, my favourite note.' For an instant he hesitated and there was a flicker of fear in his eyes, then he blew a single, brief note, soft and low.

The sound floated out into the grey dampness and seemed to enter into the very heart of everything that was there, from the misting raindrops to the glistening damp rocks. Vredech felt the presence about them change. He began to feel very afraid.

The Whistler let out an incongruous, 'Ooh!' and began gingerly rubbing the ends of his thumbs with his forefingers. 'Something nasty's coming,' he said, hopping on to the rock that Cassraw had announced as marking the point of his revelation. He squatted on his haunches, the flute at his lips, and his eyes peering hither and thither into the gloom.

A figure emerged through the rain.

It was Dowinne. She was walking slowly towards them. There seemed to be almost an aura about her, then Vredech saw that the rain was not falling on her. He, like Nertha, was soaked, the rain flattening his hair to his skull

559

and running down his face. Dowinne however, was completely untouched. And there was something serpentine about the way she was moving – half-walking, half-gliding – as if she were in another place. As she rose up the final slope to the summit, Vredech saw that in her hand, hanging idly by her side, was a long, bloodstained knife.

The Whistler drew in a hissing breath.

Dowinne paused as she reached them, then turned slowly to Nertha. Vredech made to step forward protectively, but Nertha's arm came out to stop him as she met Dowinne's gaze. The two women stared at one another for a long time, then a hint of an unpleasant smile curled the side of Dowinne's mouth and she turned to look at Vredech.

Vredech could read nothing in her gaze, though it was profoundly unnerving. It was as though someone else was looking through her eyes at him, assessing him, coldly curious yet at the same time wildly excited.

Finally she turned towards the Whistler, her head tilted to one side, while the Whistler, his flute still at his mouth, raised an eyebrow.

'You blaspheme,' she said after a moment, her voice distant and harsh. Without comment, the Whistler jumped down from the rock and skipped a few paces away. Dowinne's eyes followed him, still unreadable.

She placed the knife on the rock and then laid her hand beside it. At her touch, the rock became dry, but immediately blood began to flow from her hand. Slowly it spread across the surface of the rock, wider and wider.

'So much blood in him,' she said quietly.

The presence about them grew more and more intense.

Nertha took Vredech's arm. She was shaking.

'Release him, woman,' Dowinne said. 'He is mine.'

Nertha's jaw tautened, but Vredech motioned her to be silent, and gently eased her grip from his arm.

'How did you come here, and why have you killed your

husband?' he asked, bring a priestly sternness to his voice that he did not feel.

The blood stopped flowing. Dowinne addressed him. 'I did not kill Cassraw, I sacrificed him. As I did the others. Blood and the terror of its drawing are necessary for the heart-stone of His temple. And He brought me here, as He brought you also.' She waved a graceful hand towards Nertha and the Whistler. 'And these two are perhaps for the stone.'

Vredech in his turn began to shake. Dowinne stepped forward until she was immediately in front of him. He felt the rain stop falling on him. Dowinne opened her mouth slightly and blew a soft scented breath in his face. Suddenly he was riven with desire for this woman; old, long-forgotten desires from his youth. His trembling became different in character, and sweat formed on his forehead.

'*You* are the Chosen One, Allyn Vredech,' she said, moving herself against him. 'You are mine, we shall be joined in His name and His service, and His will shall be done through us.'

'This is madness,' Vredech said hoarsely. He raised his hands to push her away but, as if beyond his control, they merely came to rest on her shoulders. She closed her eyes ecstatically at his touch.

'No,' Dowinne said. 'The only madness would be to deny the destiny that has been laid out for us since the beginning of all things. We are His servants and we shall be rulers in this world. All will fall before us.'

'I have no gifts,' Vredech said weakly.

Dowinne smiled. 'I have the power of change,' she said, lifting a hand to Vredech's face. As he looked at it, he saw glittering silver spirals winding around her fingers, crisscrossing her hand and winding about her wrist, like a delicate and magical glove. Only as he stared at it did he realize that the shifting silver threads were water, twisting and flowing as water could not. 'He has awakened it in me. And you . . .? You span the worlds beyond. That is your gift, and that, His presence alone has wakened in you. Cassraw possessed merely a shadow of it. He was but a vessel through which He could attain me. Millennia might pass before such as we come together again to pave the way for His coming.' She reached up and put her arms around his neck. Vredech's arms moved irresistibly to return her embrace as he felt her body pressing against his. 'Come to me, Allyn Vredech,' she whispered. 'Be with me. Everything you have ever desired is before you now. We are His, and you are mine.'

Her face came closer to his.

Vredech bent his head forward.

'The hell he is, you murderous bitch!'

Nertha's angry cry accompanied her hand which appeared suddenly between them. She clamped it over Dowinne's face and pushed her violently, tearing her free of Vredech's embrace. Then, her elbow against his chest, she sent Vredech staggering backwards.

Suddenly the cold rain was falling on him again.

Dowinne's spell had gone.

The Whistler's eyes flicked between the three protagonists.

Dowinne had steadied herself on the rock. Her face became suddenly savage: teeth bared and eyes wide with uncontrollable rage. She snatched up the knife and spun round to face Nertha. Vredech had stumbled and was scrambling to his feet as he saw Nertha bend down and pick up a large rock in response.

Then, before he could cry out, Dowinne's snarl had turned into a smile. The cruelty in it froze him. Deliberately she laid the knife back on to the rock, then held out a hand to Nertha.

Nertha reeled back as if she had been violently struck. Vredech caught her. Her hands were flailing frantically and her face was contorted. It took him a moment to see what was happening, but as water had run about Dowinne's hand in a delicate tracery, now it ran over Nertha's face, a shallow, suffocating sheet, forcing itself into her tightly clamped mouth and into her nostrils. Desperately he tried to brush it away, but it flowed around his hands relentlessly.

'Stop it, Dowinne!' he cried out. 'For pity's sake, stop it. You're killing her.'

'It must be,' Dowinne said. 'His need is without end. And to be mine absoluteiy, all the affections that bind you here must be severed. As your gift drew Him here, so your incestuous love has ensured her death.'

Vredech looked down at Nertha. He could hardly hold her, she was struggling so violently. Her begging eyes seared through him.

'Whistler, help me! Do something!'

But the Whistler only watched.

'There is no help for you, my love,' Dowinne said, smiling still. 'I'll drown her in little more than would quench your thirst. It's fascinating.'

Nertha's legs went from under her and she slipped from Vredech's grip.

'No, no,' he gasped as she fell, thrashing, to the ground. Then with a furious roar he leapt at Dowinne. He had scarcely taken a pace, however, when a terrible blow struck him. He felt as though his entire body was blazing.

'I can bind you with chains of water, my love, or slowly drown you like your sister here. *Or boil the blood in your veins*. You are mine and we are His, struggle how you may. Learn that now and spare yourself endless hurt.'

Vredech tried to cry out, but could not. He looked upwards. A darkness was gathering.

Dowinne moved forward and bent over Nertha. 'See how she fights for life. See how she'll die. Revel in it. There'll be many more.' And she laughed.

Then the Whistler spoke, 'I, too, have the gift to move between the worlds, woman,' he said.

Dowinne started and spun round to face him. The pain that had suffused Vredech vanished as suddenly as it had come. And Nertha's dreadful choking became a relieved gasping as the water fell from her face.

'See?' said the Whistler. He began to play the flute, very softly.

Vredech felt the darkness overhead stirring, moving downwards. And as the Whistler played, Vredech saw what eyes cannot see, nor minds know. He saw a myriad worlds opening before him. Worlds beyond his imagining yet which he knew were within his reach. Worlds which had as their focus the Whistler and his haunted tune.

Dowinne glanced from Vredech to the Whistler, her face full of uncertainty. Then she looked upwards. 'Guide me, Lord!' she cried out.

The darkness began to close about the summit, as did the presence which had been there throughout: inhuman in its coldness, all too human in its barbarism and cruelty.

Dowinne made a move towards the Whistler and the darkness crept further in.

Then Vredech caught the Whistler's eye. There was such fear there!

He must do something. Whatever the Whistler was, he was as trapped here as himself, pinioned by the worlds he held open to save this foolish priest. Yet the ravening desire that Vredech could feel in the approaching darkness told him that he must not allow Dowinne to reach his saviour.

But what could he do?

One, two, three, four . . .

The terrible litany he had taught himself while awaiting the arrival of Cassraw returned to him.

This time, guilt-driven, he did not hesitate. As

564

Dowinne reached out to touch the Whistler, Vredech felt for his father's militia knife.

It was not there.

Panic surged through him.

'Allyn!'

Nertha's cry cut through it. She had crawled to the bloodstained rock with the same intention. But she was too weak. As he turned, he saw her slithering to the ground, Dowinne's murderous blade in her hand. Then, her face riven with despair, she made a final effort and hurled the knife towards him.

Before his mind could register what was happening, he had seized the twisting handle.

With two long strides he reached Dowinne and, gripping her around the throat, tore her away from the Whistler and drove the knife into her back.

As he did so, the Whistler's soft tune became a harsh, screaming trill. He felt the many worlds about him shimmering, moving, becoming a great whirling tumult. And then there was no summit, no Nertha, and no Whistler, save for his frantic trilling call pervading everything. And the dark presence scrabbling to seize the still-living Dowinne.

Dowinne clutched at Vredech's hand, still about her throat.

'No, Allyn, please!' she cried. 'Please!'

Pity and a lifetime's memories filled him.

'Damn you into eternity,' he howled into the enfolding darkness. Then he stabbed her again, and with what strength he had left he pushed her away from him into the chaos between the shifting worlds.

He heard her crying his name as she fell.

Cautiously, Skynner approached the fallen figure. Baton ready, he kicked the knife away from her. Then he bent down and placed his hand against her throat.

565

After a moment he looked up.

'She's dead,' he said.

The Whistler's tune carried Vredech and Nertha through the time and distance that could not be, to return them to the Meeting House. It mended many hurts and told many tales, but still Vredech and Nertha wept for a long time as they embraced one another.

Chapter 39

Privv's Sheet was quite sombre the following day. It seemed that following the assassination attempt by the tragically deranged Jarold Harverson, Covenant Member Cassraw had died of his injuries. His steadfast wife Dowinne, broken-hearted, had succumbed to her grief on hearing the news. The couple would be a great loss to the community.

After hearing the news of Cassraw's death there had been an emergency debate in the Heindral in which it had been agreed, with remarkable unanimity, that while the levy of the militia should continue, envoys should be sent to Tirfelden with a view to discussing recent events before further harm was done. The envoys were discreetly briefed to attribute the 'incident' at Bredill to Cassraw's . . . zealousness . . . if need arose. Toom Drommel sat silent throughout, occasionally rubbing his stomach.

Another item was also reported, which served to explain the comparatively modest tone of the Sheet. It seemed that, doubtless due to overwork following his energetic reporting of recent events, Privv had collapsed and died. He would be missed, but his erstwhile employees would continue with his sterling work, albeit with some slight changes in style – 'such as telling the truth,' one of them was heard to say.

No one paid any heed to the dead cat that was found by

Privv's body, though an official church order was subsequently given to the buriers to the effect that the animal be buried with him and that its name be carved on the headstone along with its owner's.

A final tiny item noted that the strange haze which had lingered about the summit of the Ervrin Mallos for the past few days had not returned when the rain had ended.

Over the next few weeks Troidmallos settled back to normal. With the passing of Cassraw, the fanaticism which he had inspired faded rapidly. His Knights disbanded when several were arrested for assaulting the Sheeters, and instigating the panic at the PlasHein Square. People who had recently been suffering from nightmares and the like found that these faded away. Negotiations with the Felden went remarkably well. The return of the survivors of Bredill had caused an initial uproar, but as one faction had instigated the invasion, so now another had its say. Judiciously, they pointed out that the aggression had been theirs, after all, and that the Madren militia was noted for its ferocity when provoked. And, as the Madren seemed quite keen not to pursue the matter, it was best to let it lie.

Vredech was appointed Covenant Member in Mueran's stead, but he immediately delegated his authority jointly to Horld and Morem as he wished to go on a pilgrimage to study the origins of Ishrythan and the Santyth.

His fellow Chapter Brothers had been somewhat taken aback, until he also announced that he would be marrying Nertha. There was some rather unclerical winking at this, and for a while the word 'pilgrimage' was spoken in inverted commas at Chapter meetings.

Darke and Tirec were more than a little surprised when Nertha and Vredech rode into their camp one afternoon. They talked a great deal. Darke's relief on hearing what had happened was almost palpable, but that it had happened at all still disturbed him badly and left him resolute to carry the news back to his homeland. The two foreigners were further surprised by Vredech's request that he and Nertha be allowed to accompany them with the intention of learning more of Madren history and other things that were happening in the world beyond Gyronlandt. Vredech also confided that he needed to learn what he could about his strange and uncontrollable gift and the part that Leck had played in it. 'And too, the darkness you've found in yourself,' Darke said to him quietly when they were alone, placing an understanding hand on his shoulder. Vredech nodded, but did not reply.

Tirec had been reluctant to agree. 'It's a long way through difficult country,' he protested at length, but Darke merely smiled a welcome and said, 'They'll learn. And I doubt they'll be as difficult as you were.'

After they had shared a meal with their new companions, Vredech and Nertha wandered off together. They came eventually to a small hillside. Vredech looked about, slightly puzzled, then he sat down. 'This is like the place where I first met the Whistler,' he said. And as the memory came back to him, so did the peace of that moment. He reached out and took Nertha's hand. There were no answers to any of the questions they had asked themselves about the Whistler – who he was, *if* he was – but they would continue to ask them.

The Whistler, sitting on a broad branch and leaning back against the trunk of the tree, played his three notes softly. He watched Vredech and Nertha on the distant hillside. After a little while he smiled, then he played the three notes very loudly so that they rang out over the fields.

Then he was gone.

Vredech started out of his half-sleep. 'What was that?' he mumbled.

Nertha was looking towards the trees in the distance.

She was smiling. 'Just the Whistler saying goodbye,' she said.

'Very droll,' Vredech retorted.

Then he twisted round and lay with his head in her lap. Relaxing into the warm summer afternoon, he stared up at the white summer clouds.